The 4th Option

The First Department 55 Thriller

Sam Draper
7.1

August 2015

A Novel

This book is a work of fiction.
Names, characters, places and incidents are either the product of the author's imagination or are used fictitiously.

Copyright Sam Draper.

2014.

Cover by Sam and Emily Draper. Images from Shutterstock.com.

Any reproduction without permission of the author is prohibited except for short quotations for use in reviews.

For Emily

Special thanks to Norm and Marcia for reading this book twice, and to Gary, Barbara, Ravi, Debbie, Lynne, Tyler, and Beth for all the feedback.

1993-1995

1.   January 12, 1993

Claire Havers stepped out of her sling-backed heels the moment the elevator doors closed. Peter Howard took her cue and pulled the knot loose on his tie. He leaned against the wood railing and watched her bend at the waist to retrieve her shoes.

"Don't get used to me filling in like that," Claire exhaled as she leaned against the opposite wall with her shoes hanging from her left index finger. "That's your world, not mine."

Peter smiled, unbuttoning his collar.

She was wrong.

Claire was the best project manager he had. She always looked great in her jeans and green Lewis & Howard t-shirts, but he'd never seen her look better than she did right now, with her long dress flowing down her small frame.

They just left a business dinner that his reputation would not allow him to attend alone. He was ranked number four on the Greenville Times list of *Most Eligible Bachelors*. Despite his partner forbidding dating within the firm, he finally had an excuse to see Claire off the job site.

She didn't know Greenville old money, and it took her some time to get used to the posh surroundings, but once she did, she was vibrant, interesting, and funny.

"You were great tonight," Peter said, enjoying her hoop earrings nearly touching her shoulders, "everyone loved you, and you really got me out of a bind."

"No," Claire looked away, "I was awkward. I never know what to say to those people." Her eyes closed and her head rested against the mirrored wall.

"Well yes, you were awkward," Peter jabbed, "but it only took you fifteen minutes to stop staring at Mr. Ashton's toupee!"

Claire shot him a shocked look. "I've never seen one in real life!" Peter knew she tried not to stare.

The elevator chimed and they both were laughing as they exited on the fourth floor. Peter produced the hotel room key card and swiped the door.

Claire pushed into his back expecting the door to open, but the key didn't work on the first try. Claire pressed her body into his back for a fraction of a second. He was keenly aware of her cheek on his shoulder.

He swiped again and the door opened so he could step forward before the pause was too long.

He turned and they were facing each other, only three inches separating them. She looked up at him, her cheeks just a bit flushed.

"I ... I", Claire stammered. They'd been in this position a few times before, close like this. Peter knew he had to take it slow, and Claire was worth the wait.

"How are we looking for tomorrow?" Peter asked, changing the subject to work.

"We were two full days ahead of schedule," Claire said, her voice still intimate. She smiled a small smile before she looked to her left, across the room to her drawing table. "Now we're two days behind schedule."

Peter felt her presence pull away from him as she focused on business. They came here intending to review construction plans for tomorrow. They both knew they were hoping for more.

Claire tossed her shoes onto the couch as she walked barefoot through the seating area.

"Now that we've got the ruling from the Bureau of Indian Affairs, I have to make adjustments so we can start work in the morning." Claire explained as she grabbed her horn-rimmed glasses from their place on the top of her board.

Peter followed and stood next to her as she slid up onto her stool. Her hand on his shoulder pulled him in close as she pointed out some details.

Peter focused. Three weeks ago, she was two days *ahead* of schedule, something unheard of in their industry. Then, the excavation crew hit something behind the exterior foundation wall of the Poinsett Hotel. There was nothing in the plans to explain a stone block, so, as required by the building code, they reported the find to the federal Bureau of Indian Affairs. It took three weeks for the BIA expert on burial cysts to make a disposition, and he just finished today.

In the meantime, Claire kept the crews working in other areas. She had the foresight to start working with the architect on an alternate design, and miraculously had only fallen two days *behind* schedule. Peter looked at her profile. She was proud of her work, and he was proud of her. She was easily the smartest project manager he had and maybe the best he'd worked with.

"Everything revolves around the waterfall," Claire reviewed the new design for the basement that included keeping the artifact where it was.

The inspector was more reasonable than anyone expected, and they only had to slightly modify their design.

They were converting the first basement level of the Poinsett Hotel into a wine bar to attract the business people flocking to Greenville's revitalized downtown. Excavation for a new fire escape revealed the burial cyst. Now the wine bar would be decorated with a Native American theme.

The inspector said the local tribe would accept the compromise rather than demanding the hotel be torn down. He only insisted a decorative box be placed over the actual carved stone block.

Claire planned to use blue light to illuminate a dramatic three sided water wall feature in the alcove around it. The result was going to be fantastic, probably better than the original design.

Claire continued, "Ronny's the best cement man we've got, and we're going to have to work all the schedules around him." She stretched across the drawings to point to the features Ronny would be focused on. Peter knew Claire was right and enjoyed feeling her right side brush against him as she pointed. She smiled but didn't look at him.

"Yes, I agree," Peter redoubled his focus on the drawings, "but don't forget the building entrance and stairways. They both have complex designs." Claire paused and leaned a bit more fully into him while considering the input.

They'd teetered on a physical intimacy that was more than professional since he stole her from another firm six months ago. Physical contact had become normal between them.

"I see your point," Claire said as she straightened up and started thumbing through the pages of the thick book of drawings. A crease formed between her eyebrows.

Peter watched as she sat up straight on the stool and focused on her work. Now he'd done it. He threw a wrench into her plans for tomorrow, and now she had to work it out. No matter, they had all night.

Peter stepped back to let Claire work through the details, he'd just be a distraction now. He sat on the couch next to her shoes.

The hotel gave his construction firm the fourth floor deluxe suite to use as the construction office during the renovations. They wanted to minimize the interruption to hotel operations while his firm installed the wine bar and made upgrades throughout the one-hundred year old building.

Claire added several drawing tables, hers against the windows, some file cabinets, and an administrative desk.

Peter knew Claire kept the bedroom mini-fridge stocked with specialty beers she gave out to her crew for exceptional work.

He stood quietly and crossed to the double doors, Claire didn't notice. The bedroom was well appointed. The bed was perfectly made.

He was disappointed to find the fridge empty.

"I gave out the last three today, before your date cancelled, and you demanded I come here and work tonight!" Claire called from her table.

Peter was pretty sure coming here tonight was her idea. He stood and moved to lean on the doorjamb. Claire paused. She smiled brightly over her bare shoulder and said, "This will take me twenty minutes, why don't you go to Barley's for some Christmas Ale?"

. . .

Ten minutes later, Peter found himself at the back entrance of the hotel with six beers. He knew Claire needed a little more time. He looked up at the hotel. The clear sky allowed the full moon to illuminate the twelve story brick façade.

He hadn't been inside the work area since they found the stupid cyst. That was a word he'd never heard before, and one he didn't care to hear again. Three thousand years ago, a guy died, and his tribe carved a non-descript stone block for him. Now, they had to work around it. Luckily, Claire worked it out.

Peter quietly stepped out of his Audi coup and crossed to the back of the building. He opened the back door and passed from the cool night air into the stale, dusty interior. No matter how much the crew tried to keep the job site clean, dust was always everywhere. He loved the smell of it. The smell of progress. He enjoyed the feel of the place as he walked down the service hallway in the second sub-basement of the hotel.

Peter imagined the sounds of construction in his mind. He'd spent thousands of hours in the hustle of work sites.

Now he was the face of Lewis & Howard, the construction firm he founded ten years ago with his best friend. He spent several nights a week at events that filled the Upstate's social calendar. The nice dinners, the glad-handing, the excuses to ask beautiful women to be his date was all very enjoyable, but fulfillment came from the hands-on detailed work. He liked watching a project come together, the noise of hammers and saws, and the sound a tape-measure makes when it's retracted.

Peter stopped suddenly.

The construction sounds he thought were in his head were not in his head at all. Someone was working up the stairs immediately to his right. He knew the stairs wrapped around to the room with the artifact that would soon be Claire's wine bar.

There was no reason for anyone to be here this time of night. Peter climbed the stairs slowly. He didn't know why, but he was trying to be quiet. His back pressed against the wall of the intermediate landing as he peeked around the corner to see that one of the double fire doors was propped open.

Conversation and light tool sounds came from the room. This was his construction site and he had every reason to be here, but something told him he wanted to see what was going on before he was seen.

Peter's eyes were at floor level and he could see the framing for the bar under construction. A man stood at a laptop computer. Peter had heard of them but never seen one before. A second man stepped into view from behind the closed door and looked over his shoulder. From behind, the two looked like twins, new construction boots, clean jeans, flannel shirts, and clean construction hard hats. Peter thought these guys were trying to look like a construction crew but not doing a very good job.

His alarm bells were starting to go off, but his curiosity was still stronger.

"Is it like the others?" Peter could hear Looking Man ask.

"So far, yes," Computer Man didn't look up but remained focused on his screen. Peter noticed his right hand was controlling a small joystick.

Peter quietly climbed two steps. A work light on a tripod lit the area out of view to the left. A half-inch cable draped from the computer towards the lighted area.

Computer Man used his left arm to push Looking Man back a bit and craned his neck to look that way, "We need to go in another six inches."

Peter crouched down so his head was below the level of the floor and moved to the other side of the step.

He rose slowly.

The work light was focused directly on the Native American artifact!

Peter saw a man on his knees next to the block manipulating the wire connected to the computer. He was gently directing the wire into a hole drilled into the cube.

The BIA gave strict orders that the cube was not to be altered in shape, location, or surface finish. Now someone drilled a hole in it? There were additional holes. A larger one near the floor even had an electric auger pulling a fine, clean sand into a pile on the floor.

They were emptying it?

Wire Man was wearing the same outfit as the other two.

It dawned on Peter that this group was here to steal the artifact. That had to be it. Briefly, Peter began to get mad, but quickly he realized these guys were doing him a favor.

"The sand is clear, we should be able to read the outer shell now," Computer Man called.

A fourth man come into view. He carried a box nearly one foot square and six inches tall and placed it directly atop the cube. He wasn't dressed as the others were. He wore dark pants and dark shoes with a leather coat. Peter's body tensed as his jacket lifted to reveal a holster with a pistol at the small of his back.

"Yes, we can see the shell," Jacket Man called. He must have been reading something from the box. "You should be able to see past the shell through port four."

"Which is four?" Wire Man asked.

Jacket Man frowned for a split second before leaning down to point at the hole centered in the cube face. As he leaned down, he looked directly at Peter.

Peter's mind began to do a lot of things at the same time, none of them telling his body to move. His heart started pounding. He felt a sense of recognition, and his ears heard Jacket Man say, very softly, "Shit."

Peter tried to decide what to do. He was on his building site. He was allowed to walk around anywhere he wanted. These guys were not supposed to be here. He was totally in the right. On the other hand, there were four of them, and at least one had a gun. Adrenaline pumped through him.

The three others in the room slowly followed Jacket Man's eyes to Peter.

"Peter Howard," Jacket Man said, "Please, join us ..."

The BIA inspector! Peter had only met him for a few moments, but it was definitely him. It made no sense for him to be here at night, and no sense for him to have a gun. This was not going to end well. "We met ... Shit! ... Get Him!"

Peter heard Jacket Man shout as he rounded the stairway landing and nearly jumped down the stairs.

The hours he spent at the gym translated into a flat sprint down the hallway. He chanced a glance back to see more than one pursuer fall out of the stairwell after him.

He was at least fifty feet ahead of them and halfway down the hall, easily negotiating the hallway at full speed as he heard them banging into tool chests and stomping loudly in their new work boots.

By the time he slammed through the outside door, he'd widened the gap enough to look around.

He closed the door, released the breaks on a tool chest and heaved it in front of the door before engaging the foot break. He stepped back and reviewed his work just as he heard a crash on the other side. The tool chest was very heavy, and while he saw it shudder, it didn't give way.

What now? Peter watched as the door opened and pushed against the tool chest. Fingers explored the small opening and gripped the door.

They were pushing.

The fingers disappeared and the tool chest rocked forward.

They were pushing harder.

Peter took three adrenaline-filled steps forward and planted his foot against the door. A man on the other side screamed as the door closed.

The pushing stopped.

Peter took a deep breath before sprinting for his car. He thought he'd bought himself enough time to get away.

He had his key in the ignition when the beer in the passenger seat reminded him of Claire. The BIA criminals, yes Peter decided they were certainly criminals, knew where his office was. They would go there, and then she would be in danger.

She'll be okay, she didn't see anything.

Peter's arm flexed to start the car, but his hand didn't turn, he had to go get her.

He looked around and jumped from the car. He struggled to walk through the lobby and ran up the stairs rather than wait for the elevator. This time the door opened on the first try.

"Claire!" he called. She wasn't at the layout table. He darted forward and could see through the double doors into the bedroom.

He stopped.

Claire had removed her long dress, dimmed the lights, and pulled down the cover on the bed. Her panties and bra were a matching green set and her white skin glowed in contrast as she reclined on the satin sheets.

For a fraction of a second, he was delighted.

Then he couldn't help but watch as her legs tensed. She held her pose but she recognized something wasn't right.

"We have to go," Peter crossed the fifteen feet into the bedroom quickly, "get dressed."

Her smile fell from her face, and her arms quickly covered herself. She turned away.

"Get Dressed!" he shouted, "Where are your clothes?" He was finally able to pull his eyes off her and look around the room.

He found her dress.

"Peter," Claire whimpered. She didn't move. She was fighting tears.

She'd get over it after he explained.

He shot to the edge of the bed and pulled her to her feet and toward the door.

She resisted.

He turned to her, looked her directly in the eyes, grabbed both of her upper arms, and kissed her.

"I'll explain everything, but we have to go," he said, still holding her arms. At first she resisted the kiss, but as he pulled back, her face was relaxed, maybe even about to smile. It had the effect he was looking for. She quickly pulled her dress over her head and stumbled after him to the door.

"My shoes!" Claire pulled his hand just as he opened the door.

"Forget them!" Peter said as he turned to exit and was met directly in the nose by a speeding fist.

. . .

Peter's eyes were watery and his nose ached as he sat on the couch next to Claire.

"Peter, I'm sorry I had to hit you," Jacket Man leaned against Claire's drawing table. Two of his men sat on the edges of the chairs directly across from them, neither looking comfortable. The knot of one of their foreheads needed attention. The third filled the doorway.

Jacket Man continued, "You must remember me, I'm with the Bureau of Indian Affairs, I'm Linus Brenner. I'm here on official business of the BIA."

"Come on," Peter interrupted, "we both know that's not true."

Linus Brenner didn't appreciate the interruption. His eyes opened a bit and Peter saw him flex to lift himself up from the table.

Peter felt himself tense.

Then Linus relaxed. After a brief pause, he exhaled, signaling that Peter could continue.

Peter looked at Claire who still didn't know what was going on. She was holding it together, but barely.

"Look, he turned back to Linus, "We don't care about that block. Actually, you guys stealing it would be a big help to me. As far as I'm concerned, you can have it. We'd report it missing, the police would investigate. We'd say we don't know anything. That won't be hard because we don't. I didn't see anything. And that would be that."

Peter thought Linus would like the plan. He continued, "People steal stuff from construction sites all the time. It would really be no big deal."

Linus raised a hand. Peter stopped. Linus spoke slowly, "First, you did see something. Something more than you know. Second, you won't be reporting anything to the police."

"Maybe the police could help us sort all this out," Peter reiterated. He moved to stand.

He didn't know what he was going to do, but he needed to regain some status in the discussion. As if by magic, pistols appeared in the hands of Linus' men. They weren't raised, but they were there. Linus let his raised hand and their guns do the talking. Peter thought better of standing. This situation was suddenly very bad. Claire's face turned white.

Linus leaned back, the guns moved from view, "Let's think about that for a moment. If you called the police, and told them someone was altering that cyst, who do you think they'd call?"

Realization hit Peter and he deflated a little, "They'd probably call you."

"Exactly," Linus said, "And, who do you think I would call if I found, let's say, someone like you messing with a Native American burial cyst after I'd ordered that it was not to be moved?"

"You'd call the police," Peter said, begrudgingly.

"That's right," Linus said, "Now we're getting somewhere!" He actually seemed happy.

"Now," Linus said, returning to his stern face. Peter could barely believe he could see out of his eyes, they didn't seem to open far enough.

"Here's how it's going to go. We're going to let you get back to what you were doing." Linus gestured to the bedroom. Peter felt the two cronies leer at Claire. She crossed her arms over her chest.

"And we're going to go downstairs and finish what we were doing down there."

Linus stepped forward from the table. His crew followed his lead and they all stood around Peter and Claire. Peter tried to sit tall, but he couldn't.

"In the meantime, you need to realize that you did see things, Mr. Howard. And because you saw those things, both your lives will never be the same. You need to know they could be much better. This could be the best night of your lives."

Peter couldn't believe what he was hearing. He could feel Claire's body shaking.

"But," Linus continued, "If you talk about this to anyone, this will be the worst night of your lives."

Claire cried.

2.   March 3, 1993

"And we were on such a roll after Greenville," Jim Williams dropped the letter on his desk. He leaned back into his high-backed leather desk chair and looked past Barbara. He reflexively ran his hand through his hair. He leaned forward in his chair. He stood. Tension rose in him. Finally, he sat back down.

His office was directly below the Vice President's, in the basement under the West Wing of the White House. Two fifteen foot long maps, one of the United States, and one of the former Soviet Union, hung on his windowless walls.

The Soviet map was covered with one-hundred and twenty-five push pins.

The US map only had five, the newest on Greenville, South Carolina.

"I thought the Gulf War ended these letters?" Barbara asked. Jim looked to the Soviet map and all its pins and then quickly returned to her face.

Barbara Atkinson stood in front of him with the first letter since the Gulf War. She'd been the communications secretary for the Vice President since Walter Mondale, and enjoyed a level of status because she'd been around long enough to be in the know. She was in her late fifties, was married to her job, and also had the special task of identifying letters written to the Vice President like the one she'd just delivered.

But she was not one of Jim's Division Chiefs. So, while the Gulf War *was*, indeed, fought over these letters, and they *had not* received one since, and everyone hoped she was actually *right*, Jim wasn't about to confirm anything to her.

"Has Thomas seen this?" Jim didn't know the exact protocol. He was the Operations Division Chief for the six years prior to his recent promotion to Department Secretary, but the department maintained strict compartmentalization of information, so he'd never actually seen one of the letters before.

For a brief second, Jim could see the disappointment on Barbara's face at her question being dismissed, but then she let it pass. "Yes, this is a copy. Thomas has the original, as is procedure. He's running the standard tests, but he's reasonably sure it's authentic."

"Damn," Jim let escape. He looked at the woman who was only

the messenger, "Thank you, Barbara. That will be all."

Just forty-three days ago, Jim joined George Bush and Dan Quayle in the Oval Office to meet his new boss. Bill Clinton was the newly inaugurated President of the United States, and Al Gore was his new Vice President. Mr. Gore didn't know it when they took the ceremonial drive from the Capitol to their new offices at 1600 Pennsylvania Avenue, but Jim worked for him.

Bill Clinton's first meeting in the Oval Office as President started with the history of letters like this one and made it to the events in Greenville.

The President didn't like it at all. The meeting ended with him throwing them all out.

Jim had not seen the President since then, but that would change today.

Thirteen months ago, Vice President Quayle promoted Jim to the position of Special Secretary for Department 55. Department 55 was responsible for all aspects of the President's relationship with LV, a relationship every president desperately wanted to end.

Jim looked to the clock over his door. Ten-Thirty. Around the perimeter of the clock, his predecessors had developed a visual indicator of the threat posed by LV. As it progressed from one to ten, the color transitioned from green to red. Jim's team of four Division Chiefs referred to it colloquially as the Threat Rose. The indicator had been at one.

"Thank you," Barbara said. She paused for a moment, hoping for a bit more information, but then she turned and left. With that, Jim took a deep breath, stood up, then sat back down in his chair and reread the letter.

> *The relationship has been strong for some time. We are saddened by the recent attack in New York City. While it would be natural for you to respond with direct military engagement against those who you believe responsible for the attack, we forbid it. Take no actions against the organizations you believe responsible for the attacks on your first city.*
>
> *- LV*

The letter referred to the bombing of the World Trade Center complex six days ago.

Jim had nothing to do with the response, but he knew the

President, and therefore the Vice President, had been preoccupied with the effort. He saw all the military brass in the halls, so he knew military strikes were in the near future.

At least they were until he got this letter.

. . .

His boss, the Vice President of the United States, took him directly to the Oval Office. The President cleared the room, even his secret service agent waited outside. The three men, Jim, Bill Clinton, and Al Gore studied every detail of the letter and tried to figure a move forward.

He knew he was dealing with two of the smartest, most accomplished men in the world, and they didn't disappoint with a profound ability to absorb information, process it, and move to the next question. Jim had been living the reality created by LV's letters for fifteen years. They had only known of their existence for six weeks, and they were asking him questions he hadn't thought of.

Jim returned to his office two exhausting hours later, after convincing the President to delay the planned military response by one day.

He looked at a note pad with an intentionally cryptic list of three questions and picked up the phone to call for help with the first. It was answered on the second ring.

"Yes, Mr. Williams?" his closest Division Chief answered.

"Please join me in my office," Jim directed.

"Certainly." The line went dead. Thomas Kirk also sat in the White House basement, but in an office across the complex. Thomas would help him with question one: *do we have to?*

Jim called to his executive assistant, who sat in his outer office, "Debra, can you get me Maxwell?"

Thirty seconds later his phone rang, "Yes, Mr. Williams?" Jim had met very few of the people who worked for his Division Chiefs but he recognized Lloyd, the assistant to his Science Chief.

"I need Maxwell," Jim said.

"Hold a sec," the informality was striking, but Jim decided he didn't care.

After a few clicks an older voice came on, "Yes, Jim." Maxwell was always upbeat. Jim had known the man for six years and never saw him down.

"Please come to my office, I need to speak with you." Jim

directed.

"Yes," a brief pause. A normal person would be looking at his calendar, but Jim knew Maxwell had everything memorized and was recalling his calendar, "I can get there day after tomorrow."

Jim thought that would be the case, "I'm going to need you this afternoon." Maxwell knew he wouldn't ask if it wasn't important.

"Then I'll be there this afternoon!" Maxwell said without a hint of contempt.

"Thank you," this time Jim hung up first. He knew it would take a little time for Maxwell to get to Jim's office from Milwaukee. Okay, Maxwell would help him with question two: *what do we do next time?*

The third question was a harder one: *What now?* Jim wasn't involved in the weeks' work to find out who had detonated a bomb in the parking garage of the World Trade Center. He didn't know who to call to work on a better plan. He knew the current plan was to return the favor by bombing the perpetrator into oblivion. He decided he would ask the Vice President.

His train of thought was interrupted by Thomas Kirk's knock and the door to his office opening.

"Thank you for coming over, Thomas," Jim exaggerated the welcome because he knew Thomas was a very introverted man and he needed to pull him out of his shell. "Please, have a seat."

Jim called past Thomas, "Debra, can you get me some time with the Vice President after this?"

"Yes," Debra's voice called back.

Jim stood and gestured to the conference table in front of his desk. Jim walked around the desk and took the seat farthest from where he was and still sat before Thomas. Without comment, his fastidious guest sat and waited for Jim to begin.

"This latest letter," Jim prompted, "Is it real?"

Thomas knew he was called about the letter and it briefly annoyed Jim to have to ask. Thomas produced the original letter from his breast pocket covered in a plastic folder. He took a pair of white gloves from his other pocket and put them on before removing the letter as gingerly as he would the Declaration of Independence. He carefully unfolded it and placed it on the table for Jim to inspect.

"Yes, it is authentic," Thomas began. "I can state this with certainty for four reasons."

"First, it came from Key West, Florida. We have never received a letter from there, and no two letters have ever come from the same city. I am sure you will dispatch a team to investigate, and I am sure they will not find any clues as to the identity of the individual who mailed it."

"Second, the paper is completely unremarkable, as is the font, the printing, the envelope, the lack of saliva on the glue in the envelope, the printing on the envelope, and the lack of fingerprints."

"Third, the limited biological material on the letter indicates that the paper was irradiated in the past five days, probably hours before it was mailed."

"Fourth, the cadence and pattern of the language and sentence structure is a perfect match."

"These are the four details we check whenever a letter arrives, and every letter has these four characteristics." Thomas looked up from the letter directly into Jim's eyes, "The only living people who know these four details are myself, the two previous Department 55 secretaries still living, and now you." Jim raised his eyebrows at this last detail.

Jim had known Thomas as a fellow division chief for six years and had grown to respect the man as the most detailed and precise person he'd ever encountered. Every detail of his appearance, of his speech, and of his arguments was measured and thought out.

"Okay," Jim started. He needed Thomas' help, "I have some questions about the content, if you don't mind."

"Certainly," Thomas was the chief of the division tasked with management of letters received from LV. He oversaw a staff of twelve archivists and forensic scientists who spent their time with these letters studying every detail. This meant he had the best insight into the motivations of the organization.

"In the past," Jim began with a question the Vice President asked him earlier, "LV has directed our Middle East policy against Iran, Syria and other state sponsors of terrorism. Now they're requiring us to not respond to terrorist attacks on the United States." Jim paused expecting Thomas to correct him or comment. The two men stared at each other and Thomas said nothing. Jim asked a question, "What do you make of this change in position?"

Thomas didn't immediately answer, but Jim could tell his silence was because he was thinking of how to answer. Jim tried to watch the man's face but instead he looked past him to the map of the United States and the pin in Greenville, South Carolina. His mind was about to wander when Thomas spoke.

"One could be inclined to believe that this latest demand is a change in position by LV. However, there are several assumptions that must be made to reach that conclusion. First, you have to assume that the bombing was not executed by our friend, Israel. It would be fair to characterize LV's opposition of the Muslim countries in the Middle East as support of Israel. Israel may have done it, and LV could be acting on their behalf." Jim felt his face cringe at that thought. "But, we know LV is not associated with Israel. In the past, they have made demands directly conflicting with the private requests of the Israeli government. So we know that while LV is a supporter of Israel, it is not an Israeli organization. And as such, they would not know about an Israeli plot to attack the USA. So, the assumption that Israel did not attack the USA is a good one."

Jim knew it was a good one, and he felt like he was just run around in a circle.

"Second," Thomas continued, "You must assume that LV is a monolithic organization. But, it could be a confederation of organizations that send demands with different objectives. We have never seen any evidence that this is the case, so the assumption that LV is a monolith is a good one."

"Third, one must assume-"

"Thomas, can we skip to the assumption that is helpful?" Jim interrupted. Thomas stopped with his mouth open a little. He closed his mouth and then opened it again. He moved his chair back about two inches. Jim immediately wished he had let the man finish. Thomas' cheeks reddened a little as though the volcano of logic that was his body was just plugged and the magma was flowing into his face. All this happened in five seconds. Over the next five seconds, Thomas collected himself, his face returned to its normal color, and he proceeded.

"As I was saying," Thomas pulled himself back to the table by grabbing the edge, "Over time, we have built a picture of what we should expect from LV based on interests expressed in their letters. We are often surprised. Based on their previous letters, their support of the terrorists may be linked to their hatred of communism, or their distaste for the United States. It may only be a coincidence that the terrorist actors are from the Middle East. Their letter could actually have nothing to do with these particular terrorists. It could very well be that LV doesn't even know who the terrorists are!"

"Wow," Jim said. He allowed himself to rock back in his chair. The US Government knew who attacked the World Trade Center because of intelligence gathering in the region. They had assumed the entire time that LV knew who did it as well, and was protecting them. It could be that they had a completely different objective. Thomas' logical approach to the problem was unique and could be right.

"But why?" Jim heard himself say. "Why would LV protect an organization without knowing who they were? What reason could they have?"

Thomas thought only a second, "I have no idea. We are far from fully understanding their motivations."

Jim thought about this. He stood again. He walked around Thomas and looked at the map. Five pins, he looked at his pin, Santa Fe.

"Thomas," Jim said, "I need you to build the argument that LV doesn't know who the terrorist are. I need it today. The President is weighing his options and I need to give him this."

"I understand," Thomas said. He stood to leave but stopped just as he stood up fully. "Jim, I hope the President is not considering ignoring a directive from LV?"

Jim didn't answer but kept facing the map.

Thomas paused a moment, "Jim, no President has ever successfully ignored an order from LV. Remember that Reagan flatly refused, and it almost destroyed us! Luckily, he was able to get Gorbachev to cave in faster in exchange, and look at the mess Russia's in now. We don't have anyone else to rely on."

"I know," Jim said. He didn't turn to face Thomas.

"Do you?" Thomas looked at him closely. Jim didn't like the question. Jim was new to his position, and he was dealing with a new administration. Thomas was implying that their naïveté could get them in a lot of trouble. Jim didn't like what Thomas was implying, but he was exactly right.

Jim turned and looked the man straight in the face, "Yes, I do. Thank you, Thomas." Thomas turned and left.

Jim checked the clock. It was almost three p.m. Maxwell probably wouldn't be in until after dinner. He asked Debra to check with Lloyd and confirm Maxwell's travel plans, then to order dinner and tell his wife he'd be working late.

With any luck, he could find his boss and discuss their

alternatives to military strikes. He walked out of his office in search of Vice President Al Gore.

· · ·

"Maxwell, I'm glad you could come to see me," Jim said sitting again at his conference table. His Science Division Chief had arrived from Milwaukee at eight p.m. and Jim was tired. Debra provided box salads and the two men were eating in Jim's basement office. He wished he had a burger, but Debra wouldn't get him one.

"I'm always at your disposal," Maxwell said as he carefully ate a large leaf of lettuce.

The meeting with the Vice President had not gone as Jim had hoped. Both the Vice President and the President were set on military action tomorrow. Thomas' argument that LV couldn't know who the terrorists were and that there must be some other motivation only angered the Vice President. *So we have to obey blindly?* Jim found himself sitting in the Oval Office while the President and his aides argued the merits and options for the military strikes. Jim kept quiet and served only as a reminder that there could be unintended consequences of a strike. On two occasions, the President almost ordered the strike immediately only to glance at Jim and steady himself. After his aides left to return to the Situation Room, the President told Jim that if he didn't come up with an alternative plan, and fast, he was going to attack later tonight.

"I need something good," Jim said after he recounted his day to his most visionary division chief.

"What do you mean?" Maxwell asked.

Jim spoke not quite sure what he meant, "I think the President is a shrewd negotiator. He sees everything twelve steps ahead. He doesn't want to accept any demand from LV because he thinks it will set a precedent that he will follow every command. He feels this issue should be small enough that LV shouldn't care about it." Maxwell paused his eating to pay attention. "The President believes that if he doesn't strike now, then LV will know they can ask for anything they want. He wants to send the message that he's not going to do everything they ask."

"That's a dangerous message," Maxwell said, "Remember what happened to Nixon when he tried to push LV around?"

"Yes, I know," Jim felt his shoulders drop.

"So, I think we agree that the President *must* do what LV tells him?" Maxwell reinforced.

"Yes," Jim stumbled getting that word out. He had briefly fallen for the seductive logic of the President that they could actually disobey and get away with it. They ate in silence for a few minutes. Maxwell was faster and finished first. He stood and Jim continued to eat. Maxwell looked at the map and the pins.

"A month ago we were all so happy to put this little pin in here. We had hope..." Maxwell trailed off staring at the wall. His face was close enough to the map that it seemed he could see the details of the South Carolina town. Jim paused for a moment but then continued to eat. He was exhausted and he needed a few minutes to recover.

Jim finished his salad, taking a moment to chew his last bite too many times and enjoy the feeling. He slowly looked up at Maxwell and saw him still studying the map.

"Hope is a powerful thing," Maxwell said after Jim finished.

"Yes?" Jim asked.

"The President is afraid that if he gives in he'll be giving in forever. That's why you asked me here," Maxwell talked to the map. "We just need to explain to him that we have options. At least that we're working on options."

"I agree we need options, because the President feels backed into a corner," Jim said.

"Tell him again about the Desertron-" Maxwell began

Jim interrupted, "He knows about the damned Desertron!" Jim told him about the Desertron on Inauguration Day. The President was not impressed. Jim collected himself, "The President knows the Desertron may yield results, eventually. But the plan is to build the thing, run it, and hope we find something we can use! That could take decades. How do we leverage what we're going to learn sooner? President Clinton needs a vision of how we can use what we're going to learn to change the situation faster ... much faster."

For a solid man, Maxwell sat down lightly. He considered his words. "History has shown that the country at the forefront of scientific discovery enjoys economic prosperity. Not only using that science, but by exporting products around the world. The Greeks, the Romans, and the British have all shown us that when a civilization allows others to catch up technologically, it will hold its leadership position for maybe a century. The US is on the verge of losing its technological edge, so we know we need the next great breakthrough to keep ahead in the world. That's the path to stay ahead of China, and also to get us out from under the shadow of LV."

Jim knew the plan. It was not a new plan, but it was the best plan. Unfortunately, it was a slow plan. He almost said so when Maxwell continued.

"While the Desertron is not our only research direction, it's the biggest and will yield the newest results. The challenge is we're going to be looking into a world no human has ever seen before." Maxwell explained.

"Yes, but we must have some idea of what we'll learn!" Jim needed some idea so he could tell the President there was a way out.

"Look," Maxwell said calmly, "We're not in a sprint. We're in a race that is centuries long. Our advantage over the past global superpowers is that we know we have to stay in the race. But it's a long race. When we win, we'll benefit for centuries."

Jim knew this, but he didn't believe it. "Yes, but the time has come for a benefit now. We need something now!" Jim shared the President's exasperation.

"There can only be one of four possible outcomes. When God created the Universe, he only gave it four rules." Jim only thought of Maxwell as his Science Division Chief. He was a scientist by training, and it was evident in every interaction he ever had with the man. It was a bit striking for him to refer to God. "So, when the Desertron is operational, we will only have four options to choose from. There are only four fundamental forces in the Universe."

"This is a little too theoretical. We need to get more practical. Is one option the best?" Jim asked.

"We're investing heavily on each of the options with the expectation that experiments like the Desertron will tell us which one will be the best," Maxwell said.

"Which one do you think is the best right now?" Jim needed something.

"You know I don't like to pick winners without the data to back them up. You also know that's why we're investing in so many technologies simultaneously. It's not the most efficient process from a financial standpoint."

"Let Mr. Jefferson worry about the finances." Jim said, "If someone held a gun to your head, which one would you pick, today, right now?"

"Don't be so dramatic," Maxwell said, "There are no guns!" Jim had just finished explaining that the US Military was preparing for a series of global military strikes that would certainly involve very large guns.

And those attacks could result in a response from LV.

Jim watched as Maxwell's posture changed. He sat up in his chair. Maxwell said, "Okay, so there are guns, let me think."

"Thank you," Jim said. He had gotten Maxwell to where he needed to be. Now he had to wait for the man to pick his best option. Jim stood and walked to the credenza below the map of the United States. He poured himself a scotch and Maxwell a cranberry juice. When he returned, Maxwell was ready to begin.

"Thank you", Maxwell acknowledged the juice, "The longest shot, but the best shot is the fourth option. *Gravity*. We'd always thought of it as the option of last resort until a new theory emerged. A student at Virginia Tech published a paper a few years ago. She was ignored by the physics community, but we immediately saw the potential of her work."

"Her?" Jim asked.

This was good. The government couldn't launch a military strike against LV, because Jim didn't know where they were. They couldn't negotiate, because Jim didn't know what LV wanted. Their only real long term hope was new technology. And Jim was beginning to agree with Maxwell, the President needed to hear about a fourth option.

"The student, she's at Virginia Tech," Maxwell continued, "Sarah Kiadopolis will be completing her PhD this year. Her ideas are revolutionary. I've been funding her work through the NSF since her first paper." Maxwell gave a brief synopsis of her idea that Jim mostly followed. The two men spent about an hour talking through how her theory would use the data from the Desertron and other places to give Department 55 an edge over LV.

Jim looked at the clock. He knew the Threat Rose would have to rise to at least three, and he knew he was running out of time. "Thank you Maxwell. You and I need to go upstairs and convince the President to not start a war tonight." Jim stood. Maxwell sprung to his feet. "Sarah Kiadopolis and her *fourth option* might just be the key."

3.   March 23, 1993

Sarah Kiadopolis adjusted her course to the trajectory of the disc and despite her exhaustion broke into full sprint. She relished the burning feeling in her legs. She could hear herself breathing hard and her heart pounding. She never thought her arms could get tired from running, but they were. That's how she knew she was getting better.

Out of the corner of her eye she saw the first group of students descending the slight incline along the path onto the Drill Field. She knew that meant her workout was over and she completed it at full speed. She allowed her concentration to break and her legs to slow. She allowed the disc to sail by just out of her reach to her opponent who caught it for the final score of the day. She slowed to a jog, a pace that would be a sprint for many on her team and left the playing field to get her things. She picked up her towel, wiped her face, and looked around. She saw thousands of students moving from one side of the field to the other. She felt part of something big. She felt like a member of a twenty-eight thousand person team. This was one of her favorite times of the week and she didn't want to miss it. Especially today.

. . .

Sarah grew up with her mother, Henrietta, in their family home. Henrietta's parents died suddenly when she was nineteen, two months after Sarah was born, leaving the two of them on their own. Henrietta completed high school and could get a stream of jobs but had difficulty holding them. She almost always worked two at a time to make ends meet.

By the eighth grade, Sarah was intensely independent. She wasn't an outcast at school, but she spent little time outside of school with her classmates. Her studies were never difficult. One spring Friday she was surprised to hear about the upcoming eighth grade dance. Sarah ate lunch with her four best friends who were all discussing their dresses and the boys who'd asked them to the dance. Sarah was only mildly embarrassed to admit that no one had asked her.

Sarah was frustrated to find she couldn't get the dance out of her head all weekend. On Monday she was intensely aware of the boys in her classes. Several were friends but she'd never thought of them as boys before. On Tuesday, she checked with the front office and determined that the eighth grade class was actually two-thirds boys. Certainly a strange anomaly that required the study of statisticians, but also an anomaly that meant Sarah should have been asked by at least two boys. Some of her male friends had mentioned dates from other towns.

By Wednesday, Sarah didn't want to think about the dance anymore, but there was little else discussed at school and she couldn't get away from it. She thought a lot about the dance and her situation at school, but she couldn't find a solution. She considered asking the son of one of her mother's friends but she decided it would be too embarrassing to ask a boy. She was supposed to be asked.

Sarah spent the night of the dance at home. Her mother arrived late from her job cleaning an office building. Henrietta sat on the sofa and stared blindly at the television. Sarah sat next to her and cuddled in, smelling the cleaning chemicals. It had not occurred to her to discuss the dance situation with her mother.

Sarah sat up and studied her mother. She was pretty enough, she guessed, but it was difficult to see. Her skin was pale and although she was in her thirties, she looked fifty. She wore no makeup. Her clothes were utilitarian, a loose t-shirt and jeans with old New Balance tennis shoes. She was thin with large breasts. In the past she had long blond hair, but now it was cut very short. She didn't brush it. Sarah was surprised to realize that her mother had given up on her appearance. Then she almost cried as she saw her mother sitting on the sofa, watching nothing, and realized she couldn't think of anything her mother hadn't given up on.

Sarah was able to look down the hallway through the open door into the bathroom and see herself in the mirror. To her sudden horror, she saw that she looked exactly the same. Her blond hair was also cut short. She wore no makeup and her clothes were entirely utilitarian. She also spent no time on her appearance.

The only difference was Sarah's tan skin, a trait she inherited from her father. Her Greek skin and Greek last name were the only things she ever got from him.

Sarah cuddled back into her mother and began to sob softly. Her mother's only acknowledgement was to softly stroke her hair.

That night she didn't sleep. For the first time in her life, she imagined her future. She decided she wasn't going to be thirty-eight years old, working two jobs, and giving up. She decided she would be different.

By the first day of high school, her only progress was a job busing tables at the nicest restaurant in Danville. Sarah met with her guidance counselor. She was devastated to find a woman who grew up in Danville and never left. She talked with her girlfriends, but their aspirations were to get married, have kids, and maybe work at the bank. Their dreams were to fall in love with a football player and ride him to the NFL.

Sarah decided her future was outside of Danville. But she had no idea how to get out. She knew the money she made at the restaurant wasn't enough to live on let alone move anywhere. She'd have to figure out how to earn more money.

By Christmas of her freshman year it had been eight months since the eighth grade dance, and she still didn't have a plan. She was beginning to worry. Two days before the winter break Sarah overheard a conversation between her biology teacher and two juniors about the Michelson Scholarship. The scholarship would send the valedictorian of her high school to the engineering or scientific university of their choice, free of charge, for four years. Sarah had not considered college. She spent the next two days in the career center researching colleges and scholarships.

By spring, Sarah Kiadopolis has hatched her escape plan. She never had a multiyear plan before and didn't know if she was someone who followed through. She would win the Michelson Scholarship. She would play sports to get an athletic scholarship as a backup.

She decided she wanted to get asked to the school dances. And to do that, she had to look like a girl.

No, a woman.

She didn't like the daisy dukes and pushup bras worn by the girls working hard on their NFL dreams. Instead, she admired the women eating in the restaurant. Not the ones hanging on the arm of a man, but the ones having business dinners. That was how she wanted to be, so that was how she was going to dress. She grew her hair out and bought some nicer clothes. She practiced wearing heels at home, and experimented with a little make-up.

Since the eighth grade dance, Sarah had paid much more attention to her mother. Henrietta brightened up when she was dating a new man. They always treated her badly and always moved on quickly, leaving Henrietta more distant than before.

Sarah tried to draw her out, to do things together, but her mother was preoccupied with finding a new man.

By Christmas of her senior year, Sarah dressed more professionally than her classmates in low heels and a pressed skirt. She worked out every day and was on the varsity basketball and soccer teams. She had her choice of boys for every school dance. She'd moved from busing tables through waitressing and even tried a few cooking positions. Now she was an assistant manager at the restaurant. Sarah had to focus on her schoolwork because it was more difficult to be first in the class than just in the top ten. She had an affinity for math and her aptitude for mechanical systems made physics her favorite subject. She'd already been accepted by the Virginia Tech Physics Department.

The Michelson Scholarship was awarded to its first female student in its fifteen year existence. She was the fourth runner up for prom queen. By her high school graduation, Sarah was happy to know she could follow through on a plan.

. . .

Today, Sarah was in less of a rush than usual. She walked with the crowd of students through the academic side of Virginia Tech to Robeson Hall. She walked lazily, taking in the Hokie-stone buildings that had grown so comfortable for her. She smelled the familiar smell of every building on the VT campus and climbed the stairs to her second floor office. Graduate students shared tiny offices but her office mate wasn't there so she changed into a fresh shirt. She spent an hour checking her simulations and left for her apartment to get ready for dinner.

. . .

College was a clean break for Sarah. The first person she met was her freshman roommate. Beth was nice enough and Sarah joined her pledging the sororities. Sarah enjoyed the generally better dress of the girls and was used to late nights and little sleep, but her straight forward approach to people and complete lack of any need to be liked didn't go well in the sorority culture. She quickly tired of the constant judgment of the members and technically she washed out of pledge week. She did not appreciate the failure. After that her relationship with Beth, a proud member of Kappa Nu, was pleasant but not close.

Sarah turned seventeen that winter. She was younger than everyone in her dorm but she was tall and her body was well developed so no one noticed. Her youth did prevent her from working at any of the bars on Main Street. She didn't want to work at the dining halls, so earning money was more difficult than it was in Danville. Without athletics, she gained ten pounds and her clothes weren't fitting right. She had a few friends on her hall, but she was startled when she realized she was bored. She decided it was time to create a new multiyear plan.

She spent her Christmas break working at the restaurant back in Danville. Her mother was enchanted by a new beau. He was a lug who talked rudely to her and hit on Sarah when her mother was out of the room. A powerful knee to the groin backed him off, but he never came back and Henrietta retreated back into her depression. By the end of the break, Sarah had a new plan.

Sarah Kiadopolis graduated in three years at the top of her class in physics, a subject she grew to love. She accepted an offer to earn a doctorate in the department. She converted the ten unwanted pounds into five pounds of muscle thanks to a rigorous gym routine and the ultimate frisbee club team. She was able to use the fourth year of the Michelson Scholarship to pay off the loans she had accumulated. Three of her friends from her freshman dorm were still her off-campus roommates. She sent money home when she could spare it and visited as often as she could get away, but her mother seemed to be slipping deeper and deeper into depression.

She continued to out-dress everyone in her classes, choosing heels and a denim skirt when the other girls, only a small handful in the physics department, chose Birkenstocks and sweatpants. She chose her clothes to remind herself of her goal, a process she learned in high school. She enjoyed the subtle attention she got from the men and boys in the department, as long as it remained subtle, and her personality was strong enough to ensure that it did. She dated a little, but she always found the boys were singularly focused. After a third date of dancing and darts followed by an hour of kissing and wandering hands, one frustrated young man told her he thought her hot body meant she would put out. It did not.

. . .

"What's got you getting all dressed up?" Angie Reynolds was

assembling a chicken salad in the shared kitchen in their four bedroom apartment. Sarah completed her shower and was in her interview outfit, skirt, white blouse, and tan heels.

"I've got my final dinner interview with Mr. Cullis tonight," Sarah said as she looked at herself in the mirror. She glanced at Angie who was looking at her as well.

"You look good," Angie said. They'd been roommates since they moved off campus junior year, six years ago. Angie was completing her MBA and had a job lined up in Virginia. The interview tonight was Sarah's best opportunity but would take her to New York City.

. . .

Although Sarah stayed at Virginia Tech, Graduate school was a new challenge, and she knew she needed a plan. She was going to graduate in four years, continue her physical activity, and make enough money so she wouldn't build any more debt.

Sarah immersed herself in physics. She taught as many classes as she could and attended all of the faculty seminars. There seemed an unlimited amount to learn. Like most of the students and professors in her department, she was drawn to the new fields created by String Theory.

String Theory was the latest attempt of physicists to find the connection between the first three forces in the universe, the strong and weak nuclear forces, and the electromagnetic force, and the fourth fundamental force in the universe, gravity.

At the beginning of her second year, Sarah was the youngest student, by age and time in the department, to be invited to the weekly String Theory debates held by the department head on Tuesday nights. Fifteen of the department's best minds, professors and students, discussed the challenges of their work. At first Sarah felt out of place. She was the only woman, and the only attendee under twenty, maybe twenty-five. After a particularly lively debate about the mathematics of Hadrian Shapes where she contributed little, she asked the department head about her attendance. She feared he would say something about equality for women, or that she brought a pretty face. She decided if any of those were his reason, she would leave the group. He laughed at her a little. He said the group appreciated her mechanical mind. He said she was the first person, student or professor, man or woman, he had met who had no trouble with the math, but approached the subject like an auto mechanic. Her focus on the physical world over the application of the math often grounded the conversation. The senior members of the group recommended her to fill an open spot because of her straight forward approach, and they were not disappointed.

Then, something amazing happened. She had an idea. She, like everyone in physics, had a near endless supply of ideas, but these ideas were quickly debated and dispatched on Tuesday nights. This idea lasted through a first Tuesday night. Then it was brought up the next week. Sarah got some homework from the group. It took Sarah three weeks to complete the homework, but when she did, it survived another debate. Quickly, the idea became the focus of her work, and grew into her thesis.

Sarah spent the next two years teaching, playing ultimate, and working with her advisors on her theory that she had named *Space Resonance*. It was a great time in her life. Her professors were supportive, she was the most popular graduate teacher in the physics department, and she had three roommates as best friends.

. . .

Now Sarah knew she was entering the transition to the next phase of her life. As she pulled onto I-81 heading toward Roanoke, she knew it was time to leave Virginia Tech. She would complete her doctoral work in two months. Her department offered her post-doctorate work, but as she thought about her future she remembered physics was a means to an end. Her time with her mother taught her she needed financial independence, and that meant drawing a large salary for her work.

Everyone in the department knew the real opportunity for physicists was on Wall Street. The mathematics Sarah needed to create *Space Resonance* could be used to develop new investment opportunities for hedge fund companies and institutional investors. The true die-hards of physics stayed in science, but Sarah was following the money and the money led to finance.

Cornwall & Wallace specialized in new financial instruments and was a pioneer in derivative product development. The firm was interviewing to fill thirty spots with the best and brightest physicists, mathematicians, and computer scientists in the country in a competitive program for new hires. Every year, after six months on the job, the team was weeded down to the ten that would be hired full time. Sarah was going to be invited to join the program, but first she had to meet for dinner with this year's team leader, Tim Cullis.

Tim wasn't an intimidating person. He had a squishy handshake and spoke in the impractical theoretical terms Sarah was accustomed to dealing with during the Tuesday debates. His talk of office politics nearly turned her off, but the money and the competitive environment were very attractive. Sarah looked forward to a pleasant dinner at one of the nicer restaurants in Roanoke. She was told she had to accept an offer immediately, and she was prepared to do so.

Still, as she sped up the highway in Angie's car, she couldn't help feel sadness that she was about to leave the best place she had ever known, and theoretical physics, forever.

4.   April 14, 1993

Claire selected a pale blue dress to offset her red hair for the grand opening of *The Artifact*. The Poinsett Hotel was delighted with what she'd done with the basement wine bar. She made the Native American burial cyst the centerpiece of the decorations and the inspiration for the name.

She was sitting at the bar with a draft beer while she waited for Peter to arrive. Her dress was for Peter Howard, but it was attracting attention from many of the patrons tonight including most of the workmen who helped her create *The Artifact*. She enjoyed their company while she tolerated the professional types trying to pick her up. She was much more comfortable in jeans and work boots.

Claire avoided Peter for a week after the run in with Linus Brenner. Peter called her every night but she didn't answer. She was either too embarrassed about what didn't happen or too afraid of what did happen to see him. She wasn't sure. She was sure she'd never been held by men with guns before, and she was terrified they would come back.

After a week, she felt secure enough to return to work. When she finally saw Peter, they decided they had no evidence of anything to report and that taking any action would only make things worse. They hoped they wouldn't see Linus Brenner or his men ever again.

Over the next two months, things returned to normal between them as they worked very closely on the project, and slowly Claire's feelings for Peter returned. Tonight Claire planned to make her feelings clear, but tonight he was going to have to make the first move. She *knew* he would … She *hoped* he would.

She looked past Ronny, her best cement man, toward the stairs up to the hotel lobby just as Peter descended them. He looked great in slacks and a sport coat. The men around him wore similar attire but they looked clumsy by comparison. He paused briefly on the last stair and scanned the room. Ronny followed her gaze. He looked back to her, but she only glanced at him and smiled softly. Claire fought the urge to raise her hand. Finally, he found her and smiled naturally. They were fifty feet apart across a sea of people but she felt like they were the only people in the room. She handed her beer to Ronny, slid down from the stool, and started to move toward Peter as he stepped down into the crowd toward her.

She wasn't seeing the people she was pushing past and was annoyed when one man wouldn't move for her. She looked over his shoulder while he looked her up and down. She tried to push past him, but he put his hand on her shoulder. She put her hand on the leather of his jacket to push him aside, but he held firm.

"Miss Havers, it's truly a pleasure to see you," Claire focused her attention on the face of Linus Brenner. "You look great, by the way." Claire stared wide eyed at the man she was the most afraid of in the entire world. She looked past him to see Peter moving toward her, but now the room seemed impossibly big, and he was still on the far side.

She looked at Linus. She knew about twenty of the men in this bar, her crew, who would be more than happy to kick the crap out of this guy if she asked. Linus had miscalculated, and she felt her wide eyed look replaced with a smile.

The room was crowded, but she'd done a good job with acoustics so it was quiet. Linus spoke softly, like they were old friends, "I've been checking up on you, and I need your help." He handed her a closed folder.

Claire looked into his face. He was about eight inches taller than she was. She'd had night mares about his face and here it was, making casual conversation. He gestured to the file. She opened it and was shocked to see it was all about her.

She reviewed her college transcript, her tax records, a picture of her house, and pictures of each of her projects. She didn't know what she was looking at, but she knew she didn't like it.

"You've got to be crazy if you think I'm going to help you."

"I thought you'd say that," Linus said, "but I've done my homework and you're my girl!" He again gestured to the folder, "I really need someone like you and you'll find I'm highly motivated." She returned to the folder. There was still a lot in it. She was a bit stunned by her own likeness when she came across a picture of a job site with her in it. Then there was a picture of her eating alone at a Ruby Tuesday. This guy was stalking her. She was about to close the folder and call her crew over when she took a double take of the last picture. She recognized the Depeche Mode poster over her younger sister's bed in her college dorm room. She felt dizzy when she saw her sister was asleep in the bed.

Claire struggled not to hyperventilate and nearly dropped the folder just as Peter reached her side and grabbed the papers.

"What are *you* doing here?" Peter asked. Claire was comforted by his presence and she leaned slightly into him. She briefly thought she had the upper hand, but with just one picture, he'd demonstrated his ability to get anywhere in her life he wanted. That one picture was a very effective threat. She might have risked a run in with the police to see her crew beat him to a pulp, but she'd never risk her sister.

"I knew you were finishing up here," Linus said, "and I wanted to come see what you've done with the place."

"Well," Peter said, "get the hell out of here!" Claire could tell Peter thought he had the upper hand. He hadn't looked through the folder. "I don't care who you are, you've got to leave, right now! And don't come back!" Peter was beginning to raise his voice and Claire could see a few of her guys start to take notice around them. If Linus got thrown out, he could retaliate against her sister. She couldn't have him angry at her. She steeled her nerves, pulled away from Peter, and put her hand on his shoulder to calm him.

"Wait," Claire said loud enough to get control of the situation, "Peter, is that any way to talk to our old friend?" She smiled at Linus and even reached out and touched his arm. She imagined her hand bursting into flames at the touch. She flashed her smile to her men around her, and they returned to their conversations. Peter looked at her with his mouth open. "It's okay, Peter. Let's hear what he's got to say." She felt like she was going to throw up, but she let go of Linus and took Peter's hand and led the men to a corner of the bar where they could talk.

They gathered in a circle like everyone else in the bar and Peter said, "Look, man, we don't want any trouble. We haven't talked to anyone. Look around, no one's ever going to know anything."

"I know you haven't talked to anyone," Linus said. Peter looked at him questioningly, but Claire felt he probably was even more thorough in his investigation than the folder led her to believe. Was he tapping their phones? "I'm here because I know what Claire's done, and I know you don't have a next project lined up yet."

"We've got some other things she can help out with, she'll be busy," Peter started, "How do you know she doesn't have more projects?"

Linus ignored him, "Claire, you're one of the best project managers around. Peter knows it. And you have a double major in electrical engineering. And you can keep your mouth shut. I've got some projects that could use someone like you."

"Look," Peter still tried to intervene, "Claire works for me, and I assign her projects!"

"I know," Linus looked to Peter, "Don't worry, I'm still going to pay Lewis & Howard for her time."

"It's not the money," Peter said, "It's you! We're not going to work with you, and we're not going to do anything illegal!"

"I'm not asking you to do anything illegal," Linus looked at Claire. She didn't want to work with him, but just like she couldn't throw him out, she couldn't really say no.

"I'm not doing anything illegal," Claire reiterated.

"I don't do anything illegal either," Linus said, "I'm not the mob!" He chuckled. Claire felt Peter's hand tighten around hers. She pulled her hand from his. She knew she'd be doing whatever Linus wanted until she could figure a way out, but right now all she wanted to do was go home, alone.

5.   April 20, 1993

Again Barbara Atkinson stood in front of Jim Williams' desk, and again she was delivering a letter from LV. The last time she was in his office, she delivered the first letter both Jim and the President ever received. That letter led to a marathon day that went until four in the morning.

At least that day ended well. With Maxwell's help, he was able to talk the President back from a direct confrontation with LV. The US military didn't attack the nations that helped the World Trade Center bombers. Maxwell was right that showing the President the opportunity *Space Resonance* offered was worth the wait, as long as it wasn't a long wait. That, in turn, convinced President Clinton to accept LV's demand and pursue non-military options. The Vice President suggested that they pursue criminal charges against the actual terrorists. This would allow the federal government to make a strong case against the countries responsible and discredit them in the international community. While it wasn't as satisfying as the military option, it was probably just as effective.

Now Jim couldn't believe his eyes. He stole a glance past Barbara at the Threat Rose. *Three*. He was just getting used to Three. Now he knew it would go up. He read the letter again.

> *The relationship is becoming strained. While you followed our last letter specifically, you did not follow the spirit. Pursuing judicial persecution of those involved in the attacks is equivalent to the military options. You will not expand the legal actions taken to date.*

> *-LV*

"Is Mr. Gore in his office?" Jim asked Barbara. There was much to be done.

6.   April 26, 1993

Sarah Kiadopolis enjoyed her familiar surroundings on the small stage in the largest classroom of Robeson Hall. The room had seating for 155 people arranged in seven arcs rising up away from her. Normally, a public thesis defense was held in one of the smaller, swankier classrooms in the Pamplin School of Business, but Sarah's popularity among the students of the Physics department required the switch to a larger space. That was fine with her. She'd taught dozens of classes in Robeson 210, and she was comfortable.

"Physicists around the world are trying to understand the relationship between all the big things like planets, stars, and galaxies," Sarah pointed to the poster that occupied the wall of the room, a collage of celestial bodies, "and all the little things like protons and electrons," Sarah pointed to the other wall with several posters of atoms and the Periodic Table of the Elements. The public defense was designed to demonstrate a PhD candidate's ability to serve as an ambassador to the public. She had to explain her dissertation to anyone who attended the event.

"If I had a powerful microscope and I looked at my arm," Sarah stood before the audience in a short sleeved white blouse, black pencil skirt and three inch heels. She lifted her arm as though reading a watch and pantomimed looking closely at her skin. "I'd be able to see millions and millions of cells, the smallest building blocks of life."

"But I'm not a biologist, so I'd go further, zooming in to a single molecule of DNA."

"Still, I'm not a chemist, so I'd zoom in to a single atom and its nucleus of protons and neutrons surrounded by its cloud of electrons." She looked past her arm at the undergraduates filling most of the first four rows. They were all silent and attentive.

"If I zoomed in further, down to the surface of a single proton, I'd get down to seeing the very fabric of space. It would look like a vast ocean expanding out in every direction." Sarah opened her arms wide. "And floating on that ocean would be strings, the smallest building blocks of the Universe. Each string would look like a tiny," Sarah looked to her left. Professor Long was watching her with a soft smile, "sailboat." Professor Long's smile disappeared at the mention of a sailboat.

Two years ago, the annual department picnic was at Smith Mountain Lake. The wind was sporadic that day and no one had much luck sailing, but Sarah and her best friend in the department, Rick, were having particular difficulty. It was like the wind whipping off the mountains was specially targeted just at them. While others were able to struggle to make it down the lake, Sarah and Rick eventually lost their fight with the wind and were both tossed overboard. The picture of Sarah and Rick after swimming back to shore, soaking wet but beaming, made it to the department website. Downloads of the picture of Sarah in a wet t-shirt and shorts overloaded the department servers, and a week later it had to be taken down.

Registration for her classes was twice the other instructors the next semester. Professor Long was concerned and offered to switch the teaching assignments, but Sarah wasn't about to shrink away from the challenge. Instead, she dressed in her normal outfit, much like today, and taught the largest classes in the history of the department. Over the next two years, she became the most respected instructor in the department because of her ability to engage the students and explain the complex concepts in a way they understood. She remained a bit of a celebrity in the college of science because of her famous sailing trip.

"Now, anyone who's gone sailing knows," Sarah saw a few in the audience whisper to their neighbors, "it's easy to lose control of your sailboat because it likes to rock side to side. In fact, I can sit in one of those little boats and rock it back and forth myself," Sarah stepped her right foot so her heels were two feet apart and shifted her weight from one foot to the other so her body rocked from side to side, "If I time my movements right, I can make that little boat tip over despite it weighing twice what I do!"

"The trick is to time the rocking of the boat with the natural tendency of the boat to rock. We physicists call the rate the boat naturally wants to rock the boat's *natural resonant frequency*." Sarah stopped shifting her weight and brought her feet back together. She looked at her audience. She'd practiced this description for two months and while she didn't want to use complex terms, she couldn't get away from it.

She recognized almost everyone in the audience, but she knew some students were bringing friends and some brought dates. She focused in on the few she didn't recognize to see that they were following along. So far, so good.

"Now, the strings floating on the fabric of space on the surface of a proton act just like the sailboats," Sarah walked to her right toward a young woman holding hands with one of her smartest students, "they vibrate around, and they have a natural frequency just like a sailboat." She stopped in front of Ethan and his date. His date looked Sarah in the eye.

"And, just like the wind can hit one sailboat with just the right frequency and send its occupants into the lake while only barely nudging others nearby," some in the audience laughed and Sarah saw her advisor shoot a dirty look at them, "a graviton can hit just one string on the fabric at just the right frequency, timed just right, to apply the force of gravity, while the strings around it with slightly different oscillations don't feel a thing."

Sarah looked back to her advisor who appreciated her analogy and his smile returned. She walked slowly back across the stage.

"Now let's imagine we wanted to knock over every sailboat in the lake at one time, how would we do that?" Sarah asked.

After five awkward seconds, Pranav, another bright student in the second row, called out, "A tornado!" Another student chimed in, "A Tsunami!"

Sarah held up her hand, "Yes, those would work, but those would each require a huge amount of energy. Let's think of a way to get them to all tip over with only the energy we have from the wind that knocked my boat over." She came to a stop at the center of the stage and looked out. She needed a student to propose a solution. That would demonstrate for sure that her audience was following her. She felt her weight shift to her right foot and let her left foot cross behind it. She looked from right to left. All the undergraduates were looking with blank stares. The graduate students had all read her papers so they knew the idea. The answer had to come from one of the first four rows. If not, she could be in danger of failing her defense.

"Ms. Kiadopolis," Ethan called. His girlfriend was leaning close to him. Sarah walked over to him. His girlfriend didn't look at her this time. "Could we get all the boats to oscillate like your boat? Somehow align all the frequencies so they all feel the same wind?"

"Yes!" Sarah was elated. She'd taken a risk asking a student to offer the next step. But it paid off! "Yes, imagine if all the boats on the lake all turned the same way, and everyone on every boat rocked the same way!" Sarah was excited and rocked her hips again, "Imagine we got every boat to rock to the left, and then timed our rock to the right to perfectly align with a wind! Then, when a big wind came, all the boats would already be rocking in the perfect frequency for the wind to add just enough energy to knock them all over!" Sarah walked back across the stage toward her advisor, this time exhilarated, "Now imagine all the strings on the surface of the proton oscillating at the same frequency and all timed together. In this perfect alignment, they would all feel the incoming graviton!"

"So the force of gravity would be stronger?" Pranav asked.

"Yes!" Sarah knew she was getting through.

"But there are millions and millions of strings," Ethan turned to talk to Pranav, "If you got them all to feel the graviton, you'd amplify the force of gravity by millions of times!"

"Could you make Ms. Kiadopolis' boat act like all the other boats?" Pranav and Ethan both turned to Ethan's girlfriend who spoke up.

"What?" Ethan asked her.

"Instead of getting all the boats to move like Ms. Kiadopolis' boat, and get knocked over, couldn't you make her boat act like the other boats and not get knocked over?" The young woman still didn't look at Sarah but twisted in her seat to look at Pranav. Clearly Ethan picked a smart one.

"Yes, that would make sense," Pranav said, "And if you made all the strings oscillate out of phase from the gravitons, you could turn off the force of gravity?"

Now there was a murmur of conversations among the undergraduates. They were all talking about possibilities of increasing or decreasing gravity. It was a fun conversation to have. Sarah stood at the front of the room and let it happen for a moment. Then Rick called from the back of the room, "But how?" The room fell silent as everyone considered this.

"You could tell everyone in each boat to rock together, get a coxswain on the shore with a bullhorn," Ethan suggested.

"Maybe," Pranav thought about it, "but I doubt you'd be able to get everyone to move just right."

"You don't ask them to do it," Ethan's girlfriend said, "you force them. You get one of those wave machines like at the waterparks, and you send out a wave across the lake that gets everyone to move together whether they want to or not!" Ethan and Pranav both looked at her like she was crazy. But Sarah knew otherwise.

"You're exactly right!" Sarah said. "You could use a wave machine to set up a standing wave in the surface of the lake. Then every boat would move up and down on the lake together, each boat rising and falling as the wave passes." The girlfriend smiled at Sarah. Sarah didn't even know her name, but knew she was brilliant.

"But how does that apply to the strings?" Ethan asked after a moment.

Sarah knew it was time for her to take back the conversation. She walked back to the center of the stage, put her feet together, and pushed a lock of her blond hair behind her ear.

"Remember, the strings on the surface of the proton are floating in the fabric of space. The trick would be to use a tiny wave machine to oscillate the fabric of space at its natural resonate frequency. Just like in the lake, we could set up a standing wave on the surface of the proton that would make all the strings bob up and down together."

"Those wave machines take a lot of power," Ethan said.

"No," Pranav corrected, "Not if we're oscillating at the natural resonant frequency. It doesn't take much energy to move something at the frequency it wants to move. Just like pushing a kid on a swing, or an opera singer breaking a glass with her voice. When you push something at the frequency it wants to move at, it's very easy!"

"Yes," Sarah said. This was easy with her bright students. "So, my work for the past two years has been to calculate the natural resonant frequency of the fabric of space. And my dissertation is the results of those calculations. The field of study is called *Space Resonance.*"

. . .

Twenty minutes later, Sarah was leaning against the heavy desk on the stage idly balancing on her heels while the students discussed the implications of her work. She made a few theoretical corrections during the discussion, but the group carried on with little of her help. The graduate students in the back of the room were taking part and the conversation was getting more detailed. Twice she had to redirect the conversation away from the mathematics, but her advisor seemed quite pleased. She was relaxing because she felt she was past the hard part.

She looked around the large room thinking this was probably the last time she'd be on this stage. She let her mind wander to her job with Cornwall & Wallace on Wall Street. She'd soon be on her way to New York City and the next chapter of her life.

"Well," Professor Long spoke for the first time since he introduced her an hour ago, "Let's all thank Ms. Kiadopolis for her time with us here. I think we all will miss her." He stood and Sarah dropped her head with a humble smile for a round of applause.

Thankfully the applause died down and Sarah welled up as she leaned back into the desk. Most people in the audience headed for the doors but a small group gathered around her for congratulations. Sarah thanked Pranav and Ethan and was happy to meet Ethan's girlfriend, a bright computer science major. She hugged each of them, and a few eager young men gathered around waiting for their hugs. They eventually left.

"Sarah, darling, you've done it!" Professor Long considered himself a southern gentleman and she knew he was pleased when he called her darling. They'd worked together for years, and he was the closest thing she had to a father figure. He was genuinely proud. "I would not have mentioned the sailing trip," he averted his eyes briefly, "but it was a brilliant move to engage your audience. And you were leading them, but they got to the theory by themselves! I've never seen or heard of a public defense where the candidate didn't have to talk for twenty minutes!"

They hugged a deep hug and he whispered into her ear, "I wish you were staying, I'm going to miss you." The tenderness from this formal man pushed her over the edge and she felt a tear run down her cheek. She pulled away and wiped it off before he saw it. His eyes were wet as well, but his smile was large and genuine as he left.

Sarah was the first person in the room one hour and twenty minutes ago, and she planned to be the last to leave. She returned to leaning back on the desk and surveyed the room. An older man was standing at the top of the auditorium probably waiting for her to leave. Sarah wouldn't have given him a second glance except for his blazing blue eyes set against his deep tan. His sharp suit perfectly fit his large frame. He was striking and better dressed than any professor she'd ever seen. She recognized him. He was the second person to enter the room. He entered and wordlessly took a seat. He watched the entire defense and now stood watching her. He gave her a small smile and a nod. Then he left.

7.   May 25, 1993

Linus Brenner   Jan 12 1993 1732   Jan 13 1993 0745

Sullivan Acer sat at his small desk in a row of small desks. He looked at the clock. Eleven-thirty. *Finally*. Normally, his diet, a feeble attempt to control his weight, made him the first one to stop working for lunch. But today was different. Today he was looking forward to lunch because of *Linus Brenner*. Yesterday, he'd found an obscure reference to *Linus Brenner,* and today he couldn't wait to figure it out.

His desk was the second in a row of five. His best friend, Bert Pickard, had seniority, so he got the window seat looking out over the parking lot. "Guess what time my stomach says it is?" Bert turned and looked over Sullivan's desk expectantly. Bert's stomach, like his, always thought it was lunch time.

"I've got to get some of this stuff done. I'm going to work through," Sullivan said.

Bert looked at him questioningly, "Okay, Erin's not going to be happy." Bert knew Sullivan had a soft spot for Erin, but Sullivan was steadfast.

"I really do have to get this done," Sullivan said unconvincingly.

"Okay, okay," Bert said, "see you later, loser." With that he stood and walked away from the windows toward the exit.

Sullivan counted to ten and looked around. No one else was there. He knew he'd be alone for at least the next thirty minutes. He closed all the documents on his computer. He looked around again.

It was funny. He wasn't doing anything wrong. Actually, he was doing his job. Sullivan sat at this desk in a row of desks in an office building full of rows of desks. He worked in the Office of Compliance at the Bureau of Indian Affairs. His office examined the activities of BIA employees from other offices looking for inappropriate behavior. His office got all the negativity that Internal Affairs got in a police department, but without any of the authority or job satisfaction.

But, it was a job.

He opened the BIA's electronic travel system and searched through it to find one entry among 1800 others. There it was.

Linus Brenner   Jan 12 1993 1732   Jan 13 1993 0745

Sullivan detested the mundane procedural aspects of his job, and he didn't care a bit about catching someone stealing pens, but he loved puzzles. He always made a point of looking at things in different ways.

Two months ago, he went on his first trip for his job, a training course in Des Moines, Iowa. He hated every minute of filling in the expense report system, reporting every drink, every meal, and every detail of his travel. But then he realized everyone else was doing the same thing. There was a vast amount of data for searching, and he decided to see what he could find. Two weeks ago, he was added as an administrator in the travel system and spent a few hours a week of his own time searching for anything that might be unusual. Yesterday, he found Linus Brenner's trip.

It took Sullivan a few moments of studying the single line before he realized what didn't look right. Linus had left at 5:30 at night, and returned at 7:45 in the morning, the next day!

Sullivan searched through the next few months' records looking for any other trips and another line stood out.

Linus Brenner Apr 14 1993 1802 Apr 15 1993 0615

So, whatever Mr. Brenner was doing on a single overnight trip, he did it more than once!

Sullivan had looked up Mr. Brenner and found he was an inspector for the BIA. The Uniform Building Code required builders across the country to notify the Bureau of Indian Affairs if they uncovered anything that might be a piece of Native American cultural heritage. If the local inspectors needed a specialist in Native American burial cysts, whatever those were, they called in Linus Brenner. So it made sense that he traveled a lot, but it didn't make any sense that he'd only travel for an evening.

He imagined Mr. Brenner could be traveling to visit a mistress, or to take bribes, or to launder money. Building permits meant buildings, and buildings meant large sums of money. Anywhere there were large sums of money, there was crime.

Sullivan looked out the window and thought for a moment. He didn't think he cared about Linus Brenner, but he did like the puzzle. He felt exhilarated that his idea to search the travel records might payoff.

Sullivan heard people returning behind him and he hastily closed out of the travel system just as Bert called, "Hey, Loser, you missed a good one!" Whatever that meant, Sullivan certainly felt he found a good one.

8.   June 4, 1993

"The President's planning to continue to pursue the terrorists, despite the directive from LV, and I'm inclined to agree with him," Al Gore said. Jim stood in the Vice President's office as his boss sat at his desk. Jim looked at the top of the Vice President's head.

Jim thought there would be more, but the VP continued to work, reviewing papers on his desk. Jim looked around the office. The office was a smaller, rectangular version of its more famous counter-part, the Oval Office. Al Gore's decorators made extensive use of the Smithsonian's collections. After a moment, Jim came back to the top of the Vice President's head.

"I don't think that's a good-" Jim started, but he stopped when his boss looked up.

"Look, the President and I agree," Vice President Gore was giving a direct order. This was not a discussion. "We know that in the past Department 55 focused all of its efforts on getting the administration to obey the orders of LV, whoever they are. But we're taking this in a different direction." Jim didn't move a muscle.

"Our policy will be to use the Roman's directives as guidance, and not policy." LV was the Roman numeral for 55, and The Vice President referred to LV colloquially. Over time, the word association never proved to mean anything to the behavior of LV, but the observation led to the origin of the name of the department Jim led, Department 55. His mind was wandering; he needed to pay close attention to this order. The Vice President continued, "We need Department 55 to get us out of this. The United States of America is no longer going to tolerate this situation. We're going to defeat them. We want the full focus of your efforts to be finding ways to minimize the impact of LV while increasing our chances of leveling the playing field."

"The Threat Rose has risen to four," Jim knew they had been stretching the meaning of LV's words already. He also knew he worked to get them out of this every day for the past fifteen years. "This course has raised the level rapidly. Thomas would tell you-"

"I'm not interested in what Thomas would tell me," the Vice President put down his pen and stood up behind his desk, "We're going to stand up to them. Not directly, but in every way we can. We've been screwing around with them for too long. They've been making threats that they certainly won't follow through on, so we're going to call their bluff."

Jim didn't know how to respond. This was a truly revolutionary approach. He had both great admiration for the man before him and incredible fear about the path which he was sending them down. The Chief Executives of the United States were gambling the future of the Unites States.

9.   June 28, 1993

Sarah drove west out of Milwaukee past the suburbs and shopping malls into Waukesha on Interstate Ninety-Four. The sun was shining at eight-thirty in the morning. Rush hour had subsided and Sarah's expectant exhilaration made her push the rental Ford Taurus to eighty miles an hour. She touched the window button. As the seal broke and air rushed in, she immediately reversed its direction and closed it. Sarah pulled the rear view mirror to check her hair. She focused through her sun glassed eyes to see that her hair had survived the brief burst of wind. She returned the mirror to its position, turned up the radio, and accelerated to eighty-five.

Sarah started her job in Midtown Manhattan three weeks earlier. She worked fifteen hours a day at a job that wasn't her favorite. But devising new financial instruments for Wall Street paid well enough for her to live in one of the most expensive cities in the world and send money to her mother.

Sarah tried to talk to her mother every day and planned to pay off her mother's debts in a few months. Then, hopefully, her mother could switch to only working one job, and then maybe start taking better care of herself. Sarah had flown to Danville just last weekend because her mother was between boyfriends and in a deep low, but it was no use.

The other new hires in the intern program at Cornwall & Wallace were intense, but she had no trouble with the work and despite the long hours, her first weeks were low stress. Her team leader, Tim Cullis, was petty and manipulative, but her work product had so far kept her out of his sights. As was her habit, she was beginning to formulate a plan for the next few years.

Then, yesterday, Sarah received an express delivery at her apartment. It was from a man named Maxwell Rassic. A short note said he enjoyed her thesis public defense and asked her to meet him the next morning, in Wisconsin! Sarah immediately figured he had to be the striking man at her defense.

The envelope also contained an itinerary with hotel reservations, rental car, and airplane tickets. There was no explanation of why she should go, but Sarah felt an irrational pang of nostalgia for physics. She checked the time and found she only had fifteen minutes to get out of her apartment if she was going to make the flight. The short time forced her to go on impulse.

She called in sick to work before she left the hotel in the morning. Tim seemed to take pleasure in receiving the call. He was probably working out how he was going to manipulate her taking a day off into some sort of political coup. Well, to hell with him.

Sarah slowed to make the exit into Waukesha and drove along

the surface streets to a large government complex set on the edge of downtown. She drove up to the guard gate and read the large sign with flowers around it that read Fort Halishaw. She rolled down her window and handed her driver's license to the US Army Sergeant manning the gate.

"I'm sorry," Sarah said, "I'm not certain I'm in the right place." He looked in her window and looked her up and down. Then he efficiently retreated to his shack without comment. She looked down at herself. She wore a white blouse and red skirt suit with black heels. The jacket of her suit draped over the passenger seat. Her hair was straight and fell down her back to her shoulder blades. She was dressed for a business meeting, but she really wasn't sure if that was what this was. She wasn't expecting this to be an Army installation and the military setting unsettled her just a bit.

The wooden gate rose in front of her car and the Sergeant returned with her license and a tag for her rear view mirror, "Dr. Kiadopolis, Lloyd Jansen is expecting you, he's in building twelve." Sarah was about to ask for directions but the Sergeant beat her to it. He straightened up and pointed into the complex, "Take the second left and follow that road until it ends." He looked back at her, "It's a long road, longer than people expect. Don't worry, you'll get there." With that he stepped back.

Sarah drove onto the base and passed large fields with men running in unison around scattered buildings. She took the second left and followed a two lane road that wound around to the perimeter of the complex. To her right were the fields and buildings of the base and to the left were trees. Eventually, the buildings ended and she drove down a road with trees on both sides. She appreciated the guidance from the Sergeant as she began to wonder if she was going the right way. Finally, she found a large three story building with floor to ceiling glass.

It was clearly much newer than the other buildings on the base. Small flowers bloomed on either side of the red brick walkway. A large American flag dominated the entrance facade. Sarah parked and walked to the entrance. She was able to inspect her suit and hair in her reflection in the glass on the way in. At the last moment, she noticed she still had her sunglasses on and slid them into her purse as she entered the building.

The entrance lobby reached to the top of the building, three stories above, and in the center was a security desk with an unassuming woman at a simple workstation.

Sarah approached, "Hello, I'm-"

The woman looked up as Sarah approached, "Yes, Dr. Kiadopolis, Lloyd is waiting for you on the third floor. I'll tell him you're here. You can go up the elevator." Everyone seemed to know who she was and she didn't even know anyone named Lloyd Jansen. Sarah walked around the desk as the woman lifted a phone. Rather than take the elevator, Sarah took the large staircase that served as the backdrop of the atrium. As she rounded the landing on the second floor, she looked down to see the woman watching her. Sarah smiled and the woman gave a half-smile back. She spoke into the phone and hung it up.

"I'm Lloyd Jansen," a tall, thin man, maybe twenty-five, extended his hand to Sarah as she reached the third floor landing. Sarah glanced over the wall to see the woman below return to her work.

"Sarah Kiadopolis," Sarah said as she took Lloyd's hand. Lloyd turned and led her to the front of the building and entered the doorway on the front right corner. Before Sarah entered, she looked back to confirm that she hadn't seen another person in the building except the woman at the entrance. She told herself that wasn't unusual for an office building at nine in the morning, but somehow she still wished there were more people around.

They entered an outer office. Sarah stood in the middle of the small room while Lloyd rounded the desk that dominated it. A door on the far wall was closed but would obviously lead to Mr. Rassic's office. A plant in the corner gave the room some color and two small chairs along the wall opposite Lloyd's desk were the only other furniture. Sarah sat softly on the edge of the chair closest to the doorway to the atrium. She wanted to project confidence, but she was nervous.

"Mr. Rassic will see you now," Lloyd said after she sat in the chair for about ten seconds. He seemed to be responding to a signal Sarah didn't see. Lloyd gestured toward the closed door.

"Thank you, Lloyd," Sarah forced a strong voice and was happy to hear that she had one. Mr. Rassic had invited her here after all. She smiled at Lloyd, stood and walked straight to the closed door. She had absolutely nothing to lose. She was only here out of curiosity, and she was sure she had nothing to fear. She opened the door and walked boldly through.

Sarah had to let her eyes adjust to the sun pouring through the eastern windows. She looked through squinted eyes and determined the room had to be twenty feet by twenty feet and had floor to ceiling windows on three sides all overlooking treetops covering rolling hills. The office included a large conference table with eight chairs, an intimate seating area, and a large glass-topped desk with a computer. A small credenza stood next to a second door.

Sarah didn't expect to be alone, and she was intimidated by the beautifully appointed room which seemed completely out of place on a military base. For an office, there didn't seem to be any place for papers. There were no decorations in the room. Not even a plant. She took three tentative steps into the middle of the room, feeling the thick carpeting, and turned to look at the deep red wall she came through. The color was in sharp contrast to the white, glass, wood, and leather of the rest of the room.

Sarah had been in the room now for about thirty seconds. She'd surveyed it and was about to wonder what to do when the second door opened and Maxwell Rassic emerged.

"Ah, Dr. Kiadopolis," Mr. Rassic said in a loud voice. He was the man from her defense. The door behind him closed before she could see where it went. He was about five-six and in three inch heels she was at least five inches taller than him. Despite the height difference, he carried himself with a confidence that made her take half a step back as he approached her. Sarah had large strong hands for a woman but her hand was lost in his. She could see high on his head that was mostly bald. He wore wire rimmed glasses and a three piece suit over a solid frame.

"Can I get you a drink?" Mr. Rassic asked. He looked her straight in the eye, and Sarah found herself forced to look straight back. "Orange juice? I'm having some."

"Yes, please," Sarah forced.

"Great," Mr. Rassic turned and Sarah felt relief that she wasn't staring him in the eyes any longer. His direct eye contact had taken her off guard. She'd have to remember that trick. She looked at him from behind. His remaining hair was short but precisely cut. The skin on his neck was tanned but not leathery. His clothes were form fitting. He was a solid man in good shape, she decided. His shoes also sunk into the thick carpet, but she could see that they were polished, maybe brand new. She watched him open a small refrigerator in the credenza, pull out orange juice and pour two glasses. He moved with a practiced precision that didn't waste any effort and she admired the way he carried himself despite the fact that they had only been in the same room together for about two minutes.

Finished with the drinks, he turned and she found herself facing him. Sarah stood tall and put her arms at her sides balancing her weight on both feet. Mr. Rassic looked her in the face with bright eyes, "Shall we sit?" He held a glass in each hand and gestured with his left toward the seating area to Sarah's right.

"Yes," Sarah said, glad for some direction. She turned and walked ahead of Mr. Rassic to the chairs set in the corner. She took the right one as Mr. Rassic set the orange juices on the small table between them and sat softly in the other. Sarah wasn't comfortable as she still had no idea what she was doing here. The chair was large. She sat on the edge with her feet on the floor and her hands on her bare knees. Her back was straight and her hair fell evenly behind her shoulders.

Mr. Rassic sat comfortably in his chair. He filled it completely and leaned back into it. Its curved back seemed to hug him. He crossed his left leg over his right and rested his arms on the arm rests.

"Well, Dr. Sarah Kiadopolis," Mr. Rassic opened slowly. He was definitely happy with this meeting, "Congratulations on the new title. I am very happy you took the time to come and see me."

"Thank you. It's my pleasure," Sarah said looking a little cockeyed at him.

"Yes," Mr. Rassic said, "Well, it's truly *my* pleasure. I trust your flight was okay?"

"Mr. Rassic, can we get to the point? I have no idea why I'm here!" Sarah blurted. She felt more tension than she was aware.

"Yes, of course," Mr. Rassic lost his smile. Sarah suddenly wished she had just told him how her flight was. "First, you can call me Maxwell." He paused and waited for her to nod. She did, tentatively. "Second, I'm very interested in your work."

"Well, Maxwell, I only saw you at my defense," Sarah forced a smile trying to get back to the light mood. It didn't work.

"I was impressed," Maxwell said. He took a moment to sip his orange juice. He put his glass back on the table and smiled. "Let me start from the beginning. I work for the United States Government. I'm part of the administration's taskforce for economic competitiveness." He paused and his eyes darted from one of hers to the other. He seemed to be checking if she had heard of it.

"I can see you have never heard of us," Maxwell said, "We're not well known, by design. We seek out technology. We don't solicit. We're tasked with creating the next generation of industries that will allow the United States of America to remain the strongest power in the world."

"Doesn't private industry do that?"

"No," Maxwell looked down, "Private industry is driven by the need to provide profits in the short term, to maximize share-holder value. There is nothing wrong with that, and the USA has benefited tremendously from the most capitalistic economy on Earth. But, the technologies that those corporations profit from must be incubated somewhere. Someone has to take the long view, invest in things that won't make money for some time."

"Okay, so you're something like DARPA?" Sarah interrupted. The Defense Advanced Research Projects Agency was one step ahead of military technology. They were responsible for looking fifteen years out while the rest of the Defense Department technology development apparatus was looking five to ten. They also funded strange projects like hooking computers together, pulse engines, and betting on when the next terrorist attack would be. She thought she was helping, but Maxwell didn't seem appreciative.

"No, DARPA is too small, you need to think bigger," Maxwell said, "And don't say NASA. Again, too small." He paused. Sarah couldn't believe he was bigger than NASA. He must have meant something else. He continued, "As I said, we're responsible for finding the industries that will propel the USA into the future. Most federal departments are interested in how they'll meet their objectives in the near term. We're not like that. We only have one, long term goal. Our goal is the economic competitiveness of the United States of America."

"Remember that the United States became the most powerful and respected country in the world through innovation. The USA is built on electricity and thermodynamics. These two fields led to the automobile, the airplane, industrialization, and the computer." Sarah felt Maxwell look at her, "You follow?"

"Yes, I had not thought of it like that," Sarah said, "but I can see it." She didn't know where he was going.

"But those innovations are in the past. Others are learning about industrialization and computers. Those fields will continue to evolve, and the USA will participate, but they are too global for us to dominate. So, I ask you, where is the next innovation coming from?" He looked at Sarah and paused. She had been thinking about what he was saying and didn't react fast enough to answer the question that she thought was rhetorical. "As you can imagine, the government is very interested in the answer to that question. We're very interested in the next field of technology that will maintain our lead ahead of the rest of the world. We're working on advanced research in materials, fusion reactions, extraterrestrial mining, and especially, gravity." Sarah had almost lost focus on his introduction until that last word.

"Gravity?" Sarah asked. Did she hear him right?

"Yes, Dr. Kiadopolis. Gravity," Maxwell said. He smiled softly. He took another drink of orange juice.

Sarah had given up on working on gravity when she left Virginia Tech a month ago. Had it only been a month? It seemed like a lifetime. She thought about where this was going while he took a drink. She had a few offers from universities around the country and even one in England looking for her to become a professor in their physics departments. She could have continued working on String Theory and gravity, but there was little interest in *Space Resonance*. There was also very little pay. It took her about two months of interviewing before she remembered that physics was just a means to an end for her. And her end was financial independence. And financial independence was on Wall Street. She doubted there was much Maxwell Rassic could say that would change her mind. Physicists working for the federal government just didn't make that much money.

Sarah knew she didn't have a poker face and that Maxwell could certainly see the disappointment she could feel on her face. She didn't know what she hoped this meeting would be about, but she didn't expect another offer to spend her career making peanuts in pursuit of a fantasy. Yet, as he put his juice down, Sarah saw him smile.

"Dr. Kiadopolis," Maxwell said in a soft voice, a voice Sarah didn't know he had, "I need your help. We need your help." Sarah cocked her head to the side. "I have a team building detectors for the Desertron. Are you familiar with that project?"

"Yes, of course." Sarah didn't elaborate. Everyone in physics knew the United States government was building the world's largest particle collider in the desert in Texas. Physicists were as good as anyone at coming up with funny names, and it got the name Desert Magnetron, or Desertron. In Switzerland, the Europeans were working on what would become the second largest. They called theirs the Large Hadron Collider. The pair of colliders would allow physicists to probe into the fundamental building blocks of the Universe to a scale never before seen. Someday, they might even *see* a graviton.

"We've been looking into detecting gravitons," Maxwell said. Sarah wondered how she was able to see where he was going. Was she ahead of him, or was he cleverly guiding her?

"Many people are working on systems to detect gravitons," Sarah probably knew of ten. This wasn't news, and none of them claimed their funding came from any secret organization.

"Ours is based on *Space Resonance*," Maxwell said.

Sarah laughed. Not a big belly laugh, but a little laugh. She couldn't help it. Was this an elaborate joke? Was he making fun of her? Was he testing her to see if she was still married to the theory she'd invented?

"That's impossible!" Sarah said after her brief laugh and a small drink of juice. She put the juice down and looked at Maxwell. He didn't laugh. He seemed completely serious. "Look, if someone was working on a *Space Resonator*, they would have contacted me."

"Imagine they had not," Maxwell said, "You're not as famous as you might think."

That stung a little. *Space Resonance* wasn't a mainstream theory. No one else had spent any time on it. Sarah was the only physicist who published any papers on the theory, and she had great difficulty getting them into any journals. Anyone working on it would know it was hers.

"Look," Sarah was now serious like Maxwell, "Even if someone were building a *Space Resonator*, it wouldn't work to measure a single graviton released from a single collision in a particle accelerator. The theory requires the full field of actual gravity, the billions upon billions of gravitons emitted by stars! What you're suggesting is ludicrous." Sarah wanted to leave. She wanted to tell him she wanted to leave. She took a deep breath and sipped the orange juice she held in her lap. "Okay, now, I know you know what I just said is true. You paid for me to fly here, so I did, but I'm going home on my flight tonight. So why don't you just ask me what you want to ask me, so I can get back to my day job."

Sarah knew she took a risk being so direct. But she decided she wasn't risking anything. Whatever Maxwell Rassic wanted, he wasn't going to get it, and Sarah wasn't going to waste any more of her life on *Space Resonance*.

Sarah checked out of the conversation. She briefly looked out the window. It was a beautiful day. Maybe she could get out of here soon enough to walk along Lake Michigan. She didn't think to bring her bathing suit. Maybe she could buy one at the mall on the way back to the highway.

"You're correct that we can't use a *Space Resonator* to detect a single graviton," Maxwell said. He was very serious and leaned forward in this chair. "The team I have working on it doesn't know that. They won't know it until it doesn't work when the collider starts. But they do have a prototype and they're working to miniaturize it. In the meantime, I've planned a test that they won't know about."

"Okay," Sarah said. She could see he was serious now, but where was he going? She forgot about the bathing suit.

"I plan to test the Resonator by looking at distant stars," Maxwell said.

"Yes, that's the best way to start," Sarah had thought about this, "but there are problems. I don't know how to make a resonator at all, but if you figured out some of the basics, you must have realized that it would be contaminated by the atmosphere and earth's gravitation. One of my papers went through some of the math on that, but the reviewers refused to allow me to publish the application to the resonator. I could only show the theoretical math."

"I've reviewed your papers and agree with your assessment," Maxwell said, "That's why I plan to launch a resonator into space."

"That's highly unlikely," Sarah said. She was now enjoying the conversation even if she knew he had an ulterior motive. Maybe she could get that bathing suit. "You'd also have to shield the detector from electromagnetic interference. I only came up with one option to do that. It was diverting electromagnetism and light away from the detector. The only system with the power to do such a thing is the Hubble Space Telescope. I looked into it. The Hubble cost tens of billions of dollars to build."

"Yes," Maxwell said, "In two weeks, NASA is going to announce Hubble has a problem. They're going to say the Hubble has a design flaw that needs to be corrected. They'll announce a space shuttle mission will be diverted to correct the problem. This is a cover. The actual mission will be to install a *Space Resonator*."

"Uh huh," Sarah said. She felt her body relax. She knew the only money available for scientific projects like that came from international collaborations over decades, not a secret division of the government operating in a few years. He was after something, but she knew it wasn't a *Space Resonator* on the Hubble Space Telescope. She felt her back touch the curved back of the chair. "And you want me to install it? Be an astronaut?" She was back to thinking about the bathing suit. Somehow, this guy thought he was going to get her excited about something and then get her to agree to help him with something else. Bait and Switch.

Then Sarah figured it out.

Cornwall and Wallace had a big competitor, Michael Smith, LLC. This guy must be from Michael Smith and trying to get her to switch companies. She'd heard of there being a lot of pride between the two, and some games being played, but nothing this elaborate.

"Don't be ridiculous, I can't make you an astronaut!" Maxwell considered, "Well, maybe, but no, I need you to process the data, to create the specifications for the final build."

"Uh huh," Sarah said. She crossed her right leg over her left and put both hands on her right knee. Her skin was naturally olive and she didn't need much sun to get her summer tan. She didn't get out enough in New York, so an hour on the beach here would do the trick. "I have a good job now with Cornwall and Wallace. I don't think you can afford to get me to switch to your project."

"Yes, I know Mr. Wallace. I understand you're doing quite well," Maxwell said. He had his elbows on his knees now. Sarah was sure this was not going as he had expected. His mention of Mr. Wallace, the partner in the firm she worked for confirmed that he was with the competition. This had to be an elaborate scheme. He continued, "I'm certain you will make it through the intern program and get hired full time. I'm also certain that you will eventually get bored of the work you do there and will start looking for another opportunity. I just can't wait."

"Oh, and you have something more interesting for me to do?" Sarah asked. She knew Michael Smith would do exactly the same thing as C&W. Otherwise, there would be no rivalry. Maxwell didn't seem to understand her comment. He looked at her questioningly.

The questioning look only lasted a moment, "Sarah, I'm very serious. I would like you to come and work for me. My boss is highly motivated to get you to help us. I'm aware of your financial situation and know that you are in the financial industry to make money. I know what Mr. Wallace pays, and I'm going to double it."

Playing hard to get was working. Double it! She would have to consider this. This was no longer just a game. She held her face and her pose still. Maxwell looked at her. Despite her attempt to hide it, he seemed to know he got to her.

"Sarah, I want you to go home and think about what I've said," Maxwell said, "But know this, if you mention this to anyone, there will be no offer from me, and I'll be forced to discredit you to cover up what has happened here. We have powerful reasons to keep out of the public eye." Sarah had no reason to mention this to anyone, so she nodded agreement as Maxwell stood.

Sarah was a little surprised by the abrupt ending of the meeting, but she was exhilarated to leave. She could get a suit, work on her tan and swim in the lake for an hour, and still make her flight.

Five minutes later, her jacket was off, her sunglasses were on, the radio was blasting, and her hair was blowing in the wind as she accelerated onto the highway back to Milwaukee. Double it! Just maybe she'd be back.

10.   July 4, 1993

"Peter!" Linus Brenner called as he stepped out of his rental car. It was a Porsche Boxer and he decided he would never rent one of them again. He didn't think he'd notice the difference in power, but the Carrera had so much more. He saw Peter Howard across the laydown yard. Linus stepped toward the edge of the yard from the parking lot and remembered his New & Lingwood boots. They were designed for exceptional style, something he needed in his next meeting of the day, but not here. Linus looked around and found an indirect path to the construction office without stepping in any mud puddles. This just made him mad by the time he reached the trailer Peter ducked into.

"Peter!" Linus called as he climbed the two steps into the trailer that served as the office. His eyes adjusted quickly and he found Peter in the office looking over some papers at one of the administrative desks. A woman in a business suit, probably a lawyer, was with him. "You dog!"

It had barely been six months since he interrupted Peter with Claire, and Peter was already working on another one. And based on how close they were when he first came in and the few inches she moved away from Peter when she saw Linus, it seemed he was good at what he was doing.

"Jill," Peter said to the lawyer, "Can you give us a minute?" Linus sat down on the couch next to the door and watched as the lawyer collected her papers.

"I'll see you tonight," She touched him on the arm on her way out.

After she was gone Peter looked at Linus, "What do you want?" Linus couldn't tell if Peter was happy to see him.

"I need you tonight," Linus said, "We're going to Phoenix."

"Tonight? You've got to be kidding," now Linus knew Peter wasn't happy to see him. "It's the Fourth of July, we're trying to get out of here early." Peter looked a little coy, "I've got plans!"

Linus appreciated Peter's priorities, but he didn't care about them. "No, you don't. Jill will wait, I'm sure she'll be just as happy to do you tomorrow night."

"Hey," Peter seemed to want to defend Jill's honor, but they both knew what the plan was. He calmed, "Hey, why don't we try this? Why don't I go with you tomorrow night?"

"My boss wants it done tonight, so we do it tonight," Linus said, "I'll be back in an hour." Linus stood but Peter wasn't done.

"I'm not going with you," Peter said, "I can go tomorrow night."

"I have something to take care of, tell Claire she's coming too," Linus didn't like being talked back to. His position had enough stress without his subordinates giving him a hard time, "I thought I made it clear, I'd need your help from time to time."

"Yeah," Peter said. Over the past few months, Linus had made a point of stopping in to ask Peter and Claire to review some technical drawings, or some project plans with him. Everything he had them do was completely legitimate.

A month ago, Linus asked Peter and Claire to review plans to inspect another site like the Poinsette Hotel. Claire didn't like it and at first she refused. A subtle mention about her sister brought her around. They'd reviewed the plans, and Claire actually made some good suggestions.

"Look, I pay you well, don't I?" Linus asked. He paid Peter very well for both his and Claire's time. He actually slowly increased the payments until Peter said it could be an issue. "Should I alter that arrangement?"

"No, it's not that."

"Look, Peter," Linus explained, "You and Claire helped me make the plans, now I need the two of you to come help me execute them. We'll be in and out in one night, you'll be back by morning."

"I told you," Peter said, "We don't want to do anything illegal."

"You made the plans," Linus said, "was there anything illegal in them? I'm the BIA inspector, who else says if something is illegal?"

"If it's not illegal, then why do it in the middle of the night?"

Linus knew he would need to use this sooner or later, "Your partner, Frank Lewis?"

"Yes?" Peter leaned forward from his position against the table. He was trying to look intimidating, but Linus thought he looked silly. Linus stood, exasperated.

"Frank's not been a very good boy," Linus said, "He embezzled some money from a client a few years ago." Linus studied Peter's face. He could tell this wasn't news to Peter. He was too calm. But it did take half a heartbeat for him to realize what it meant that Linus knew. "I already knew that. So what?"

"Does the client know? Does the IRS know? Do the Police know?" Linus asked. He knew all the answers were no. Peter looked without saying anything. His silence was welcome as he figured out what was going on.

"I'll see you in an hour," Linus said. Peter looked like he was about to say something. Linus raised his hand, "If the next and only word out of your mouth is not *Certainly*, then I'm going to ask that you bring Jill with you tonight."

The two men looked each other in the face. They were both standing and Peter moved to about a foot away. His eyes were darting back and forth while he weighed his options. Linus didn't think he was being unreasonable. It was only one night, and he was going to pay him for his time. Peter opened his mouth to speak and closed it. Linus smiled. Sometimes it was fun to wield such power.

"*Certainly*," Peter said. Linus waited to make sure there wasn't anything else. Peter looked away. Linus left.

11.   July 7, 1993

Eustis Jefferson should've been annoyed sitting alone in the private room of Nathan's Chophouse. Ten years earlier, he would have been pacing around bothering the waitresses. Now he enjoyed what he expected to be ten minutes alone after a long day.

Mr. Jefferson, as the rest of the group called him, had spent the day in Washington DC a guest of the Securities and Exchange

Commission. He was part of an exclusive twenty member team assembled by the SEC to review the vulnerabilities of the US financial system. Today the team met to conduct a series of tests. The Defense Department would call them *war games*. They simulated scenarios where fraudulent activities had the potential to sink the economy into a depression. It was exhausting work, but some of the most fun Eustis had at his age. He found he looked forward to these exercises all year.

At ten minutes after eight, the dinner was supposed to start at eight, the second attendee arrived. The second to arrive was Pete Elliot, the CEO of Elliot Financial. The two men didn't care for each other. After a polite nod, he stood near the door and waited for the waitress to offer him a drink. He didn't wait long. As he gave his order, three other team members arrived.

The third to arrive was Herbert Wallace. He and Eustis were good friends and spent time together whenever they were in the same city. Eustis also had another reason to speak with Herb, so with only the slightest eye gesture, he called Herb to the seat next to him.

"That was a tiring day," Herb said, "I'm not sure I can keep this up." Herb and Eustis were both in their sixties and among the senior members of the team. They both said this would be their last war game every year, and they both knew it would not.

Eustis removed the heavy glasses from his face and pulled a handkerchief from the small pocket of his vest and cleaned them. It was a habit. They were already perfectly clean. "Did you get the envelope I left in your briefcase?"

"Yes," Herb looked at his friend. He'd seen the envelope during a break a few hours before. He recognized the handwriting from Eustis. Whatever it was, he was sure it was important.

"You have an intern in your new hire program, whatever you call it," Eustis said, "A Dr. Kiadopolis." He looked at Herb who didn't seem to recognize the name. That was not unexpected. "I need to borrow her."

"That's all?" Herb said, "I thought we were going to do something interesting!"

"Well, I might need to borrow her for an extended period. I understand she's probably the best in your class this year."

"I'll look into it," Herb said, "But I'm sure we can spare one intern, even if she's the best. I'll follow your instructions." Herb looked around the room and flagged a waitress.

"Please, I know I don't have to ask you to keep this to yourself."

"No, you don't have to ask," Herb said just as the waitress arrived at his side, "I'll have wine."

"Red or white?" the waitress asked.

"Whatever goes with the meal."

"The chef recommends a California Mon Lis Pinot," The waitress said smartly.

"Excellent," Herb said. Eustis put his glasses back on his face just as a group of younger team members filled the table. He was pleased to see that the youngest member of the group chose to sit next to him opposite Herb. There were all levels of skill in this group, some were the brightest, and some were the second brightest. This young man, the CFO of an energy trading company, might be the brightest in the room.

"Good evening, I'm glad to get to sit next to you," Eustis said to the young man. Herb didn't know him. "Herbert Wallace, may I introduce the Chief Financial Officer of Enron, Jeffery Skilling?"

12.   July 14, 1993

The offices of Cornwall & Wallace occupied the forty-third through fiftieth floors of a midtown Manhattan office building. Sarah sat in the bull pen, an arrangement of twenty desks on the forty-third floor. As members of the intern program washed out, the remaining members of the program absorbed their desks into their own workspaces. Many of the desks were assembled into a large conference table and as their numbers dwindled there was more and more room for each of them. What started as a cramped work area was becoming spacious. In another few months, only ten would remain in the area that originally held thirty-five. No one bothered to maintain the rows or organization that they started with so the desks were haphazard, like they had been dropped from the ceiling.

When the program started there were four women. Sarah started sitting next to one of them and when she washed out Sarah took her desk and networked her computer to her own. She was able to program on one and run simulations on the other. Few knew she had two computers and no one knew what she did with them. The result was she could produce about thirty percent more output than she could have with one. She was also a faster programmer than most, so she was working about fifty percent faster than anyone else in the office.

Tim Cullis had turned out to be even more petty than she expected. As the head of this year's internship team, he could have built a cohesive team with strong bonds, but instead he did everything he could to foster divisions and play political games. He constantly tried to force the team to gang up on one another. He directed interns to secretly find errors in each other's work or to outwit each other's economic simulations. Then, when they went before the chief economics board, Tim would spring the other team's work on them to undermine the primary presentation. He said it made each presentation stronger, but it really only made the office political and manipulative.

When Sarah had called in sick to see Mr. Rassic, Tim went straight to the chief board and moved up her presentation two days. When she returned to the office with a new tan, he moved her presentation up by another day. She had to work all night, but she was able to pull it off and had anticipated the counter attack Tim prepared.

In the end, the board even commented that she seemed relaxed and refreshed and she appeared to be the only one in the bullpen that ever got out. They said she was outsmarting Tim and making it look easy. Rather than working to take credit for his team member's success, Tim got mad. Now, he made things as difficult as he could.

"Mr. Wallace would like to see you at six-thirty tonight, in his office," Tim said in a smug, loud voice. Too loud to only be for her. Sarah couldn't believe she'd washed out, but that was the only reason Mr. Wallace asked to see interns. She was shocked but would be damned if she let Tim see it.

"Thank you, Tim," Sarah said as loudly back. She wished she had something smart to say, but she didn't. She returned to her work and waited.

At six o'clock Sarah went to the building workout center. She showered and changed into the fresh skirt and blouse she kept in her locker. She fixed her makeup and hair. At exactly six-thirty Sarah stepped off the elevator onto the fiftieth floor fresh and ready for her fate.

The fiftieth floor was a different world. It was broken into mahogany walled offices and smelled of leather. A lovely woman about fifty sat at a reception desk.

"Mr. Wallace will see you immediately Dr. Kiadopolis," the

woman said and gestured with her head to the open door with his name next to it. Sarah walked directly into the plush office. It was full of heavy wood, a large desk, wooden walls, and heavy leather couches. She didn't like it at all. She'd never seen Mr. Wallace before. Much as she expected, he was a tall, thin man, probably in his sixties. He'd removed his suit coat and stood in suspenders and tie fumbling with the remote to the television.

Sarah became aware of her dress when she saw the fineness of his clothes, double stitched and perfectly tailored. It wasn't often someone out-dressed her, and she was keenly aware that her clothes were not in the same class as his.

"Karen!" Mr. Wallace shouted and turned toward the door, seeing Sarah for the first time. He looked her up and down and smiled, "I heard you've been making this internship look easy." Sarah smiled inside but wondered why he would say such a thing to someone he was firing. He shouted again, "Karen, I need the TV on!" Sarah stepped forward and wordlessly took the remote from him. She studied it for two seconds and turned the TV on. "Forget it, Karen!"

Mr. Wallace looked more directly at Sarah. "Dr. Kiadopolis." He paused and started again, "May I call you Sarah?"

"Of course," Sarah said to the question that only had one answer.

"I want you to relax, you aren't washing out today," Mr. Wallace had certainly not gotten to where he was without people skills and despite her efforts he could read her discomfort.

"Thank you," Sarah said. *What?*

"No, thank you!" Mr. Wallace said, "It's not often I get to do a friend a favor!"

Sarah didn't understand that.

"Can you put on CNN?" Sarah worked the remote as they both stood in the middle of his office. Sarah got CNN on. She looked at it for just a second then turned to Mr. Wallace. He was looking only at her and smiled.

"Sarah, you and I share a friend I believe," Mr. Wallace said, "and he tells me you will be interested in the news broadcast at six thirty-nine."

"Okay?" Sarah said. What could he be talking about? They continued to stand. The time on the bottom of the screen read six thirty-seven.

"My friend has asked me to put you on special assignment," Mr.

Wallace said, "This is not normal for an intern, so I'll have to take you out of the intern program."

"But you said I wasn't washing out?"

"You aren't. You are, right now, a graduate of the intern program. You're hired. You will be on assignment for the next six months. At the end of six months, you can return to the team, whoever is left on it, or you can continue with the assignment. The choice is yours."

"I don't think I understand," Sarah said, "Who's your friend?"

"Sarah, you and I both know we were going to hire you at the end of the program anyway. This just gets it over with. While the rest of the team is earning their spots you can begin to contribute more fully right now," Mr. Wallace said.

"What will I be doing?" Sarah asked again, "Who's your friend?"

"Oh, I thought this was all clear to you!" Mr. Wallace said, "Oh, look, its six thirty-nine. Let's sit down."

They both quickly sat on the edge of the couch to see the talking head on the television.

"NASA announced today," the talking head said, "that they've been working on a long term solution to the difficulties that have emerged with the Hubble Space Telescope. It seems the lenses were not properly machined and this is causing the images collected from the ten billion dollar satellite to be blurry. The fix will take a year and a shuttle mission will be diverted from its original schedule to make the repairs. In other news. . ."

Sarah stared at the screen wide eyed. "Who is your friend?" She asked.

"Sarah? Are you alright?" Mr. Wallace asked, "Your color is draining right out of you. Do you need a drink? We don't want to miss the story." Mr. Wallace returned to watching the television. Sarah knew she'd seen the story she was meant to see. The next story was about a dog in Texas saving his master. The one after that was about a company that made pocket watches. They watched for five minutes. Sarah turned the TV off after she found the remote was still in her hand. "Well, I hope you've seen what you're supposed to see," Mr. Wallace said.

She had thought little about the silly trip she took to Wisconsin until this moment. She decided the bump in pay Mr. Rassic had offered was interesting, but she understood that her pay would increase rapidly once she left the intern program anyway.

So Maxwell Rassic did know Mr. Wallace. He knew about the Hubble telescope and just contacted her through CNN. He must have nothing to do with Michael Smith, LLC or Mr. Wallace wouldn't call him a friend.

"He asked me to give you this," Mr. Wallace walked back from his desk. Sarah didn't see him go, but now he handed her an envelope. Sarah looked at it and recognized it immediately. It was just like the one Maxwell had sent with the itinerary to travel to Wisconsin before. She knew she would be returning to Wisconsin in the morning. "You're to report only to him, don't talk to anyone here about your assignment, even me. Your salary and benefits will continue uninterrupted and you are still an employee of this firm. You can return here to work at any time." Mr. Wallace looked down at her kindly. Sarah looked up at him from the envelope but said nothing. He smiled and nodded, "Good evening, Dr. Kiadopolis."

13.   July 17, 1993

"I'm Sullivan Acer," Sullivan Acer stood at his table in a training room with thirty others, "Let me see, two things I like and one thing I don't," This was the ice breaker at a training class on personalities everyone had to attend, but no one wanted to. The bright-eyed consultant leading the class acted like she was hanging on every word of everyone's introductions. "I like the Wisconsin Badgers, I like teaching my son how to swim, and, uh, I don't like watching Discovery Channel shows about space!" It was the only thing he could think of. He should have said he doesn't like public speaking, or training classes.

Sullivan sat down and didn't listen at all to the next three people's introductions. Instead he thought about last night. Sullivan's son, Danny, was five and since he was three, all he talked about was space. He loved Star Wars and his backpack had a giant green Yoda on it. Last night, they had to leave the pool early to get home to watch a special on black holes and the latest images from the Hubble Space Telescope. They ended up eating dinner at the coffee table so they could see the beginning.

Six years ago, Sullivan went on one date the summer before he started college with Danny's mother. Leanne had been a cheer leader at their high school and paid no attention to Sullivan while they were there. She was much easier than anyone else Sullivan dated and he couldn't believe his good fortune when he lost his virginity to her that night. They saw each other a few times after that, several times more than Sullivan would have if not for the sex. He realized that while he and his friends were planning to go to college and looking forward to the adventures ahead, Leanne was not. She didn't seem to have any plans. Actually, Sullivan decided she liked hanging around with him and his friends because of the excitement and anticipation in the air.

Sullivan was embarrassed to remember that the first time she didn't have sex with him after a date he decided not to see her again.

He was home at Christmas time that year and ran into Leanne working at the grocery store. He thought she had put on weight, her grocery store uniform was not flattering, but she still looked good. He hadn't had any luck with the girls at college, which wasn't unusual for him, so he happily accepted when she asked if he wanted to get together again.

He was walking her from her parent's door to his parent's car when she told him she was pregnant. He thought that explained the slight bulge in her belly and was disappointed that that probably meant they wouldn't be having sex that night. After he closed the car door and was rounding the front of the car to the driver's seat the realization hit him. Leanne was implying that the child was his.

He was right. They didn't have sex that night. They waited until their son was born and got married the following summer. Sullivan moved into married housing at the University of Wisconsin and they made a run at family life. Sullivan's parents were liberal about this sort of thing and quite supportive.

"You love your son no matter what he does," his father had told him. At the time, he thought he was disappointing his father. But then he said, "You make it easy. I'm proud of you." His parents weren't rich but they helped out as much as they could, and Leanne worked various jobs around the University. With that, they were able to get by for two years.

Then Leanne's parents decided to leave Wisconsin and move to Tennessee. Her parents were less liberal and had never been supportive of Sullivan. They were never openly hostile, but they always pointed out any failing. They seemed to blame him for Leanne's situation; a situation Sullivan thought was actually pretty good. When they decided to move, they asked Leanne to come with them, and she wanted to go.

She told Sullivan she was going and taking Danny with her. It was devastating for him. He pleaded but quickly he learned that she was going to pick her parents over him and there was nothing he could do about it. He struggled with the thought that his marriage was over, but it was. He considered going with her, he was only a year from graduation and maybe he could finish down there, but that would set a difficult precedent. He would always be subservient to her parents. No, if she was choosing them over him, then they had no future. Luckily his father had a friend who was a lawyer and he advised Sullivan that Leanne couldn't just take Danny to another state. Leanne quickly decided to give up her rights without much of a fight.

Sullivan, Leanne, and Danny took one final trip down to Florida that summer. Sullivan hoped that a nice vacation would convince her to stay. It was an expensive trip, but it was his last hope. On the last day in Florida, they went to the Kennedy Space Center. None of them was that particularly interested in the center but they heard they couldn't take a vacation in Florida and not see it.

It was the last good time they had together as a family.

Now, Sullivan figured that was why Danny continued his love of space. So they spent many nights watching the ridiculous, sensationalized Discovery Channel space shows.

Sullivan was pulled back to the training class when he heard a man at the next table introduce himself, "I'm Linus Brenner. I like traveling. I like wintertime. I don't like being in Wisconsin in the summer!"

Linus Brenner.

There he was. Sullivan had tracked Linus Brenner and found he took several more overnight trips. With his other leads, he managed to correlate odd behavior with criminal activity, but not with Linus Brenner. So far he could tell he took odd trips, but couldn't find anything else odd about him.

The class was a day long and had a number of interactive exercises. By the end of the day, Sullivan and Linus had spoken several times. Sullivan figured Linus was very good at talking and sounding like he was saying things while being very careful to not convey any information. The man could easily be hiding things.

14.   July 19, 1993

As expected, Sarah met with Maxwell the next day. That was four days ago. He only told her four things.

First, he told her that he was serious about her developing the algorithms required to design and use a *Space Resonator*. He'd be installing one at the repair of the Hubble Space Telescope, and he needed her to get the data and process it.

Second, he told her he rented her an office in Reston, Virginia. She had to move there and get set up. He would pay her rent so she could keep her New York apartment, or she could quit her job in New York and he would pay her twice her salary. She said she would keep her New York job.

Third, he told her she was to return to Wisconsin and meet with him in four months, on November first at eight a.m.

Fourth, he told her that she could not tell anyone what she was doing, not Mr. Wallace, not Lloyd, not her mother, not anyone. She was to keep all of her work in her office. He pointed out that he had never shown her any papers, and she should never show him any either. He told her Cornwall & Wallace would maintain her cover. He said that if anyone found out what they were doing there would be an international technology race, similar to what happened with the space race and the Cold War.

The entire meeting was held with her standing in front of his desk and him sitting. There was no attempt at greetings, no orange juice. It took only five minutes. He looked forward to seeing her in November. She tried to ask a question, but he waved her out saying that she would figure it out.

Over the next four days, Sarah bought a car, opened a bank account, and rented an apartment in the same complex as her college roommate, Angie Reynolds. Now she was sitting on the floor of her empty office in a stylish building three miles from Dulles Airport in Reston, Virginia.

The building was unremarkable in that all the buildings in the area were stylish. As the area around Washington DC developed, the money available was so large that the contractors were competing for the most extravagant spaces. The building was remarkable in that it had no large tenants, and no listing of its tenants. The guards were expecting Dr. Kiadopolis and identified her with photographs that were obviously taken in Lloyd's office while she waited to see Maxwell. The guards gave her a badge and also coded her fingerprints into the lock on her office door. She was escorted to her office door and the fingerprint scanner was tested. The guard left her alone with a large packet of information.

The eighth floor of the building was a continuous hallway that wrapped in a "D" around the curved building. There were interior and exterior offices and Sarah was relieved to find she had an office with windows at the sharp end of the top of the "D". The floor inside the office was tile just like the hallway, and the office came unfurnished. Sarah took off her heels and sat on the floor resting against the door and opened the folder provided by the guards.

The first page was the list of rules.

1. Do not discuss work outside your office
2. All deliveries must go through the guard desk
3. No modifications to the exterior walls, exterior of the office doors, or hallways
4. No listening, recording, or bugging devices
5. All data lines into or out of the building must go through the data center
6. Do not use last names except the building staff

Sarah thought the last rule was odd, but the others seemed standard. She knew Maxwell was very interested, excessively interested, in security and secrecy. She imagined that the other tenants of her building felt the same way. She set the rules on the floor next to her.

Next she reached into the folder and pulled out a VISA credit card. It had her name on it. It looked like a personal card, not like the university credit cards used by the professors that said *For Business Purposes Only*.

The remaining piece of paper in the folder was a note from Maxwell saying the card was for her business expenses including furnishing her office, computers, and anything else she needed. She looked out the windows into the bright blue sky and wondered what she would do next.

Sarah ate lunch at a McDonald's next to an Ethan Allen furniture store. She bought a desk, a chair, and a large bright red plush area rug to be delivered the next day. She went to an office supply store and bought a dry erase board, markers, paper and notebooks, pens, pencils, and some file folders. She bought a powerful desktop computer and two monitors and had them also delivered the next day. She went to Home Depot to buy the mounting hardware for the dry erase board and a hammer, electric drill, and screwdriver set.

The guards in her building looked at her funny with the dry erase board but let her pass. It took three trips to get all the stuff to her office and she realized she needed to return to the Home Depot for a three-drawer tool chest. She made some noise installing the board but no one commented. It was seven in the evening, but she was happy to finally start mapping out a plan.

Standing barefoot on the hard tile floor under harsh fluorescent light, she pulled out the green dry-erase marker and set to work.

15.   August 4, 1993

Punching Peter Howard in the face was very satisfying. After two failed attempts, Claire had given up at a chance with him, but her feelings for him still frustrated the hell out of her. They spent a lot of time together, but they never moved past what was becoming a deep friendship.

"Now body blows!" the boxing coach shouted. Claire concentrated on her footwork and tried to land her punches past Peter's blocking arms. Boxing was much more difficult than she expected. It was exhausting and required a lot of concentration. Luckily, she was able to get all her frustration out here, in the ring, so their day-to-day relationship didn't suffer from her feelings that just wouldn't go away. She knew he felt the same way, but somehow Linus Brenner seemed to always show up at the wrong time.

Linus Brenner. Thinking of him made her punch harder. He occasionally asked for help investigating burial cysts. *Asked.* She hated that he *asked* every time, but that she didn't really have a choice. He never mentioned the picture of her sister, but the threat was delivered as effectively as the punches she delivered to Peter's face.

At first she didn't even want to review his plans, now they were participating. And Linus was paying Peter too much money for their time, so now they were complicit. But complicit in what? So far they didn't think they'd done anything illegal. It just felt illegal with all the sneaking around.

When Peter suggested that maybe they should learn to defend themselves, Claire was appalled. But as she thought about it, it seemed a wise precaution with the side benefit of spending more time in very close proximity.

"Good Claire, now back to the face!" the boxing coach called out. Peter's job was to wear headgear and a chest pad and act as the boxing dummy while she danced around the ring. Claire redoubled her focus on the smirk on Peter's sweaty face and tried to land a punch on his right cheek.

"Okay, that's enough," the instructor, an old man leaning on the ropes, called. Peter looked to the instructor and for just a moment, his guard was down. Claire took her chance and landed the blow she was looking for. Peter hit the mat harder than she'd wanted. Claire nearly burst into tears at what she'd done. She wanted to be close to him, but certainly not to hurt him! She dropped to her knees over him. He lay on the mat, a little dazed, and just smiled at her. She wanted to touch his face, but her gloves prevented the tenderness she wanted to convey. She fought back the rush of tears.

"I'm okay," Peter whispered. He reached his gloved hand and touched her thigh. She was going to lean in and kiss him. She paused a moment.

"Okay, that's enough," Claire knew she'd paused too long when the instructor called to them. She smiled instead and looked up. The good feeling evaporated when she saw it was Linus, and not her instructor, who told her it was enough. He was sharply dressed in a form fitting suit. He looked like a gangster with is black hair brushed straight back. Just like that, her perfect moment was dashed, again. Damn Linus Brenner.

Claire saw he had a bag in his hand, "Claire, put this on." He held the bag out, "We have an appointment."

"We're not done here," she said. She knew she'd be going with him, but she wanted to resist.

"Oh, I'm sorry," Linus said, feigning concern, "You are done here. Get dressed, today is your first day of your new job." She sat back on her heels while she thought of what her options were. Peter sat up slowly. She could try to run out the back through the locker room and disappear. No, she knew she couldn't disappear. She had no idea how fast Linus could get to her sister, but she was sure he could beat her. "I don't have a lot of time, let's go!" He snapped his fingers. Claire looked at Peter, wishing she had not paused a moment ago. An eternity ago.

. . .

A few moments later, Claire sat alone in the locker room. She was terrified to look into the bag to see what Linus had picked for her to wear. She figured she would run if she couldn't stand the implication of the outfit. Relief poured over her to find a polo shirt and slacks. She quickly showered and met Linus in a black two door Jaguar.

"Boxing?" Linus asked as he pulled onto I-385 toward Greenville.

Claire wasn't sure she wanted to have a conversation with Linus Brenner, and it occurred to her she'd never been alone with him before. They looked just like any two people speeding down the highway. "Yeah, it occurred to us that we might be in some danger on your assignments, so we thought we'd learn to take care of ourselves."

Linus laughed. "Claire, if I think there's any danger, I don't bring you on a job. I've got plenty of muscle. I call you when I need brains. I can train all the covert-ops guys I want. I've got you protected, don't worry." Claire didn't ask who was going to protect her from him.

Linus pulled into an industrial park closer to downtown Greenville, off Woodruff Road. Rows of low buildings, some with garage doors, and some with small storefronts, were all surrounded by small parking lots. She had little idea where she was.

Claire exhaled fully for the first time since she saw Linus when they entered one of the buildings and she saw a normal-looking office with cubicles. As they walked down the row of cubicles, Claire saw the backs of normal-looking people working at normal-looking desks. She tried to look at their computer monitors and could only see that they were engineers of some kind. She could tell because of the technical drawings and calculations she saw on many of the screens.

Linus burst into the walled office at the end. Claire noted that he didn't knock. A small Indian man with a bald head sat with his back to the door. He was working not at a computer but at a work table with electrical equipment scattered around.

"Ravi!" Linus boomed. Claire could tell Ravi knew who was behind him. She could also tell Ravi felt the same way about Linus as she did. He stopped working and his shoulders tensed. He turned slowly around to face the two in his office. Claire thought he was soldering because of the smoke coming over his shoulder. She was surprised to see he was assembling a circuit, but he was also smoking a cigarette. She couldn't smell the smoke and realized Ravi had a fume hood over his workspace sucking the smell out of the room. He almost snarled when he saw Linus. Then he saw Claire, and his face softened.

Ravi stood off his stool and turned to face his guests. He was short. Maybe just over five feet and he carried a large stomach. Claire thought he gained the weight recently because his clothes were too tight and he looked sloppy. He wasn't a practiced heavy person. He mashed his cigarette into an ash tray.

He exhaled loudly and asked in a deferential tone, "Yes, Mr. Brenner, what can I do for you?"

"This is Claire Havers," Linus put his hand on Claire's shoulder. Claire didn't like it but she only smiled at Ravi. "She works here now."

"What?" Ravi's expression turned quizzical, "I've got all the help I need. I'm barely getting by as it is. I do have actual customers, you know!" Ravi spoke with the precise British accent of those raised in India.

"You don't have to pay her," Linus said, "She's going to work on the cell signal processing project." Linus didn't wait for any more discussion. He turned to leave. As he reached the door he turned and said, "One more thing, she works for me, not you." With that he opened the door and closed it after himself.

Claire and Ravi were left staring at each other. The only thing they had in common was Linus, and neither of them seemed to like that man or what he did. Ravi looked down at his desk and pulled out another cigarette. He pushed the box out to offer Claire one.

She shook her head no.

He lit it and let out a long breath of smoke. It wasn't under the hood so Claire could smell it. It smelled awful but she could tolerate it because the motion seemed to relax the man and his shoulders slumped. After about thirty seconds Ravi asked, "So, you're here to watch me?"

Claire didn't know how to answer, "I'm a construction project manager. At least I was this morning. Linus picked me up and told me I worked here now." She thought that would make it clear to Ravi what her situation was. He looked out the side of his head squinting one eye.

"So, what do you know about signal processing?" Ravi asked.

"I double majored in electrical and civil engineering at Clemson," Claire answered. Ravi's eyebrows rose. The double major was impressive and Claire often got that response.

"Fine. So we'll make the best of it," Ravi said. "Come over here and I'll show you what I'm doing."

He turned and faced back to his work bench. Claire walked around the desk and stood next to him. She could smell more cigarettes from here and it took her a moment to get used to it. The table was covered with electrical components. She saw breadboards, power supplies, volt and amp meters, and many integrated circuit chips, resistors, and bits of wire.

"Tell me what you see," Ravi said staring down at his creation after perching himself back on his stool.

"I don't know what this is."

"Don't look at the whole thing, break it down into its parts," Ravi instructed.

"Okay," Claire studied the components. She enjoyed the laboratories at school and she tried to focus, "That's a radio transmitter. No wait, it's a receiver. And there's a processor. Power supply. Those are RC signal conditioners." Claire leaned in to see the circuits more closely. "Between the processor and the receiver, are those multiplexers?"

"Exactly," Ravi smiled and Claire was on a roll.

"So you're using the RC circuitry to isolate a particular frequency from the rest of the signals coming in from the antenna," Sarah looked around, "Where's the antenna?"

"I don't need to make one of those, we're going to install this on cell phone towers," Ravi said.

"But cell phone data is digital, it's bundled into packets," Claire remembered from school. She thought of her sister. She looked away for just a moment but Ravi seemed to catch on to her change of attention.

"What?" Ravi asked. He seemed to be more aware of her than his earlier anger at seeing Linus would suggest.

"It's nothing, a lot's going on," Claire said, "so you're going to piggy-back on the cell phone towers, but you're going to filter out the cell phone data. What for?"

"The clue is the multiplexers," Ravi said. Claire looked at him for a moment. He seemed to really be genuinely enjoying sharing with her what he was doing.

"I don't know," Claire admitted.

"Multiplexers are much faster at capturing discrete data, but they can't store much. So I must be looking for a signal that's small but I don't know when it's coming in," Ravi said.

"What signal?"

"Linus gave me a signature of the signal. I'm using this signal generator to reproduce it and this cell phone circuitry to create the background cell phone noise." Ravi pointed to a bunch of equipment on the shelf over the table.

"What's the signal for?"

"I have no idea," Ravi said. His face darkened, "and I'm pretty sure I don't want to know." Claire looked down at the board. She didn't want to have this conversation.

"So what's next?" Claire asked.

"We're going to test this circuit on a six-cornered cell of the cell phone system as soon as we can get it all working," Ravi explained. He took a deep breath and Claire could see his face brighten, "So I need . . . I guess *we* need six working systems packaged and ready to go. We also need a portable signal generator to emit the pulse."

Claire looked at Ravi. She looked around his office. She had no idea what was going to happen when Linus appeared at the boxing ring and short of Peter beating Linus to death, she decided this was as good an outcome as she could have expected.

16.   October 21, 1993

Jim tried to walk calmly toward the Oval Office. He carried a new letter in his breast pocket. He had just convinced the Vice President that there was no realistic option but to comply. The Threat Rose was up to five and this demand was too public and too specific to hide.

> *The Relationship is damaged. The continued parsing of our meaning is troubling. We need to trust each other. Stop all work on the Super Collider currently under construction in Waxahachie, Texas. Destroy the work to date, and do not begin construction of another machine.*

> *-LV*

Jim knew exactly why LV would want the government to cancel the collider. The Desertron was the best chance to advance science in America. When it was up and running the US would move decades ahead in the areas of science with the most promise of leading to the next global technology revolution. It could be the best chance they had to neutralize LV's threat.

He didn't know how LV figured it out.

Uneducated Congressmen regularly railed against what they called a waste of money, but the Desertron didn't appear in any specific line item in the budget. Department 55 funded it entirely, and Department 55 didn't show up in any report. The Desertron was one of Department 55's largest expenditures and it was a feat of accounting genius for Eustis Jefferson to keep it undetected under such scrutiny.

Someone must have leaked something. Jim paused on his way through the ornate halls of the West Wing at the realization that someone must have leaked something. Damn. He'd have to improve Department 55's security precautions.

Three secretaries staffed the room. None knew what Jim Williams did, but they all knew that he was allowed to pass unquestioned into the Oval office at any time. Jim knew there were exactly seven people with that privilege.

He entered unannounced and stood next to the door.

The *Resolute* desk of the President dominated the top of the room in front of the windows overlooking the Rose Garden to his left. Six people sat on the couches directly in front of him debating. It took Jim a moment to recognize the President sitting to his right in a high-backed chair next to the fireplace opposite his desk. The President's head was down and he didn't see Jim enter.

Jim recognized that two of the people on the couches were congressmen and he listened long enough to learn they were arguing the details of earmarks for their districts. Something about two million dollars in one project versus two point five million in another had the President staring at the floor. Jim spent more than that every day. He didn't think the conversation should involve the President of the United States, and judging by the President's posture, the President agreed with him.

Suddenly President Clinton looked up and saw Jim. For the first time since they met on Bill Clinton's Inauguration Day, the President looked happy to see him. He stood, "I have to ask you to excuse me, I'm sorry."

"But we're not done!" the feisty congressman closest to Jim blurted. He thought better of it when the President looked him squarely in the eye from a standing position. The meeting broke up and the six quickly filed past Jim out the door, probably wondering who he was.

After they left, the President addressed the Secret Service Agent stationed next to the door, "Mike, give us a moment?" Mike didn't hesitate.

If Jim thought Bill Clinton looked happy a moment ago, he was wrong. The President's face returned to the scowl to which Jim had grown accustomed. Jim stepped up to the couch and handed the copy of the letter to the President. He waited while the President read it.

"Al Gore?" The President asked without looking up. Jim nodded. The President exhaled loudly, and Jim saw him age before his eyes.

"Do it."

17. October 30, 1993

Working with Linus was lucrative. He paid Peter for Claire's work despite her not doing anything for him. Peter was paid for his time. At first, it was frustrating when Linus asked Peter to do something, but Peter quickly learned the things he asked for were usually fun.

Mainly Linus needed help with job sites. The same kind of work Peter accidentally found him doing that night at the Artifact. At first, Peter and Claire just helped with planning. Now they were involved in the jobs. Slowly, Linus asked for more and more. So far, he never asked either of them to do anything illegal. It just seemed like they were.

Linus was certainly looking for something inside those burial cysts, but they never found anything but dead Indians. Peter told Linus that if they did find something, he and Claire would not help break the law. Linus assured Peter that he'd bring in different crews if they ever found anything *interesting*.

In the beginning, it didn't make any sense for Linus to coerce Peter and Claire into helping him. He seemed to have plenty of people to do his work. But after a while, they realized Linus' people were inefficient. What took three of his people ten hours, Claire and

Peter got done in three.

And then there was Claire. The night of The Artifact opening, Peter reserved a room in the hotel despite living less than a mile away. When he arrived at the bar, she was looking for him as much as he was looking for her. He knew that night was one of those rare times when a fledgling relationship got a second chance. Her blue dress set off her red hair, and for a moment, they were the only people in the crowded room. Somehow, Linus interrupted again. After that, Claire cooled, and Peter thought they were definitely through this time. Peter wasn't one to dwell on things and he tried to move on, but he couldn't shake his feelings for Claire.

Yesterday, Linus showed up at his trailer again with a special assignment. Peter was to travel to a wedding. One of the bridesmaids knew things Linus wanted to know. Information was a valuable commodity, and he was willing to pay for it. Linus provided an invitation to the wedding and the name of the bridesmaid. Peter was to make contact with the woman so that they could develop a lasting relationship. He was to gain her trust. Linus said he saw how well Peter handled women, and that this one was a scientist, so he needed someone with Peter's background. Peter knew he didn't have a choice, and he couldn't see anything illegal about attending a wedding and meeting a woman.

Peter watched the wedding ceremony with interest. They were on Palm Beach in south Florida. The balcony of the Breakers Hotel overlooked the ocean. He wasn't looking at the ocean, but instead enjoying the game of trying to figure out which of the five bridesmaids was the one he was here to meet.

The beach setting for the wedding meant the bride and her entourage spent the last few days in the sun. Three of the bridesmaids were burned. Clearly they were from up north and got too much sun. They were not heavy, but their dresses didn't do them any favors and they didn't hold his attention. The other two, positioned furthest from the bride, were different. They were striking women whom he enjoyed studying. They were both tall and thin and clearly more careful about the sun. The first was angular like a model with smooth creamy white skin and no sign of a burn. The second was tan and strong, probably a marathon runner. They both stood slightly out of position to get in the shade of the building. Peter hoped one of these two was the woman he was sent to meet, but he thought realistically it was probably one of the burned ones.

Peter spent his time avoiding the advances of the single women during the reception while the bridesmaids attended to the scripted events. He was a little older than the wedding party but younger than the parents. He took care of himself and knew he looked good in a nice suit, and his easy conversational style served him well in these situations. He knew he could enjoy the company of any one of about half a dozen women, but he didn't want to complicate things with meeting another woman. This was actually fun!

Finally the official activities concluded and he was talking to one of the burned bridesmaids. "I'm an old business associate of the groom's uncle," Peter told Gale. He figured that was close enough to justify being here, but far enough that no one could question it.

Gale was a little tipsy. Peter was handing her another drink, "Okay, are you staying here at this hotel?" Gale was aggressive and while Peter had no intention of taking advantage of it, he knew she could help him meet his mark. He made small conversation with her until the tall, striking model bridesmaid joined them. Now he was getting somewhere.

"Gale, who've you found?" the model asked with a smile that didn't reach her eyes, accentuating the angles of her beautiful face. She put her hand on Gale's shoulder as she looked straight into Peter's face, "What would John think of you spending all this time over here with this suave guy?" Her voice was kind, but her look was not. Gale's face fell at the mention of John.

"John can go to hell!" Gale blurted. This was not what Peter wanted. He couldn't be seen as a man preying on some vulnerable woman at the wedding.

"My girlfriend couldn't come to the wedding either," Peter didn't have a girlfriend, but he had to not be a threat, "I was telling Gale, I couldn't wait to get back to her tomorrow, that I was looking for a souvenir to bring back to her." That wasn't what he was telling her, but Gale went along with it because she didn't want to look desperate either.

"Yeah," she wasn't a good liar, "I wish I was as excited to get home as, as, what was your name?"

Perfect. Peter reached his hand out to Model bridesmaid, "I'm Peter Howard."

She didn't seem to want to meet him, but it was a wedding, and she was a bridesmaid, so she had to, "I'm Angie Reynolds." Damn. Peter was holding out hope she was the one. But she wasn't. "Are you okay? I'm sorry to disappoint!" Angie's face told him she wasn't sorry at all. Peter's face must have shown his disappointment.

Now Marathon, the fifth bridesmaid, came over to see what was happening. She put her arm around Angie and the sleeveless dress revealed a surprisingly strong bicep.

"Gale, are you meeting new people?" Marathon asked. Her genuine smile reached all the way to her eyes. "You know you're supposed to be on your best behavior! Come on!"

"It's not like that, Sarah!" Gale said. *Sarah.* Marathon was his mark. "Why do you girls always think the worst of me? I wasn't going to take Peter up to my room!" Actually, Peter knew that was exactly what she wanted to do.

"Well, now," Sarah said, "it's bad form to tell this poor guy you're not going to sleep with him." She looked at Peter for the first time. Her smile remained. "Maybe I'll have to take him upstairs to make it up to him!" Peter was knocked off his game with that comment and struggled to find words. Sarah knew it and her bright smile showed she was enjoying it.

Peter was saved by the music starting up again, "Ha! Why don't you three go and dance. You can decide who's taking me upstairs later!" Sarah laughed with Peter. It was a comfortable laugh of two people who now shared an inside joke. Angie didn't laugh and looked at her friend in shock. Gale liked the dancing idea and struggled to get off the barstool gracefully.

Sarah winked at Peter as the three women left him for the dance floor. His work here was done.

18.   November 1, 1993

Sarah returned to Wisconsin for the first time since she accepted the job in July. Her arrangement with Maxwell Rassic was coming to an end and she was only getting started. Although she had accepted the assignment begrudgingly, this project was much more fulfilling than the Wall Street stuff. She wanted to continue the project and had prepared a detailed description of her work plan focusing on the future.

The same secretary greeted her in the atrium and watched Sarah climb the stairs with the same half-smile. "Good morning," Lloyd greeted Sarah at the top of the atrium stairs. "It's been a while."

"Yes, it has. Long enough for the weather to turn cold," Sarah couldn't think of much to say to this man she barely knew. He turned, and she followed him to the outer office.

Lloyd turned and faced her inside his office, "Your coat?" He held out his hand.

Sarah unbuttoned her red overcoat and as she pulled it off she followed Lloyd's eyes down her body across her chest under a tight knit sweater to thick skin colored stockings and beige heels. She really didn't know what to wear. She was afraid it would be colder in Wisconsin in November than it ever got in Virginia or New York. She didn't own a pant suit and this was her warmest outfit. Lloyd himself was wearing a high-neck sweater with a zipper zipped up all the way. Sarah knew she caught him staring, and she could give him a hard time, but she also knew it would serve her better in the long run to take a different tack.

Sarah bent her knee letting her heel come out of her shoe as she let her coat slide from her shoulders. When Lloyd's eyes moved back up her body he found her staring straight at him with a small smile. He smiled back only for a moment before he took her coat and turned to hang it up.

"The weather's turned cold, but it's going to get colder," Lloyd said to the coat rack, "I'm from this area, I'm used to it. You can always put clothes on, but you can't always take more -" He stopped himself before he said *off*; Sarah knew. After he finished with the coat, his shoulders drooped and he moved back to his desk.

"I agree," Sarah said. She knew he felt self-conscious, "But I would still choose laying out on a beach to freezing my ass off any day!" She talked brightly knowing she was drawing attention to his awkwardness further. She smiled at him and brushed her hair back from her shoulders.

"Dr. Kiadopolis," Mr. Rassic said, standing to her left in his open door, "I'm sure Mr. Jansen here would like to hear more about your beach vacations later, but you and I have other things to discuss." His voice was his normal boom. She was sure she looked at him wide-eyed. As much as she was enjoying embarrassing Lloyd, she felt equally embarrassed with Mr. Rassic. He raised an eyebrow with a small smile and turned into his office. Sarah and Lloyd shared a look. Sarah mouthed the word *Sorry* to him. He smiled sheepishly and sat.

Sarah followed Maxwell into his office. She was glad he led her to the comfortable seating area and not to stand in front of his desk.

He had already set out glasses of orange juice. She made a point of sitting more comfortably, trying to look less nervous than she was.

"So, you've been buying a lot of computers?" Maxwell dove right in. Crap. Sarah had been spending a lot of money on Maxwell's Visa Card. She needed the equipment to make the calculations she knew he needed. She'd spent more money in the last four months than she did during her entire graduate school program. If he was worried about the cost, this conversation was going to lead to her returning to New York. She wanted to start this discussion with her work, not what it was costing him.

"Yes," Sarah said, "I researched the format of the data transmitted from Hubble. I've gotten an account on the file transfer protocol site so I can -" Maxwell raised a hand.

"I don't care about the computers. Buy whatever you need." Sarah thought she would have to argue about this. That was easy. She didn't know what to do next, so she just looked at him.

Maxwell looked exactly as he did the last time she saw him. His three piece suit was a throwback to an older time, but it fit him well. Sarah guessed he was in his mid-fifties. Lloyd didn't wear a suit and the receptionist downstairs dressed similar to Sarah. She still hadn't seen anyone else in the building, but she guessed Maxwell was the only one dressed this formally. He sat with his left leg over his right presenting a well-polished shoe. Sarah noted his hair was perfectly cut and his neck was shaved. She heard that some men got haircuts every few days instead of shaving themselves. Maybe he was one of them. His thick frame filled the chair he was in where Sarah knew there was at least six inches on either side of her.

"What can you tell me about my *Space Resonators*?" Maxwell asked.

Sarah smiled. This was what he was paying her for. He sent her off to think about the problem of decoding the data. He was paying her to get a head start on the work and to make sure there wasn't something he needed to account for in the design. But there was.

As she worked at her dry erase board deriving the methodology to decode the images that could come in from Hubble, she realized the thickness of the resonator was a key variable. It took her two months to derive the ideal value. She was glad to have the answer ready for this moment, "The resonator's thickness must be exactly eighty-seven point three millimeters." She didn't explain further.

Maxwell held up his large hand and extended his index and thumb about as far as they would reach. Then he moved them closer together. He examined them and tried to gauge eighty-seven point three millimeters. "About three inches, right?"

"About three and a half," Sarah said.

"I've been building a five inch *Resonator*," Maxwell said.

"No, I'm sorry," Sarah said, "that won't work. If the *Resonator* is thinner, the gravitons will pass through and not be amplified sufficiently." Sarah assumed they were using the conceptual design she had suggested in her thesis. Dr. Long had asked her to remove that part of her dissertation, too much science fiction, but Sarah insisted and he let her put it in as an appendix. Now that appendix had to be how he was doing it.

"I knew that, is there a problem with it being too thick?"

"Yes," Sarah said, "It's a little counterintuitive. One would expect that thicker would mean more data, and I thought the same thing. But the math tells me that if we make it too thick, the gravitons will agglomerate."

"They'll stick together?"

"Exactly," Sarah said, "I can't think of anywhere that could happen in nature, but if it does, the *Resonator* would still be affected by them but the data would only show a blob."

"A Blob?" Maxwell said, "Is that the technical term for it?"

"We're talking about something no one else in the world has ever talked about. There is no technical name for it." Sarah said, "We could call it a *Maxwell* if you like." Sarah lifted her juice to her lips to cover the smile that she couldn't stop.

"Yes," Maxwell said. His eyes also brightened. "I'm sure we'll discuss something a little more valuable in the future, so I might save *Maxwell* for something a little more prestigious, if you don't mind!"

"Okay."

"Anything else?" Sarah was a little disappointed Maxwell was done with that conversation, but she was beginning to learn he was focused only on results. She only shook her head no.

"Now, some very practical matters," Maxwell said. Sarah returned her glass to the table between the chairs as it was empty now. "Your time with C&W has come to an end. They'll take you back whenever you want, but I'll be paying your salary starting in two weeks. You should move out of your New York apartment." Sarah looked at him.

How did he know she still had her apartment in New York? He had offered to pay for her Virginia apartment, but she decided to pay for it herself because of how much money she was spending on her computers. She was both happy he had assumed she was going to stay and a little disturbed that he knew something that she didn't think he would. In the end, she decided it didn't matter and wasn't that private a piece of information, "Okay, thank you," was all she said about it.

"And we've experienced a leak of information. The need for security is no longer a theoretical construct, but unfortunately has become a real concern," the levity on his face disappeared. He was very serious.

"A leak having to do with my work?" Sarah couldn't imagine how she could have leaked something. She didn't communicate with anyone. That was turning out to be more difficult than Sarah thought it would be. She was used to working with other people, playing ideas off her colleagues. It was difficult, but she had not told anyone what she was doing.

"No, not you, but my boss asked me to remind you that this all has to be kept to yourself," Maxwell said.

"Mr. Rassic," Sarah said, "I've told my friends that I'm on assignment from C&W in Washington. They didn't fully understand what I did there anyway, so they don't ask a lot of questions."

"Good, keep it that way" Maxwell said, "Although you're working for me, your paycheck will continue to come through C&W. If someone calls there, they will confirm you work there." Sarah was at first surprised, but she remembered Mr. Wallace had called him a friend. "Have you spoken with your mother?"

"I talk to her regularly," Sarah looked at him sideways. Why would he ask about her mother? "Why?"

"It's important that you live a normal life," Maxwell said. That was weird. She was living a normal life. Who said anything about her not living a normal life? She worked on a special project for the government, what was abnormal about that? Everyone in her building did that. Maybe everyone in her building worked for Maxwell for all she knew. Maxwell smiled, "Sarah, you've maintained your New York apartment. I'm asking you to get rid of New York, and fully accept the job I'm offering you in Virginia. I need the *Resonator*, and I'm sure you want to give it to me. I believe we have settled your financial concerns, and your mother's, so you can focus."

Sarah looked at him but didn't have anything to say. She didn't know if she liked him thinking about her personal life, but he seemed to be trying to help her.

"Sarah," Maxwell said, he leaned forward, "The work you're doing is very important to me. It's very important to the United States. That means several things. First, you are important to me, and I want you to be as productive as possible. If you encounter any inconvenience that can be resolved with money, don't hesitate." He looked at her to make sure she understood.

"Okay," Sarah said. She felt like she was a little girl talking to her father.

"Second, if your work is important to the United States, then it would be important to many other governments if they knew about it. This department is not new, and over the years we have learned that keeping this work under wraps is critical. The people that ran the CIA and KGB have trained a new generation of spies, and they aren't looking for military secrets. They're looking for secrets that will put their countries ahead economically."

"Am I in danger?" Sarah asked. Maxwell stared at her. He was measuring his response. The longer he thought about his answer the more silly she felt. Again, she felt like a child.

"No," he finally said, "you're not in danger. We haven't had any issues like that. The most recent leak resulted in canceling the Desertron."

"The Desertron?" Sarah blurted. She knew the Desertron was canceled. Rick Patterson lost his job and his life's work, that day. "*You* canceled the Desertron?"

"No, *I* didn't", Maxwell said, "The leak forced my boss to tell *his* boss to cancel it, and it got canceled."

"How? What was the leak?" Sarah was taken aback.

"We live in a complex world where we struggle to maintain the smallest technological advantage," Maxwell said, "Do you understand?"

"Yes," Sarah didn't, but he got his point across. Keep everything secret, got it.

"Third," Maxwell said, "I don't have a backup for you, so don't think I want you to stop working on this project. If you're thinking about leaving the project, for any reason, let me know."

"Okay," Sarah said.

"If you're getting offers for a new job, if you feel like relocating to California, if you get pregnant and you want to be a full time mom, let me know," Maxwell looked her straight in the face expectantly.

"I'm not pregnant and I'm not moving," Sarah said.

"Good, do you have any questions for me?" Maxwell asked.

Sarah thought for a moment. She had only met this man, her boss, four times. She was expected to work independently until January without any contact. "No, I'm clear."

Maxwell smiled his little smile, "Excellent." He stood. Sarah took it as a cue to do the same. They shook hands and without anything further, she walked to the door. With her hand on the knob she looked back to see him walking back to his desk, his back to her. She opened the door and left.

Lloyd helped her into her coat. They shared a smile. She was only in the building for thirty five minutes.

. . .

Linus Brenner never got tired of traveling. He was free to do whatever he wanted to meet his objectives. He never traveled for pleasure but was on the road almost constantly for work. He drove up Route 267 toward DC from Dulles Airport. He'd memorized the directions to take him directly from the airport to his destination. It was late in the evening, and the roads should have been clearing, but Northern Virginia traffic was notorious for rush hour lasting until 10PM. Tonight, he had a job to do three miles from the airport and he had plenty of time to make his 8AM flight the next morning.

He wore a button down blue shirt, slacks, loafers, and a new sport coat, no tie. It was the standard uniform for business men on the late and early flights, and he looked exactly like eighty percent of the men at the airport. He was anonymous if not invisible.

The secret funding of the Desertron showed how determined the US Government was to find any technology that could help them in their struggle with LV. Linus didn't know how LV's scientists determined that the Desertron could lead to their demise, but he knew it required a source of information from inside the US government. It was his job to seek-out any other sources of information coming from the US government that would help LV by any means necessary. Linus liked jobs that were *by any means necessary.*

Linus watched the mileage on the car and knew his left turn into the upscale apartment complex was approaching. He had called ahead to learn that twelve four-story buildings were arranged in concentric rings around a community swimming pool. He drove directly to the specific unit and selected the reserved parking spot of the owner whom he knew was out of town. He lifted his briefcase from the passenger seat, stepped out of the car, and walked to the building. He was looking for 404 and walked up the outside stairs. At this hour the young single people were out and the young married people were getting ready for bed so he was alone in the stairway. Once he reached 404, his skill with his lock-pick set got him into the apartment in fifteen seconds.

A light shone in the window making a pattern across the vaulted ceiling. He made his way through the apartment and closed the blinds before turning on the light near the front door. He'd reviewed the layout of the apartments from a brochure and related the actual space to the image in his head. From the doorway, he looked past the small dining area into a larger space that was half living room and half kitchen. He knew the closed door to his left went to the laundry and the door to his right to the only bathroom. The bathroom connected to the bedroom. The main door to the bedroom was out of his view, ahead and to the right. Windows on the right of the main living room looked out on a balcony. The space seemed large for an 800 square foot single bedroom apartment. He appreciated the high ceilings and now understood that the climb up three flights of stairs was worth it.

He stepped forward to a small desk against an angled wall opening into the large living room. The desk had a tidy pile of mail. He confirmed the address and the tenant and shuffled through the mail with gloved hands. Nothing interesting, but he laid them all out and photographed them nonetheless.

Linus picked up a picture frame on the desk to study. Two people were in the picture, likely the woman and maybe her grandmother. She seemed happy in a summer dress although her grandmother's look was vacant. She was nice looking, good legs.

He looked through all the cabinets in the kitchen and read all the titles in her 'library' which was the shelf made by the top of her kitchen cabinets. At first glance, they all looked like cookbooks. Upon further investigation, most were texts on all topics. Again, nothing interesting, but again, photographs. Her refrigerator was normal; there was frozen meat in the freezer, some ice cream, and Tupperware containers. Her living room was simply decorated, a couch, a chair, a television, some pictures on the walls.

He set his briefcase on the counter in the kitchen and pulled out a number of listening devices, small cameras, a network hub, and a set of small tools.

It took him twenty minutes to cut a small opening in the back panel of the top, corner cabinet with a hand saw. He had to be quiet because the wall abutted the neighboring unit. He routed the connection wire from the network hub down the space behind the cabinets and into the fixture of the under-cabinet lighting. He spliced the power supply into the power feed for the light and mounted the hub in the wall. Supply power was always the challenge of long term surveillance. He replaced the panel using wood putty to fill the cracks and returned the contents of the cabinet.

He replaced one of the GFI outlets in the kitchen with a camera module and another with a microphone module. Both still were functioning outlets. From there, he'd be able to hear and see everything in the kitchen and living room. He installed microphone modules in the bedroom and bathroom. He then installed bugs in each of the two telephones in the apartment. He'd been in the apartment for two hours and completed the technical work.

Linus retrieved his camera from the peninsula and returned to the bedroom. He sat in a small chair in the corner and surveyed the room. The room had double doors opening to the living room, a door to the closet, and a door to the bathroom. A queen sized bed was in the traditional position in the center of the room and a dresser was in the corner. A bookshelf next to the dresser had no books but served as a display case for sports trophies, pictures of some college girl-friends laughing, and other assorted memorabilia.

He was supposed to find anything out of the ordinary, so he looked through her closet, dresser, and laundry. There was nothing unusual for a woman. She had plenty of shoes, skirts, and dresses. She seemed to exercise a lot, she was a member of a gym, had basketball, soccer, running, and cross training shoes that all looked worn, and she had several jerseys.

She had a few lacy bra and panty sets but no leather or cuffs. Her underwear was pretty but not sexy. There was no evidence of a man in her life.

There were no work papers, her computer didn't have password protection, and there were no messages on her answering machine. There was no sign she worked from home or had anything from work in her apartment.

There was no evidence of anything useful for blackmail. No

safe, no pile of overdue bills, no revealing photos. There were no pictures of children or boyfriends. There was a bottle of wine and a few expensive beers in the refrigerator, but no evidence of drug use. There was nothing in the back of the toilet, nothing in the top of the closet, nothing shoved into the toe of a shoe, nothing in the washing machine or behind any of the heating vents.

Linus photographed everything in the apartment.

Satisfied he knew a lot about this woman, he set about to see that he had left no trace. He re-opened each drawer to see that everything looked as neat as he had found it. He re-examined the closet to see that the shoes were all arranged and the clothes were not bunched. He checked the outlets he modified to confirm that they worked, and studied the floor below them to see that he had left no dust. He picked up his briefcase, turned off all the lights, opened the shades, and returned to the doorway. He looked back to confirm that he had not left footprints in the carpet, and he left. He had three hours to get back to the airport and make his return flight.

19.   December 8, 1993

Kathryn Thronton couldn't believe the bad luck she had over the last five hours. She was focused intently on the detailed work in front of her. She was trying to remove a small nut from a shaft with an electric ratchet. She'd done this about two hundred times before but this time the nut was stuck on a burr. She was frustrated that her gloves prevented her from grabbing it.

Tom was around the other side completing his work and would be done any minute. Kathryn was at least thirty minutes behind and she still had another task to complete, a task Tom didn't know about.

Kathryn closed her eyes and listened to the sound of her breathing. She had to calm down. After she felt calm, she opened her eyes and looked to her right.

Two hundred miles away Kathryn could see the Horn of Africa speeding by at 17,000 miles an hour. She gave herself ten seconds to look at the view, the blue of the Indian and Atlantic Oceans spectacularly sharp on this cloudless day in South Africa. She looked slightly to the left and saw the radiation panel of the Hubble Space Telescope about fifty feet from her. Her legs were stiff because they hadn't moved in three hours. Her space suit boots were magnetically fixed to the platform below her to give her a solid footing for her work. She was repairing the Hubble Space Telescope. She knew if she looked to the left she would see the cabin of the Space Shuttle *Endeavour* with the crew beginning to watch her expectantly. She didn't look.

She reversed the direction on the electric ratchet and drove the nut at full power back onto the stud. She then reversed it again and at full power drove the nut off. With that speed the nut broke through the burr and came loose. Her relief was short lived as she saw the nut come loose from the ratchet and float past her visor. She thought about grabbing the nut traveling slowly past her but decided against the sudden movement. She had a spare. The nut disappeared over her shoulder. She smiled as she thought that in five thousand years, that nut could be part of Saturn's rings.

With that nut free she was able to complete the task she was here to do. Two days ago, on her first spacewalk of this Shuttle Mission, she'd installed a new instrument on the Hubble Telescope. This entire mission was about fixing the Hubble and the entire crew was here for that purpose, but Kathryn had been asked, very privately, to install a new instrument. She was able to practice the other details of her mission in the deep space simulation water tank in Houston, but she was doing this part for the first time. With the new instrument in place she had to connect the power and data cables to the main busses. She stood at this panel because she was also out here to finish the repairs everyone else was here for. She thought it would be easy to also connect the busses but she had not planned for this stupid nut.

With the nut off, she was able to quickly connect the power and data cables. She replaced the nuts and was closing the panel when Astronaut Tom Akers appeared around the side of the Hubble Telescope.

"You need a hand?" Tom asked. She knew he was joking. In their huge suits there was no way they could both work inside this panel. She also knew he couldn't see what she had just done.

"Nope, I just finished," Kathryn said as she pushed the hinged door closed. "I'm just going to put these two bolts back in and we can go inside."

"No problem for me!" Tom said. Protocol required Tom to wait for her and they return together. Kathryn knew he would do what anyone would do in his situation. He took the opportunity to look around and allow his body to float in space.

20. December 9, 1993

Peter Howard turned forty-one yesterday. He didn't feel old except when he exercised. When he was twenty, he didn't know why people warmed up. He could show up to a softball game and throw as hard as he wanted the first time. He played catch with everyone because that was what everyone was doing, not because he needed it. That changed when he turned thirty. He found he needed to warm up or he'd hurt himself. By the time he was thirty-five, he began to feel sore after exercise and he couldn't play two or three sports a day. Now he could only workout four times a week or he'd build up injury and develop nagging issues. If he didn't work out four times a week, he could feel his muscles weaken and his stomach bulge.

And Peter Howard wasn't going to have his stomach bulge. He maintained a tan year round, colored his hair; thankfully his hair greyed and didn't fall out, and maintained a thirty-two inch waist. He was keenly aware he was starting to show his age, but he was going to do everything he could to slow it. Luckily, a sixty year old man looked good if he took care of himself.

Peter and Frank's business was thriving with unlimited demand for new construction projects. Peter was even starting to consult for other builders who needed help getting permits or other issues with county, state, and even federal agencies. He wasn't sure, but he thought Linus might have been steering business his way. Sometimes Linus would mention a business deal he shouldn't have known about. But then again, Linus Brenner knew about a lot of things that weren't any of his business.

Peter was staying outside of Washington DC for a meeting tomorrow morning with the Federal Housing Authority. He was consulting on a project outside Charlotte, NC. Whenever he traveled he found gyms with reciprocity agreements with his own in Greenville. Linus called him earlier today and told him Sarah Kiadopolis would be working out at this particular gym in Reston, Virginia tonight. Linus asked that he meet her again and take her out for dinner. He wanted Peter to develop a relationship with this woman, and he didn't mind that it took a while. Peter certainly couldn't object to meeting Sarah again. Unfortunately, it meant changing his flights to come in early and he had to miss boxing with Claire.

While Peter was beginning to see past the jerk that was Linus, Claire didn't like Linus Brenner at all. In fact, Claire said she wanted to kill him at least three times. Peter thought he knew her pretty well, and he thought she was deadly serious. Since Linus had interrupted their attempts at getting together twice, Peter didn't think he'd ever get another chance. Still, he found himself thinking of her often. Peter thought of himself as a lifelong bachelor and considered Claire the closest he'd ever get to a wife. They weren't even dating.

"Peter Howard?" Sarah was scheduled to take a Yoga class tonight. How Linus knew that, Peter couldn't imagine. Peter timed his workout to be at the pull up bar strategically located between the Yoga studio and the locker rooms when the class let out. He was struggling past four pull-ups when Sarah finally passed him and called his name. He pushed through and got twelve then dropped lightly to the ground. His arms were burning, but he didn't let it show.

Sarah stood before him with the same genuine smile he couldn't stop looking at in Florida. "Well, Sarah," Peter picked up a towel, "Right?" She looked great with a light sweat and her hair pulled back in a ponytail. Peter wiped his face, his arms protesting. "What are the chances?"

"I could ask you the same thing!" Angie Reynolds leaned into Sarah. Peter recognized the model bridesmaid from the wedding. She wore the same suspicious scowl. What had Peter done to her? "What are you doing here?"

"I'm washing my car," Peter glanced at Angie and offered an obviously silly answer for an obviously silly question.

"I thought you lived in South Carolina?" Sarah asked. Her smile was still there.

"I do," Peter said, "I travel to this area for work a lot. I just found this gym, - Hey, how do you know where I live?" Peter was careful not to mention where he lived to anyone in Florida.

This question made Sarah look away for an instant. Peter couldn't help but look down to the Virginia Tech stretched in pink across her chest. His glance was only for a moment, and he was sure Sarah didn't see it, but when he looked up, he looked directly at Angie who definitely did.

Angie glared at Peter as though he had just reached out and honked her breasts rather than steal a glance. Angie crossed her arms over her chest. "She checked up on you after the wedding. Is there something wrong with that?" Sarah's smile switched to a look of shock, and she whirled around to face her friend.

"Why'd you tell him that?" Sarah asked her over protective friend.

"It's okay," Peter said, "I like an industrious and resourceful woman." Sarah's smile returned. Peter had softened the situation and turned Angie's comment designed to end the conversation into an angle. Sarah seemed open to it because she turned back to face him. The toe of her bright blue running shoe touched the floor allowing her strong calf to relax. Her hand rested on the railing of the workout station. She was relaxed and open. A case study in contrast with Angie's firm battle stance with arms crossed. Peter decided if he didn't move soon this would become awkward. "What are you doing later? I'm here on business and my dinner fell through. Care to join me?" Sarah's face stayed relaxed as she looked to Angie. Angie looked horrified. "You can tell me everything you learned about me, and how you learned it."

"We've got another engagement," Angie said, "We do have to get going."

"She's right," Sarah said. She looked genuinely disappointed, "I'm afraid it'll have to be another time." Sarah looked at the clock. "And we do have to go, I'm sorry. It was nice seeing you again, Peter Howard." Peter struggled to not show his disappointment.

"No problem," he didn't think there would be another time, but he didn't think there was anything further he could do. Peter stared at the legs and asses of the two women as they walked away. Sarah turned and caught him checking her out from about twenty feet away. He'd learned a long time ago that when you were caught, own up to it. Don't look away. He looked her directly in the face and smiled. He nodded slightly. Sarah said something to Angie and walked quickly back.

"Our thing only goes until about ten tonight. I could meet you for a quick drink at Charlie's then," Sarah looked at him expectantly.

Peter smiled but not too broadly, "See you then."

21. December 10, 1993

"Do me next! Do me!" Sullivan looked up from his drawing he'd just completed. Erin, one of his best friends in the world, hurried over in a red Santa cap.

"Hold on," Sullivan said, "I'm just finishing up Travis." It was the annual office Christmas party, and as had become a tradition, Sullivan was drawing caricatures of everyone in the office. Travis sat with his wife for five minutes while he drew bubbly characters emphasizing Travis' solid build compared to his wife's petite figure. Sullivan liked drawing, he was good at it, and he liked the idea of spending five minutes studying Erin's pretty face, but he was getting tired. He signed his name to the bottom of Travis' picture, and the happy couple thanked him and returned to the party.

"What would you like me to do?" Sullivan asked as he ate another Christmas cookie. As he popped the cookie in his mouth, he tried to remember how many he'd eaten. Damn, he'd lost count. He wasn't fat, but he was getting more rounded than he liked.

He watched Erin sit across from him. She was always nice, and after Bert she was his best friend in the office. He thought she had a crush on him at one point, but it had passed. Still, maybe?

"Wait," Erin said. She stood back up and surveyed the crowd. "John, get over here!" She waved a man over. Sullivan didn't recognize him. "Sully, this is John!" John sat in the chair and Erin sat on his lap. Maybe not. Maybe if he stopped eating so many of these damned cookies! She wrapped her arms around his neck. Sullivan exhaled and turned down to begin drawing.

"Erin, why don't you give Sullivan a break," Harold, Sullivan's boss saved him from another drawing, "I need him for just a moment." Sullivan looked up to see a pout flash across Erin's face.

"I'll get you later," Sullivan interjected.

"Okay, boss," Erin recovered and stood up. She pulled John's hand, "See you later, Sully." They disappeared.

Sullivan closed his drawing book and stood up, "Thanks."

"No problem," Harold said. He handed Sullivan a cup of punch. Sullivan took a drink and confirmed it was the good stuff. "You know, when I see you doing these drawings, I'm a little sad you didn't stay in art school." His boss was referring to Sullivan switching from art to history in college. Sullivan was about to say something but Harold continued, "Just a little."

"I do like drawing," Sullivan didn't know what to say. Harold was over six team leaders, each with six people on their teams. He didn't have much time for the people on those teams.

"Look, Sullivan," Harold took a sip and looked around the room to see no one was watching them, "That work you're doing with the travel system. Its good work. Damn good."

"Thank you, sir."

"I don't know if you know it, but you've given me more leads to refer to the fibi's than anyone else," Harold was talking about the FBI. When Sullivan got a lead, he built a case and gave it to Harold. Harold could refer it to someone on his other teams for detailed investigation and prosecution in the case of internal issues, or refer it to the FBI for criminal matters. "Actually, you've made more solid referrals than everyone else on the team put together. And you know that's what gets me noticed."

"I'm happy to help," Sullivan was happy his boss was getting good credit for his work. He didn't care about getting credit. He wasn't planning on working here forever, certainly not making a career out of it.

"I need you to give me more," Harold said, "I want you to quietly make me a list of the people you'd like to work on *your* team. And I'm going to start having you talk directly to the FBI. I think you'll work better that way."

Sullivan wasn't sure if his boss really just wanted to reduce his own workload, but he was happy for the opportunity. "Thank you. I do have this one case, it's not really a case yet, it's more of a hunch about this one guy. He's taking all these overnight trips."

"That's great, we can talk about it next year," Harold had clearly finished the conversation and looked around the room. "Erin, come on back!"

22. December 15, 1993

Lieutenant Roger Minetti scanned the horizon out of habit. He could see only clouds in every direction to the horizon. He knew that was all he would see. His heads up display told him so. He had been on station in his F-18 Hornet aircraft for forty-five minutes and he hadn't seen anything around him. At his altitude of thirty-five thousand feet, well above the clouds, he knew he could see about forty miles. He also knew he was not alone.

Lieutenant Minetti was part of the third air wing aboard the USS Nimitz. He was patrolling airspace over North Africa as part of a UN peace keeping mission. Whenever the United States sends a fighter aircraft anywhere it's supported by a huge infrastructure. For the Lieutenant to be flying there, right then, twenty men aboard the carrier were responsible for the maintenance of his fighter, two AWACS aircraft provided a real time map of every aircraft within a thousand miles with their giant dome radar dishes, four thousand men and women made the Nimitz function, and twelve destroyers, subs, and other support vessels made up the Nimitz battle group. He was the tip of an immense spear.

His flight was scheduled to leave its patrol airspace and return to the Nimitz in fifteen minutes. The Lieutenant loved to fly but sometimes, when he was up here alone, he looked forward to getting back.

"Charlie-One," the headset inside his helmet called, "this is Home-Hawk, over."

"Home-Hawk, Charlie-One, over," The Captain responded. Home-Hawk was the AWACS aircraft providing air traffic control for his flight.

"New target designated Ground-Five," the voice said, "Acknowledge."

Lieutenant Minetti looked at his display. A small red square appeared just outside of his missile range off to his right. "Acknowledge new target, Ground-Five, over." The AWACS Controls Operator, Specialist Jason Beard, had placed the target on his display and he was confirming the Lieutenant had it. It was number five because he had passed four previous potential ground targets in this mission without taking any action. He banked gently to the right to line up his flight path with the potential target and closed in on it. He'd done the same for the previous four.

Somewhere down on the ground, below the clouds, someone had decided that something might need to be destroyed. It could be a covert mission with a marine detachment lighting up a potential target with a laser targeting system, or it could be a car with a tracker that was placed by a CIA operative two weeks ago, or it could be a building targeted by a bureaucrat in an office in DC. He didn't know, and the beauty was, he didn't have to. In the six months the Nimitz had been on this mission, he had flown one hundred sorties, targeted eight hundred thirty times, and fired seven missiles. He never knew what he fired on, his job was to be the tip of the spear, and stab when commanded.

The target moved down his display and entered into the projected pie wedge ahead of the symbol of his aircraft indicating the range of his weapons. "Charlie-One, Home-Hawk, target is hot, over."

"Home-Hawk, Charlie-One, target hot, confirmed, Fire, I repeat, Fire," the Specialist called.

"Charlie-One, Home-Hawk, confirm authorization to fire on Ground-Five," Lieutenant Minetti double checked according to his protocol.

"Home-Hawk to Charlie-One, fire on Ground-Five Authorized. Fire. Fire. Fire."

Lieutenant Minetti flipped the safety cover off of his control stick, took a short breath, and mashed his thumb into the button. His aircraft shook just a bit, like a small speed bump, as the ground attack missile dropped from below the left wing. He could see it hanging there below the aircraft for a fraction of a second before the rocket engaged and it jumped out ahead accelerating to two thousand miles an hour. Within seconds, all he could see was a trail of white smoke making a gentle arc up and ahead and then turn down just before the horizon. Someone, or something, was going to have a bad day.

23. January 3, 1994

Our relationship is faltering due to continued disrespect. While we do not condone the actions of Mr. bin Laden, his accomplishments suit us. Accordingly, you will take no further actions to harm him.

- LV

President Clinton stood in the middle of the Oval Office. He still wore his overcoat damp from the fog outside. His breathing was slowing after running in from Marine One, his helicopter. He had been about to attend a fundraiser in New York City when his Secret Service Team received the signal that he was needed back at *The Nest*. They raced here, leaving the preparation suite of the hotel in lower Manhattan one hour and ten minutes ago.

Bill Clinton read the letter again.

Jim faced him and felt the strain in the President's clenched jaw in his stomach. The President handed the letter back to him and turned back towards the helicopter.

24. January 5, 1994

Sarah looked out the window of her eighth floor office again. The weather was cloudy, but she didn't think it was going to rain. It was dark and cold in January so looking out the window was little help. She looked at the clock on the bottom of her computer screen. Six-thirty. Crap. She looked to her computer monitor and studied the data processing readout. She couldn't decide what to do.

Angie Reynolds, her best friend since college, was picking her up downstairs in ten minutes for their club soccer match. They were likely to win, and that win would guarantee them a spot in the playoffs in no small part due to Sarah's midfield play. She'd only missed one other game so far this season, and their team lost badly.

The *Space Resonators* installed in the Hubble were generating much more data than Sarah anticipated, and Sarah worked seven days a week to keep up. She was simultaneously developing new mathematics, new numerical methods, and new user interfaces to work on these problems. She was a reasonably competent computer programmer, but at Virginia Tech, she could always walk over to the computer science department in McBride Hall for help. Here, she was on her own.

Her computer processing was scheduled to complete in thirteen minutes. She opened the comparison data. The best available scans of the Crab Nebula were also provided by Hubble. The space telescope could see details of the stars previously hidden by the distance between Earth and the interstellar structure. With the best optics and best detectors and best computers in the world, the Hubble Space Telescope was powerful enough to differentiate what was happening in the north, south, east, and west of the star. This capability allowed study of the interactions of the star's surface with its neighbors and also gave some of the first clues about the presence of planets around those stars. There was just not enough data in the stream of electromagnetic radiation received by the Hubble Space Telescope to give more resolution about any one star. Hubble relied on the hugeness of millions and billions of stars to give the magnificent images that were on the cover of every scientific journal of late. When looking at a single star, four pieces was by far the best physicists had achieved in hundreds of years of trying.

Sarah's comparison image of a specific star was only four pixels.

She blew them up so they took up half of her screen. She plotted the density distribution in those four quadrants across the star. She'd collected the electromagnetic information just before and just after she used the *Space Resonators* in her latest scan five days ago. The conventional image showed the northern quadrant of the star had higher density, probably a solar flare, bursting from the surface. The conventional data was very consistent just before and just after the *Space Resonator* so her gravitational data should match.

Six minutes until the scan was scheduled to complete. Sarah couldn't sit still. She stood in the middle of her office. She kicked off her heels and stood barefoot on the area rug. She crossed her right leg over her left and attempted to touch her toes. Normally this was no difficulty for her as she stretched before every practice. Today, her skirt was too tight and her motion was restricted. She reached to her left hip and unzipped her skirt giving herself the room to touch her toes. After a minute of alternating legs her palms rested flat on the floor with her legs straight. She was able to stretch her quads and her arms but there was no way her business clothes would allow her to finish her warm up. She would remember to bring her soccer uniform to her office next time. Luckily, she'd asked Angie to pick up her uniform and a dress for later, and pick her up on the way to the arena.

She looked over her shoulder during a calf stretch against the door and froze. Her processing was complete. She stumbled back to her desk chair and stared at the screen. The four blocks of the comparison image hadn't changed. It was the new results on the right of the screen that held her attention.

"Are you coming down here?" Sarah was temporarily confused by the sound of Angie's voice. She'd answered her office phone without realizing it. Angie must have been in her car outside.

"I'll be right down," Sarah said, not quite meaning it.

"I picked up the dress you wanted," Angie said. Sarah had a dinner reservation with Peter Howard after the game tonight but she wasn't thinking about that now. "I'm glad you're trying to get a man's attention, but Peter?"

The new image on the screen was a circle. It was blown up to the same size as the comparison image, about five inches across. Where the comparison was broken into four sections, the *Space Resonator* data was broken into one hundred sections. Her image looked like the comparison had come into focus.

"You know what you should do?" Angie was still talking but

Sarah was barely listening. "Tell him to pick you up at your apartment. When he comes to the door, tell him to come in, don't quite be ready. Make him wait a few minutes. Then walk right up to him and in your best girl voice, tell him you're sorry for making him wait. Tell him you really want to make it up to him. Then kneel down and give him a great blowjob. He'll do whatever you want after that." Sarah knew that was Angie's move. She was very direct in all things. Sarah admired that.

Since they met at the gym, Sarah had seen Peter three times. Each time, she'd offered to cook him dinner, her move, and each time he refused. He would not come to her apartment, so even if she wanted to try Angie's move, it wouldn't work. Besides, three dinners wasn't too long. She wasn't even sure she was interested in him. Damn it, Angie was distracting her.

"I'll be right down!" Sarah said as she hung up on her friend. She took a moment to study the image no one on earth had ever seen before. She could see that there was, in fact, a solar flare emanating from the top of the star. She could see that the eastern hemisphere was comparatively docile. The southern section had a dark region that she couldn't explain right then. She was taking advantage of one billion billion times more data available in a gravitational signature to create the higher resolution image of the distant star.

Sarah had done it. She was looking at a spatially-resolved image of a distant star, vastly exceeding the capability of the best electromagnetic equipment humans had ever conceived. And all this was made possible by the use of *Space Resonators*! She couldn't wait to tell . . . She couldn't tell anyone. Certainly not Angie. She wouldn't be able to tell Peter later tonight, either, even though he'd ask if anything interesting was happening at work. Okay. She'd tell Maxwell on January 10th at their scheduled meeting. It was only five days away.

In the meantime, she had a soccer game to win.

25.   February 27, 1994

"What the hell is this?" Thomas Kirk threw a crumpled up newspaper at Jim as he stepped out of the conference room and closed the door. Jim struggled to remain calm. He'd just been called out of a meeting to talk to Thomas, who'd apparently followed him here. He stared at the door for a moment to let his eyes adjust to the indoor lighting.

Jim was in New York visiting Eustis Jefferson at his office. He'd been inside the conference room for the past six hours with Eustis and his team of accountants responsible for the finances of Department 55. The room opened up to a tenth floor view of Central Park on the upper east side of Manhattan. Jim always arrived to any meeting in this room thirty minutes early so he could get used to the spectacular view and study the history laid out before him.

Thomas Kirk, on the other hand, had an office across the White House complex from Jim's.

"How could you-" Thomas dove in. He stopped when Jim raised his hand. Jim waited another beat before he deliberately bent down to pick up the newspaper. He continued to face away from Thomas as he looked at the paper. He immediately saw the headline that upset Thomas.

US Treasury Declares China a Currency Manipulator

He made no indication that he knew which article was bothersome and instead flipped the paper over and was looking at the other side as he slowly turned to face Thomas. Jim looked up at his subordinate with a questioning look.

"You know damn well you're looking at the wrong side!" Thomas could barely keep his voice down.

"Yes, Thomas," Jim said in his calmest voice. He didn't want to escalate the situation. He knew Thomas would be mad, but he didn't think he'd hop a plane to confront him. "I do know about this." Jim walked away from the door to a small seating area expecting Thomas to follow.

"How could you let this happen?" Thomas pleaded. He was still talking loudly, "You and I have been over this!" Jim was almost to the seat and Thomas hadn't moved yet.

"Thomas, come over here and take a seat. And calm down." Thomas quickly followed the direction and sat next to Jim. He was calm by the time he got there. Clearly, he'd been angry the entire trip. It spilled out more suddenly than he thought it would. He probably surprised himself more than he surprised Jim.

"Jim," Thomas said after taking a breath, "Three weeks ago, we received a letter from LV demanding that we *do not interfere with the internal affairs of China.* And now we go and insult them by declaring their *internal* monetary policy to be unacceptable to the international community?"

"No, Thomas," Jim had been over this with both the Vice President and the President three times. They were steadfast in their decision to proceed with their declaration. It had been in the works for months. "We did not declare their *internal* monetary policy unacceptable. We declared the way they manage their monetary policy in relation to other *external* currencies unacceptable. China's been pegging their Yuan to the Dollar for decades. In the beginning, we were helping a struggling economy emerge from communism. Now, we're helping a global economic giant maintain a trade imbalance that isn't good for us or for the Chinese People. Only the Chinese Central Committee and their handpicked capitalists are getting rich on a system that's both illegal and detrimental to the *Global* economy."

"You know that's parsing words," Thomas sneered.

"No, it's following directions to the letter."

"No, to the letter would have been to leave China alone!" Thomas looked to his lap with frustration, "You're playing with fire here. This parsing of words hasn't been appreciated. We're seeing the preamble of the letters grow increasingly firm."

"Listen to yourself," Jim knew Thomas was right about his assessment, but he was incorrect in his belief that Jim could do anything about it, "You're talking about the preamble of letters. I'm talking about the foreign and economic policies of the United States of America. I'm talking about the President of the United States having the ability to execute the duties of his office without interference from outside agents." Thomas lifted his head and the two men stared at each other. "Thomas, President Clinton has made it clear that he is going to follow the exact requirements of the letters. But he's not going to go past that. He doesn't care about the sentiments conveyed in the preamble of the letters." Jim looked at Thomas expecting some reaction. Thomas looked incredulous.

"If you read this article," Jim tried to change his approach, "you'll see that the administration has laid out its arguments to the world. You'll also see those arguments are clearly targeted to LV and clearly show that the US isn't interested in the internal affairs of China. LV will do its homework. LV will see that the United States is following instructions. But, LV must understand that the United States isn't going to stretch the meaning of their words to cover other things that they couldn't possibly have foreseen."

"LV can do whatever it wants," Thomas said. Jim agreed with that so he didn't respond. Jim couldn't admit that he actually agreed with Thomas and that he thought the President was being particularly belligerent with this latest letter. Instead, he stood. Thomas continued, "I'm going to have to increase my Threat Rose recommendation. I think everyone will."

"I agree," Jim said as he walked back to the conference room door.

26.   May 27, 1994

It was Friday night, and Sullivan was on his fifth date with Liz. Things were going well until she started asking about Erin.

"No," Sullivan said over the filet at Outback Steakhouse, "I never dated Erin." Liz stopped chewing a bite and looked at him skeptically. "Okay, maybe I had a little crush on her, but that was years ago. She's on my team, we're not even allowed to date!"

"That's not a good answer!" Liz said, "You're supposed to tell me she's ugly!"

"Oh, yeah," Sullivan said, "and she's ugly." In February, Harold made Sullivan a team leader. It wasn't really something he was looking for, but it did mean he got to pick the people he worked with. Bert and Erin both happily accepted his offers. Sullivan knew he and Erin had moved past any chance at a relationship, and the three of them continued to be good friends.

She demonstrated her feelings for him by setting him up with Liz, one of John's friends. She suggested they double date, but Sullivan said he'd like to have a few dates alone before being subjected to such scrutiny.

"There are three movies I would see tonight," Sullivan tried to change the subject.

"I'm sure we'll pick a good one," Liz said with disinterest as she took another bite. Under the table, Sullivan felt her foot rub his calf. "I'll enjoy anything we see."

"Okay, then," Sullivan said, "I guess we'll see Forrest Gump." Sullivan was trying to continue the conversation as she slipped her shoe off. Liz touched him all the time. While they had done little in private, her hands roamed all over him when she taught him to play putt-putt golf. He liked it. His ex-wife never touched him in public.

"Why don't you tell me how your day went?" Liz said. Above the table she was focused on eating her salad, but below the table, her foot slid into his lap. She rubbed his thigh and smiled a little smile.

"Uhh," Sullivan stammered. She took a sip of her beer and didn't look at him.

"Uhh, what?" Liz asked, "You went to work today, didn't you?"

"Yes I did," Sullivan cut a piece of steak. After a sip of his beer, he described his day, "I had a few meetings, Erin, Uh, Erin has been developing new tools to evaluate the travel system at work, and she's coming up with some good leads." Sullivan wasn't sure what he was saying, "I've got my first meeting with the FBI in two weeks, and we need to have some solid leads for them."

"And that's why you've been working late?" Liz asked.

"Huh?"

"You've been too busy to go out with me for almost two weeks. I've been getting worried," Liz said. "I'm here to make sure it won't be two weeks before our next date." With that she extended her toes.

"Yeah, most of the time I'm bored off my ass, but lately it's been pretty exciting," Sullivan said.

He hadn't told her about his six year old son, Danny, yet. He actually spent most nights at home with his son. He found women had one of two responses to his telling them he had a son. Either they wanted to run away, or they wanted to go to his house right then and start playing mom and dad. He didn't want either reaction from Liz, so he decided to wait.

27. June 8, 1994

This was the sixth cell phone tower she climbed and Claire still couldn't believe how windy it was one hundred and fifty feet from the ground. She wore a hardhat and full safety harness so she wasn't afraid, but the wind was making the top of the tower sway three feet side to side. She stood on a four foot by four foot platform at the top of the ladder. Electrical boxes acted as the railing and large receivers blocked half the view of the surroundings. At this height, the gaps between the receivers gave her a view for miles.

Claire took the time to look out to the next tower. She knew it was three miles away. Actually, she could see two towers, one hundred and twenty degrees apart. She knew there were three other towers she couldn't see that formed the hexagonal shape of this cell of the nationwide cell phone system.

She repeated the same procedure on each tower. She installed the hand-made electrical devices she and Ravi concocted to allow the cell to act as a giant detector. The detector was designed to detect a specific signal that could be emitted from a remote anywhere from the ten square miles of ground within the cell below.

"Claire, are you up there yet?" Ravi called on the two way radio Claire wore in her ear. He was at the bottom of the tower configuring the system to process the data.

"I just got here," Claire puffed between deep breaths, "You know, if I'm taking too long, you could be up here, and I could be down there!" She knew Ravi was afraid of heights, something they discovered at the first tower.

"I'm tired and hungry," Ravi said, "Let's get this done so we can run the diagnostics overnight and test tomorrow."

"Okay, Okay" Claire smiled to herself. Over the past year, she had developed a deep respect for Ravi's technical abilities, but she couldn't believe how much he was a slave to his vices. If they ate a meal fifteen minutes late, he was complaining. Of course, he was down in a windowless box, and she was high in the air enjoying the view across the horizon. It occurred to her that the sun was setting behind her, and she turned to see one of the most spectacular sunsets in her life.

Their plan was to get these devices installed on every cell phone tower in the country. Linus demanded that the system report a detection of the signal within ten minutes. Ravi and Claire were certain they'd know which cell received the signal within two.

He also demanded that no one be able to tell the system was installed. In order to simultaneously accomplish these two requirements, Ravi had designed a system that replaced the standard power converter module for the inbound signal receiver. It was a highly standardized part of the system, and no one would notice the extra circuitry.

Six weeks ago, Ravi and Claire tested a small system in their lab in Greenville and showed Linus that they could detect the signal. Linus was excited and told them he'd pulled some strings to get them access to this particular cell to test. The race was on for them to construct a full-scale six tower demonstration. They had succeeded, and tomorrow, they would drive around the cell with a small transmitter testing the signal reception.

Unfortunately, Ravi realized that the modification of the system he created would only work with the exact system configuration of the cell towers at that time. That meant any upgrade of the cell system would require a complete rework of their technology. Linus assured them he had people in high places at the FCC that would help him make sure any upgrades were very slow coming.

Standing up here, literally on top of the most impressive achievement of her career, Claire was annoyed she was thinking about Linus Brenner. She hated Linus for the power he held over her. She hated the way he threatened people. She hated the way he looked. But, she had to admit, Linus was driven. Claire found she admired his single minded focus on his objective. She also admired how he never talked to anyone about his objective. Once she figured out he was so focused, she began to predict his behaviors, and once she knew what he was going to do, she could work within his plan.

She still didn't know what his plan was, but he seemed to have far too many resources to be part of the mob, and his search was much too sophisticated to be part of a drug cartel. He made a lot of threats, but she'd never seen him act on any of them. She knew she could be working on a lot of different projects, but both she and Peter agreed, this was something important. They both also agreed that they didn't know if they were the good guys or the bad guys, but at the moment it was revealed, they would choose to be good guys. Whatever that meant.

"Are you done?" Ravi called.

"Hold your horses!" Claire called back, "I might just sit up here for another half hour and wait for the sun to set!"

"If you don't get down here in the next ten minutes, I'm locking you up there for the night!" Ravi threatened. Claire laughed out loud so Ravi could hear it. His formal accent and generally soft spoken demeanor didn't fit with trying to yell. "I'm serious!"

Claire started the process of installing the equipment, "You can't leave me up here all night. You don't like eating alone." She knew she would be back down in ten minutes, but she liked poking at her small teddy bear.

28. September 22, 1994

"I can't stop looking at that necklace," Peter said as he took a small bite of salad. Since they met for drinks a year ago, Sarah and Peter spent time together any time he was in Northern Virginia. He was in the area about once a month, and they'd gone to nice dinners together, she'd attended a Builder's Association Meeting with him, they went to Redskins' pre-season games, toured the Smithsonian, everything a couple would do. Everything except become a couple.

Peter asked her about her work. Cornwall & Wallace still maintained her cover and that included sending her details of Tim Cullis' work. She studied before meeting with Peter and found she could easily describe what she was really doing for *Space Resonance* but use the language of the financial markets. He asked her very detailed questions about her work and she responded in kind. He told her about his various projects in Greenville and his consulting work that brought him to DC. They shared stories. He listened attentively and made good jokes. He always dressed nicely, like she did. He still ended their evenings with a kiss on her cheek.

Sarah estimated he was somewhere between ten and fifteen years older than she was. She found that liberating. He was young enough that he was very handsome and his body was still strong, but old enough to not hit on her constantly like the other men she met. In fact, he wasn't hitting on her at all.

"People tell me it brings out my eyes," Sarah said. She was very comfortable with their friendship, but she couldn't help but want more. She dated a few other men, but they were so focused on sex, she never got past a second date.

"It certainly isn't drawing my attention to your eyes!" There it was. Sarah had selected the necklace because it hung low on her chest. She wore a low cut black dress and the pendant was resting on the skin between the tops of her breasts. No one ever said it brought out her eyes. Sarah wore the necklace and the dress and the heels to draw his attention to her body and as she walked up to him at the table tonight, it had. She found his slow play with her very attractive and she enjoyed how they seemed to be dancing around their attraction to each other. She liked that he wasn't in a rush.

"Well I wore this necklace to focus your attention. I was afraid you were spending too much time looking at my calves!" Sarah took a bite of her salad trying to stay as casual as Peter. Three months ago, they'd played racquetball together. He played a lot and beat her easily but her strength and speed definitely scored her some points. He'd commented that *I had no idea serving a racquetball was so sexy.* She caught him stealing glances often, and she did the same. Since then he'd mentioned that they should play racquetball several times. She smiled at herself. Peter looked up to her face, glanced down at the necklace, and back to her face.

Peter finished his bite and said, "Well, after dinner I'm taking you up to my room where I can give that necklace the focus it deserves!" He looked her straight in the eye. Sarah didn't detect any joke. He broke the look and returned to his salad after the half a heartbeat it took for him to convey to her he was serious but before the full heartbeat that would have put her on the spot. He was good, and she was fully bought in.

"That's exactly what we'll do," Sarah said as the waiter arrived with their entrees. As they ate, the conversation returned to normal and her necklace was not mentioned again. Sarah was strongly aware of it resting against her skin and she could feel it every time he looked at it.

They ate dinner at the restaurant of Peter's hotel, and as they walked through the lobby, Sarah was afraid he would walk her to the valet. She hoped he couldn't see her face blush as he turned to the elevators.

As soon as they entered his hotel room, Peter dropped his keycard on the floor and guided her gently against the wall.

He looked her straight in the eyes.

She held her breath and thought her necklace was going to burn into her skin.

Peter lowered his eyes to her necklace. He leaned down and kissed her neck. Sarah leaned against the wall as Peter kissed her all over the exposed top of her chest. She reached for the buttons on his shirt, but he took her wrists and raised them over her head. He looked her in the eyes to wordlessly convey his intention, and she held them there. She felt his hands reach around her back pulling her chest slightly away from the wall. She closed her eyes and lifted her chin to give him full access to anything he wanted, allowing her right leg to bend and press the heel of her shoe into the wall. She stretched her arms up against the wall, aching for him to touch her in places her dress covered.

She was breathing heavily when he stood up and again looked her in the eyes. "Thank you," he said. He kissed her once, gently on the lips, their first kiss, and he drew back from her. She wanted to throw her arms around him and press herself to him, but she knew that was not his plan. She waited, she dared not move, hoping for him to continue with her. Her mind liked that they were taking things slow, but her body wanted him to go fast, very fast, right then.

She focused on slowing her heart rate on the elevator ride to the lobby. They both faced forward. If they started anything there, she knew she wouldn't be able to stop. He walked her to the valet on wobbly legs, and she drove home with the windows down.

29. October 15, 1994

"Jim, I asked to ride with you because I think you're going down a dangerous path," Thomas sat next to Jim on his way to the airport. Thomas would return to his office with the White House car.

Jim looked to his left at the man in his perfect suit looking back at him over his glasses. While Thomas was impeccably dressed, he somehow didn't seem comfortable sitting in the back of the town car. He seemed out of place, like he wasn't supposed to be there.

"What are you talking about?" Jim asked. Since the incident with the Chinese currency, Jim had worked with the President to address the two letters they received. The President continued to barely meet the precise demands while making sure to select details that would not satisfy the spirit.

"I've been reviewing patterns in the letters." That was all Thomas ever did, so this wasn't news. Thomas continued, "Since President Clinton took office, we've received seven in a row over the course of almost two full years where LV has characterized the relationship in a continually deteriorating fashion!"

Jim was aware of this. He thought about it every day. He actually found himself hoping for another letter, probably the only person in the world hoping for a new letter, one that said the relationship was better. The Threat Rose was at six and Jim knew it had never been there for long before. He also knew it was that high in part because of Thomas' recommendation of eight pulling the average up. But it wasn't getting better. It was because the President was steadfast in his efforts to not quite follow instructions. At every opportunity, he would bend the limits of the definitions of the words. It made Jim uncomfortable, but as the Special Secretary of Department 55, he didn't think he could let Thomas know that.

"I know there's been some tension, but that's not unprecedented," Jim said. He tried to sound confident but he was actually asking.

"Jim, we've never gone this long with a negative trend on the relationship," Thomas stressed, "I checked." Jim knew Thomas checked every statement he ever made. He'd seen plots of the tone of the letters versus time. Jim knew there were times when the tone of the letters dipped, and the United States had to make some concession and the tone would improve. Surely, this could not be the worst time?

"Surely this isn't the worst time in our history?" Jim said. He tried to say it and not ask it.

"At this time, there is debate in my division. Every member of my team believes now is the worst time in our history. I disagree with them. But they're convincing me," Thomas reported gravely. The car turned off the highway toward the airport, the conversation would end shortly.

"Well, Thomas, I don't need a debate, I need something I can take to the President," Jim pushed back.

Thomas was a bit taken aback, "What?"

"The President isn't going to tolerate being pushed around by The Romans on a whim," Jim said, "He doesn't think their recent demands are really that important to them, so he doesn't think he really has to respect them." Jim needed to turn the President. He needed another Greenville. He couldn't just sit and hope something happened. He needed Maxwell and that physicist to deliver! It had been months since Maxwell told him her system was working, now what were they waiting for?

"I don't know why the President would think that," Thomas said, pulling Jim back to the conversation, "There's no evidence of LV ever asking for anything on a whim." Jim and others referred to LV as The Romans, Fifty Five, or the Bastards. Thomas didn't like inferring anything, so he only called them LV. Jim knew that lack of imagination was prohibiting Thomas from following his argument.

The car was pulling up to the departure gate. Jim needed something to restore the relationship. He needed the President to respect LV's wishes. "Thomas, I need you to figure out why The Romans are so interested in Osama bin Laden and China. What the link is. Then we can tell the President why they're serious."

The driver opened the door with Jim's bag. Jim stepped out and leaned back into the door. "Thomas, this is the second time you've come to me with this concern. This is the second time you've come to me without anything I can use. I want to convince the President to change his course. I need something convincing!" Jim left Thomas in the car without a good-bye.

30. November 12, 1994

Sergeant Mike Abdul-Kan had been sitting on this roof top for two hours. He'd been in Sudan for three months. He was part of the Army Rangers' Special Unit Buckeye. He held a high powered sniper rifle and watched down a long road between buildings leading to the edge of town. He knew the last building he could see was half a mile away and he was careful to monitor the wind. Periodically he checked his scope. He was sweating profusely and he had to keep the eyepiece clear.

His team had been in Sudan monitoring the motions of Osama bin Ladin. They replaced the previous team. They watched him eat. They watched him sleep. They watched him play with his kids.

Special Unit Buckeye also watched him meet with his lieutenants. They knew he was releasing a video because they watched him film it. Sargent Abdul-Kan watched through his scope with cross hairs on bin Ladin's forehead while the man threatened to kill Americans and talked about how everything from America had to be destroyed.

Over the previous two months, the Sergeant asked for permission to fire eleven times. Eleven times he could have easily rid the world of this pesky gnat. Every time he was told no. They were there to observe and to train. Some bureaucrat in Washington had some agenda that stopped him from taking care of business. But he was a professional. He followed orders.

The Shithead must have finally pissed someone off. Today, the Sergeant asked for permission and was told yes. He was cleared to take the shot.

"The convoy is moving." The ear bud nestled against his eardrum repeated the voice of Specialist Kaliq. The team was spread up and down the street waiting for the convoy they knew was on its way.

The first Mercedes SUV came into view at the edge of town. The few people on the street quickly cleared at the sight of the speeding vehicle. The first vehicle was followed after ten seconds by three tightly packed identical Mercedes.

"The package is in vehicle two," Specialist Kaliq reported. His team was all of Arab descent so they could move around the town unnoticed. Specialist Kaliq was outside the first building looking like one of the many unemployed men in the town.

The Sergeant noted that the Specialist was the only person still on the street as the convoy passed his position. He realized the Specialist stood out as the only one who didn't take cover when the first SUV sped down the street. The oddness of the view was just registering in the Sergeant's mind when a muzzle flash erupted from the side of the third car and the Specialist dropped to the ground.

"Shit!" Lieutenant Solomon screamed into the ear bud, "Engage!" The three vehicles accelerated. The Sergeant only intended to fire one shot today, into the passenger side of the second SUV, killing Osama bin Ladin, but the convoy was moving too fast now. Instead he targeted the driver's side of the first SUV and fired three rounds rapidly into the glass. The bullets had the desired effect. The SUV veered to the right hitting the building and bouncing back into the narrow road. The two following vehicles slowed, and the Sergeant fired into the windshield of the second vehicle.

The doors of the first vehicle opened and three automatic rifles emerged firing forward in the Sergeant's general direction. This forced him to pause in his firing and assess that he was actually not in any danger. None of his team was in danger either, so he didn't bother to engage the four in the first vehicle.

The third and second SUVs began to move in reverse. Four more shots into the windshield of the second car had no effect. He stopped firing and studied the scene. The windshield must have been bulletproof. The glass now had seven bullet impacts but the vehicle continued in reverse. Suddenly the two vehicles stopped.

Sergeant Abdul-Kan was briefly distracted as the rest of his team engaged the first SUV quickly silencing their fire. When he refocused on the stopped vehicles he was shocked to see the third vehicle was stopped next to Specialist Kaliq's dead body and the back door was open.

"They're taking Kaliq!" the Sergeant shouted. Then he started firing into the windshield of the third SUV. He only got one shot off before the vehicle began moving again. It didn't hit the driver because the vehicle proceeded under control. He changed tack and began firing into the hood of the car.

As quickly as it started, it ended. The two vehicles disappeared out of town.

Sergeant Abdul-Kan sat on the building blinking. He didn't know what to do next. He waited for his Lieutenant.

31.   December 1, 1994

Peter looked up from his computer as Sarah let herself into his hotel room. They'd seen each other often and he propped the door with his room key.

"Yes," he said into his headset, "We're going to make the deadline, you can count on it!" He was studying a construction schedule on a conference call from his hotel room outside Washington DC. He needed a few more minutes to get this done. He looked at Sarah who pointed to the bathroom. He nodded; glad she was okay with him running long. Some women wouldn't understand.

"I've got the plans here, and I think we can make it," Roger, Peter's project manager was saying. Peter winced.

"*You Think!*" the project owner screamed.

"I … I," Roger tried to recover.

"Bob," Peter intervened, "We don't think, we know." He hated when people *think* they could do something. Either you can or you can't. He wished Claire was on this project. "Bob … hold on a sec …"

The bathroom door opened and he was going to tell Sarah he needed a few more minutes, but no words came out of his mouth when he saw her.

Sarah dropped her dress from her shoulders. Her full breasts were fighting her bra, the muscles of her stomach led to the top of her small panties, the curves of her tan legs were accentuated by the rise of her heels, and Peter's heart skipped several beats.

"Peter," Bob called into his ear, "Are you still there?"

"Yes, yes," Peter struggled, "I'm here." Sarah walked slowly to him. She leaned down presenting her cleavage to him, and began to unbutton his dress pants. "We've got everything under control. Roger, can you go over the…" Peter couldn't continue when Sarah's hand pulled him from his boxers.

Their relationship had heated up quickly and Peter enjoyed Sarah's playful sexuality.

"What?" Roger asked. Peter really needed Roger to take over.

"Go over the schedule, step-by-step," Peter got out as Sarah released him, stood, and turned to face away. He was glad she gave him a moment.

As Roger started talking Sarah looked over her shoulder with a mischievous smile. She backed over his knees and straddled him.

He put his hand on the small of her back, needing to push her away, but wanting to pull her closer.

"Roger," Peter said, "Go back to the delivery details," as he talked, Sarah lowered herself onto him, the thin material of her panties the only barrier between them. He forced himself to keep talking, "Show him the cement schedule." As he talked, Sarah slowly moved against him.

"No, the second set of deliveries, show how the foundations will be done with two days to spare," Peter needed Roger to take over, but he had to help. He struggled to describe details of the construction schedule for a few minutes as Sarah worked herself against him.

Whenever Peter stopped talking, Sarah stopped moving, pausing on his lap. He could see her rib cage expanding with her heavy breathing.

"No," Peter had to interrupt again, "Bob, Alan's a good friend of mine. Those trucks won't be late!" Sarah moved again. She was timing her motion to his talking. It was delicious torture. Luckily, Roger was handling the conversation now.

"Okay, Bob," Peter said, "We'll talk more tomorrow." He disconnected the phone and pushed Sarah to the bed.

32.   December 23, 1994

"Where's Ops?" Thomas asked. He was the last to arrive in Maxwell's spacious office overlooking the woods of suburban Milwaukee. Every time Jim came here he remembered Maxwell and Eustis, Science and Finance, had refused to relocate to Washington DC. From this view, he could see why.

Four men sat at the large conference table next to the single red wall in Maxwell's office, and they were each looking out different windows across the trees as the sun came up.

"He's not coming," Lloyd answered as he set down coffee for Thomas and orange juice for Maxwell. Maxwell looked at him with almost imperceptible sternness, but both Jim and Lloyd got the message and Lloyd quickly returned to his outer office.

"He told me he doesn't want to weigh in on this," Jim said, "he wants us to make the decisions, and he'll execute."

"That's not how it's supposed to work," Thomas said. He was highly process oriented, and Jim knew this would make him uncomfortable. Jim was enjoying the view, but couldn't help watching the precision with which Thomas added cream and sugar to his coffee. He didn't think the man had ever spilled anything.

"He's in Idaho," Maxwell said taking a sip from his orange juice, "Should I call him, we could all wait?" Maxwell was making a joke but Thomas thought it was a good idea.

"Look," Jim said, "we've got to proceed. I'm not sitting here all damned day!"

"But maybe he would come," Thomas looked up from stirring his coffee.

"If I was him," Eustis said, "and I didn't want to voice an opinion, and you forced me here," The older man spoke slowly but everyone waited. "I would simply convey the opinion of the average of the rest of us. That way I could be here, but not make a difference." Eustis was a game player. He could find a way around any rule, any system of checks and balances. That was why he was so good at what he did. Jim felt himself smile.

Thomas thought for a brief moment before he acquiesced, "Fine."

"Fine," Jim said. He addressed the other three men. They were each older than he was, and each of them had been in their positions longer than he had, and each of them knew exactly what they were here to do, and had done it more times than he had. "We're here to update the Threat Rose. You all know I stare at the thing every day. We last left it at six."

Jim didn't want to go first, but his predecessor liked to go first and he set a precedent. "I'll start." He looked for an objection and thought he was going to get one from Thomas.

Thomas seemed more uncomfortable than usual.

"I've been working closely with the President over the past two years," Jim began, "and his plan seems to be working. He's been able to comply with the letter of LV's requests while parsing the words so he can minimize the impact on his policies."

"A dangerous game!" Thomas blurted. The other three men looked at him. It wasn't customary for someone to be interrupted. Thomas' eyes opened wide as he looked back at the other three men. Jim figured the nonverbal rebuke was sufficient. Thomas took his first sip of coffee.

"I believe," Jim continued, "that the President is right. He's picked a series of issues LV wasn't married to, and he's pushed back. I thought we were heading down a very dangerous path, but then he completely complied with the Desertron demand. He destroyed the thing! So, while the letters have been confrontational in their tone, I think we've struck a new balance of power, and we're reaching a new status quo. I think with this new status quo, we'll never get the threat rose as low as in the past, but it will be stable. Today, I give it a four." Jim looked around the room and no one reacted except Eustis.

"Stable isn't always good." Eustis said almost to himself. He was small with an almost bald head. He sat back from the table with his right leg over his left and his coffee cup held with both hands in his lap. He was cradling it, like he was collecting its warmth. He slowly looked up with a smile. "I guess I'm next."

"Well, go ahead!" Maxwell was happy to push him to next. Maxwell was full of energy, like he always was, but was ready for someone else to talk. Jim decided to watch Maxwell while Eustis talked.

"Okay," Eustis slowly set down his coffee. Everyone waited while he leaned back and took his glasses from his face. He rubbed them with his silk handkerchief to pass a few moments of time. Jim thought Maxwell was about to interrupt, but he also knew these two men were good friends. Eustis spoke slowly but allowed a bit of his carefully concealed Creole accent to get through, "A calm before the storm. . . All is quiet on the western front. . ." He completed rubbing his already spotless glasses and returned them to his face. "It has always been human nature to assume that because the enemy is not attacking it must be withdrawing. I fear we are dealing with a snake that is coiled and ready to strike. The question is this: has the snake cocked its head and bared its fangs? Or is the snake resting its head on its coiled body waiting for us to get too close? The trouble here is we can't see the snake. And the worse trouble is it only takes one bite. There is no second chance." Eustis looked at the face of each man.

Jim felt his stare even though he was focusing on Maxwell. Jim tried to read the man, but couldn't get anything from his large face. If Maxwell was affected by Eustis' comments, it didn't show. That's good. Jim didn't want these men to be affected by each other.

"Jim," Eustis drew Jim back to him, "I think we're dealing with a snake that's lifted his head. Seven."

Jim knew Eustis wasn't easily pushed above seven. Seven meant a recommendation of changing course. It meant that the path they were on had the potential to lead them to catastrophe. Eustis was a game player; he looked for the long play and he had already calculated the impact of his recommendation. He rarely wanted to change paths so a seven from him was quite remarkable. Maxwell's face broke and Jim could see a bit of shock on him as well. Jim checked Thomas who had his first very small smile. Thomas was looking at Maxwell in anticipation and Jim followed his lead.

"Okay," Maxwell said. Then he abruptly stood and walked to his minibar. Jim was now sure Eustis had surprised him. If not, Maxwell would have simply jumped into his comments. The three men waited for Maxwell to refill his orange juice.

"Do you need a refill?" Eustis asked Thomas. Eustis knew as Jim did that Thomas had only taken one sip, but he was trying to calm him.

"I'm fine," Thomas said. Then he realized Eustis was asking for more. "I'm fine."

"How's Bethany's Dream?" Eustis asked.

"I'm headed there right after this." Thomas seemed to relax. He and his wife had planned to sail in their retirement. Seven years ago, they learned that breast cancer wouldn't let them live their plans together. Five years ago, Bethany died.

All the Division Chiefs attended the funeral.

The next morning, Eustis arranged for the group to sail on the same type of boat Thomas had talked about buying for years. At the end of the sail, Eustis told Thomas the boat was his.

The group all knew Eustis had an exclusive set of friends, many of whom could give a boat away, but they also knew Eustis had access to nearly unlimited wealth. Thomas was a stickler for protocol and normally wouldn't have accepted. But a day after burying his wife of twenty-five years, he looked at the four men he was closest with in the world and accepted.

Jim knew mentioning Bethany's Dream could either force Thomas from the room or draw him in. Thomas smiled and took a second, deeper sip of his coffee. Maxwell returned.

"I have an idea," Maxwell said, "Next time let's do this on the bay!" Maxwell had just invited himself and the rest of them onto Thomas' boat.

"Good idea," Thomas genuinely liked the idea. Good. Jim knew the security implications would be difficult to overcome, but it could be done. And Thomas was back with them. "Now," Thomas said, "Let's hear it, Maxwell."

Eustis had relieved a level of tension. He had taken a risk and it paid off. Jim needed to learn how to do that. Maybe it was just experience.

"Six," Maxwell said.

"What?" Jim asked.

"Six, that's my number."

"I think you should say some more words than that."

"Okay," Maxwell's large face had a broad, mischievous smile, "Should I tell you about snakes? Or boats? Or the President's strategy? NO. The Romans don't know anything about any of those things. We need to look at this from their perspective, and deal with the data we have at hand." He looked at Jim, "What the President is thinking is irrelevant." Then to Eustis, "and we can't assume we know whether a snake is sleeping!"

Maxwell was a scientist. He dealt with scientists every day. This was how scientists think.

"Let me start with what we know. The Romans have been making specific demands. The government of the United States has been complying with the letter of those demands. LV has called us on the spirit of their demands, but they shouldn't expect us to know the spirit of their demands because we don't know who the hell they are!" He paused for a sip of juice. "So, is LV getting what they want? Maybe not. But, they are getting exactly what they ask for. Are they affecting our positions in their favor, whatever their favor is? Yes." He looked at the other men. "They make demands. We follow them. We're not very good at following them so they need to get better at making them. They are making progress. If we stop their progress, we're going to be in deep trouble. So, stay the course, but err on the side of meeting their demands. . . Six."

Jim changed his mind. He hoped Maxwell's comments would affect Thomas. He knew Thomas was very concerned with the current path. Maxwell made an excellent technical argument that LV had options. Even Eustis would agree a snake doesn't attack if it has other options. The team looked to Thomas. He was smiling, but the smile seemed to drip off his face in the next few seconds. He spoke carefully.

"Gentlemen, I believe we are in uncharted territory. Over the past two years we've received letters with increasing discontent. We've never before gone for two years with a constant unsatisfied tone. LV's made a series of demands over an unprecedented three topic areas. While you mentioned that we dismantled the Desertron, we are redeploying the science to the European collider under construction at CERN. It will be much less effective, but we're continuing the research. We took another stupid shot at Osama bin Ladin in the Sudan desert, and somehow, LV learned about it. And China, we haven't pushed them on human rights, but we're trying to get them to move on Taiwan, Tibet, and economic issues. So we are ignoring the obvious intent of the letters if not the exact words. The President believes he can ignore the demands because he thinks they're just random. Just because we haven't found the connection doesn't mean there isn't one."

"We've never been so far from compliance for so long. I know you're each looking at this as a game, or a philosophical puzzle, or as a science experiment, but this is none of those things. This is the fate of all of us. This is serious. I believe this President is not taking this seriously. I believe we are in the midst of the most dangerous threat our nation has ever experienced, and we're not taking sufficient action. I am forced to set my number at ten."

Jim knew Thomas was uncomfortable, but he didn't think he'd go there. He tried to not go wide eyed.

"I've never heard a recommendation of ten," Maxwell was flabbergasted. He raised his glass of orange juice to take a drink but change his mind and returned it to the table. Then he stood. He walked around the back of his chair. Eustis sat quietly and quickly pulled his glasses from his face. Maxwell rubbed his face with a large hand. "Thomas, it can't be ten. Ten is . . . Um . . . ten's crazy. Ten's . . ."

"Ten is treason," Eustis said in a quiet voice. Maxwell froze with that word. Jim thought it through. Seven was change course. Eight was change leadership in Department Fifty-Five, basically fire Jim. Nine was undefined extreme action, and ten was replace the President.

There had only ever been two consensus tens.

"It's not treason!" Thomas exclaimed, "I'm only suggesting that we all do more. It's only treason when we're all in agreement!"

"If we were all in agreement," Eustis said calmly, "and every one of us recommended a ten, would you change your vote to a nine?"

"No."

"Then it is, in fact, the definition of treason," Eustis said. Thomas looked like he wished he could take back the No. Not the ten, but the no.

"Okay, that's enough of that," Jim needed to keep some control, "Thomas is not going to act alone. So we're not talking about treason. Thomas, are you sticking with ten?"

"Yes," Thomas said, "Ten."

33.   January 10, 1995

"That can't be possible," Sarah studied Maxwell's face for some sign of a joke. She hadn't seen him in exactly one year and she still wasn't comfortable with him yet.

"It is possible, and we did launch the second Hubble four months ago," Maxwell repeated, "It's in a polar orbit and is ready to begin transmitting data. It's called *Kite String*."

"It has Space Resonators?"

Maxwell nodded. Sarah looked down to her skirt trying to piece together a timeline. They sat in the comfortable chairs in his office at her second annual progress report. The trees outside were covered with six inches of snow and her drive in had been cold this morning. She'd expected cold but not zero degrees. That was cold enough that her quads froze on the short walk from her car into the building. Lloyd laughed at her while she sat in his outer office and rubbed her thighs.

Lloyd was much more comfortable with her this morning after she'd asked him to take her out last night. They went downtown to play darts and pool. She leaned into Lloyd a few times when men came to hit on her. She enjoyed flirting with him and he flirted back, but she was serious enough with Peter that there was no chance of anything further. He got a few looks from women. When Sarah returned from the bathroom to find two young ladies moving in, she impulsively walked up and kissed him to mark him as hers. She pulled away, immediately regretting it, but thankfully there was not awkwardness this morning.

Maxwell was drinking orange juice. Lloyd made Sarah strong coffee. She increased the resolution of her *Space Resonance* system to one hundred times that of the Hubble Space Telescope. She had a long way to go as the available data in the graviton stream was still a billion times larger. She thought she would have the big news, but Maxwell showed her up.

"We only completed the first installation on Hubble a year ago," Sarah said, "I'm just here now to describe my progress, and you've already sent up a second satellite?"

"Yes." Maxwell was letting her think things through and seemed to be enjoying himself.

"The *Space Resonator* can be the last piece to be configured, as we showed with Hubble, but you must have begun construction of *Kite String* years ago, while I was in grad school…" She looked out the window across the tops of the trees.

"We started construction the day you moved into your office in Virginia. It's not uncommon to engage in parallel development."

"Parallel development," Sarah looked up, "you're talking about ten billion dollars!" She blurted. She paused. Maxwell looked at her without expression despite her disbelief. It seemed she had been staring down at her lap for some time, and Maxwell had actually reclined in his chair as she was becoming more animated. She watched him take a drink of his juice. He seemed to do it slowly for effect. She couldn't tell if to gather his own thoughts or to allow her to gather hers.

Then he began, "I told you, my boss is very interested in your work."

"You've told me that before! You can't spend so much! How can you spend so much and no one know about it?" She was instantly angry with herself for interrupting. Then she wondered why she was so angry? It just didn't seem to make sense. He paused, looked out the window briefly, and returned his gaze to her with renewed focus.

He continued, "Sarah, we're very interested in your work. You have come to understand that. What you don't seem to understand is the level of interest." Sarah felt him look into her eyes. He was looking for acceptance, and she couldn't determine why she didn't want to give it, yet.

"You yourself have written about the importance of the search for the Unified Field Theory, that it will *explain the Universe*. That it will 'tell us where we have come from, and therefore help us understand where we're going'." Maxwell recited words Sarah wrote in college.

Maxwell took another drink, apparently deciding to approach this from another angle, "Do you watch the Discovery Channel shows about space, Dr. Kiadopolis?"

Sarah was a bit bewildered by the question, but quickly remembered professor Long's recent interview on 'How the World will End'. She answered, "As a kid, of course, but the shows seem to be a bit more sensationalized now."

"Yes, Discovery is trying to make their subject matter interesting," Maxwell said, "so they take images of distant galaxies and explain how the image proves the world might end in one billion years. The audience is expected to forget about the billion years because they're flashing computer animations of the world blowing up. They're struggling to draw near term value out of the images created by Hubble and other scientific endeavors. They're trying to make it interesting. The irony is that they're reporting on the most important work done anywhere in the world, the work that will change the nature of mankind's interactions with its surroundings, and they are failing to make it interesting."

Sarah thought a moment. Discovery had the same challenge as the introduction of every astrophysicist paper; space is too big, too far away, and too abstract. "I've experienced this challenge myself. Not that I don't think it's interesting, but that it's hard to make it relatable to everyone."

"Yes, it's evident in your writing," Maxwell said dismissively, "The reality is that the work you're doing could not be more important to the United States today."

"How?"

Maxwell bunched up his lips and leaned forward. He put both elbows on his knees. Sarah thought the lights got a little dimmer but that must have been her imagination. He had her attention.

"Ten thousand years ago, humans moved from hunter-gatherer animals to farmers. Three thousand years ago, humans started using metals. Two hundred years ago, steam engines and machines moved us into the industrial revolution." Maxwell's bright blue eyes were on fire. Sarah knew the history, but wasn't quite following where he was going. "At the turn of the century, Carnegie, Rockefeller, and Mellon were masters of the mechanical world. They knew how to take advantage of thermodynamics and structural mechanics. They knew how to respond to the world, just as Newton did when he wrote his laws."

Newton wrote that *every action has an equal and opposite reaction*, and that *a body in motion tends to stay in motion*. Sarah knew those were the laws Maxwell was referring to. She looked at him, forcing a smile.

"But then, two amazing things happened at nearly the same time," Maxwell was excited. "These two things were only possible because we'd moved from reacting to the forces of the Universe to actually understanding them!"

Sarah, like all physicists, was well versed in the four fundamental forces of the Universe, and she knew one of the amazing things, "We split the atom."

"Exactly, Doctor," Maxwell smiled, "We split the atom. To do that, Einstein had to figure out how two of the fundamental forces of the Universe worked. The strong and weak nuclear forces. And he had to begin to relate them to another of the forces. Coincidently, we were also mastering the force of electromagnetism!"

"Yes," Sarah followed, "but electricity was known much earlier, Benjamin Franklin toyed with it in the 18th century."

"Toyed with it," Maxwell picked up, "you're correct. Edison put it to use with its obvious first application, lights. When Edison lit up Wall Street, he began the transformation of nearly every human activity. Lights and motors quickly had impacts, but the real transformative value of mastery of the electromagnetic force came with the transistor. Edison could never have predicted computers or the Internet. The car you drove here, the satellites we're discussing, and the clothes you're wearing would not exist as they are without our mastery of the electromagnetic force."

"Yes, I see all that," This was a nice topic of discussion for freshman physics students. "But what does this have to do with our work on..." she stopped short. She glanced down at her hem-line. Benjamin Franklin toyed with electricity, trying to figure out what it was. Now, two hundred years later, she was trying to figure out gravity, the fourth and final fundamental force in the Universe. Now she saw it. Benjamin Franklin flew a kite and learned about electricity when lightning traveled down his kite string. Now Sarah and Maxwell were flying a much higher, more technological, much more expensive kite. And now they were waiting for *Kite String* to give them the clues they needed to master gravity.

"The United States is struggling in the world. We're losing our technological edge. Much of the world is looking for the next

Internet, the next *big thing*. They're looking in the wrong places. To transform the world, we need to be looking for the next *electromagnetism*. That's what I'm paying you to do. We're looking for *gravitation*. The country that's the pioneer in gravitation will be the leader in the world for at least 200 years, and we want that country to be the USA."

Sarah knew all this. She hadn't put it together quite as eloquently as Maxwell just did, but she knew it. She also knew the government didn't spend money like this without some immediate opportunity for return. He wasn't telling her everything, but she was happy he told her what he did.

Sarah looked up to meet his gaze as he summed up, "We're not looking for the next Internet. We're looking for the next *America*."

34. March 11, 1995

Jim Williams again slipped quietly into the Oval Office. The President sat in front of the fire and was leaning forward, both feet on the floor. Jim didn't know everyone, but he knew HUD Secretary Henry Cisneros, and the rest were probably his staffers.

"Henry, it's vital to me that you save money, but it's also vital to me that you keep people moving up in the world, not down," the President directed. Jim knew the President couldn't get into every detail. There were too many of them. All he could do was set the top level direction. Jim tried to emulate this President in his own leadership. President Clinton set his overall objectives, and he had fourteen cabinet secretaries to meet those objectives. Still, he was inquisitive and smart, so he got into details when he needed to.

"Of course," the HUD Secretary answered. Henry knew as well as Jim did, when the President of the United States told you how he wanted something to go, you didn't argue with him. His second lieutenant, Eleanor Baker, a career bureaucrat at the pinnacle of her career, did not.

"Mr. President," Eleanor said, "You must realize that some of these cuts will result in some people losing benefits, but most. . ." Eleanor continued speaking, but the President saw Jim. Jim knew he needed no introduction. He only came into this room unannounced for one reason. The President dropped his head and it hung for a moment as he looked at the floor. Eleanor stopped speaking abruptly. The room was silent for a moment.

When the President lifted his head, he saw Henry's face had gone white. Eleanor looked like she was going to pass out. The other three had not said much in this meeting, and they were not about to start now.

"Eleanor," the President looked at her. Jim knew her future rested in his hands at this moment. A slight jab, and she would never come in this room again, and all of the clout she carried in her department because she was occasionally invited here would be lost. She would likely retire within two months. She looked directly at him, awaiting her sentence. "Eleanor, I always appreciate your honesty. I apologize for having to break this meeting up early, something else has come up. I look forward to seeing you at our next update." With that, the President stood. Jim watched the color return to Eleanor's face. Jim's respect for President Clinton continued to grow.

"Thank you," Eleanor said, "Mr. President." Henry raised a subtle hand to indicate that she stop talking. Then he quickly swung it around to shake the President's hand.

"Thank you for your time, Mr. President," the HUD Secretary blustered. The team was elated that they had not made anyone mad, and quickly closed their attachés and almost ran from the room. Jim held the door for them as they left. The President moved to his desk and sat down in his plush leather chair.

"So, what is it this time?" The President was in a good mood, "Do the bastards care what we feed the French Prime Minister for dinner tonight?" Jim wasn't sure the good mood would last. He crossed the large room to the chair sitting next to the desk and facing out the windows behind it.

He handed the copy to the President and took a seat

Our relationship is reaching a breaking point. There is an upcoming election in the Chinese Island you have been mistakenly calling The Republic of China. China is right in its desire to retain the island under its control and anyone who interferes would be meddling in the affairs of a sovereign nation. The USA will publicly denounce any effort of the ROC to separate from the Chinese mainland. Further, the USA will stop any efforts, diplomatic or military, aimed at interfering with Chinese missile tests in the Straits of Taiwan.

-LV

"Again with China?" The President said quietly. He looked at Jim, "Is this some kind of joke?"

"No sir, this is a genuine letter from The Romans."

"I don't think you're trying to make a joke!" the President's good mood was gone. "What are The Romans trying to pull?" Jim didn't know how to answer. He didn't think the question was actually for him. Jim knew the President was processing the authenticity of the letter, just as Jim had done. He also knew he would come to the same conclusion Jim did. It was authentic, and it wasn't a joke. It was a demand and they would have to follow it. "I met Mr. Lee, and I want to help him." The President said, almost sadly. Jim knew he was coming around.

Lee Teng-Hui was the defacto leader of Taiwan and he was about to succeed at having the first free elections in all of China. Jim knew the US had been supporting those efforts from behind the scenes as well as publically supporting the Taiwanese. He also knew China didn't like it and was threatening military rocket tests to scare the Taiwanese into voting to maintain the status quo. In the last hour the Vice President had told Jim that the President was a strong supporter of Mr. Lee's efforts in Taiwan. The President saw it as a matter of global importance to stand up to the Chinese as a demonstration of peaceful transition to democracy in the face of a powerful anti-democratic foe.

"This isn't just about China," the President said. Jim waited patiently, so far the President wasn't yelling at him. That was a good sign.

"Jim," the President looked Jim in the eye, "We're going to have to comply, and we're going to have to set thirty million people back in their quest for democracy and freedom. We will publically comply, at least. But I have means that are not public, and I'm going to use every one of them! And I'm going to hit China with everything else I can come up with!"

Jim didn't think that was a good idea, but the President wasn't asking for his opinion. Just as Eleanor barely made it out of here, Jim wanted to get out of here soon.

"How can some hidden group of people be telling me what to do? How come I don't know who any of them even are? I know you're working hard to find these fifty-five Romans," the President said, "but I need you to stop coming in here and telling me about all the things you're working hard on! I need you to come in here and start telling me you're succeeding at something! Get Out!"

35.   March 15, 1995

"This is Kimali King with an exclusive from Honolulu, Hawaii," a young woman reporter announced on the television in Jim's office. A central office of several hundred staffers combed through stories from around the world and compiled a review based on key words provided by a number of the Administration's senior officials. Jim had two staffers in that office who compiled a tape for him. Jim judged that Kimali was probably not her real name, she had a tan, but was not Hawaiian.

Kimali continued, "Last night, Lee Heng-Hui, the unofficial President of Taiwan, landed here in Honolulu to refuel his plane." She stepped to the side so her cameraman could see past her to the airport in the early morning sun. In the distance was a Gulf Stream jet that could have belonged to anyone. "Normally, a dignitary of Mr. Lee's importance would have received an official welcome from the US State Department, but today, he will wake up on that plane. He wasn't allowed off his plane because the US State Department not only didn't welcome him, but it didn't allow him permission to enter the country. Not even for the night! This snub certainly sends a signal to the Taiwanese government that *America is not its friend!*" The camera man returned to Kimali who was looking sternly into the camera, her pretty face crinkled, "This is Kimali King, reporting an exclusive for Honolulu's best KRBT." Her face broke quickly into a smile just as the tape was cut to another story.

Jim leaned into his chair and looked up at his clock over the door. It was seven-thirty in the morning. Thomas was right. The President was walking an ever thinning line between following LV's demands and disobeying. The Threat Rose around his clock read seven, indicating the consensus opinion of his Division Chiefs was that a change in direction was necessary to avoid calamity. The problem was this President of the United States was different than all of his predecessors. Somehow, Bill Clinton didn't accept the demands placed on him by this abstract authority. He didn't accept at face value the words on the pages of the letters he received. And that meant he was always trying to find a way out of them.

Jim could do no more than he had done to influence the President of the United States. So he had redoubled his efforts to find another way out from under The Romans' thumb. The challenge was he didn't have many tools at his disposal.

Thomas and his team were studying every word of every letter. He had teams across the country and across the world looking for any association between the various demands and any organization that could be associated with them. He funded half the think tanks in Washington to work out the underlying motivations of the organization to find any clue to their identity. He funded two thirds of the research into speech patterns and linguistics at all the universities across the country to try to develop the scientific methods required to decode these letters and find their origins. Still, they had nothing.

Maxwell was working to level the playing field with The Romans. For thirty years, Department 55 knew that the ultimate path to ridding the world of the influence of LV was through technology. While Maxwell was pursuing many avenues of technological advancement, the young physicist from Virginia Tech had become the face of his efforts.

Sarah Kiadopolis was making steady, if slow, progress on her *Space Resonance* theories. Maxwell assured Jim that his path with her was the best course, and they were progressing faster than could have been expected. Jim's impression was Maxwell was slowly putting more and more of his focus on this young woman and her Fourth Option. Unfortunately that option was some time away.

So the leadership of the United States was playing poker against an opponent it didn't know. Jim liked to play poker, but he liked to look his opponents in the eyes. He also liked to have a few cards go his way. This game was only one way. LV held all the cards and all the US could do was call their bluff. His job was to get some cards, and so far, he was a complete failure.

36.   April 1, 1995

"Why won't you come to my apartment?" Sarah leaned back into the sofa in a thick terrycloth robe. Peter extended a trip in Boston for a trade show and asked Sarah to join him. She flew in early in the day. They walked the Freedom Trail, played Frisbee with some college kids on Boston Common, and ate dinner at Parker's.

It had all the makings of a perfect day.

But somehow it wasn't.

"Not this again!" Peter said. He sat next to her in a matching robe. He shifted away. Over the past months, Sarah was beginning to wonder where their relationship was going because Peter refused to come to her apartment.

"Yes, this again," Sarah insisted, "How can we be this serious," Sarah waved her hands around the hotel room, a nice suite overlooking the Common, "and you've never seen where I live?"

"You've never seen where I live!" Peter retorted. Sarah was shocked that he was right. She'd never seen his apartment.

"That's different, I've never even been to Greenville," Sarah said. Was it different? "If you want to go, let's go, right now." Sarah moved to get up.

"Don't be ridiculous," Peter said. He stood and went into the bedroom. They'd both taken showers separately, getting ready for an evening they planned to spend in, and out, of their robes. By the looks of it, they'd be spending most of the time in the robes. Sarah thought that might be best.

The last time she'd been on a date with anyone other than Peter was Lloyd in Milwaukee, and she knew then that it wasn't really a date. She was committed to being with Peter, but she was realizing he was not committed to her. He wouldn't come to her apartment. That wasn't it, but it was just the symptom of a deeper problem. Anytime she thought they might be getting more serious, he always seemed to make a little comment, or a joke, to keep it light.

At dinner, he mentioned his project manager, Claire. A woman he'd known for years. There was something about the way he talked about her. Sarah couldn't imagine him talking about herself that way. Somehow, Sarah thought he had stronger feelings than he would admit, maybe even to himself, for his project manager.

She couldn't shake the feeling as they walked back to the hotel, and now she was putting it together. Despite their fantastic physical chemistry, and the genuinely good time they had together, he just wasn't that into her. It was a strange feeling for Sarah, a problem she'd never felt before.

"Why don't you come to bed?" Peter returned from the bedroom but didn't come around the couch. Sarah was shocked to find she was almost asleep.

"Why won't you come to my apartment?" Sarah looked at him through watery eyes.

"Come on," was all Peter said.

"I think I'm fine here," Sarah said. She looked away from him.

This was supposed to be the weekend where they got really close. Instead, Sarah realized, it was the weekend where they got apart.

Sarah fell asleep on the couch and took a taxi to the airport before Peter woke up.

37.   April 15, 1995

"Sullivan," FBI Agent Hector Feliz called over the phone, "Where have you been?"

"I got held up, sorry," Sullivan knew Agent Feliz was waiting to begin an operation tonight based on the data Sullivan was going to provide.

"Did you get the last set of travel information?" Hector asked. He had a slight Hispanic accent that Sullivan found pleasant. Sullivan's team had delivered five cases over the past six months to Agent Feliz that led to arrests. Sullivan's boss was continuing to get kudos for his work, so he had plenty of leeway to get things done. Hector and Sullivan had developed a mutual respect.

"Yes, Mark Roth hasn't traveled to Westmont in five months," Sullivan said. Mark Roth was a BIA inspector responsible for the Tulsa, Oklahoma region. Erin had discovered a local builder that was getting permits more quickly than usual with little or no travel by Mr. Roth to the site. This didn't mean anything, but a little more digging found that Mark Roth processed by far more permits with by far the least travel of any inspector in the region. Crest Builders was the recipient of all of the rapid permits, and Sullivan calculated that Mark's rapid processing allowed Crest to get deals ahead of its competition worth millions.

Hector looked into Mr. Roth using the FBI's resources and legal authority and found Mr. Roth was receiving non-monetary favors including a regular set of prostitutes in exchange for the permits. Unfortunately, while the favors were unmistakably linked to the permits, they didn't have proof. Both Crest and Mr. Roth were very careful.

"Okay, we're going in tonight," Hector told Sullivan.

"What's the plan? Do we have any direct evidence?"

"No, that's why we're going in," Hector often had plans like this and Sullivan marveled in his cleverness, "I'm going in with another agent, a new man on the team. I'm telling Mark I need his help investigating an internal matter involving criminal activity at the

Westmont building site. I'm telling him that the agent who's with me is part of the criminal enterprise and I need to flush him out. I need Mark's help. That'll get him to the site and we'll call in the leadership of Crest and get them twisted around each other. I'll just be there to pick up the pieces."

"Isn't that entrapment?" Sullivan asked.

"No, I'm going to tell him I'm with the FBI. I'm not going to ask him to do anything illegal. I'm just going to confuse him and let his confusion do him in."

"That's good," Sullivan said. He hoped it would work. "That's really good." Sullivan imagined the operation. Hector's ideas always seemed like there was little chance they would work, but they almost always did.

"How's Liz?" Hector asked. He was done talking about work.

"Liz is great," Sullivan answered. He wasn't quite done with work, but he could work it in. "She's been talking about moving in for about two months now. Danny loves her, but I'm not sure."

"Why not?" Hector asked. He'd met Liz once when he came to Wisconsin to meet Sullivan's team. "She's way better than you, and you'd better put a ring on her finger or someone else will!"

"Let's not get ahead of ourselves, Hector," Sullivan said. He'd married the first girl who slept with him, and it didn't last. Liz was still very happy to explore him during their dates, and Sullivan was actually afraid his feelings for her were still too sexual. After a brief moment, Sullivan pulled himself back to his meeting with Hector. "But, speaking of long-term commitments, did you look into the latest stuff I sent you on Linus Brenner?"

Hector groaned. They'd talked about Linus before. Hector even looked into him. There wasn't anything to find. He wasn't receiving payouts. He wasn't getting hookers. He wasn't receiving favors of any kind. So far, he just had strange travel habits.

"If we tried a trick like this on him," Sullivan said, "maybe he'd let something slip." Sullivan had been tracking Linus Brenner for two years but had never been able to put together a case like he had just handed off about Mark Roth.

"To pull off a trick like this, I need to have some idea what he's into so I can design the play," Hector said, "not to mention I bring ten agents with me. It's expensive. So I need to show a return. I need to know I'm going to get the guy. Heck, it doesn't even appear to be anything to get him on!"

"I know." Sullivan wasn't happy about that, but he knew

Hector was right.

"Why don't you follow him, see what you can come up with?" Hector asked. Sullivan couldn't believe that in two years he'd never thought of following Linus himself.

38.   April 18, 1995

A half century ago, Colonel Burkett developed a taste for excessively strong coffee with one square of Hershey's Chocolate in it. It was an innovation he learned from the American company he was adjunct to in North Africa. He had few happy memories of his time there, but he couldn't shake the flavor. He got in the habit of carrying a Hershey's Milk Chocolate bar with him everywhere he went just in case he stopped for a cup.

It was two forty-five in the afternoon and the traffic was beginning to increase on the street outside the small diner. He used the mixing straw to push his chocolate square around the bottom of his cup as he looked out the window and down the block. Although he was a tall man, still over six feet, he had long since discovered that his eighty years gave him a camouflage that meant he could sit here for hours and no one would notice him.

"Can I top you off, young man?" The waitress looked to be in her sixties but was probably in her fifties. She came by, he knew, out of duty because he was the only customer in the diner this quiet afternoon.

"No, thank you," the Colonel carefully covered his accent and spoke slowly.

"Well, you just let me know," she looked past him to the package he had on the seat in a neat bag. It was a smallish box wrapped like a child's birthday present, "It looks like you have something good planned for this afternoon." She said with an expectant smile.

Americans were always so nice when they were working for their precious tips, "Yes, something very nice." He considered referring to her as *darling*, but he thought he couldn't cover his accent well enough. Besides, she was probably going to be working tomorrow, so it didn't really matter what she thought of him that much. He waited for her to leave before he let his face grimace.

The package next to him served two purposes. The first was to give him an excuse to sit here waiting. If pressed, he would tell the waitress he was waiting to meet his great grandchild for the first time. He would say he had just learned about him and that his granddaughter said she would drive in from out of town either today or tomorrow. He would say he was happy to sit and wait. He had nothing else to do. The waitress would say she was happy for him, but as the time passed, the waitress would become sad and sympathetic to the non-descript old man waiting for the meeting that didn't seem to be coming. If she remembered him and mentioned him to anyone tonight it would be a passing reference. Tomorrow, she wouldn't mention anything to anyone.

The second purpose was the small electronic transmitter built into the toy inside the box. The remote controlled car would work if inspected but a carefully designed series of manipulations of the steering wheel and accelerator on the remote would cause the radio transmitter to emit a very specific signal.

He had these buttons before. His team disguised them several different ways over the years. But he had never pushed the button before. It bothered him how many of his lieutenants volunteered to come here and perform this function. Some seemed to relish the thought, like they'd been secretly hoping to wield such power. One does not volunteer for this type of assignment. When he selected his successor, that behavior would weigh heavily.

He'd hoped it would not come to this. He never planned to be here today. He struggled to find a way to avoid it, but he conceded that the larger goal was worth this sacrifice. Still, it was a sacrifice he would commit to, and carry out, himself.

Colonel Durkell was deeply disappointed in the President of the United States. Bill Clinton was infuriating, even for an eighty year old man who had seen a lot to infuriate him. He reminded himself that his anger had nothing to do with what he was doing.

The Colonel sent the President a series of letters getting more and more specific about what he wanted. Each letter was more explicit than the last, each further emphasizing the importance and the urgency of complying. And this President found a way to not quite comply with each one. It was now apparent that Bill Clinton was going to continue to disobey. That would not do.

The Colonel had very specific objectives as well. And he had dedicated his life and his eternal afterlife to achieving his objectives. The President needed to know that LV's objectives were more important than whatever Bill Clinton or the government of the United States was trying to achieve.

Bill Clinton was the first US President Colonel Burkett dealt with to never serve his Federal Government under the shadow of the Cold War. That meant he didn't understand the full seriousness of the obligations of the office. Colonel Burkett paused in stirring his coffee when a realization hit him.

It was the Colonel, through his authority as head of LV, who brought about the end of the Cold War. It was the Colonel who demanded the collapse of the Soviet Union allowing Bill Clinton to be elected without having to carry on fighting the Cold War. It was Colonel Burkett who created the situation he was in right then. Maybe Bill Clinton was only the inevitable consequence of the Colonel's own actions? That didn't matter now. He was here now and he was happy and proud of the state of the world he'd helped to create. It was closer to *His* endgame than it had ever been.

The Colonel looked out the window of the diner as a lone woman emerged from an office building across the street. She was but the first of thousands that would be leaving the office buildings for home in the next few hours.

He visited Christine last night. Christine worked in one of these buildings. The Colonel didn't know which one. She was a paralegal, a mother of two, and a trusted member of LV. She had an office overlooking the street outside, but she wasn't there today. She called in and told her boss that she, her husband, and her kids were going on a spur of the moment vacation. They left this morning. They would be gone for a few days. The Colonel would take it from here.

At two fifty-eight the Colonel reached subtly into the package though a small flap cut in the bag that no one could see. He was able to reach into the wrapped box and manipulate the remote control car's steering wheel. He began to turn the wheel. The sequence took about one minute to enter and took all his concentration. His fingers were old but he had practiced this action about two hundred times in the past month. He knew his mouth moved slightly as he talked through the right-left-left-right-stop sequence. He heard an almost imperceptible beep from the box. The beep signaled that the code was properly entered. He needed to pull the trigger on the remote.

He wrapped his finger around the trigger as he had practiced many times, but this time he paused. He looked out the window. He reached into the pocket of his tweed sport coat and grabbed the small cross he'd carried for fifty years. He said a small prayer and with his *Amen* he squeezed the trigger. A small beep forced him to open his eyes wide. It was done. 18:00:00 . . . 17:59:59 . . . 17:59:58 . . .

39. April 19, 1995

Jim Williams lived on a quiet street in McLean, Virginia. He picked the area for the schools and access to public transportation to get into the city. At first he drove the five blocks to the metro station, but he quickly found his unpredictable schedule meant he often had to work late into the night and missed the last train home. He found himself getting the White House drivers to drop him off at the station so he could get his car. If he walked to the station in the morning, it took an extra few minutes, but it meant the drivers could just drop him at his house.

Jim's wife, Molly, was a school teacher when they lived in Santa Fe fifteen years ago. He was able to pull some strings and get her a job with the Department of Education in DC. She didn't have to work, Jim could pay himself anything he wanted, but she liked what she did. This morning they walked to the subway and rode in together.

"Do you have a busy day?" Molly asked once they were sitting on the subway. They both liked riding backwards.

"Nothing special," Jim said. His wife thought he was a speech writer, "I'm working on a draft for a speech a few weeks out, no pressure." One of Jim's direct staff was responsible for keeping track of what the President was doing and providing Jim tidbits about upcoming speeches so he could hold his cover. "Should be a normal day, and I should be home in time for Paul's game."

"Right, Paul's game," their son was on the high school baseball team, and Molly wasn't a fan of the sport. She felt some guilt about not wholeheartedly supporting her son in his activities. She went to the games and made an effort to look interested, but Paul knew she couldn't stand them. Jim enjoyed them so he made sure he attended.

Molly was reading a draft report for work and went back to it. Jim sat and thought. He knew Molly couldn't understand how he could just sit there. It actually bothered her a bit. He reviewed the situation with LV in his mind, struggling to find a way out of the current mess.

The stops became a blur, and passengers got on and off. Jim

held his wife's hand and watched out the window. Molly nudged Jim, "You better get off." It was McPherson Square.

"I love you," Jim said as he pulled himself out of his trance and jumped from the train just as the station signaled *Ding Bong* and the door closed. He looked back into the train as his wife mouthed the words "I love you, too." She smiled and returned to her report.

Jim enjoyed the walk to work, tolerated passing through security, and appreciated the splendor of the White House on his way to his basement office. He pulled up his calendar to see what the day had in store for him.

He was meeting with the chief scientist from the Texas Supercollider who had flown in for the meeting. Then he had a budget meeting, he was going to exceed his spending mandate and he needed to update the President. That was more of a formality because his funds didn't come through Congress. Then a brief meeting with his speech writer to give him an update on the speech he was supposed to be writing before he went to lunch with his wife.

After lunch Jim scheduled the entire afternoon with Thomas' team reviewing the letters in detail looking for any hint of why LV would be so interested in China, Osama, and the Desertron. Thomas kept telling him there didn't need to be a common thread. Jim kept telling him there had to be because they were all of interest to LV, and LV must have had something they were trying to accomplish.

At first Jim enjoyed the debates with Thomas' team, but he was losing patience as the months went by and the Threat Rose increased.

Jim looked at the Threat Rose around his clock. It had been a constant seven for the past three months. It didn't matter much what this threat rose said. The President decided the threat was not significant, so he wasn't going to respond. That didn't mean Jim could sleep at night. Every morning for the past three months, Jim had gone through this same thought process. He wanted that level down, Thomas wouldn't let it, and the President wasn't going to budge. All he could do was continue on.

. . .

"I don't see why any of this matters anymore," Rick Patterson was frustrated, "Bulldozers have been plowing our work into the ground. Not only are we not continuing, we're wasting some of our remaining money destroying any progress we'd made!" The head of the Desertron Project brought his brightest young star with him to the meeting. They'd been working on the last details and writing reports since the Desertron was canceled. Jim wasn't surprised that the bull dozers were there, he'd sent them. Thomas suggested a visible sign of contrition. Jim sat with the sad scientists in the immaculate Roosevelt Room of the White House listening to them tell him what could have been had they run the supercollider.

"It matters because we can get you into the CERN," Jim responded, "It's not as big as ours was going to be, but it'll have to do. The question is can you get anything out of working there?"

"The CERN was all the Europeans could do," Rick said, "It was going to be a child's toy compared to the Desertron. Now you're asking me to go spend the next ten years playing with their toy?"

"It's all I've got," Jim said. He was sorry, but there wasn't anything else he could do. As it was, he was going to have to funnel several hundred million dollars into the CERN program through a shell sponsor to get Rick the appointment.

"I'm not sure I can accept, I'm not sure the CERN will have the power-" Rick stopped, he read Jim's face. Jim looked over Rick's shoulder to the door that just opened. It was Barbara Atkinson. Jim liked her, she was always happy even though she was delivering unwelcome news.

Jim glanced at his watch, it was just before ten in the morning, pretty early for her to have already processed a letter, but that was the only time she ever talked to him.

Her face was sheet white, and she was sweating.

"Are you okay?" Rick asked Jim.

"I'm fine," Jim knew his face must have been mirroring Barbara's and Rick could read that something wasn't right. "Doctor Smith, Doctor Patterson," Jim addressed the two scientists without looking at them as he stood and rounded the table, "Thank you for coming in. Rick, you'll accept the position because it's the best chance we've got. Now, please excuse me."

Barbara reached out her hand with a folded sheet of paper.

Jim raised his hand briefly to signal *not here* and walked past her out the wide door. He felt her following him as he walked down the hallway. He was heading to the basement but he didn't think he could wait.   Janet, the Vice President's executive secretary, was at her station but didn't put up any resistance as Jim walked into his boss's office with Barbara on his heels. Jim knew Al Gore was out of the office today.

Barbara handed him the letter. As he read, Jim felt the color drain from his face. He found the nearest seat and fell into it.

"What is this about?"

. . .

At exactly 9 AM, the countdown reached 00:00:00. The circuitry performed flawlessly, connecting electrical current to an amplifier circuit that released capacitors that charged firing caps on twenty-four discrete sets of explosive charges. The explosive charges were set in a spherical arrangement and designed to implode and crush a sphere of plutonium 239 precisely.

A ball of plutonium 239 could rest in an enclosure for many years with little or no change. While some of the plutonium would decay due to the unstable nature of the element, the atoms would be spaced sufficiently apart that the neutrons released by the decay were unlikely to strike another atom, in turn causing it to decay and release neutrons. If the temperature is raised within the ball, the plutonium atoms begin to vibrate with more exuberance, increasing the chance that they will catch a passing neutron. If the pressure is increased dramatically, the atoms are pressured closer together, making it much more likely that a neutron from one plutonium atom would strike another, causing it to release yet another neutron. A *chain reaction* begins when the density is increased sufficiently that the interaction of one neutron with the next atom becomes an exponential increase in reaction. This density threshold is colloquially called the *critical mass*. At critical mass, the plutonium decays rapidly, releasing vast quantities of energy.

The objective of the explosive charges around the plutonium ball was to raise the temperature and pressure sufficiently to reach critical mass and cause an uncontrolled fission reaction, or nuclear explosion. This particular device was produced in a factory in the former Soviet Union forty years earlier. The high explosive charges came from another factory in another part of the Soviet Union. As with any communist enterprise, the employees of the factory had little or no interest in improving the quality of their products, and as such, the workers in this high explosives factory were more interested in food than in making explosives. The batch that went into this bomb was mixed incorrectly and overheated during manufacture, reducing its explosive power to less than a third of its design.

When the explosives fired the temperature and pressure within the device rose to only thirty percent of the design. This was enough to cause only a small fraction of the plutonium to begin the chain reaction and the resulting explosion was less than two percent of design strength. The resulting force was projected upward through a truck parked outside the Alfred P. Murrah Federal Building in Oklahoma City.

. . .

Jim only had a few moments to think about the letter before the commotion began. First Jim and Barbara heard loud footsteps in the hallway. Then they could hear the walkie-talkies. Jim walked toward the doorway. Janet was standing behind her desk with her hands folded in front of her. Jim stepped toward the hallway to look out just as two Secret Service agents ran past toward the Oval Office. A third agent appeared in the doorway and stopped him. He wore a flak jacket over his suit and rather than a pistol he carried an M16 assault rifle.

"Back into the office!" The agent commanded. Jim obeyed. Jim and Janet were ushered into the Vice President's office ten agents with their pistols drawn escorting the President of the United States down the hallway. He knew the end of the hall had the stairway down to the Situation Room and the cold war era secure vault designed to withstand multiple intercontinental ballistic missiles.

Jim looked at Barbara, "Who else has this?"

"I followed the protocol," Barbara said, "Thomas has the original." Jim knew neither Barbara nor Thomas told anyone else about the letter. So how did the Secret Service know to collect the President? And what exactly was the letter about?

Jim decided he needed to go with the President and moved to pass the agent.

"I'm sorry sir," the agent said, "we're on full lock down."

"What's going on?" Jim asked.

"I don't know, something about a bombing," the agent maintained his solid stance in the doorway but listened to the radio transmitter in his ear, "not here in Washington, but it's a big one!" Shit, this is it. Thomas was right.

The office erupted with noise. Jim turned to see Barbara turn on the television. A perfectly coifed news reporter sat at a desk,

"Again, we're reporting live from Oklahoma City where a massive explosion has destroyed ten buildings in the heart of downtown!" Jim let the letter fall from his hand to the floor as he listened, "Let's go live to Mike Lutjen, Mike what are you seeing?"

Mike filled the screen and towered over the crowd gathered around him. "Emergency responders are on the scene of what appears to be a massive explosion. As you can see behind me," the camera panned off of Mike to the face of a building reduced to a huge pile of rubble. "The federal building here in Oklahoma City is completely destroyed! Emergency responders are rushing through the rubble as hundreds of people are carried out and thousands more are feared trapped."

They watched for about five minutes as Mike tried to relay what was happening. Jim realized the story was changing quickly, but the basic facts were that a large explosion destroyed at least one building. This had to be what LV was referring to. Jim picked up the letter and turned to leave the office.

"No sir! We're under full lock down," the agent said.

"But I have information relevant to the bombing!" Jim cried as he tried to move past the agent.

"Sir, it doesn't matter what you know, or what you convince me of," the agent didn't raise his gun, "there are marksmen in the hallway that will shoot anyone without their Asset Pass clearly displayed." Jim knew he was right about one of the joys of working in the White House. In the event of a lock down, the Secret Service would shoot anyone walking around the halls and ask questions later. The only exception was someone with an Asset Pass. The Asset Pass was a colored three by five card and it had to be displayed over the heart to move in the halls. Only a few people had the cards, and Jim was one of them. The color changed every day and an agent was tasked to deliver the new colors to the offices each morning. Jim was supposed to carry it everywhere he went, but he often forgot. He forgot today.

"My Asset Pass is in my office," Jim tried, "I'll go get it!"

"If you leave that door, I'm under orders to shoot you," the agent said, "I might miss, but I'm sure there are five agents between here and wherever you're going who won't!" Jim weighed his options. He had none.

Jim sat with Barbara who was regaining some color. Janet was beginning to cry. Actually, Barbara and Jim were two of only a few people who knew there was no more danger. There would not be another bomb today. Janet might be afraid another bomb was about to go off in the White House. Barbara held her hand and that calmed her a bit.

Jim used the Vice President's phone to call his wife. He told her everything was okay, they were on lock down. His wife was on lockdown too, and he didn't need to tell her it meant two different things between the Department of Education and the White House. They decided it was best to stay where they were, and to leave their son in school. Jim said he would probably have to work late.

What would he do if he had his Asset Pass? He would report directly to the President. Would the President do anything differently than whatever it was he was doing now? Yes, he would know they were not in danger. Jim didn't know what advice he would offer, but he did know he had information that the most powerful man in the world needed right now.

"Thomas!" Jim called. He saw the man walk past in the hallway, "Thomas Kirk! Come back here!" The agent looked sternly at Jim. Jim wanted to run to the door and call again but he couldn't. Then Thomas appeared in the doorway. His florescent pink card pinned to his chest allowed him to move. He entered the office. The agent let him pass.

Thomas walked straight up to Jim. He was briefly afraid the older man would hit him in the face, but instead he wordlessly unclipped his Asset Pass. The two men looked each other in the eye. Thomas had warned that LV would respond in some way, some catastrophic way, and that they must be obeyed. Jim had felt his pressure, but had failed to persuade his boss. Now Jim could see a tremendous pain in Thomas' face. The man was not here to gloat about being right. He was right, and it destroyed him. Thomas handed Jim the pass. Then Thomas turned and sat next to Janet. He was taking his position with those who had done everything they could, and were now spectators.

Jim hurried down the stairs past three rifles trained on him. Even the third time, he didn't enjoy it. The pass got him to the outer access to the Situation Room, but he needed more ID there. He showed his normal office badge and pulled a special card he carried from his wallet. This was his first time down here, and the tension was not eased by the marine who kept his M16 trained on him while the marine behind the desk looked him up on the approved list. The list included photographs and the marine compared Jim's face to the file photograph. He thought if there was any question he would signal to his compatriot, and Jim would be put down.

"Thank you, Mr. Williams," the marine said. He handed his IDs back and pressed a button that started the mechanical process to open the heavy doors before him.

Jim stepped through. He found himself in another outer room. This one had several doors off of it and half a dozen marines in full battle gear. None had their weapons raised.

The large double doors directly across from the entrance clearly lead to the Situation Room and to the President. Jim slowly walked toward the doors watching the marines who watched him back. He opened the door and slid inside.

. . .

While outside everyone moved slowly and cautiously, inside the Situation Room was a flurry of activity. He entered the room along the long end of a large conference table. To the left on the wall were several projected images and that end of the table seemed to be full of the technical team processing data. Panning to his right were slowly increasing ranks of military officers from each branch starting with two stars and rising to the four star Joint Chiefs. After that were the suits. Jim recognized the National Security team including the heads of the FBI, CIA, and NSA. Finally, at the head of the table was Bill Clinton, the President of the United States.

"I want to know everything there is to know about this guy!" The President was saying.

Jim looked back to his left at the screens. One screen had the TV coverage just as he was watching in the Vice President's office with Mike Lutjen now down at the blast site. Two screens showed military readouts of threats across the region and the globe. One screen showed a camera view of the lawns outside the White House including the path Jim had used to walk to work this morning. There were marines in full battle dress everywhere. The last screen showed a picture of a man. It was a driver's license photo of Timothy McVeigh. Jim followed the conversation that somehow he was involved and was miraculously picked up only moments after the bomb went off.

Jim felt the strange feeling of someone looking at him and panned back to his right. Only one man was looking at him, it was Bill Clinton. The President of the United States had just recognized that his Special Secretary for Department Fifty-Five was in the

Situation Room. The two men looked each other in the eye for a few seconds as the rest of the room hummed with activity. Jim watched as various emotions crossed the President's face, and he finally saw realization cross it. The President's eyes opened a bit wider than normal.

The President stood. Everyone at the table stood and the room fell silent.

"Carry on," the President commanded and turned from the head of the table to walk past Jim.

"Mr. President!" one of the four stars called. The President looked at the man who was rarely in a room he did not command. The man closed his mouth and remembered his place. The President walked out the door and Jim followed him.

The six marines in the outer room snapped to attention but the President didn't notice. Instead he went to one of the other doors and walked in. It was a small auxiliary meeting room with a small table packed with nine analysts poring over documents and computers. They were clearly feeding information from here to the technicians inside the Situation Room.

"Out!" the President said. The nine looked up and immediately scurried from the room. After they left, the President disconnected the power to the four computers and pulled the phone cord from the wall. Then he stood with his back to Jim and slowly turned around, steeling himself for what he was about the see.

Jim handed him the letter.

The relationship is broken. We have been forced to act in an unprecedented way. We regret the loss of life, but it was necessary to remind you of the importance of the relationship. You will not discuss today's events except as a matter of domestic terrorism. You will take no action to interfere with the Chinese national aspirations. You will take no action against Osama bin Ladin. We are not happy to repeat ourselves. Any actions to the contrary will result in more unfortunate events.

- LV

The President of the United States folded the letter and wordlessly handed it back to Jim. They both knew the letter meant the two of them were responsible for the deaths in Oklahoma City.

This made all of their efforts to decode the letters, to parse words, to recruit physicists, to manipulate financial markets, to attempt assassinations, to do everything else they had been doing...

Irrelevant.

They failed.

The President of the United States wept.

1998-2001

40. November 10, 1998

"Damn," Al Gore crumpled. He'd been traveling for a week so Jim delivered the latest letter directly to the President.

> *The relationship is improving slowly. Certain factions within the Congress would like to leverage Ken Starr's investigation to impeach the President of the United States. Allow them to succeed.*

> *-LV*

In the three years since the Oklahoma City bombing, the President followed every command from LV to the letter. Bill Clinton had called LV's bluff and LV had the cards. Luckily the device malfunctioned, but a malfunctioning nuclear weapon still killed over five hundred Americans. The public face of the President was still the confident swaggering leader, but in private he had not recovered. He questioned every decision. He was constantly afraid. He relied heavily on Jim Williams. If Jim so much as hinted that a course of action might be contrary to a directive, it was immediately scrapped. Jim was now the President's most important advisor and sat in on every meeting.

Jim knew this letter didn't have anything to do with President Bill Clinton.

"What the hell am I supposed to do?" The Vice President slouched down on one of the couches and stared at the copy of the letter in his hands. Jim had never seen him like this. He was the most composed, most prepared, and most determined man he'd ever met.

"Al," Bill Clinton sat next to his friend, "We can still win this."

"How?" Al sat up and composed himself. He looked at the President, "Remember when this all started? Remember when you called me to Little Rock and we talked about everything we'd do? You were going to get things started, and then I was going to really get it done? We were going to have sixteen years!" He looked up at Jim. He knew Al Gore was remembering the first time they met, in this room, the Oval Office, on Inauguration Day. They didn't know it, but all their plans for their four terms, two for Bill and two for Al, were changed that day.

"I've spent most of my time in office chasing LV," Al leaned back into the couch, "Whatever progress we've made, it's nothing I can use on the campaign trail. Even if I mention some of the profound technological advancements we've made, I can't take credit for them. I was going to have a resume."

"Al," Bill said, "Vice Presidents get their resume by being Vice President. You've been a part of everything that's happened in the past six years, and you can be proud of it. We'll make the country proud of it."

"I was going to champion business innovation," Al wasn't listening now, "I was going to be a champion of the environment! Remember that?" He again focused on Jim, as though Jim was LV, "Remember the Kyoto Protocol? We negotiated the most advanced set of environmental protections the world had ever seen. Sure we were going to combat Climate Change, but with that we were going to clean up the air and water around the world for billions of people! Then we got that damned letter!"

Just before Al Gore went to the Kyoto Climate Change summit, LV had sent a letter demanding that the US not ratify the treaty. There was no choice but to comply, but Al Gore was too invested to walk away. He was allowed to sign the treaty knowing that the US Senate could not ratify it. Jim and the President engineered a 95 to 0 vote to deny ratification of the Kyoto Protocol signifying to LV that their demand was met.

"I know why we didn't ratify," Al still looked directly at Jim, "but now every moron who doesn't believe in the scientific method tells me I was wrong. Damn it. I don't know what's worse, the idiots who don't understand how science works, or the smart people who are so easily manipulating them to protect their own financial interests?"

"Al," Bill had more empathy than most and he shared Al's pain at his impending realization, "It's going to be okay. We're still going to win this. We're still going to have sixteen years."

"No," Al said, "We're not. LV doesn't care about Kyoto, they did that to hurt me!"

"We don't know that," Jim interjected. When his bosses were talking, his role was to keep their facts completely accurate.

"You might not know it," Al said, "but I've thought it all along, and this letter confirms it! Why the hell else would they want you to be impeached? They clearly said impeached, not removed from office, so we'll work some more of our legislative magic and get the Senate to acquit, it will be easy because this is all stupid. So you'll be okay. It's going to kill me, though. I won't be able to use your accomplishments anymore. My resume as the Vice President will be destroyed. They're doing this because they don't want me to be the next President."

Jim and the President had been studying this letter for four days. Al Gore came to their conclusion in one minute. There wasn't much left to talk about.

41.   March 28, 1999

The last time Dr. Sarah Kiadopolis sat on a stage ahead of a crowd was her public thesis defense, five years ago. She enjoyed teaching then, and she expected she would enjoy this lecture today. That didn't stop butterflies of anticipation from stirring her stomach as she waited for the lecture hall to fill.

Sarah asked Mr. Rassic if she could start to reintroduce herself to the physics community in January of 1998, at their fourth annual meeting. Their work was progressing well, she was the only person in the world who could see the spatial distribution of elements in distant stars, and she thought they could start to tell the world about it. She'd improved her resolution to ten thousand times that of the best images anyone else could make and she hadn't shown anyone. Besides, Maxwell had her working on other things.

He said no.

This January she was ready to ask again, she'd prepared arguments, but it wasn't necessary. Maxwell surprised her with an invitation to speak at the Society of Women Engineers, SWE, at their annual meeting in Orlando. He said he knew he wouldn't be able to keep her bottled up forever. Women Engineers wasn't exactly what she was thinking, but Maxwell asked her to think of how she could get a better offer. She decided to take it.

As part of their annual meeting, SWE invited women in science and engineering to give talks on their work. There were several lecture tracks and Sarah was in the track for *Alternate Careers*. She'd be sitting on a panel with four other women who each studied science and engineering but had taken careers in other fields. The session was two hours and each of the five women was supposed to give fifteen minutes of introductory remarks about how their technical training led to their current careers. Sarah wasn't thrilled by the topic, but she was sure she could make a good impression, and she needed to get some practice under her belt.

Today, she chose her red skirt just above the knee with white sleeveless blouse and white heels over bare legs. She was in Florida after all. The room was arranged to hold about two hundred people, and she was surprised that it was filling up.

The other four women on the panel all had engineering degrees and three of them were managers of engineers. She didn't think that really counted as *Alternate Careers*. The last woman, a short, stout woman with striking black hair, had trained as a chemical engineer and was now a physician. Sarah was looking forward to hearing from her.

The three managers went first and Sarah was fourth. After a simple introduction from the moderator, she was alone at the front of the stage with four women on chairs behind her. There was a podium but Sarah instead walked directly to the front center of the small stage.

"Good morning, I'm Dr. Sarah Kiadopolis," Sarah said, "I've been with Cornwall & Wallace of New York for the past five years. I've been developing financial derivatives and other monetary instruments, and I'm going to tell you how I got there. In order to do that, I need to start at the beginning. I earned my PhD in Physics at Virginia Tech," Sarah waited. She hoped for a bit of a response but the room was silent. She was the fourth woman to speak.

"To explain how I'm using my physics education in the creation of financial instruments, I need to make sure everyone knows the answer to three questions," Sarah introduced.

Several women were actually taking notes.

"One. Which is stronger, the force of gravity or the electromagnetic force?"

"Two. Why do we care about the answer to question one?"

"Three. Is there anything we can do about it?"

Sarah never looked away from the crowd. She was holding most of their attention so far. A good sign, she hoped.

"Fifty-thousand years ago, the first people on earth knew the answer to question one. Let's think about Grog, one of the first men hunting and gathering in central Africa." Sarah added an aside, "Despite fifty-thousand years of progress, he's just like most of the men I've met in the last year." That got a rise and some laughs from the crowd. Good. "Grog used rocks to sharpen sticks and grouped together with his friends to defend themselves against lions. Despite being slow, weak, and dumb, just like today," a bigger laugh, "and not having big teeth or claws, Grog and his friends were able to use tools, group effort, and brain power to dominate the animals and the landscape. He didn't know it but his life was controlled by two important forces. The first was gravity. The second was electromagnetism." The writing in the room stopped. She thought they would be surprised by electromagnetism, and they were.

Sarah had been taught to stay still while presenting, but she liked to move around and she turned slightly to walk to the corner of the stage. She used her arms to animate her discussion. "The first humans knew that when something went up, it always came down. They lived in a world, in a Universe actually, where gravity kept them firmly on the ground. They lived in a Universe where spears thrown into the air always fell back down. If they were good at it they could predict fairly well where they would fall. Grog was good at it and often hit his target. No one could modify the force of gravity, and Grog didn't know where it came from but he did know how to use it to reliably pull his spears to the earth. Grog also knew that no matter how high he threw his spear, it always came back down. Today, physicists don't know much more about gravity than Grog, but we'll get to that in a moment."

Sarah knew this talk was purely for entertainment value and so far the women in the room were entertained.

"Luckily for Grog, gravity never pulled him through the surface of the earth to its core. Luckily, the bare soles of his big feet never passed through the surface of the ground. Grog knew they never would. Grog also knew that until he touched it, he could hold his foot as close to the ground as he wanted and he would not feel it." At the corner of the stage, Sarah planted her left foot and let her right foot rock back onto her three-inch heel. She slowly brought her toe close to the floor pantomiming Grog's knowledge. Many in the audience strained to see the example. "Grog knew there was a force counteracting the unnamed force of gravity that reliably held his feet up once they came into contact with the ground. He also knew that force only worked across very small distances while the force of gravity seemed to reach out forever." She let her toe come close to the floor, allowing it to pivot left to right. Then she let it touch the floor and hold firm.

She'd rehearsed this talk several times in her apartment, but she didn't account for the larger size of this room as she walked to the podium. The room watched her walk the ten steps.

"As I described the knowledge of the first humans, all of us in this room are comfortable in the knowledge that we not only know what Grog knew, but that the same rules still apply. Grog probably didn't spend much time pondering the nature of the force that kept his feet from falling through the ground. He probably didn't ponder much of anything between his insatiable desire to reproduce and the tremendous effort he put into messing everything up!" She paused. This was the third day of the conference and she was right to assume the male bashing was in full swing. She received more appreciative laughter. "Let's not blame Grog entirely, though. He couldn't have pondered the force holding him up much because it took over forty nine thousand years to figure it out." Many in the room wrote, probably the number.

"So we need to jump forward to Ben Franklin. One day, he tied a key to a kite and flew the kite in a thunder storm. Today, this is not advisable, but then he had no idea that he would be allowing a massive charge of electrons held statically in the clouds to pass through the key and form a current, flowing to the ground and dissipating into the earth. Luckily, the current didn't pass through him on its way."

"Over time, scientists learned that matter is made up of atoms, and atoms are made of electrons orbiting their nucleus made of protons and neutrons. The electromagnetic force makes electrons repel electrons and attract protons. That same electromagnetic force makes protons repel protons and attract electrons." Sarah had jumped ahead a long way and waited for everyone to catch up. "In the toe of my shoe, just like in the sole of Grog's foot, the atoms have the same number of electrons and protons. This means their charges are balanced out."

Sarah stepped out from behind the podium and stood facing the side wall of the room. "So, when I lift my heel off the floor, the billions of electrons in the tip of my heel are trying to repel the billions of electrons in the floor. At the same time the billions of protons in the tip of this heel are trying to attract those billions of electrons in the floor. The result is that I don't feel any electromagnetic force on my heel because the repulsion of the electrons exactly equals the attraction of the protons."

"Now, as I bring my heel close to the floor, there's an atom at the very tip of my heel. It's the first one to get close to the atom that is closest to it on the floor," Sarah allowed her heel to drop closer to the floor and looked over her left shoulder to the audience. She saw several women in the audience lean forward to see the gap get smaller between her heel and the floor. "We need to remember that electrons are tiny particles that orbit the nucleus of atoms. The protons are trapped in the nucleus. So, in the two atoms that are now getting close to each other, their electrons are much closer to each other than their protons."

"We could think of it like this." Sarah let her heel fall to the floor, and turned to face the audience. She paused while the women leaned back in their seats and looked up to her face. "While the protons in my heel are still very far from the protons in the floor, their electrons are beginning to bump into each other. So the electrons repel each other with much more force than the protons attract the electrons because they are so much closer. Luckily for me, the force of those electrons pushing against each other is strong enough to hold me up and keep my heel happily away from the center of the earth!"

"As I stand here on my heel the force of gravity is trying to pull not only my heel, but my hair, my arms, and more and more the skin on my face," Sarah considered making a comment about her breasts needing her bra, but the skin on her face comment got enough recognition from her audience. "Unlike electromagnetism with its protons and electrons, gravity only has gravitons, and gravity only attracts. So there's no counterbalance to the force of the entire earth pulling me to its core with all its might. No counterbalance except the tiny layer of electrons in the heels of my shoes using the electromagnetic force. So, the electromagnetic force contained in the heels of my shoes is strong enough to overcome the gravitational force of the entire earth!"

Sarah looked at the crowd triumphantly. She'd worked on this explanation for weeks. A few in the crowd nodded. "It turns out that the force of electromagnetism is billions of billions of times more powerful than the force of gravity!"

Sarah paused and looked at the crowd. She still held their attention. Several women were taking notes as she walked to a stool on the far end of the stage and took the cup of water from it. She took a drink and sat on the stool, holding the cup in her hands. One of her toes touched the floor and her other heel was hooked on the bar of the stool.

. . .

Claire Havers sat in the fourth row of the auditorium and listened to Sarah Kiadopolis talk about Grog. Sarah was a pretty good speaker, her story was good and she engaged her audience much better than the three managers before her.

Claire studied Sarah's face and body looking for any blemishes. Her white blouse and heels accentuated her tan and her tight red skirt showed her curves. Claire had felt her own bicep when Sarah extended her arm during her explanation. She thought herself a strong woman, but Sarah was stronger. Her legs were muscular too. She stood out among the other four women on the stage.

Claire was supposed to be paying attention to the talk for any revelations about her work, but all she could think of was the time Dr. Sarah Kiadopolis spent with Peter Howard. He was getting better looking as he aged, a phenomenon reserved exclusively for men. She knew she was still in love with him. She had not allowed herself to use that word, even in her own mind, until she mentioned Dr. Sarah Kiadopolis to him.

Two weeks ago, Linus asked her to come here and listen to the doctor. She mentioned the assignment in passing to Peter and was shocked to learn that Peter knew Dr. Kiadopolis. Peter and Claire talked every day. He was the only person she could open up to about all their assignments. He knew everything she was doing for Linus, but he had never mentioned his *Dr. Sarah Kiadopolis* assignment.

Since that revelation, Claire thought about Peter constantly. Yes, she loved him. She dated other men, but nothing serious ever developed. She knew Peter saw plenty of women; he was always open about it. Ravi knew them both and quickly decided she loved Peter, but she wasn't ready to admit it to herself.

Peter told her he saw the Doctor for about two years, on and off, but that was years ago. He said he had not seen her in some time. It was no big deal. Linus had asked him to meet her and see if he could learn anything from her. It was just like Linus sending Claire here now. Now that she was looking at the Doctor, she knew it was nothing like that.

The way Peter talked about Dr. Kiadopolis, Claire expected her to be an overweight, pale, dorky lady. Nothing Peter would like. Maybe that's just what she hoped. Now the better looking she was, the more confidently she spoke about physics, the brighter her smile, the nicer she seemed, the more Claire hated Dr. Sarah Kiadopolis.

. . .

"Now that I've taught you something you've known your whole lives, and that everyone has always known, and that has been true as long as there has been a Universe, we move to Question Two: who cares?" Sarah began again after ten seconds on the stool, "How is this knowledge going to do anything for me? How is it going to help America compete in the world? Why should The United States Government, or any other government, spend a dime to figure this out? To answer this, I'm not going all the way back to Grog. I'm going to start with Ben Franklin. Ben knew electricity, lightning to him, was important, and that it should be explored, but it would take over one hundred years for someone to understand electricity well enough to do something with it."

"In the late eighteen hundreds, Thomas Edison, George Westinghouse, and Nicola Telsa argued over the best way to deploy electricity to the world. Thomas Edison had the light bulb, a marketable use for electricity. He knew he needed money, so he arranged to create the first electrical grid on Wall Street in New York City. The electric lights were a hit, and the race was on to electrify the world." She was comfortable on the stool and she stayed there. "When he first thought of electricity, and its uses, he thought of light bulbs and motors. He couldn't possibly have foreseen that as we developed a better and better understanding of the nature of electricity and electromagnetism, we would be able to build transistors, computers and now the Internet."

Sarah spoke slowly and calmly recounting the story. The women were all listening.

"Soon after Edison electrified New York, another man had an idea," Sarah said, "Albert Einstein published his papers on Special Relativity in 1906. This time it took just under forty years for the world to be shook by the impact of his understanding of nuclear energy. At one moment, the atomic bomb both ended World War Two and started the Cold War. Just like it was difficult to understand the full impact of understanding electromagnetism, we only now understand that mastering Einstein's Relativity and the Nuclear forces also gave us Carbon Dating and Global Position Systems."

"Here we are with two scientific discoveries that have changed the world. We have two fields of study, electromagnetics and the nuclear forces that have led to much of the vast wealth and geopolitical dominance of the United States in the past one hundred years. How could two areas of study be so important? If we can understand what is unique about these two fields, electromagnetics and nuclear energy, then maybe we could try to find another field of study that was like those and focus our efforts there. If we could identify what these two have in common, and what makes them so special, we could study the progression of those special features to predict how others would develop."

Sarah took another sip of water. She was a little concerned that she was losing her audience, but she continued. She stood and walked to the edge of the stage.

"Physicists have identified what is unique about these phenomena. Physicists have determined why they are so important, even fundamental. We now know that all the interactions in the Universe, from us not falling through the floor to the center of the earth, to the chemical reactions that form memories in our brains, to the phenomenal temperature created in stars, to the near stopping of time at absolute zero temperature, can all be boiled down to four forces." She held up four fingers on her right hand.

"Let me say that again, everything that happens in the world, and everything that happens in the Universe, can be explained by four forces." Sarah paused.

"Many of you know what these forces are. The first force is the strongest, the electromagnetic force. So, it makes sense that the understanding of the electromagnetic force would have nothing less than a profound reshaping of the world as we know it. Understanding of any fundamental force will have that effect on you. In fact, understanding forces like these will have effects on you that you can't predict, just as Edison couldn't possibly have foreseen the computer." Sarah dropped her index finger leaving three.

"The second and third forces are related, and we will call them the nuclear forces. These are best characterized by the bombs that Einstein's theory made possible, but those bombs are only the light bulb of the nuclear forces. They're only the beginning of what can be achieved with these forces." Sarah dropped her next two fingers leaving her pinky alone.

"So now we have three of the four fundamental forces. We have basic understandings of their operations, and we have the knowledge to manipulate them to our benefit, or ultimate destruction. The understanding of these forces has reached into every part of our lives, they've changed the way we see things, they've changed the way we communicate, and they've changed the way governments relate. The economic impact of our understanding of these forces is incalculable."

"But there is one more fundamental force."

Sarah waved her pinky. "It's the weakest force by billions of billions of times. It's the force Grog knew about. He knew how to live with it but couldn't explain it. It's also the force that we, today, also know the implications of, but not how to control."

"Gravity." Sarah looked at her pinky. She stood on a large stage under a soft spotlight with her feet together. Her hand was raised with her elbow bent like she was taking an oath except that only her pinky was raised.

She looked back to the audience. Several women were looking at her pinky too. She spoke softly. "Imagine the impact of understanding the last Fundamental Force in the Universe. Sure, just like the light bulb and the atomic bomb; gravity will have some obvious applications. If we could manipulate gravity, we could hover. Imagine transportation without gravity. Imagine the ease of space travel without gravity. Imagine the elimination of roads and bridges. Imagine how much less building materials, oil, and pollution would be created. We could even selectively increase gravity if we needed to."

"That's the good news," Sarah let her hand fall, "The bad news is that we're pretty far from understanding gravity sufficiently to make these kinds of modifications. We might be hundreds of years away."

"The challenge is that gravitons are just too damned small, they're so weak we can't even see them. We're looking for something that's a billion billion times smaller and weaker than an electron!"

"That's why we're looking deep into space with advanced telescopes. We need to look at sources of vast quantities of gravitons. We're looking for clues that will help us find gravitons in the hearts of distant stars." Sarah wanted so much to tell this audience that she had found them. She wanted to show them what she had done. But Maxwell had been adamant.

Sarah took a deep breath and looked to the back of the auditorium. The doorway was open; some women had come and gone.

Peter Howard?

She required a double take, but Peter Howard was leaning on the door jam. He smiled at her and nodded like he'd seen her just yesterday. Sarah had not seen Peter Howard in four years.

Not since they took a weekend trip to Boston. Since then, she'd been on few third dates, but, despite Angie's urging, had not been intimate with another man.

She only remembered the good times with Peter, and seeing him now reminded her of the heat they'd shared, but didn't realize she missed until just now.

She forced herself back to the room and hoped no one noticed her distraction. "And, uhmm. We're using those clues to look into the centers of atoms. We're using the most advanced supercolliders on the earth to search the structure of matter itself. Soon, the CERN will complete the Large Hadron Collider. This is where we hope to find new clues to find gravitons. We're on a hunt for the smallest force in the Universe."

Sarah moved back to the chair, "That's why governments are racing to find the graviton. The country that finds the graviton will be the country that leads the world in the next century. That's why we care!"

Sarah paused and looked around. The women were still paying attention. Many were smiling, but some seemed to be looking concerned that she was reaching too far. Oh well. She thought about her third question. Her intention was to be even more abstract than this previous discussion, but she feared she would lose this audience quickly. She took a different tack. One she would be able to defend with Maxwell.

"So, we have one question to go. What do we do about it?" Sarah wasn't quite going to answer that question. "It turns out the small size of the graviton is both a challenge and an opportunity. Hopefully an opportunity we can capitalize on."

"The smallness of the graviton means that it can be used to see very small things. Let me put it like this. If you're trying to measure the distance between here and Seattle, you would use miles. If you want to measure the distance between me and you, you would use feet. The distance between my hands, inches. To measure the distance between two molecules, we use electron microscopes. But how do we see details of an electron? The answer is we can't because we'd need something smaller than an electron to see any of those details."

"If we could see gravitons, we would see billions of them for every electron. We would be able to see an electron with the same resolution we can see each other in this auditorium."

"So imagine a computer that worked not on electrons, but on gravitons. It could be billions of billions of times more powerful. Imagine a hard drive that worked with gravitons. It would be able to store billions of billions of times more information!"

She wanted to say what would happen if she looked at stars. She looked at the crowd.

They were waiting for her punch line, but she knew she would not deliver the one she'd built up to.

Instead, Sarah looked to the back of the room to see a friendly face, but the doorway was empty. Her heart fell until she realized she still remembered his number.

. . .

There is was again. Claire looked over her shoulder to the back of the room following Dr. Kiadopolis' eyes. What was she looking at?

. . .

She wanted to tell them what she had done, how she was much closer than anyone in this room could imagine. But she couldn't. She wanted to tell them that there was a *Space Resonator* on the Hubble Space Telescope right now. She wanted to tell them that she could see distant stars ten thousand times better than anyone else, but she couldn't. She wanted to tell them there was a second Hubble, *KiteString*, orbiting with a second set of *Space Resonators*.

She wanted to tell them that she had not looked at a distant star in two years. Two years ago Maxwell told her to turn *KiteString* around. Maxwell gave her specific coordinates on the earth and told her to tell him what she could see. She knew Maxwell was interested in commercial applications of the technology and she indulged him on what she thought would be a short assignment.

Now, two years later, she was frustrated to know that while her system worked perfectly in space, it didn't work at all on Earth. She'd spent the past two years struggling to see a tiny bit of Earth and no time looking at the stars.

The pause dragged longer than she was comfortable with. She felt that her face had fallen. She quickly collected herself and looked out to the audience with a smile. She wanted to tell them all what she had done, but instead she carried on with her cover.

"So, I spent years researching the origins of gravity at Virginia Tech," Sarah said, "And while I wouldn't give that up, I found I had to wait for the technology to catch up to the theories. I needed the Europeans to complete the Large Hadron Collider. And, I needed to make some money!"

Sarah still met with Tim Cullis at Cornwall & Wallace every few months to maintain her cover story. He was still a weasel, but he helped her. Sarah described how her description of physics was applied to her work on financial derivatives. This discussion took the last few minutes of her fifteen minute allotment.

. . .

Two weeks ago, Peter Howard was shocked by the juxtaposition of two different times and places when *Claire Havers* said the name *Doctor Sarah Kiadopolis*. Over the past six years, Peter shared everything with Claire including who he dated. It bothered him when she dated, but he had no reason to be jealous and he was glad she shared it with him too. In that time, he'd only kept one thing from her. It just wasn't ever the right time to tell her about Sarah.

Now, seeing the way Claire looked at Sarah, Peter knew it was a mistake to mention it ten days ago.

It was Sunday night, the third night of the conference that was to last until Tuesday, and the women were in full networking mode. It took Peter an hour to make his way around the reception hall, and he didn't see Sarah anywhere. Maybe it was a bad idea to come here anyway.

"Excuse me, ladies," Peter stepped away from a group of civil engineers from Houston who were very interested in leaving Houston. He answered his new Motorola Razr cell phone without looking at the display, "Hello, Peter Howard."

"Peter, this is Sarah Kiadopolis," her unmistakable strong voice had not changed a bit, "The US women's soccer team just missed another corner kick against Mexico. If you want, I'm in room 1220, come up."

"Okay," Peter said, but she hung up.

Twelve minutes later, he pushed the door to 1220.

It gave.

He smiled when he saw she'd propped the door with the plastic room key. Her room was a suite and he crossed the living room.

"Dammit!" he froze when he heard her shout as the television erupted with a collective groan. He could see the bedroom was illuminated only by the random flickering of the television. As he approached the bed came into view.

Sarah was on her knees on the center of the bed. She still wore her blouse from her presentation today, but she'd removed her skirt. Her hair was tussled but she was intently watching the television. Her hands were on her knees and she leaned forward slightly. With her butt raised from resting on her feet Peter could make out her panties. Her quads and biceps were both flexed in tension as she focused on the television before her. Peter leaned against the door jamb to enjoy the view of the sexiest woman he'd ever met.

"The US Women line up for another corner-kick," the announcer called, "Brandi Chastain takes the kick ... Mia Hamm is there! It's ... just over the goal." Peter couldn't see the television, but he didn't care. Sarah's face dropped with the miss. When it came back up, she glanced to her left and met Peter's eyes. Her scowl broke into her beautiful smile, and she wordlessly waved him over. He walked slowly to the edge of the bed as she watched the television and crawled toward him.

He didn't know where this was going, but he was going with it.

Sarah didn't take her eyes off the game while she started undressing him. She kneeled on the edge of the bed while he stood just at the edge. He followed her lead and removed her blouse. Once she had him down to his boxers, she tore herself away from the television long enough to kiss him deeply and pressing her body to his. She fell backwards onto the bed, pulling him down with her. She returned to watching the game while guiding his head to her breasts.

42.   May 8, 1999

Sullivan Acer sat on a lawn chair on the tiny piece of grass that was Hector Feliz's backyard on the outskirts of Albuquerque. They watched as Danny, Sullivan's son, played soccer with Hector's three kids at the end of the yard. Danny was eleven now, and Hector's oldest son was eight, but Juan was a natural player and the game was even. The two younger kids were trying to keep up, but they mostly just ran around. Beyond the yard the grass ended and the desert stretched to the mountains in the distance. It was ninety-eight degrees and Sullivan basked in the warmth that he rarely experienced in Wisconsin.

Today was Gloria's birthday. Hector's wife was a proud Honduran woman, and she was inside with her mother and sisters. Sullivan and Hector enjoyed the retreat to watch the kids outside. Their professional relationship had grown into a friendship.

Sullivan was having a rough time after his break-up with Liz, and Hector invited Sullivan to bring Danny to the party. They were together for three years. She moved on quickly, and he didn't.

Hector invited them to stay at their full house, much to Gloria's frustration. He needed a man in the house to help protect him from all the estrogen. A few days and fifteen hundred miles away was just what Sullivan needed.

Sullivan brought his drawing pad and delighted the women with the pictures he drew of each of them. Now he was idly drawing a picture of his friend while they talked.

"People breakup," Hector said. They'd gone over the breakup late into the evening last night, and Sullivan had brought it up again. Sullivan could tell Hector was growing tired of it. "Look, you said it yourself. You were fighting all the time. Not about anything, sounded like she was just into playing games. She wanted all of your attention when she wanted it, and when you gave it to her, she treated you like shit! Always fighting is no way to live, man."

"Not always," Sullivan said. He looked down at his drawing, "Make-up sex."

"Look, all guys like make-up sex," Hector said more loudly then Sullivan was comfortable with, "But dude, there's more to life. You need to be happy the rest of the time too."

Sullivan shouldn't have told him about that, but he was trying to figure out his feelings. Hector wasn't buying it. He thought they should have ended things a long time ago. Hector was right. Unfortunately, Sullivan had a track record of getting into relationships with women too soon, and then staying with them too long. Next time would be different. He'd take it really slow.

"Hey, I heard Crest Builders finally went under," Hector changed the subject. Sullivan was glad to move on.

The trick had worked on Mark Roth, and Hector arrested both Mr. Roth and the head of Crest Builders. They were both serving time in Oklahoma. The company tried to hold on, but it couldn't. It was one of the largest busts in BIA history thanks to Sullivan and his team. He continued to find new leads. Hector took those leads and made fifteen high profile arrests in the past two years. Now Hector was about to be promoted to head his field office.

"Thank you for what you did in Cheyenne," Sullivan said, referring to the most recent arrest of a BIA agent taking bribes. Hector had to chase the man and ended up spraining his ankle badly. Sullivan couldn't quite get Hector's ear to look right in his drawing.

"Next time, I'm going to send you after that guy!" Hector said. Sullivan had never been in the field. His team gathered the leads, and Hector's team followed them. Sullivan hated that part. He wanted to get out of his little office, but at the same time he was terrified of leaving it. He was absolutely in awe of Hector's field experience.

"I'd love to go, but I can't ever get away," Sullivan complained.

"Bullshit. You've been saying that for years now," Hector jabbed. He was right. Sullivan could go out in the field if he wanted. Hector prodded where he knew it would hurt, "What if it was for Linus Brenner?"

Sullivan had been focused on the ear and his pencil. He stopped at the mention of Linus Brenner. He put the pencil in his left hand

and looked out to the mountains. Sullivan didn't have any official cases of his own, they were all assigned to his team members, but he still followed Linus Brenner. The man was completely clean on paper. Sullivan knew he was dirty in real life. There was something going on but he couldn't find anything. No clue of any inappropriate behavior.

"I haven't thought about that guy in two years," Sullivan said. He didn't look to his friend.

"That's a lie!" Hector laughed a bit and took a sip from his long-necked beer. "You sent me his travel itineraries two months ago!"

"Okay, but that was out of habit, not because I'm thinking about him." Sullivan was lying. They both knew it.

Luckily Gloria interrupted, "That's fantastic!" She looked over Sullivan's shoulder at the picture. "When you finish that, I'm framing it and putting it in my office!" She put her hand on Sullivan's shoulder and looked out to the kids, "Hey guys! Next goal wins! Food's ready!"

Hector was light on his feet and jumped up. He and his wife watched as the kids ran past into the house. They turned but Sullivan didn't move.

"You come'n, brother?" Hector asked.

Sullivan barely heard. It had been eight years and he'd never moved on Linus Brenner. Why not? He'd never gone into the field. Why not? What was he afraid of? He hated that he was afraid.

"Yeah, I'm coming," Sullivan said. He wanted to look to his friend but found he couldn't look at the man who did what he was too afraid to do.

43. June 1, 1999

"He's here?" Sarah asked unintentionally.

"Yes, Ma'am," The security guard on the other side of the phone answered, "Should I sign him in?"

"Yes … of course … I'll be right down," Sarah hung up the phone and stood to leave. At the door, she turned to look at her office. It was full of computer equipment, but clean. The light shining in through the windows made trapezoids under the five wheels of her desk chair. She quickly returned to push in her desk chair, turned off her lights, closed her door that automatically locked behind her, and walked down the hall. In all the time she had worked for Maxwell Rassic, he had never been here.

The sound of her heels clicking on the tile floors reminded her of her quick pace. She passed an open door and the inhabitant looked up. She'd seen him around, but they'd never spoken. Apparently, she didn't normally walk so fast.

In the elevator she calmed her breathing. She had no idea why he was here, but she didn't think he would be happy. In January, she told him for the second year in a row that her system wasn't working.

She used the elevator ride to assemble her mind for what might be a difficult discussion. She'd checked with the satellite team and they assured her that the data was good, but she was unable to resolve any usable information from the scans. She re-tasked the satellite back to space, collected more data from the stars, processed, and got good results, but she couldn't figure out how to get good data from the earth scans.

Maxwell sat in the lobby on one of two visitor's chairs. He didn't have anything with him and was wearing his normal conservative three piece suit. He looked sharp but anyone walking through the lobby wouldn't give him a second glance.

As Sarah approached, her heels on the tile floor alerted the guards, and all three looked up. All three watched her as she walked over to Maxwell and stood in front of him. He remained seated and didn't react to her presence. His eyes were closed.

Sarah waited thirty seconds before she glanced back to the guards. All three quickly made themselves look busy. The first time she met Maxwell, she felt she had ended the discussion with the upper hand. Each meeting after that, he'd demonstrated an ever-increasing command of her field, what appeared to be limitless influence, and a mildly disturbing insight into her personal life. She stood before him in the lobby of her building a grown woman and a PhD physicist, but feeling like a child waiting for her father to pause and kiss her on the head good night. Just as she was considering sitting in the other chair he abruptly opened his eyes and stood.

"Hello, Sarah," His voice commanded the attention of the guards and didn't give her a warm feeling about the visit, "Let's go to your office." She turned and led him to the elevator. They stood side by side in the elevator facing the door like strangers. She was looking down at the ground trying to think of something to say to break the ice. Work discussions were not permitted in the elevators or public areas of the building.

"Does your boyfriend like you staring at the ground like that?" Maxwell asked. Her head shot up and she stared wide-eyed into her reflection in the steel door.

"I don't have a boyfriend!" Sarah blurted. Then her face grimaced. It was none of Maxwell's business if she had a boyfriend. She looked at him and he just smiled back at her.

"Okay, Okay," Maxwell said.

Sarah thought maybe he was thinking of Lloyd, his assistant. They'd made plans to go out every time she was in Milwaukee. They had a good time, but they were only friends. Did Maxwell think they were more? She opened her mouth to ask, but caught herself. If she mentioned Lloyd, she knew she wouldn't be able to deny it. So she just closed her mouth. She still couldn't think of anything else to say.

On the other hand, the US women's soccer team was quickly approaching the World Cup matches in July. The team was playing regularly, and since the night in Orlando, she'd invited Peter to join her for each match. They explored each other's bodies making a game of keeping each other on the edge for the first half of play. Half time was a spectacular release for each of them followed by food, drink, and a few minutes of catching up. Then they'd start again for the second half.

She was delighted to run into him in Orlando because she had not been delighted with any man since Peter. Sarah knew they were not becoming boyfriend and girlfriend. Their relationship was physical first and social a distant second. She was very happy to continue under those parameters. He certainly felt the same, no boyfriend stuff. He still wouldn't come to her apartment.

Sarah pushed those thoughts out of her mind as the elevator binged. Why was she thinking about that now? She hoped Maxwell didn't read anything into the blush on her cheeks. Thankfully, the doors opened and Sarah led the way forcing a slow walk. She operated the biometric scan next to her door, and she held it open for Maxwell to enter. She closed the door and turned around to find him sitting in her chair. She made the awkward realization that there was only her chair in her office and she was forced to stand in front of him again, repeating the scene from the lobby.

"I've improved the algorithm with each scan. I reprocess the previous data from space with each revision of the system. The images are getting sharper and sharper," Sarah explained, glad to be able to get to business. She hadn't told him about the improvements to the space images and hoped it would help, "I can show you how I've improved the resolution of the scan by an order of magnitude, and reduced the time to process the data by two orders."

"Yes," Maxwell said, "But that's not helping the earth scans. I'm thinking of having another researcher take your data and try to find a pattern in it." Sarah felt her chest constrict. He'd come here to take away her work. And he was probably right to do it. She took a step back as though punched in the stomach. She felt her back against the door. It felt better to have some support, and the slight lean allowed her to look down at her skirt while she thought. She heard Maxwell exhale loudly.

"I can continue to improve the algorithms, they're getting better every day," Sarah was talking to her skirt.

"Okay," Maxwell said. Sarah had been told many times that her emotions showed too easily, and Maxwell must have been able to see he had upset her with the comment about the other team. "I'd like to see the space images, show me."

"While the processors worked on the scans of Earth," Sarah explained, "I also ran the new algorithms on the data from space to confirm that I wasn't changing the results. The good news is that the results got more and more defined. As I decrease the bandwidth of the Fourier series, I get more resolution in each series allowing more defined data." She was happy she'd taken the time to prepare the images and compare them to the previous results. She pointed to the workstation on her left, his right, "I have images on these screens."

He looked to his right, "Ah, yes," he rolled the chair to his left, taking up about half the space between the two stations. He held the command position, and wasn't going to give it up.

She moved to the workstation and keyed in her password. The two screens before her came to life. She worked to pull up the images but was having difficulty typing bent over her desk. She looked out of the corner of her eye. He was watching her hands and the screens intently, but was either oblivious to the difficulty he was causing her, or was doing it on purpose. She didn't think he was oblivious to anything.

After mistyping for the second time, she gave up and knelt down. Her skirt didn't allow her to go on one knee, and she put both shins flat on the floor. The carpet was plush and clean. In this position, her desk was at chest level and her arms rested on the desk. She had to look up to see the screens, but her hands were in proper position to type, and she was quickly able to bring up the images she was looking for. She leaned on the other workstation desk to rest her knees and allowed Maxwell to look at the twin screens.

The left screen had a picture of the Sun. The image was clear, showing the turbulent surface with its dark and light spots and a solar flare bursting from the surface. The caption read, *Our Sun with SOA optics.* State of the art optics provided a bright, clear image of the sun familiar to the public due to its availability on the Internet and use on the cover of National Geographic and other magazines. In a smaller box on the same screen was a white blurry dot made up of four pixels. The caption read, *H1595-9531, Hubble SOA.* This star was the largest star at the edge of the known Universe, and the focus of most of her recent space scans. The Hubble Space Telescope had extended the ability to see the Universe and in effect back in time, to nearly the beginning, but those things seen at the edge were only tiny specs.

Two images also filled the right screen. The smaller image was about 25 times larger than the small spec from Hubble, about fifty pixels across. The caption read *H1595-9531, Space Resonance Hubble, 1.0.* The image was fuzzy, but there were contours across it and the details of the star were defined.

The final, larger image on the screen was the new one, the one that held Maxwell's interest. It looked much like the picture of the Sun on the left screen. It was large, nearly filling the screen, and the image showed in great detail the surface of a star with all its bright and dark spots where nuclear reactions were reaching the surface from deep inside. The caption read, *H1595-9531, Space Resonance Hubble, 23.3.*

Maxwell looked at the screen for about two minutes. Sarah was certain he knew what he was looking at. She looked down to try to think of something to say about the earth scans. Her knees were red and had the pattern of the carpet. She reached down to rub them. Maybe he would forget about the Earth scans as he saw what she had on her screen. His shoes abruptly came into her view in front of hers as he spun around in the chair.

"This is truly remarkable," Maxwell said. Sarah looked up. He clearly liked what he saw, but he wasn't as excited as she hoped he'd be. "The improvement in resolution is tremendous work…"

"Yes," Sarah was anxious to build on that sentiment, "The image of H1595 is not of light, it's the distribution of density across the surface. I set the color to replicate what we see in the solar image for effect."

Much to Sarah's dismay, Maxwell's eyes drifted to the computer monitors that were now behind her, the other workstation was processing the data from the latest earth scan. It was using the same version of the software that created the images she wanted him to look at, 23.3, but she had little hope the results would be any better than 21.5, the version that reduced the previous data set. That effort resulted in nothing but white noise and she didn't want to focus on it.

Maxwell studied it long enough to make Sarah uncomfortable.

"What's that computer doing?" Maxwell asked.

"Processing the last scan of Earth," Sarah didn't realize her hands were moving around as she was describing the work on the space scans until they hit her hips and she deflated into the desk she was leaning on, "The routine won't complete its work until about 9:30 tonight, but I don't think it'll look any better, just noise."

Maxwell squinted at the screen, "I have some matters to attend to downtown. I'll be back here at 9:45."

With that, he stood and left her office as quickly as he had entered. Sarah was startled with his departure and didn't quite know what to do with all the space.

Sarah exhaled and flopped down in her chair. At least now she got to sit in it. She continued to deflate, put her elbows on her knees and her face in her hands.

Her anxiety all caught up with her at once. Maxwell's visit was like the exclamation point on a sentence that she was dreading to hear for some time.

You failed! Maxwell didn't say she was out, but he did say he was going to bring others in. She'd never failed at anything in her life before this moment.

She looked up. She looked directly at the white noise. There was a spot in the image. The pit in her stomach lifted, and her heart skipped a beat. She now squinted her eyes as Maxwell had done not three minutes before. In the upper left-hand corner, the picture wasn't completely random. The image wasn't done being formed, and it was still very blurry. As she'd said, it wasn't scheduled to be complete until tonight, but there was a bright spot. What she thought was Maxwell thinking about taking her project from her was him squinted to see a spot show up in the image. She sat up and pulled herself over to the workstation so she could look more closely. The closer look didn't improve the image, but helped reassure her that it was really there. She knew it was there because she knew Maxwell saw it too!

Her hands sped across the keys on the keyboard as she used the other screen to interrogate the numbers behind the image. She didn't know what the image was of, but the dot had to be dense, much more dense than its surroundings to be showing up as a bright spot while everything else was so neutral. She scanned the density ratios in the area. They were all between 1 and 50, and bouncing around at a nearly random pattern. In her space scans, once she eliminated the blackness of space, the densities were always in that same range, corresponding to the atomic weights of the first 50 elements, the most common. She checked the bright spot. It was in the 200's.

She checked the time-history of the bright spot. Each iteration of the software moved the value higher. The values closely approximated the atomic weight of the substance. The data passing two hundred meant there must be some error in her processing.

"Damn," she said aloud. She checked the numbers again. Yes, her system was going out of control. She briefly considered canceling the run, but she knew Maxwell needed to see it.

Her heart sank again. The last hour had been an emotional roller coaster, and Sarah felt ready to get off. She pushed back from the desk and rolled her chair to the center of the room, positioned equidistant from each workstation and the door. She had to think, and fast. She knew she had to relax to get anywhere.

Sarah pulled the pencil out of her hair and let her hair fall over her shoulders. Had she had this pencil in her hair the entire time? She couldn't remember putting it in, but she often put her hair up with a pencil without realizing.

Focus! Not on her hair but on fixing this problem. She closed her eyes. Her head fell back so that if her eyes were open she would see the ceiling. She breathed deeply. She'd tried yoga but didn't like it, but sometimes the relaxation techniques helped her clear her head.

After about three minutes, nothing came to her. She decided she would start a second set of processors to decode the data. Then she decided she would just sit for five more minutes.

. . .

Sarah was startled by the knock on her door.

No one had ever knocked on her door before.

A few hours ago, Sarah borrowed a chair from her neighbor and that was the first time she talked to anyone else in the building.

Sarah was surprised to see Maxwell when she opened the door. She expected to see her neighbor looking to continue their brief conversation. How did he even get into the building?

"The scans aren't right," Sarah blurted, "I need more time!" Sarah looked at Maxwell, "Why did you come back?"

"I said I would return at 9:45," Maxwell said matter-of-factly.

Sarah fought the urge to check her watch. What time was it? "Of course, come in." She stepped aside so he could enter. As he passed, she checked her watch and discovered that ten hours had passed without her notice.

Déjà Vu. Now the windows were dark, the two monitors for the right workstation were laid face down on the desk, and Maxwell was sitting in the chair she'd borrowed.

"Rough day?" Maxwell asked.

"I've been working on finding the error in the scans of Earth that made the dense spot you saw," Sarah again pulled the pencil from her hair and let her hair fall back to her shoulders. She moved to her desk chair. She sat so they were facing each other with her facing the desk and the window and him facing the door.

"Why do you think there's an error?"

"I realized that the density of the spot is too high. It passed two-hundred so I started looking for an error in…"

"What's wrong with two-hundred?" Maxwell interrupted, "Did the scan finish processing?"

"I couldn't bear to look at it," Sarah waved her hand at the downed monitors over her shoulder, "I'm sure it's complete. I've run a lot of cases that finish but are useless."

"You could've turned the monitors off."

He was right, it had crossed her mind, but laying them down was more permanent. She'd considered taking them out of her office. Maxwell stood and awkwardly reached past her to lift the monitor that displayed the white dot ten hours ago. Sarah didn't want to look at it, so she just waited for him to return to his seat. She was sure she would see blobs of data, probably not all white noise, but still random. She knew she would spend months trying to make sense out of the mess. She hoped she would get to keep working on it, at least.

When the monitor was up, Maxwell looked at the screen for about one second before he sat back down. Sarah searched his face. Where she expected to see dissatisfaction, she saw a pleasant smile. He nodded slightly and despite herself, she turned to look at the monitor.

She was completely unprepared for what she saw.

The screen showed the density of material in the specified area about one hundred feet across, just below ground level. Sarah knew the area was in a town, she'd checked the coordinates. The picture was perfect. The image looked like an x-ray of a building. At Maxwell's direction, she had set the scan to cut a slice through the basement of the building. The walls of the foundation were visible, thick concrete along the edges. The interior walls were wooden two by fours in some of the walls, metal studs in others. She could see refrigerators, wiring in the walls, maybe several tables. She looked at the upper-left corner. The high density object was still clear. It was the highest density object in the image by far, 239.

"It worked," She said, still staring, "but…"

"Yes, it worked." Maxwell looked at her, waiting for her to comprehend.

"But what is that?" She pointed at the dense part of the image, "Why would enriched plutonium be in a building in Upstate South Carolina?" She looked directly at Maxwell, "How did you know? You knew about the plutonium?"

Sarah could see that Maxwell was pleased. She could also see that he wasn't going to answer her questions. At that moment, she didn't care. It worked!

44. July 5, 1999

"Peter, can you push it in a little further?" Mark Posley, Linus' computer man called. Claire Havers leaned against the wall in the basement of the First Fifth Bank in Boise, Idaho. Recent renovation work had uncovered a Native American burial cyst. The building code required Linus Brenner to inspect it, and tonight he brought Peter and Claire to help Mark.

"No, the other way," Mark called out. He studied his computer screen as Peter pushed the end of the borescope into the hole they'd drilled into the large block. Peter exhaled deeply. Claire was equally frustrated.

"Are you seeing anything?" Linus Brenner asked. He stood next to Claire and asked every few minutes from their waiting position. Four years ago, Linus asked Claire to look over his project plans for an upcoming inspection of a burial cyst. Three years ago, he'd asked them to assist with an inspection. It was slow and cumbersome working with men who clearly weren't trained to use the equipment. If Claire could use her team from a job site, this task would take two hours. It was lucky they got out that first night in nine.

"No," Mark reported, "Peter, two inches out?" Peter pulled the cable out. Claire knew the man was watching a video display from the camera mounted in the end of the cable Peter was manipulating. "No, I mean in!" Peter pushed it back in. Claire was about to pull her hair out.

By the fifth inspection, Claire and Peter had taken over the drilling and borescope activities. Linus still wouldn't let them see what was on the screen. Claire found she ended up standing against the wall with Linus sometimes for six hours while Mark, or whoever else he brought to operate the computer, guided the borescope.

"Who is Sarah Kiadopolis?" Claire asked Linus. Peter and Mark would be busy for some time.

Linus looked at her, "She's a physicist, like I told you." Linus looked at Claire through squinted eyes.

"No, she's not," Claire said, "She's in finance, she used to be in physics, but you knew that, Peter's been filling you in for years." She looked at Linus and he smiled at her.

"You're right," Linus said, "We'd be very interested if that changed."

"What is it you asked Peter to do with her?"

"Didn't Peter tell you?"

"No."

"I think he should."

Claire exhaled. She wasn't going to get any information from Peter. And she guessed this was something Peter had asked Linus not to share with her.

She decided to try a different approach.

"Peter told me he liked the assignment. Do you need more help?" Claire didn't think Linus could squint his eyes any further, but he did.

"Are you seeing anything?" Linus turned and asked Mark.

A year ago, she explained to Linus that she knew they weren't looking for bones in these cysts. She'd led the installation of the signal detectors on every cell phone tower in America, and now every new tower included the circuits Ravi designed. She knew they were looking for something electronic, not something Native American. She told him that she and Peter could do this work themselves faster. It bothered her that Linus told them to come. He'd switched from threats to paying them too well to say no. He had them plan out the work, but he didn't trust them to look at the screen. They didn't know what they were looking for, but all she needed to be able to do was tell the difference between electronics and bones.

Tonight, they'd completed the drilling process in a fraction of the time it took the thugs Linus had used earlier. Now they had to wait while Mark Posley, a large black man, tried to direct Peter. He was probably a superhero with a gun or a knife, he had huge arms, and if someone walked in on them, Claire was sure he could take care of it, but he didn't seem to know in from out.

"Linus," Claire leaned over to whisper to him after watching for about fifteen minutes. At this pace, they'd be here another three hours. "Why don't you let me help Peter? If we find electronics, Mark can take over. You'd kick us out anyways! Then we'd get out of here faster."

Claire was surprised to see Linus glance down at his watch. "Okay. Get inside the box. Once you see bones, we're done. If you don't find bones, Mark will take over."

Claire was ecstatic. She stepped forward and Mark happily stepped aside. He didn't like fumbling through this anymore than Claire liked watching him.

Claire studied the computer screen and recognized the circular video display characteristic of seeing out the end of the small tube. She could see the tube was in a small passage inside the cyst and after about three seconds found Mark's problem. "Peter, go forward about an inch and a half and pull to the right." She knew that would push the tip through a small gap to the inner chamber. The image didn't move and Claire looked to Peter.

Peter looked back over his shoulder from his crouched position in front of her. Their eyes met and Claire could see both relief and pride in his eyes. They shared a long second that still put butterflies in her stomach before he efficiently executed her command.

They were looking inside the cyst in two minutes. A task she'd watched consume over an hour the last time. She and Peter were a good team. They shared everything together. Their work with Linus and Ravi. The few men she dated and the many women he did. That closeness augmented their technical skill like a tennis doubles team allowing them to anticipate each other's moves and accomplish the task in record time.

She felt the edges of her mouth frown at the thought of the one thing he didn't share with her. That woman. Doctor Sarah Kiadopolis. Peter mentioned that they dated a few years ago. Linus asked him to *get to know* her, to see what she was working on. He said she didn't tell him anything and he stopped seeing her. Claire asked why he didn't tell her about it at the time. He didn't have a good answer. He just said he was through with her. Still, there was something there. She must have been special or he would have told her.

"Linus," Claire called after another twenty minutes, "I've got bones." She looked at the clock on the screen. It took just under four hours to confirm that this was, in fact, a Native American burial cyst. She was now certain it didn't have any electronic equipment in it. She'd beaten the previous record by over two hours.

Claire was proud, and she could tell Linus was too.

45. August 5, 1999

In his capacity as the Science Chief of Department 55, Maxwell Rassic spent more money than DARPA, more than the Department of Energy's advanced project directorate, and more than NASA other than the space station. Since the Oklahoma City bombing, he discussed his activities with the President of the United States twice a year. This time, Maxwell had taken a commercial flight to Washington DC for a series of meetings on various topics. At the end of the first day, a black sedan drove him forty-five minutes to Andrews Air Force Base. The car was part of a special fleet used by the President to pick up those who would travel with the President on whatever trip he was taking. Maxwell didn't know where they were going, and it didn't matter to him because his meeting was scheduled to take place on Air Force One.

Markings on the license plate sped the car through base security as Maxwell watched out his window. He was able to catch glimpses of Air Force One between a few buildings on their approach. The driver stopped the car under a covered drive next to a small building adjacent to the plane. The reporters and other public passengers entered the building through a main entrance and waited in a lounge with large windows overlooking the plane like they had box seats at the Redskins game. Maxwell was not taken to that entrance, and would not mingle with the other VIPs in the lounge.

Inside the building, Maxwell went through security where his invitation was inspected by US Marines who took their job very seriously. The invitation didn't have a name on it, and no identification was shown in the entire process. The Marines knew that the holder of the invitation was to be cleared of any weapons and allowed to pass without discussion. He was shown to a smaller lounge where three other men sat at small tables. Maxwell recognized his friend Eustis Jefferson at another table, but as protocol dictated, he took a separate small table and looked out his own small window.

Eustis Jefferson was a seventy-four year old black man from Alabama. He was raised poor and outside of work he would let his language slip back to a hint of his southern accent. Maxwell knew he had served in the military and went to the University of Connecticut on the GI Bill. He graduated top of his class in accounting and was one of the brightest securities and derivatives brokers at Goldman Sachs when he attracted the attention of the Securities and Exchange Commission.

He designed a method of generating profit for Goldman so complicated that while it set off the flags with the SEC, no one there could determine what he was doing or whether it was illegal. The SEC brought in the Attorney General to compel Goldman to force Mr. Jefferson to divulge what he was doing and how he was doing it. At the time, the chief counsel for Goldman was a golf buddy of President Johnson's Chief of Staff, William Watson, and he asked Watson to ask the Attorney General to reconsider.

These events were coincident with Johnson's efforts to conceal tremendous spending on Department 55, and the President asked Watson to bring Mr. Jefferson in for a chat. Eustis left Goldman Sachs in 1965 and by 1970 had devised the largest money laundering scheme in history. He'd taken over as the Chief

Controller for the Bureau of Indian Affairs, convinced President Nixon to authorize Indian casinos, and created the infrastructure to launder hundreds of millions of dollars in federal funds through the casinos to wherever they were needed. The operation had scaled to thirty billion dollars a year and Eustis once told Maxwell he was confident he could double it. Throughout the twenty-five years and seven presidents Eustis had been the Finance Chief for Department 55, he'd never failed, or even been cited, during an Office of Management and Budget audit.

Over the next ten minutes, two others joined the small group, each taking private tables and keeping to themselves. A stewardess offered each man drinks from the bar in the lounge next door. Maxwell drank a cranberry juice, his after work beverage, as the sun set over the crown of the 747 in front of them. A marine opened the exterior door out to the Tarmac, and the men wordlessly walked out to the plane. Several of the men carried suitcases that they placed on a dumbwaiter to be retrieved at the top of the stairs. Maxwell carried no luggage or briefcase, he memorized every detail he needed to know, and didn't need to take notes. At sixty-three, he'd led the Science Division for eighteen years and his memory was still strong. He climbed the stairs to the entrance to the plane and walked inside.

Aboard Air Force One, a female airman dressed pleasantly with her hair in a bun directed him toward the back of the plane. Her silk blouse didn't hide the strength of her forearms. She was selected for this post because of her physical strength as well as her pleasant demeanor. She didn't need to check his invitation, as only those in his class of travel were boarding at this time. He walked back toward the rear of the plane past the President's office, Secret Service detail station, conference rooms and rest rooms. He could see straight ahead to the rows of seats in the back similar to those on any commercial aircraft reserved for media. Thankfully, he didn't make it all the way there.

He turned into the last small room before that section. In the small room were eight cubicles, four on each side and two windows to the outside. The space was designed so eight men could work quietly, and privately. Maxwell chose the cubical closest to the windows and the front of the plane. He handed his jacket to another airman similarly dressed and equally as strong as the first who disappeared with it. He sat in his chair as the other men did the same. Many set up computers or started making calls. Even though these men knew they weren't going to introduce themselves to each other they would all work to look like the alpha male in the room. For the younger men, this was accomplished by looking the busiest.

Eustis Jefferson selected the other chair next to the windows and the two men sat down leisurely. They only shared a brief glance. Eustis carried a small attaché case and set it on the desk behind him without opening it. Maxwell enjoyed a cranberry juice and the company of his old friend while they sat wordlessly facing each other and looking out the window as the plane sped down the runway to wherever they were going.

The plane leveled off and the airman collected Maxwell's empty glass. Three minutes later, Vice President Al Gore appeared in the doorway. When Maxwell's eyes met the Vice President's, Mr. Gore tilted his head in a gesture that meant the President was ready for them. Maxwell expected to have to wait until the wee hours of the morning. He glanced at Eustis who took the initiative and stood. Eustis paused for the briefest moment to sure his footing, pulled down the corners of the vest of his grey three piece suit, picked up his attaché without looking and walked to the doorway, disappearing toward the front of the plane. Maxwell looked out the window for a few more minutes before he followed.

Maxwell looked aft at the doorway and saw the media cabin was full. He retraced his steps toward the front of the plane. A Secret Service agent sat in the chair across the hall from the President's private office, indicating which room he was in. As Maxwell approached, the agent sized him up and returned to his sheaf of papers. The first airman appeared nearly startling Maxwell as he approached the office door.

"Good evening," Maxwell said. She smiled at him as she opened the door, stepped into the room ahead of Maxwell and stepped to the side.

The 747 afforded about fifteen feet for the width of this room, and it was probably twenty feet from fore to aft. Maxwell had counted the twelve windows on a previous visit. Tonight they were all dark.

President Clinton sat at his well-appointed, but not fancy desk at the forward outside corner of the room. A white leather sofa was against the windows. Jim Williams sat on that sofa next to the desk. Another sofa was empty on the wall just to Maxwell's right

Eustis was seated at a desk chair next to the President's desk and the two of them reviewed the documents he'd carried with him.

Jim knew everything they were reviewing so he only half paid attention. Maxwell knew Jim was with the President almost constantly. The President seemed to rely on him more and more. Mr. Gore stood at the end of the desk also reviewing the documents. Maxwell waited a moment until the President looked up, followed by the other three men.

"Thank you Beth," President Clinton said to the airman, "That will be all."

"Yes, sir," Beth quickly, but smoothly, left the room, closed the door, and Maxwell heard the latch lock. They were not to be disturbed. Good.

"Maxwell," the President turned to him with a quick smile, "Please, have a drink," he flicked his head toward the mini bar in the forward inside corner of the room, "We need just another minute to review the financials." He remembered once listening to Eustis go over the financials, and that he couldn't think of a worse way to spend the next three minutes, so he took his time getting a glass, some ice, and another cranberry juice from the fridge. He then took a seat on the sofa next to the door and looked out the window for a moment, wondering where they were going.

"Excellent," the President said without enthusiasm. He was a smart man, and Eustis was practiced at making his presentations short and to the point, but the complexity of what he was talking about always came through and it was taxing to keep up. The group broke up. Eustis stood, secured his footing, and shuffled to the sofa in front of the windows next to Jim. The Vice President moved to the far aft wall and leaned on the small bar under the projection screen mounted there. It occurred to Maxwell that in all the time he had known Al Gore, he rarely saw him sit.

"Now, Maxwell," President Bill Clinton looked directly at him, "Jim tells me you have some good news?"

"Yes, sir," Maxwell began, "As you know, Eustis has been providing funds to invest in a wide array of technical efforts to bring the end of LV."

"Yes," the President was well aware of the efforts to explore theoretical physics and accelerate any potential lead that could help find the graviton. He also understood that experimental physics was one of the most expensive endeavors in modern time, and that Eustis and his team worked to cover the money Department 55 was spending.

"We've had a breakthrough," Maxwell said. The President

leaned forward. "As you remember, we've been making *repairs* to the Hubble Space Telescope." The President nodded that he did remember. "Actually, we aren't making repairs. We were making a series of modifications based on work in the field of *Space Resonance*. Six years ago, we installed a *Space Resonator* on Hubble. Four years ago, we used that *Space Resonator* to detect gravitons coming from distant stars." Maxwell managed eight other experiments like this one, and didn't give the President details unless there was a breakthrough. He was shocked to realize that he had not discussed *Space Resonance* with the President since the night they talked him down from attacking the World Trade Center Bombers. "Immediately after that, we turned the *Space Resonators* around to look at the Earth."

"Yes, I remember Doctor K-" The President had a great memory. Jim might have talked to him about this, "a woman if I remember, from Virginia?"

"Yes, Dr. Sarah Kiadopolis from Virginia Tech," Maxwell said.

"The Hubble can turn around?" The President asked.

"Actually, we have a second Hubble, called *KiteString*, and they both can," Maxwell continued, "So, we tasked the satellite to study the site in Greenville, South Carolina."

"It's still there?"

"Yes, we have a number of well hidden nuclear devices around to experiment with detection systems," Maxwell said.

"I see. Good idea."

"Yes. We tasked Dr. Kiadopolis and *KiteString* to search for that device. We didn't tell her what she was looking for." Maxwell looked to Al, Eustis, and Jim. They were listening, and seemed to be understanding. "At first we were disappointed that she was unable to process the data and find anything. I gave some of the data to Lawrence Livermore's Advanced Computing Center. They didn't know what they were looking at but they did notice a sixty hertz harmonic interlaced into the signal." Maxwell was aware that he was getting too deep because the President was starting to frown. No one stopped him to ask a question. "When we looked into space at a distant star, the signal had no interference. When we looked at the Earth, there was a sixty hertz interference that scrambled the sensitive *Space Resonators* making it impossible for them to resonate at the prescribed frequency." He looked at the President, then the VP. Al's face changed as he had a moment of realization.

"The electric grid?" He asked.

"Exactly, yes!" Maxwell was almost proud, "The electrical grid of the United States runs at sixty hertz, sixty cycles per second. The signal from the grid renders the *Space Resonators* ineffective if the grid is active in the area we're scanning."

"How do you know it's the grid?" the President asked.

"And what do we do about it?" the Vice President chimed in. Eustis was quiet, but smiling, because he and Maxwell had discussed this at length over the past three months.

"We ran a test," Maxwell said, "We turned off the grid intermittently over several days in Greenville, timed for *KiteString* to make the scans."

The President sat back and considered what he just heard. He frowned. He looked at Maxwell for a moment, then at Al and Eustis. He finished with Jim. Jim looked back with a confident smile. That reassured the President and he returned to Maxwell.

"So, what happened?" the President asked.

Maxwell continued, "The image was so clear Sarah easily identified the plutonium core from space!" Maxwell knew he didn't need to go into all the details. He collected himself and continued, "The bottom line is that we have a satellite orbiting the earth that can look down and detect anything we want to find anywhere on Earth."

A huge smile crossed the President's face. Maxwell watched as the man seemed to shed five years. Tension in his forehead he had long grown to live with faded away. His eyes opened wider than they had in years. He began to rock in his chair. Abruptly, he stood up and moved to the minibar. He made himself a drink deliberately as the room watched in silence. Five hundred people were killed in Oklahoma City on his watch, he had been impeached six months ago, and finally he had a shot at getting to the people who had forced those events on him, and on the United States.

Eustis and Maxwell looked at each other. Their smiles were also large, but they knew there was more work to do. Jim was waiting for everything to play out and remained quiet. They heard the President drop ice in the glass and deliberately pour a drink. They watched as he turned around and leaned on the bar. He raised the glass to his lips, and just as it was going to touch, he paused and pulled it away.

"The electrical grid? We need to turn it off any time we want to use this system?" The President asked. And there it was. Two months ago, Maxwell knew everything he just told the President.

He didn't know how to solve the problem of the power grid, so he went to Eustis. Now it was the quiet schemer's turn.

"Yes, the electrical grid," Eustis said. He was still relaxed, leaning back in the couch speaking almost so softly Maxwell couldn't hear him. He hoped the President had better hearing than he did. Eustis continued, "The solution to the electrical grid is not a technical one. We will use the markets to create a reason to turn off sections of the electrical grid."

"We don't need a reason!" the VP said, "I'll call over to the Federal Energy Regulatory Commission and tell them to turn the grid off whenever we need it!"

Eustis glanced at Al Gore, but quickly returned to facing the President, "Yes, we considered making up some reason for turning the grid on and off, some sort of system check. That would be very hard to justify. There are too many interests involved in electricity. Too many smart scientists and too many engineers wouldn't buy some need to test the system, or any other excuse. There would be uproar, and we would attract unwanted attention."

Maxwell looked at the Vice President who accepted the truth. He was a little surprised that Jim had not fully briefed his boss before this meeting.

"The reason for turning off various parts of the electrical grid has to be the most nonsensical power in the world," Eustis said, "federal regulation!" Maxwell winced. Eustis was a Republican, but he was normally more careful around the more liberal people he met.

"Now wait!" Al said, "You just told me it couldn't be a directive from us. It couldn't be a new regulation!"

"Yes, I did," Eustis turned to Mr. Gore, "We're not going to create a new regulation. We're going to do something that can be just as damaging. We're going to deregulate." Eustis took off his glasses and wiped them while everyone in the room considered his statement. "Maxwell and I have already paid a visit to your friends at the Federal Energy Regulatory Commission. They described the patchwork of regulations that control the grid and grid pricing in some areas, while allowing limited free market activity in others. We, Maxwell and I, propose that we destabilize the electrical grid through market forces, not through technical requirements. We'll start with the most regulated markets and rapidly deregulate them. The deregulation will allow the separation of the power generators from those who are responsible for delivering power to customers."

The President looked to Al. Neither man had a background in finance. They thought about this for a few moments and the Vice President asked, "Isn't the electrical grid market already moving this way?"

Maxwell thought about answering, but he knew this was Eustis's area, "Yes, Mr. Vice President, many grids are moving toward deregulation, and many are experimenting on a small scale with allowing the companies we traditionally call power companies to separate themselves from the companies that generate the electricity. Some areas have developed spot markets like the stock market with people on trading floors trading megawatt hours. There is, however, a critical difference with electricity."

Eustis looked to Maxwell because this was a technical detail. Maxwell said, "The electrical grid has no capacity to store electricity. That is, when electricity is generated, it is consumed at the exact same instant as power travels through the system at near the speed of light. For other industries, like chocolate chips, for example, there are manufacturers who make the chips and send them to warehouses. Then the distributors draw from the warehouses as needed. The warehouse serves as a buffer to match supply with demand, and allows the time of production to be different from the time of use."

"With electrical energy, there is no warehouse. That means that any change in use of electricity must be matched by a change in production instantly. This also means that any change in production must be matched by a change in use instantly."

"So," Eustis took back over, "currently the supply of electricity is matched with the demand every six-minutes, and it is carefully regulated. When we deregulate, the market will still attempt to match supply with demand on that basis, and it will succeed most of the time. There will, however, be instances when the demand goes up high enough to potentially exceed the available supply. We will design the pricing structure of the deregulated market in a way that will allow us to obscure the matching of supply and demand, allowing for an impression of an overly tight market. With this newly installed instability, we'll then be able to use some minor additional events, like a power plant unexpectedly needing maintenance, or an unusually warm summer requiring more power than expected, and we'll be able to cause brown outs as the way to stabilize the grid."

The President had moved back to his desk and sat. Maxwell was surprised to see that his eyes were closed. He had a small smile on his face. Was he not paying attention? That was his prerogative, Maxwell guessed. The drink sat on his desk in front of him, still full. With the President resting, Vice President Gore led the conversation.

Al Gore was sharp and said, "We'll need someone on the inside, someone in the power industry who could help us create these markets."

"Over the past two months, I've been discretely inquiring through some of my contacts in the accounting industry," Eustis explained. "I have a close friend at a natural gas trading company who's been helping me figure out the details. Of course, he has no idea we want to destabilize the grid, he's just in it to make a huge amount of money."

"And this close friend thinks he can do that?" Al asked.

"Yes," Eustis spoke slowly and quietly, "Over the last seven years, he and I have worked with the SEC on evaluating different schemes, different ways of manipulating markets. It's a special project that we both get to participate in as members of the SEC Select Council of Advisors. We've been evaluating and designing schemes for a decade and he's quite good at it. I'm actually quite certain he's been designing a few of those schemes and executing them within his company to artificially boost profits. When applied to the natural gas pipelines, he can make a fair return, but if he can apply it to the whole electrical grid, he could stand to make billions, maybe tens of billions."

"What are the risks?" The President asked without opening his eyes.

"I'm not sure we'll be able to create the instability these guys are expecting," the VP said. Al Gore was quick on the uptake, but Maxwell was beginning to suspect Jim had briefed him before and they were helping guide the conversation for the President. The Vice President was playing the role of not understanding to draw out the details so the president could process everything.

"If we do not create sufficient instability," Maxwell said, "then we just have to come up with something else. There would be nothing lost except time."

"I don't want to waste any time," the President said, "I want this to end!" The President's eyes shot open and he looked at Al Gore. No one said anything and the President resettled his eyes.

"We'll be able to create tremendous instability," Eustis said,

"The instability will be a function of the money involved. The beauty of this scheme is that we can control it by adding money. That means we can force it to become unstable. If it's not unstable enough, we can add more. This is the same principle the Federal Reserve tries to employ to manage the entire economy."

"I'm not convinced this is going to work, we should study it some more," Vice President Gore said half-heartedly.

"No!" Bill Clinton sat up. He took the glass from the table in front of him. Everyone watched him. He took a slow sip. "I don't want to wait. I want this to work now. Do it." Maxwell now saw that the Vice President took a bit of a pessimistic stance to get the President to push him. He saw it on Al Gore's face.

Maxwell and Eustis had achieved what they came for, and they knew that it was time to go, "Thank you, Mr. President," they said almost in unison. They stood.

"No. *Thank you*," The President was happy. They moved to the door, "Oh, you said we are going to make someone a billionaire, who's your lucky friend? I might need something later."

"I go way back with Jeffrey Skilling," Eustis said quietly, "He's the Chief Operating Officer of Enron. We're going to destabilize the California energy markets."

"Well," The President raised his glass, "Here's to your Mr. Skilling!"

46.   October 14, 1999

Sarah had been working twelve hours a day for the last four months. The time passed quickly. As soon as Maxwell saw she could process images of the earth, he tasked her to reduce the time the electrical grid needed to be off.

In order to make the pictures they saw, the *Space Resonators* had to be trained on a particular portion of the earth for ten hours. The challenge was that the satellite was traveling through space at seventeen thousand miles an hour, and made a complete loop around the earth every hour and a half. That meant the satellite would only see the same point on the earth for ten minutes per orbit. So, to capture ten hours of data, the satellite would have to be tasked to the same point for ninety hours. The electrical grid either had to be off for ninety hours or turn on and off every hour and a half for four days. So while the system worked, it was impractical to deploy.

Two months ago, Sarah realized she didn't need the power off for every satellite scan. She could collect a large data set with the power on. She could then take data from three scans with the power off to build a key that would unlock the rest of the data. That meant she only needed the power off for about three hours to create a key. That key could wait until the data from the other eighty-seven hours was collected. The large data set could be processed and then the key could be applied, revealing the pure results. It had taken her two solid months, working every day, to make it work. She tested the new algorithms on stored data sets from Greenville, processing failed scans and using only three scans from the successful power-off set to make the key.

The hours were long, and she missed her regular exercise routine most days. She'd taken to having food delivered to the security desk for almost every meal. She did push-ups and sit-ups in her office while the system was running, and even considered installing a pull-up bar into the ceiling.

She knew she was working too much when she fell asleep on the floor of her office. She couldn't take her work home so she considered sleeping here, but there were no shower facilities in the building.

Finally, after sixty days straight, the key worked and she was able to perfectly recreate the successful run with only three samples of power-off data. She tried to get it to less than three, but she couldn't find a way through the mathematics. She decided that could be left for another marathon, and that she was going to spend some waking hours outside of the office.

Excitement at leaving her office was building as the computers powered down.

Maxwell would be delighted at their January meeting.

That was three months from now. Damn. Her enthusiasm curbed.

She decided to chance sending Lloyd an innocuous email about good news and left her office with her spirits rising again.

She drove home squinting and it took her ten minutes to realize this was the first time she'd been outside during daylight in over a month.

What to do? It was early afternoon. *Late lunch?*

A stolen glance in the cosmetic mirror of the Civic confirmed she wouldn't be going out for food. With frizzy hair, no makeup, pale skin, and puffy eyes, she wouldn't be eating out anywhere.

She needed sun, and she needed to run.

Bursting into her apartment, Sarah dropped her purse on the pile of neglected mail and stripped off her skirt and blouse on the way to the bedroom.

She had two bathing suits, one for exercise and one for sunbathing.

Bikini.

Barefoot on the warm cement walk with towel and keys dangling from her lazy finger, the warm sun almost made her reconsider swimming.

Three moms sat together on the lounge chairs talking and half watching their four or five kids play in the shallow end. Their scowls weren't invitations for her to join them, so Sarah dropped her towel and keys lazily on a lounge chair and unceremoniously dove into the pool.

Thankfully, her bikini held on, but it required some subtle adjustments made as she began to swim laps.

The heated water felt even better than the sunlight.

She focused on counting strokes and the precision of her motions as the tension of sixty days of intense calculations, programming, and processing flowed from her.

Touch, turn, plant feet, push, one, two, three, four, breath, five, six, seven, twenty six, turn.

She swam in this pool maybe half a dozen times each summer, and her record was fifty-one laps.

Today, she stopped at one-hundred and seven.

She felt her pulse in her arms and legs leaning back on the lounge chair faced into the sun.

The moms got the kids ready to leave. Her breathing returned to normal by the time the three women herded the kids past. Two of the women were older. They worked out, fighting the battle with their bodies, but not quite winning. They looked at Sarah as they passed, but didn't smile. The third woman was much younger, probably a nanny. Young enough to not be in any battles, she smiled brightly.

Sarah returned the smile and a little nod.

The sun felt great, but she would only sit in direct sunlight for a few minutes. She closed her eyes and savored it on every inch of her body it touched.

Without a watch, she limited her time, and returned to the pool for forty-seven laps of backstroke.

When she got out of the pool this time, there were two dads with two kids.

They smiled.

She smiled back and took her time toweling herself dry.

Fighting the urge to run, she walked barefoot down the path back to her apartment. It must have been about four in the afternoon, people were returning home from work. She passed a few men on the path to her apartment and decided that maybe she would call Peter.

They had not talked in two months and she didn't know when he would be in town next. With any luck, he'd be in town tonight. Since the Women's World Cup, they had continued to see each other when he was in town. They both knew they weren't going to end up together, and that knowledge allowed them to enjoy each other without any expectations. Their relationship was easy and very satisfying.

She could use it, tonight.

She entered her apartment, tossed the towel into the laundry room to her left, and went to the drawer in the small table to get Peter's number.

There was a knock at the door.

Without thinking, she stepped one step to the door and put her hand on the knob.

Then she realized she was still in her bikini. She took a moment to look around.

Another knock.

"Hold on!" Sarah announced. She threw on a t-shirt from the laundry room, and stepped to open the door.

A man in a crinkled suit, the type she imagined a police detective would wear, looked her straight in the eye.

"Yes?" Sarah asked.

"Sarah Kiadopolis?" the man finally asked.

"Yes." Sarah responded. She decided she wanted to close the door. The man was holding an envelope, and he extended it to her.

"This is for you." Sarah kept her right hand on the door and was ready to slam it if necessary. She took the envelope in her left hand.

"Thank you," the man said. With that, he turned and headed back toward the stairs. Sarah watched him step down the first step and then closed the door. She'd been on a high when she got home, and the little run in with that man had her heart pounding. She pushed the thought of him out of her mind as she leaned on the inside of her door.

What was she doing? Peter's number, right.

She stepped back to the drawer that was still opened and went to reach into it when she remembered the envelope in her hand.

Without thinking, she turned and walked the three steps to her kitchen table. Before she got there, she made herself take a breath.

She sat down and opened the envelope. A hand written note said ...

> *Sarah, I look forward to hearing about it tomorrow morning at eight am.*
> *-Maxwell.*

What? How had he gotten this to her so fast? She didn't know exactly when she left her office, but it must have been only about two hours ago! The envelope also contained plane tickets to Wisconsin and hotel and rental car information. Crap. She checked the flight information. She was leaving Dulles airport in an hour and a half! Double Crap. She looked around her table. She saw the small candle holder that served as her center piece. There was no candle, but a rolled scrap of paper, and she immediately remembered that it had Peter's phone number.

Well, another time, Peter, Sarah said to herself.

Luckily, Sarah was able to focus her nervous energy on showering, dressing, and throwing together an overnight bag.

Sarah's exhilaration didn't diminish on her flight. She enjoyed the flirtations from a nice looking businessman on the plane.

After two drinks in the hotel bar, and a few more flirtations from a few nice-looking men, one almost interesting enough to continue, she retired alone to bed.

. . .

"You didn't call me when you got in last night," Lloyd took her coat and didn't hide his admiration of her legs.

"It was so late, and aren't you still seeing Sally?" Sarah sat in the chair against the wall and let her shoe dangle from her toes.

Lloyd walked around the back of his desk and sat. "Actually, yes, we're engaged now!" Lloyd was smiling broadly at delivering the news, but he was having trouble pulling his eyes up from Sarah's legs.

"That's wonderful!" Sarah stood. She wanted to hug Lloyd, but he was behind his desk. He didn't move from his position. It was probably for the best.

Sarah realized she'd always considered Lloyd a friend, but the kind of friend that was a candidate for more.

She pushed the slight disappointment from her mind as she entered Maxwell's office. She walked straight past the conference table to the comfortable chair seating area near the windows. She sat in one of the club chairs and crossed her right knee over the left. Her right shoe briefly dropped to hanging from her toes, but she decided that was okay with Lloyd, but not with Maxwell, and she flexed her toes to cover her heel.

Maxwell looked at her, his mouth slightly open. Ha! She thought, she'd finally surprised him. "Something to drink? A martini maybe?" Maxwell said. He stood and circled his desk to the mini fridge. He wore a thin blue suit with a vest. He had taken off the jacket. Sarah remembered it hanging in Lloyd's office.

"Orange juice," Sarah said. Maxwell was already pouring it.

"So, you said you have good news?" Maxwell asked. Sarah continued to feel very relaxed as Maxwell crossed the room and took his seat. But when he looked directly into her eyes with his dazzling stare, she was shaken back into the situation and she reflexively sat up.

"Yes, very good," Sarah said. Maxwell waited for more. She explained that she could now collect ninety-five percent of the data with the power on, process it, and then collect three scans with the power off to create the key to unlock the gravitational image. Over the next half hour, she explained how she had tested the algorithm on the Greenville data, and that three scans was the minimum.

"Okay, this is good," Maxwell said. He seemed happy, but not ecstatic. He asked no more questions for probably three minutes, and they sat quietly. This had happened before while he thought things through. But this was different. She was anxious. She didn't know what she hoped he would say.

She took a sip of her juice. Then she drank the whole glass. She stood and rounded her chair to look out the windows across the landscape thinking of what she might do next. She considered turning back to the stars. Maybe she'd be able to find a black hole. Maybe she'd publish a paper.

"Sarah!" Maxwell stood next to an open cabinet on the far wall of his office, at the head of the conference room table. She didn't see him move. She focused her eyes as she crossed the room, looking at the board. He'd been writing calculations on the board.

1200 miles / 0.1 miles per scale = 12,000 scans
12,000 scans * 90 hours per scan = 108,000 hours ... 4500 days
4500 days per satellite / 2 satellites = 2,250 days
2,250 days / 365 = <u>6 years</u>

Maxwell was calculating how long it would take Hubble and KiteString to scan a twelve-hundred mile tall swath of the Earth's surface if the *Space Resonators* were set to collect data continuously. The calculations disappointed Sarah because they meant her five minute old plans would be put back on hold for apparently six years.

"Right?" Maxwell asked.

Sarah cleared her plans from her mind, bit her lower lip, and studied the numbers, "They look correct."

"Good," Maxwell said, still thinking fast, "But six years is too long. We'll need more satellites!" Sarah didn't know how serious he was, "Can we begin creating the background data set today?" Sarah thought a moment.

"What are you looking for that we need to start a search today?" Sarah asked. "This is really cutting edge science. Could we take some time and see what these new algorithms could do in space?"

"No," Maxwell answered without a moment's thought.

The rejection struck her and she paused. Sarah thought they were developing a system that could be used for something in the future. What she just learned was Maxwell wasn't developing this system for a theoretical future use. He wanted it for a specific use right now.

She focused on his request.

"Switching from searching a particular location to searching a wide area poses two problems," she said, "First, I'm here. I need to run some numbers to get the runs set up. Also, I would need a target area."

"The Continental United States," Maxwell said with a dismissive wave of his hand. Maxwell shouted, "Lloyd!" Sarah stopped for about one second before Lloyd opened the door, "Lloyd, Dr. Kiadopolis needs the next available flight back to DC."

Lloyd nodded and closed the door without comment.

"There's a second issue," Sarah said. The speed Maxwell wanted to get started caught her off guard. She wasn't sure he wanted to hear another issue, but it was important.

"Yes?" Maxwell asked. He stared right through her. She waited for his eyes to focus on her face.

"If I get back to the office today, I could get the flight paths ready tonight, and we could begin scanning tomorrow, but we'd be receiving data at a rate that we couldn't possibly absorb! My servers are large enough to get data in ten minute bursts, with as much as twenty hours of total storage time. So, my servers would be full in less than a day. We could send the data somewhere else, but"

"No, we won't be sending the data anywhere else," Maxwell cut her off and thought quietly.

"Look, even if I had servers, I don't have the space to put them. My office is completely full," Sarah added, "And even if I had the space, I can barely keep the servers I have working. I'm not a network engineer. I only know enough to get by."

Maxwell looked at her. He then left her standing next to the dry erase board and walked back to his desk. He sat and thought. Sarah didn't know what to do with herself. All the spunk she had when she walked in drained away. She wasn't excited about collecting this data, but she was certain she had little choice. She considered asking if Maxwell could get someone else to do it. At $425,000 a year, she earned more than twice what she could at Cornwall & Wallace, and five times what she could in any other job a physicist could get. Nope, she wasn't going anywhere. She walked back across the office to the club chairs and retook her seat. She took deep breaths as she looked out the window over the tree tops to the horizon.

A soft knock at the door disrupted her thoughts. Without any response from inside, Lloyd opened the door and entered quietly. He walked directly to Sarah and handed her a letter sized envelope stuffed with folded paper. "Dr. Kiadopolis." He looked at her with concern. She smiled at him with her mouth only. He retraced his steps and left. Sarah opened the envelope and unfolded the papers to see her return travel itinerary had been changed. Her return flight left in just under ninety minutes.

"Sarah," Maxwell focused his eyes on her, "I'll take care of the servers. You get the satellites tasked." He stood, but didn't come around the desk.

"Very well."

. . .

By one-thirty in the afternoon, Sarah's heels clicked along the tile floor of the hall leading to her office. Twenty-four hours ago, she'd walked the other way on her way to the pool.

As she rounded the long curve of the corridor to the top of the *D*, Sarah became anxious at the sight of sunlight spilling from the normally-closed office doors. Her door was tucked into the top of the *D* and an office door was within ten feet of either side of hers. While her door was closed, both of her neighbors' were open. A box appeared from the first door as she passed it.

One of the three men from that office poked his head out. He was the one she borrowed the chair from four months ago when Maxwell visited. They said hello to each other in the hall, but that was the extent of their relationship.

Another face appeared from the other open door. Sarah didn't know him but recognized him as her neighbor.

"Get moving, Sarah," the first man said. His name was Aaron, "We all have to be out by five!"

Sarah stopped and looked into his office. Boxes were everywhere. He'd been packing for some time. Most were closed with labels on them but two were open on his desk.

She walked past her door to look into the other open door. This office was in much worse shape. She didn't know what was done in this office, no one knew what anyone else did, but every tabletop was covered with mechanical and electrical parts. Only a few boxes were packed.

"What's happening?"

The neighbor with all the equipment answered, "We got notices that we were moving this morning. We were supposed to be out by noon. We protested and they gave us until five." His face betrayed panic.

"We'll be okay," Aaron said referring to the team of three that shared his office, "but he seems to have a lot of junk to move." They all knew they couldn't help each other.

"Yeah," Tinkerer said, "but all my junk has just the right place. I'm in the middle of a critical assembly! I have pieces in a particular order, and I can't just pick up and move! I tried to explain it to the building manager, but he said the movers were coming!"

"I don't know how you're going to move all those computers," Aaron commiserated. Sarah didn't like that Aaron knew what was in her office, but how could it matter? She also had a suspicion she wouldn't have to move anything.

"We'll see," she said and moved to her door. She opened it with her biometric scan feeling self-conscious that they were both looking in after. Maxwell was the only one who had ever set foot inside except her. She smiled at the two men as she closed the door.

She confirmed that she had received no notice to move and immediately began to process the requirements for the scans Maxwell requested. The process was tedious, but one she'd done many times, so she could move through it quickly. She set her stereo to a mix of Def Leopard and Guns and Roses, her mind on autopilot, and went to work.

By six p.m., well ahead of schedule, she completed the work and submitted it to the *Hubble* and *KiteString* servers. It would take the satellites three hours to respond to their new orders and by nine p.m. the data would begin to fill the servers surrounding her in her office. Maxwell would have to come through by around noon tomorrow, or the collections sweeps would have to be postponed.

. . .

The next morning, Sarah was shocked to find the neighboring offices transformed. Racks of servers filled both rooms floor to ceiling. Maxwell had accomplished another miracle and they had not missed a second of scanning time. He must have mobilized a dozen computer engineers to get the servers ready that night.

She found a request in her email to allow the maintenance crew into her office to drill holes through the walls large enough for fiber optic data links. By noon, the servers in the other two offices were collecting data. Sarah spent the rest of the week inventorying the system, calculating that there was about eighteen months' worth of storage in the two rooms, getting the biometric access to the offices, and confirming the security precautions with building management.

47. December 25, 1999

Sullivan and Danny rested at the table after the Christmas gorging at Sullivan's parents' house three miles from their own. Danny was twelve so there was not as much magic, but they had a nice time. His parents invited their old friends, a couple from down the street. Sullivan invited Bert. Bert was going to bring a date, but she backed out at the last minute.

Sullivan's mother enjoyed making a full dinner for the seven people in attendance.

"We're going to have to leave soon," Danny leaned over and whispered to his father. Sullivan could see his mother's happiness and didn't want to leave. But he knew Danny had been looking forward to this afternoon for three weeks.

NASA had a spacewalk broadcast on the new NASA cable TV channel. Danny hadn't lost his love of space and they couldn't miss it.

"What?" Sullivan's mother asked. She couldn't possibly have heard.

"NASA's fixing the Hubble Space Telescope today!" Danny announced.

"On Christmas?" Sullivan's Mother asked, "Shouldn't they take this day off?" She was not happy with the idea of them leaving.

"They're in space, Grandma!" Danny said, "They can't waste a whole day!"

"It's a very special day," she said quietly.

"I know, they're going to televise the whole thing," Danny said, "It's one of the first times they're going to show us what it's really like up there!"

"From what I heard," Bert chimed in, "It's pretty boring. It's going to take them five hours to install a new wire." Danny's face fell. Sullivan shot a dirty look at his friend. Bert knew Danny's interest in space was really his connection to his mother. Bert knew Sullivan hoped Danny would lose interest but so far, he had not. Sullivan was just happy he hadn't asked to see his mother in four years. He thought that if Danny lost interest in space, he'd start gaining interest in Tennessee, and space was much easier to deal with.

Four years ago, the last time Sullivan had seen his ex-wife, he drove to Tennessee to pick Danny up. She lived with her parents in a two bedroom ranch on thirty acres ten miles from town. They were doing okay, but they weren't doing great.

Leanne had mentioned keeping Danny maybe for the next school year. The thought terrified Sullivan, but he didn't have a clear reason to say no. He just wanted his son with him.

"And if he came here with us, you could help us get a nicer place," Leanne said after dinner that night, "we do need more room if Danny's coming to stay with us. He needs to stay with us, I don't want him growing up to be a wimp, like you."

Sullivan was sickened to think Leanne was only angling to get Sullivan to give her some money. But money was what she was after. Since then, Sullivan had sent Leanne a few hundred bucks a month and in return, she never asked to see Danny. Danny didn't ask to see her, and everything was okay. All he had to do was watch NASA.

"Okay," Sullivan said, "Mom, we're going to have to get going. I'm sorry we're going to miss dessert. Can we come by tomorrow?"

"Sure you can," Sullivan's father said. Sullivan's father was the only person he had ever told about the situation.

48. June 10, 2000

Doctor Hans Walters walked into one of the many Starbucks in downtown Seattle. Claire Havers knew he would be coming in because she'd been following him for the past three days.

It took a year of badgering, but Linus finally gave Claire an assignment like the one he'd given to Peter.

It was Thursday, and she'd been in Seattle all week. She wanted to get back to Greenville by the weekend, but Linus told her she couldn't come home until she made contact with Dr. Walters.

So far, she'd discerned he was an average looking twenty-eight year old who talked to his friends about video games too much. He worked at a small mechanical design firm and she had no idea why Linus wanted to know what he knew.

She did know, Linus told her, that Peter was again meeting with Doctor Sarah Kiadopolis, and he wasn't telling her about it. She felt a little betrayed, but she still didn't have any logical reason to feel that way. So when Linus asked her to meet Doctor Walters, she jumped at the chance to not tell Peter about it.

She decided to approach him at this Starbucks. He stopped here each morning on the way to work. She bought a tight but professional dress and rain boots. Every woman in Seattle wore rain boots. She sat at a high table near the front door and positioned herself so that her crossed leg stuck out into the aisle.

She knew her position worked because several men stopped to try to talk to her.

Dr. Walters looked at her several times while he waited in line, and she tried to make eye contact, but he wouldn't.

She knew he saw her, so she couldn't try to approach him somewhere else.

He made his way through the line and Claire watched him leave the shop, turn left and disappeared from her view.

"Damn," she said under her breath. She'd have to stay another day. That meant not getting home until Saturday. She had a date tomorrow night, but now she'd have to postpone.

"You okay?" a nice looking professional man with a big smile asked. He must have overheard her.

. . .

The next morning Claire tried jeans and a rain coat with a University of Oregon baseball cap. She sat at the high table again reading the newspaper.

"Go Ducks," Doctor Walters said when he got next to her in line.

"Go Ducks!" Claire responded. She looked him directly in the face with a false bright smile. He looked at her, returning her smile, but as she watched his smile disappeared and after an awkward moment he looked away. Damn.

"When did you go?" Claire asked, trying to make conversation. It was a little risky.

"I graduated six years ago," he said, "I try to get back once a year. You?" There it was.

"Oh, I didn't go there," Claire answered, "I dated a guy from there..." again there was nothing further. He was about to look away. Claire panicked and looked down to the newspaper. It was opened to the want-ads. The first heading she read was for *apartments*. "I'm new to Seattle, just moving in. You wouldn't know a good place to live, would you?" This was an obvious ploy, but men were normally receptive to obvious ploys.

"Oh, yeah, I know a few places," he moved in to look at the newspaper. He read down the list. "I wouldn't look there, it's a dump!" He indicated the second listing. He pulled a pen from his shirt pocket and went through about twenty of the listings marking ones she should go see. He was oblivious to the line backing up behind him. Claire gestured to the people waiting that they should go around.

"Where's that one? It seems nice," Claire knew exactly where it was. It was the building Doctor Walters lived in. She'd been there going through his apartment and installing listening devices three days ago.

"Actually, it's nice," he said, "I live there."

"Oh, what a coincidence," she looked at him doe-eyed.

"If you don't have anything going on, you could come by," Hans looked at her sheepishly, "you could come by after work if you like."

"That would be fantastic!" Claire didn't have to fake her enthusiasm. Linus had been very clear she had to make contact with this guy. She'd go to his apartment, probably have dinner with him. Get to know him a little and get out of there.

49. June 15, 2000

Sarah sat on a new couch under the windows in her office. Sufficient sunlight shined in over her shoulder so that she didn't need the fluorescent overheads. She read the Wall Street Journal and enjoyed a cup of tea. She occupied this office for the last seven years but never thought of it as a place to enjoy until the last few months.

She had no trouble convincing the building managers to open doors in the walls so she could get from her office into each of the others. Next to the doors she asked for, and received, windows, creating the feel of a larger space. She moved the smaller servers out of her office and bought the couch. She put a monitor on a small table next to the couch so she could watch the progress of the satellites and replaced the seven year old rug. She even had a pull-up bar installed above one of the doorways.

Sarah's workload slowed as the satellites orbited and transmitted data every day, all day. She automated the data reduction process so her computers and servers built the locked files and stored them ready for the opportunity to create keys. The locked files required a fraction of the space of the raw data so the servers in her expanded office had the capacity to store the entire world's lock files. She created a few projects to work on, continuing to streamline the software, but she was able to work only forty hours a week.

It had been four months since she started collecting the data and Sarah had gained three pound of muscle and recovered her tan. Her indoor soccer team traveled to a tournament in Florida and came in third.

When she wasn't working or working out, Sarah spent a lot of time with Angie. Her friend was very involved in the Center for Performing Arts, and Sarah helped her with some of the administrative work. In return, Angie took her to the evening fundraisers.

Peter continued his regular visits. They met for dinner and then move to his hotel room to watch a sporting event. Sarah still picked soccer games, but she was getting into watching basketball with him.

They took turns bringing each other to the very edge of release for as long as possible, Sarah holding Peter on the edge for the entire first half, and Peter returning the favor for the second half of whatever game they were watching. Then they would enjoy each other fully after the game. The pattern was freeing and they both took opportunities to ask for exactly what they wanted.

Heavy air conditioning cooled Sarah's office suite to just over sixty degrees and despite the cold, Sarah felt her face flush at the thought of their last night together.

The temperature was perfect for the hardware but sent Sarah to the couch to soak in the sunlight streaming in the windows. She'd kicked off her shoes and was reclined on the couch with her legs tucked under her. She enjoyed the sunlight and left the blanket she used when she slept in her office in its place on the other cushion.

The Wall Street Journal printed headlines down the left side of the front page and Sarah was in the habit of reading every one. She often read a detailed article or two if they caught her attention.

Today, one did in particular. The article described rising instabilities in the recently deregulated electrical markets in California. The detailed article described the market for buying and selling electricity on the *spot*, every six minutes. The idea was to match the least expensive producers with the demand, allowing market forces to create the most efficient system. What was happening, though, was that the grid was experiencing brief times when the supply did not match the demand, and the frequency was beginning to fluctuate. As the summer was driving the daytime temperatures up, people were turning on their air conditioning and increasing the demand for electricity. The grid couldn't keep up with the demand. The system operators were considering brownouts across the state to avoid a massive blackout of the electrical grid.

Sarah couldn't believe it. She was collecting data with the power on hoping for the power to be turned off, and they were planning to do it. On purpose.

Whatever Maxwell was looking for, he had her searching all over the USA, including California. She'd need to know when and where they were going to turn the power off. Maxwell could probably help her with that.

Sarah sent a note to Lloyd telling him she was itching for a vacation. She knew she'd be greeted at her apartment tonight by a man in a wrinkled suit with airplane tickets.

50. September 22, 2000

Linus was not as happy with Claire as she thought he would be after she had dinner with Dr. Walters. Linus was at her house the morning she got home. He wanted to know what Dr. Walters was working on. He thought it was clear to her what her assignment was, that he gave the same assignment to Peter, and he'd managed to get it done with Dr. Sarah Kiadopolis. She'd asked for the assignment, and he needed her to succeed.

Linus impatiently explained that the best way to get information from a man was sex. A man would talk about anything if he thought it would lead to sex. Linus embarrassed her by reminding her that he found her in her underwear trying to attract Peter seven years earlier. He was certain she'd improved her skills since then. He horrified her by telling her some of the intimate details of her relationship with her last boyfriend. Claire looked quickly around her living room before she stopped herself. Linus must have had cameras in her house!

"Have you ever heard from that physicist from Virginia?" Claire sat on the couch in Peter's condo overlooking downtown Greenville. She'd been back to Seattle a few times since her conversation with Linus. Dr. Walters was always happy to see her, and he clearly was hoping for more than a friendship. Claire hadn't been able to go beyond friendship and she couldn't explain it. She genuinely hoped Peter could help her out, despite not wanting to hear about his past.

"Claire," Peter handed her a glass of wine. She knew she was in love with him, and she was pretty sure he was in love with her, but it seemed neither would ever do anything about it. He sat down right next to her and looked out at the skyline. "Sarah is my friend."

"*Is?*" Claire asked, "I thought you hadn't seen her in years?" Peter didn't look at her but kept looking out at the river.

"When you and I lasted talked about her, over a year ago," Claire didn't like that he was being careful with his words, "I had not heard from her in some time. Then, I bumped into her, and we started being friends again."

"Friends with benefits?" Claire asked.

"Yes," Peter looked at her now, "Why?" He took a sip of his wine.

"You never talk about her," Claire weighed whether to tell him about her assignment, and decided against it, "It seems strange." She leaned into him because she wanted to feel close, to make this conversation less confrontational. "That's all."

"Look, Claire, at first Linus asked me to go visit her. He kept asking me to do more with her, get her to open up. At first, I didn't want to sleep with her. It was weird, I mean, you know what she looks like, I should have jumped at it. But there was something about Linus wanting me to." Claire looked up at him. He was being sincere. "But it happened. Then, when I reported to Linus that she didn't talk, he lost interest. Then I could see her on my own. We dated for a while, but it didn't work out. I hadn't seen her in years, just like I told you, and then we met up, and we see each other every so often."

Claire had talked to Peter about women before. He'd given her this type of detail before. But somehow he didn't tell her about Sarah. She wanted to think. She rested her head on his shoulder and wrapped her hand around his bicep. She wouldn't tell him about Hans.

"Are there others like her?" She asked while they were both looking out to the Reedy.

"No."

"Would you tell me if there were?" Claire had to wait for a moment.

"Yes, if you asked, I would tell you."

Claire left his apartment at about ten in the evening. She wanted to stay with him, and she thought he wanted her to stay.

51.   September 28, 2000

"Now look here, you know I'm a good Christian, and I love Israel as much, more even, than the next guy," George W. Bush grumbled at Joe Lieberman, "but shouldn't the voters get to decide an issue like this?"

It was four days before the first Presidential Debate of the 2000 election season and the four candidates met for a fifteen minute session in a hotel room in Daytona Beach, Florida. All four candidates had Secret Service Details outside.

George enjoyed campaigning, and he was beginning to think he could win. He didn't want to meet with them, but Dick Cheney, his running mate, had insisted. Around the small conference table sat George Bush and Dick Cheney, the Republican nominees for President and Vice President, and Al Gore and Joe Lieberman, the Democrats. If the media caught wind of this meeting, there'd be hell to pay. George thought they'd be discussing some rules of the debates, not the fate of Israel.

"No, George," Al Gore, the sitting Vice President of the United States said, "The voters will get to decide lots of things, but not this." George thought he saw Al look at Dick. They seemed to have something going on. There was no way he was going to ask about it. He was just paying very close attention.

"Okay, okay," George said, "I'd be in favor of supporting Israel whatever you guys said."

"Yes," Dick said, "I know we all would." Again he was looking out the side of his head at the Vice President. "The important thing here is to show the world that there isn't any daylight between us. The factions that oppose the United States and Israel around the world will read even a hypothetical debate on this issue as a quantum shift in our position. We all need to make sure this doesn't become a pissing contest."

"Fine." George said. "That's just fine."

"Joe," Al said, addressing his running mate, "We're all agreed? No fighting over Israel? We're all equally in absolute agreement that we're on the side of Israel, no matter what?"

"I'm absolutely in favor of our unwavering support of Israel, but this is a differentiation issue for me. I'm Jewish for Christ sake!" Senator Lieberman said. The three other men looked at him.

"I know we all want to take every opportunity to point out how stupid everyone else is at every opportunity," Dick looked around the table, "But on this issue, we all have to be together."

George was already on board, he was actually happy that Joe wouldn't get to use the issue. This would work out for him. Joe knew it too, and he didn't want to go along. George could understand everyone's position around this table except Al Gore's. Why would his opponent give him this issue, one that his running mate could use against them? He thought it could be a trap, except that Dick seemed to know why Al was on board. George decided he'd ask his running mate about it later.

"I'll let you win our debate," Dick said with a little smile.

"Let me win?!" Joe nearly fell out of his chair. "You asshole, you used to be in this game, but it's been a long time!"

"Wait," George said, "We don't need to go that far." Dick looked at George. George looked at Joe. They were trading the debate between the running mates to get nullification of Joe Liebermann's unique position as the first Jewish Vice Presidential contender and George couldn't decide if it was a good trade.

Dick seemed sure it was.

"Okay," Joe said. George had the unsettling suspicion that it didn't matter what he said in this meeting.

52.   January 10, 2001

Sullivan Acer ran through the parking lot to his rental car. He just watched Linus Brenner get off his plane at Dulles International outside Washington, DC. He knew Linus had to get his own rental car and he knew which rental car agency he was using. He also knew that if he lost Linus at the airport he had no hope of figuring out what he was doing in Washington DC tonight. Sullivan retrieved his car from the hourly parking lot and drove around the large loop at the terminal, stationing his car at the exit from the rental car center. Sullivan didn't like the song on the radio but he was too afraid to look down to change it.

I don't want him to be a wimp, like you. Leanne had stung him with those words. He would have said something, but he was a wimp.

Well, it took him a year, but he was following Linus Brenner now.

Sullivan noticed that Linus traveled to Washington DC every year on or near January 10th, and decided that would be the trip he'd follow.

It was eight thirty in the evening and cars were regularly coming from the car rental parking lot. Sullivan inspected the driver of each. After ten minutes he thought he'd missed him. Finally, Linus emerged in a BMW 3-series. The government didn't pay for such a car, but anyone could pay the difference for an upgrade. Sullivan didn't know anyone who ever did.

Sullivan followed as Linus pulled onto Route 29. He stayed a few cars back and tried not to look suspicious. If Linus spotted him, there would be no way of explaining what he was doing here. He expected Linus to head for the nearest highway to get into Washington DC and had to swerve off the on-ramp.

The car in front of Sullivan stopped at one of the endless line of stop lights along Route 29. Linus was getting away. Sullivan strained to see Linus pull into a left turn lane and wait. If there was a break in the traffic, Linus would make the turn and not be seen again. Luckily the traffic was still heavy for the evening rush.

Sullivan's grip on the steering wheel tightened as he waited for the progression of the light. The car in front of him took a seemingly infinite second to begin moving when it got the chance. Sullivan willed the car to move forward. His heart nearly stopped when he looked past the car inching forward in front of him to see that the turn lane was empty.

Linus had made the turn.

Sullivan hit the accelerator hard when a gap in the traffic allowed him to pull around the slower car. Then he found himself right where he had last seen Linus, waiting to make the left. He was encouraged when he saw the left turn entered into an apartment complex. Maybe he could find Linus' car. It occurred to him he should have taken down the license plate. He'd be fine, how many black BMW's were in this lot? An opening in the traffic allowed him through.

The road dropped down from Route 29 and came to a tee at the complex rental office. The three spots in front of the office were empty. He could see through the large windows of the office to a court yard and pool. The neighborhood was a series of four story apartment buildings on both sides of a street that made a loop around the courtyard. In the early evening the parking lot was full but there wasn't any traffic.

He was about to turn right when he saw the BMW emerge around the building on the left. Linus must have circled the neighborhood. He pulled directly into a parking space facing a building on the outside of the complex.

Linus looked down in his lap for a few moments. Whatever he was looking at was bright.

Was he watching television?

He put it in the passenger seat, stepped from the car, and pulled a backpack from the back seat. Linus wore a heavy overcoat over a blue business suit. He looked like everyone else at the airport.

Sullivan realized he had been sitting at this stop sign for some time. Luckily, no one was behind him, but he had to move or he might attract Linus' attention. He pulled forward directly into one of the three open spots and looked out of the corner of his eye.

Linus crossed the parking lot and entered one of the stairwells on the inside loop of the complex.

Sullivan took a deep breath.

Now what?

He knew where Linus went, but had no idea why. Who was he visiting? Was this just the first stop on his way into the city? He could imagine several things he was doing here, and could not imagine him coming all the way here for only a few-second visit. Sullivan decided to go see what Linus was looking at in his car.

Sullivan stepped out of his gray Ford and walked toward Linus' BMW. Two inches of snow had fallen that day and the parking lot had mounds of snow all around it. Sullivan and Linus both traveled from Wisconsin and Sullivan had no trouble navigating the ice as he crossed the street to the side where Linus had parked.

As he walked he tried to look at the building on the inside of the loop. With his head turned up and to the building, he shifted his eyes so that he could look to the stairwell Linus had entered. He could also see the balconies on the building.

He could hear every step he made, the sidewalks weren't cleared and he crunched through snow. His senses were hyper-aware. If Linus were to emerge from the building, he couldn't just turn and run, and he couldn't keep going forward, he'd be seen. Linus would certainly recognize him, and he'd have no excuse for being there. He was completely exposed.

He felt better as he passed the building entrance. At least his face was away from the stairs. Finally he approached Linus' car.

Any relaxation he felt about passing the door instantly vanished as he had to turn to walk next to the car and look into the window.

When Sullivan was young, his father worked at the university near his home where he grew up. As an employee, he could use the facilities and every morning he went swimming. In the summers, Sullivan would get up at five in the morning to go with his father to the pool. He didn't swim laps, but instead went for the diving board. The diving team practiced in the same pool and there was a 5 meter and 10 meter platform. The first day of the summer Sullivan would stand at the top of the five meter platform and stare down at the water. It would take him several minutes to talk himself into stepping off. The second time up the ladder, he would only wait a few seconds for his nerve to harden. He began to imagine an opening. An opening that once he passed through it, his nerve was firm and he began to accelerate to the edge of the board. Once he passed the opening, there was no slowing down. As the summer went on, the opening moved back down the platform, eventually down the ladder. It never went away, but it waited at the foot of the ladder for him. By the end of the summer, he would pause at the bottom of the ladder to mentally pass through the opening, climb the ladder and flip off the ten meter platform without hesitation.

Sullivan mentally placed an opening at the edge of the sidewalk next to Linus' car. He paused a moment just before the opening. He looked one last time to see that no one was coming down the stairs. He stepped through the opening off the curb.

He walked quickly down the length of the passenger side of the car. He glanced down into the passenger seat.

A laptop.

He planned to walk down the length of the car and cross the street in a natural pattern, but there was something connected to the laptop he needed another look at.

At the end of the car, he turned and walked back toward the front. He got another look into the car. A short range antenna, like the kind on walkie-talkies, protruded from the side of the computer.

He paused for a fraction of a second.

It was time to get out of there.

He walked quickly onto the sidewalk and directly toward the building on the outer ring of the neighborhood.

As Sullivan approached the building he saw Linus descending the stairs to the ground floor in the reflection in the sliding door of the apartment next to the walkway. Sullivan forced himself to walk slowly into the opening of the building directly ahead.

Passing through the breezeway to the far side of the building took forever, but he finally came to the sidewalk around the outside of the complex, turned left and headed back toward his car. This sidewalk was not shoveled and few people had walked there today. His shoes were trudging deep in the snow.

Sullivan ducked behind the corner of the building when he saw Linus' BMW pull into the turn lane and wait to pull back onto Route 29. He waited until Linus pulled away continuing in toward Washington.

There was no way he would make it back to his car in time to catch up.

Linus was gone, so Sullivan begrudgingly walked back to his car. He needed to figure out what he was going to do next. He had no idea where Linus was going. Sullivan had no idea how to find him except that he had a return flight in the morning. He walked slowly, dreading getting to his car and having to decide where to go.

Sullivan returned to his car and still had no idea what to do next. Linus surprised him by being in the apartment for less than five minutes. That surprise caught Sullivan out of his car and made it impossible for him to follow Linus out of the parking lot. He should have stayed in his car! Now all he knew was that he visited someone in that building for a few moments before he continued with his plans. Whatever those plans were, Sullivan wouldn't see them because Linus left too fast. Now he had no way of picking up his trail. He'd have to return to Wisconsin with nothing and wait until Linus made another trip like this.

At least he'd done it. He traveled into the field and followed Linus Brenner. He'd imagined following him to Washington DC for years, expecting to see him meet with some mob bosses, or deliver a wad of cash, or take a bribe, or visit a woman. Instead, Sullivan learned, he drove straight to this apartment complex and visited one of the apartments for five minutes.

Sullivan took a deep breath, closed his eyes, and rested his head against the headrest. It was Wednesday night, so most of the young professionals in this complex were probably in for the night.

The laptop in Linus' car had a short-range antenna. Whatever Linus was looking at, the signal had to come from nearby.

He was watching a signal transmitted from inside the apartment!

There must be surveillance equipment inside that apartment.

Linus was checking to make sure the apartment he was visiting was empty!

Sullivan looked down the row of cars and saw that every space was full. Every space except the one recently vacated by Linus. Sullivan jumped out of his car, adjusted his coat to repel the cold, and walked down the sidewalk on the inside loop of the complex.

The spaces were numbered and Linus was in space 402. Sullivan looked up at the building. He could see lights on in every apartment on this face of the building. He walked to the covered stairway of the building. He noted the numbers on the doors of the apartments and saw that 402 faced the pool, not the parking lot. He passed through the breezeway to the pool area. The pool was fenced but he was able to walk around the outside of the fence to the far side of the complex. From there, he looked back at the building to see that only apartment 402 was dark.

It wasn't conclusive, but the coincidences were piling up. From there he went to the mailboxes and found apartment 402 was occupied by *S. Kiadopolis.*

Now he felt this trip wasn't wasted. He'd discovered an important clue. He now knew S. Kiadopolis was important enough to Linus Brenner for him to travel here once a year for the past eight years.

He also knew S. Kiadopolis didn't know Linus Brenner was doing it.

53. January 15, 2001

Claire visited Seattle every other week since October. She was working with Ravi on a new electrical design, and she worked remotely during the day. She spent most evenings with Hans. She didn't push anything, she just talked about her work, carefully not giving any specifics, and let him talk too. Hans had disappointed Linus by not revealing any details about his work, but Claire was delighted. Claire knew Hans was the kind of dorky guy she wouldn't have given a second look at, but now she knew he was a pretty great guy.

Two nights ago, he took her for a nice dinner before they walked to the movie theater. It was cold and rainy, as it often was in Seattle, and they lingered under dry overhangs.

The first time they were alone at an overhang, Hans surprised her with a quick kiss.

Two overhangs later Claire was anxiously returning the kisses and pulling him to her. They made out in the elevator up to her apartment before saying goodnight.

They weren't planning to see each other last night, but Claire asked and Hans quickly canceled his plans. They were going to go out, but instead they went straight to the couch and made out. Shirts were hastily discarded and soon Claire was straddling Hans while he focused all his attention on her chest. Her breasts were small and most men didn't spend a lot of time on them, so Claire thoroughly appreciated his enthusiastic attention.

Tonight Claire ate dinner alone while Hans spent the evening with his friends playing an online interactive game as he did every Monday night. She smiled while thinking about the past two nights and the pleasant turn of her relationship. She hadn't been touched like that in, she thought about it, in too long. And Linus was wrong, he didn't talk about anything. Then again, he didn't have much of a chance to talk.

She frowned.

Damn it.

She thought she was done thinking about Linus Brenner. She thought she would report that Hans didn't talk, just like Peter had with Sarah, and then she'd be free to pursue a relationship without Linus breathing down her neck. She decided it would take a little more time to satisfy Linus. That would be okay.

No, it would not be okay. She wasn't looking forward to reporting what she'd done here, and she sure as hell wasn't going to want to report what she planned to do over the next few months!

No, this was going to end tonight. She was going to give him the opportunity to talk to prove he wouldn't, once and for all.

Claire finished a bottle of wine and dialed his apartment.

"Yes?" Hans answered.

"Hi, it's me," Claire said, "Are you done playing with your friends?"

"Yes, we just finished, I won!" Hans often won, but he was still happy with himself.

"Well, that's great," Claire bit her lip. She decided she would go for it, "Do you want to come up here and we can celebrate?"

She knew Hans liked her in her jeans, so that was all she was wearing when she answered the door.

"So, tell me about it, how did you win?" Claire said over her shoulder as she walked into her apartment as though nothing was out of the ordinary.

"I, uh?" Hans followed her slowly.

Claire sat on her couch in her living room. She forced herself to lounge with her arms at her sides and her bare ankles crossed on the floor. The cool air made her nipples erect and she knew she looked good.

Hans stood with his mouth open.

She patted the seat next to her and Hans walked over and sat down. She'd thought he would jump right in, but her forwardness was putting him off guard. Good.

"So, tell me about your day," Claire said as she put her hand on his thigh.

"Um, Today I was designing a bracket," Hans stammered.

"Uh Huh," Claire said as she reached over and started unbuttoning his shirt. "Tell me more about this bracket."

"Well," Hans said. The encouragement was working, "It's a really cool bracket, and actually it's more of an electromechanical system!"

"Really!" Claire couldn't really work his buttons from next to him so she slowly slid off the couch to a kneeling position between his knees, "an electromechanical system you say!" From there she was able to quickly open his shirt. She leaned forward and kissed his nipples and stomach. He stopped talking. "Tell me more about it!"

"Okay," Hans was beginning to breathe hard, but he kept talking, "I've been working on a project for about four years, we've made several prototypes." Claire was beginning to lose herself in what she was doing, but she had to focus to listen to what he was saying. Nope. He wasn't saying anything interesting about his work. She sat back and looked up at him with a smile while she opened his belt and button fly.

"The bracket's for a sensor we're installing on the Hubble Space Telescope." She'd planned to keep prodding him, but she was not interested in what he was saying any more. She kissed down on his stomach until she reached the edge of his purple boxer briefs. "It's a special detector designed to find gravitons."

"What?" Claire looked up at him. He didn't just tell her what he was working on, did he? She must have not heard him right.

"Yeah," Hans looked down at her. He interpreted her question as encouragement when really she didn't want to hear about his work at all, "There's a detector that can actually see gravitons."

Hans was struggling to keep talking through heavy breathing. Claire didn't want him to continue talking. She looked back down, rubbing one hand across him while she kissed the skin her other hand exposed by slowly pulling the elastic of his boxers.

Hans mumbled now, "And I'm helping with the latest installation."

Claire stopped moving, her lips against his skin.

She lifted her hand from him.

She slowly sat back trying to unhear what she just heard. He'd definitely just told her what he was working on. This was not going to proceed as she'd hoped.

Suddenly she wasn't interested in continuing the evening. She stood up, crossing her arms over her chest.

His eyes opened with confusion.

She turned away from him, "I think you should go."

. . .

Claire cried for a solid hour after Hans stumbled out of her apartment. She didn't get back to Greenville until the following evening. She didn't want to talk to Linus even though he would be happy for the news.

She didn't want to go home either. After picking up her car from GSP airport, she drove straight into Greenville to Peter Howard's apartment.

"Claire!" Peter was surprised when he answered the door. For a fraction of a second, he looked like he wasn't going to let her in. Maybe he had another woman over this evening. He was dressed in a nice suit.

In that fraction of a second, Claire felt her heart breaking apart.

But then he stepped aside, "Come in!"

Claire pushed into the apartment but instead of moving past him, she moved straight into him and despite herself her eyes let the flood gates back open.

His arms closed around her and she decided right then she wouldn't be in another man's arms ever again. She leaned back. He looked down at her. She lifted up onto her toes and kissed him. They had not kissed since the night they met Linus, and all of that emotion poured through her lips into his.

The kiss was hard and she was breathing fast when it ended. She looked up to see Peter looking down at her, his face full of emotion. She couldn't tell him about Hans. She didn't want to either. On the way here, this was about Hans, but once their lips touched, it was about them, these two. She pushed up again and kissed him again, and she felt his urgency rise with hers.

She'd missed too many opportunities to let this one go. She tore at his clothes and he tore at hers. Normally, she waited to see who would take charge in this type of frantic encounter, but not this time. She only paused pulling at his buttons to lift her hands over her head so he could pull her t-shirt off. He was moving fast and she felt her bra disappear. She decided to skip the shirt and he let out a low hum when she reached inside his pants.

She pulled her hand free and wrapped her arms around his neck when he lifted her off the ground. He moved her quickly to the ottoman they'd rested their feet on countless times. She lay on her back as he pulled her pants and panties off in one swift motion. She was naked and breathing hard.

He entered her quickly and they both didn't last long against the climax that had been building for eight years.

Peter canceled his plans and they spent the evening together. They ate and talked and kissed into the night. When it was normally time for her to go, they moved into his bedroom like they had done it that way for years.

54. January 17, 2001

Sarah told Maxwell about California last June. He already knew. At their annual meeting on January tenth, she'd updated him on her progress.

The Independent System Operator that ran the California grid had to create a report of likely locations for brownouts for the following day and post it to a secure internet site. Maxwell arranged for Sarah to receive access to the site and Sarah checked it each morning for the potential locations of brownouts in California.

KiteString had a polar orbit and traveled the length of California each orbit from south to north, so Sarah had little difficulty building the tracking files to prepare for the brownouts. She had the files ready each morning by nine AM, in plenty of time for the heat of the afternoon to get the air conditioning blasting all over California.

Other than the hottest part of the day, the satellite continued its background scans somewhere over Nevada.

Sarah added a second screen next to her couch to report the status of her satellites and also the status of the California grid.

This lunchtime, Sarah set a new record of eight pull-ups on her bar, completed one hundred sit-ups and twenty push-ups. Tired, she sat down on her couch to eat a burger and read the paper. Just after lunch was usually the most interesting time for the California grid, and she had to be ready to task the satellite if the power went down.

Halfway through her burger, the power went down in a large part of San Francisco.

KiteString was ten minutes from passing the area.

She threw her burger to the side, cursed under her breath as it made a mess of her blanket, and moved to her desk.

She worked quickly to task the satellite. The brownouts tended to last just three hours. If she missed this pass, she would likely not have time to collect the data she needed.

The commands were submitted as the satellite passed over Tijuana, Mexico.

There was little time for the satellite to reposition. There was nothing further she could do but watch.

She turned to the screen with the display showing the paths of her two satellites. The Hubble traveled in its equatorial orbit and was currently over the Mediterranean on its way to Syria. *KiteString* diverted north-westward into Southern California.

It would be close.

Sarah held up the edge of a piece of paper to her computer screen attempting to extrapolate the new path to see if it would make it. The new path seemed to pass directly into the Bay Area. She felt tension, but she was only a spectator now.

Over the next five minutes, *KiteString* reached the center of San Francisco and turned due north passing into Northern California. Sarah watched the path move into Oregon.

She turned her attention to the processing computers. Network routers sent the data to her servers over an encrypted connection eight minutes after it was collected in space. She could tell immediately whether the electrical grid was off or on.

If it was on, the swath of collected data was white on the green background of the map. If the data was collected with the power off, the swath turned red. The swath moving northwest was white as it entered the San Francisco area. A vertical break between white and red moved from the left of the screen to the right as the satellite passed into the brownout region. The brownout region was large and the entire swath turned red. This was rare as the previous brownouts she mapped were smaller than the one tenth of a mile covered by the satellite. The path of the satellite returned to north and after a few moments, a white horizontal line moved down the screen as the satellite exited the brownout region. Sarah had missed some of the brownout, but had captured much of it.

Sarah realized she was standing and nearly holding her breath. She exhaled happy. She counted the collection of most of the data as a win.

Sarah was under orders to report to Maxwell each time she created a key for any part of California. She was to study the resulting images, fly to Wisconsin, and report anything she found from memory. This was her fourth trip and there was never much to report. On her own initiative, she scanned for various things.

She scanned for plutonium because of the search in Greenville. She had never found any more of that, and didn't expect to.

She scanned for a few chemical weapons like mustard gas and VF gas. She never found any of that either.

She scanned for cocaine, methamphetamines, and pot. The pot scans came up nearly solid in some areas. Meth and cocaine showed up with some here and there. She noted a few locations and committed the coordinates to memory.

She began to scan for endorphins. Endorphins are key chemicals enabling the transmission of nerve signals throughout the nervous system of all animals. The human brain is full of them. By searching for endorphins, she could locate living human brains that were either in high concentrations or not moving much. This method allowed her to identify bed ridden patients in hospitals. She figured that any gathering of people that stayed stationary for around ninety hours should be looked into, like maybe people held by human traffickers or other criminals, or people in hiding, or people trapped under rocks in the desert.

Maxwell asked if she had found anything suspicious, but so far nothing she reported was of interest to him.

Maxwell's urgent approach to her scans told her he was looking for something, but he refused to give her any idea what it was.

Sarah called her travel agent and scheduled a flight to Milwaukee for the next evening. She knew she would need tonight to process the data and most of the day tomorrow to study the results. As she hung up with the travel agent, she found herself standing in the middle of her area rug barefoot. Adrenaline made her want to do something else, but she needed to wait for the computers to work. She ran forward three steps, jumped, and grabbed the pull-up bar. She pumped four pull-ups out before she dropped from the bar. She rubbed her bare arms and returned to her seat next to the burger she had dropped on her couch.

55.   January 19, 2001

Sarah smiled awkwardly at Lloyd in Maxwell's outer office. She wore her gray skirt just above the knee with a cream sweater under a gray blazer. Thick cream colored stockings warmed her legs. She'd been here for her annual review just the previous week and knew it would be cold. She sat in the small wooden chair in the corner of the room.

Lloyd smiled wordlessly back. Lloyd invited Sarah to his wedding two years ago. Sally was a pretty girl from Sheboygan.

After the wedding, she told Lloyd she didn't want him seeing her outside the office. It was unfortunate that they were uncomfortable now, but she understood.

He'd already looked at her twice before, each time, drawn to her tapping foot. She stopped, and he returned to whatever he was doing. She wasn't nervous last week. She hadn't been nervous here since the scans started working.

This time was different. Not that she was not successful, the scans worked perfectly. She'd run the full data reduction a second time to confirm that it was run correctly. She was also in the process of building error checking systems, and she ran all of those as well. Sarah looked down at her nails. She had practiced not biting them in high school, but she had to fight the urge now.

"Sarah," Lloyd called. Sarah looked up to see him hanging up his phone. "Maxwell's ready for you now. Please go in." Sarah told herself she wasn't nervous, just anxious. She stood and brushed her hands down her suit.

"Good morning, Dr. Kiadopolis," Maxwell was sitting at his desk as he always was. He looked up and instantly sensed the difference in her. Sarah walked across his office to the club chairs next to the windows, as she always did.

Maxwell stood and watched her cross the office.

Sarah always dressed professionally to visit him, but today she was wearing her suit, and she suddenly felt like she was at an interview. She sat and immediately started talking.

"I found something. Two days ago. There was a brown out in the San Francisco Bay Area and I got *KiteString* over it just in time. I processed the data twice, so I am sure."

"Dr. Kiadopolis," Maxwell interrupted, "Sarah, would you like a drink?" Sarah just frowned. "Okay, why don't you tell me what you found?"

"Mr. Rassic," Sarah said sitting straight-backed with both feet on the floor, "I, we, I found an atomic bomb in the foundation of a building in downtown San Francisco!" She looked for a reaction.

She got none.

He just looked back at her, standing behind his desk. After a few seconds, a small smile began to break on his face.

"I checked the data reduction twice! There is definitely a plutonium core surrounded by heavy explosives. It is literally a textbook nuclear device. I looked it up." She was talking, but she just stopped as a brief moment of recognition crossed Maxwell's face. Did he know about this bomb? No, it wasn't recognition, it was relaxation. The look only lasted two seconds before he returned to his smile.

"Sarah," Maxwell said as he rounded the end of his desk casually, "this is excellent news!"

"How could a nuclear weapon under a building in downtown San Francisco be good news?"

"I didn't mean that," Maxwell said, "I meant it was good news that you found it. Your system is truly working. What building?"

Sarah told him where it was.

He had never asked where anything was before. When she reported on drugs, he asked a few questions but never where they were. Now, he asked where the nuclear weapon was. She watched him sit in his chair with practiced casualness. She watched him closely.

"Did you find any more cocaine?" Maxwell asked. Maybe he wasn't interested in the bomb.

"*NO*," Sarah said with some frustration, "Aren't you interested in the nuclear weapon? Doesn't that concern you?"

"Of course it does. I have a friend at the Department of Energy. I'll let him know we found it. He'll confirm whether it's supposed to be there or not. We can't go after every cocaine dealer, but if you find an enormous stash, we'll report it too." Maxwell smiled.

Sarah told him she didn't find any chemical weapons or hidden people. Certainly nothing as interesting as a nuclear weapon!

"Last time we talked, you told me there was something specific you were looking for," Sarah said, "It would be much easier for me to find it if you told me what it was."

"Sarah," Maxwell explained. His face stayed open and clear. "I told you I was searching for things. I'm searching for anything you can find. When you find things, I report them to the various departments who could use the information. I don't want to presuppose what you can find. You're already running searches I didn't think were possible. I don't want you to focus on just one thing."

That made a lot of sense. The presence of a nuclear weapon had thrown her off her game. It was certainly a big find, but there could be lots of other things she could locate. There had to be an explanation for why a device was there. Maybe it was a leftover from research, like the one in Greenville.

Sarah stayed with Maxwell for another hour and they discussed other things she could search for.

As she left for the airport, Sarah couldn't shake the look on his face when she told him about the bomb. Nothing else had that reaction with him. She couldn't quite pinpoint the look, but she was sure that bomb was more important to him than he was letting on.

. . .

Claire was groggy in the middle of the night in Peter's bed. She heard him talking on the phone.

"Look, you don't need to find Claire, I know where she is!" Peter said into the phone, "What's that supposed to mean? That's none of your business. Look, I'm still doing my job, so it shouldn't matter to you... No, you can't ask her that! … No … Yes its different than with me!" Claire rolled over and sat up. She'd told him about Hans. He was very understanding, but he didn't like it.

He softened to her touch. "Okay, okay, what do you want us to do? … Okay, we'll be there. … No you don't need to keep looking for her. I know where to find her. … We'll see you tonight!"

Peter hung up and laid back down. Claire tucked under his arm. She pressed her body against his and wrapped her arm around him.

He put his hand on her arm.

"San Francisco." Peter said.

56. January 20, 2001

Jim Williams sat alone in the Oval Office. He'd stood outside while the movers made the miraculous transformation from the Bill Clinton Oval Office to the George Bush Oval in less than two hours. In that time, the carpet, drapes, wall paper, and every piece of furniture was changed. George Bush had just completed his inaugural address and was making his way down Pennsylvania Avenue to this very room. Bill Clinton and Al Gore attended the inauguration and would join him here soon.

LV had sent a letter telling Al Gore to drop his objections in Florida, but the Vice President had already decided to concede.

The eight years since the last inauguration had been shaky, but he thought this meeting would go well. They had positive results to report, and Thomas reminded Jim that Vice President Dick Cheney already knew about LV.

The door opened and the former President and Vice President entered the Oval Office, maybe for the last time.

57. February 5, 2001

Sarah Kiadopolis pulled into her reserved parking space outside her apartment building. In a single rehearsed motion, she set the parking break, put the manual transmission in neutral, and killed the engine with the key. She was in a rush, but she was always in a rush when she was driving. She had a soccer game in 20 minutes. She had to change and drive 20 minutes to the indoor field.

She checked her rearview mirror and saw a man standing near the stairs to her apartment. He studied her car and apparently decided it was the right one and started to walk toward her.

It was just after work, still daylight, and there were others getting home in the parking lot. She looked at him. He was medium height, white, and dressed in a nice but not expensive suit under a nice but not expensive overcoat. When he was studying her car, his face had a look of determination, but once he decided to approach, a genuine smile broke across his face. She got out of her car and moved to the back on her way across the parking lot.

"Ms. Kiadopolis?"

"Yes..." He knew her name? Was this another of Maxwell's delivery men? She didn't think she had any reason to run back to Milwaukee tonight.

"I'm Sullivan Acer," he held out his hand. Sarah moved her keys to her left hand and forced herself to take his hand confidently. Not a delivery man. "I'm with the Bureau of Indian Affairs."

"Okay," Sarah decided to let him explain his presence, her immediate fear left her.

"I work in a unit that investigates fraud in building permit practices," Sullivan explained, "and your name has come up in an ongoing investigation."

. . .

Sullivan saw Ms. Kiadopolis' eyes go back and forth searching his eyes. She stood in front of him in a sharp professional suit under a forest green coat. He thought she tensed as soon as he mentioned the building code. He must have found the right apartment. He realized that the people in this apartment were not Linus' friends, and likely were in some sort of trouble with some difficult people for Linus to be watching them.

The reserved parking space made it easy for Sullivan to find S. Kiadopolis. She wasn't what he was expecting. He was actually expecting a man in the building industry. It was unusual for pretty young women to be involved in building permit crimes.

"Are you involved in the building industry?" Sullivan asked.

"No," she continued to look him straight in the eyes. She wasn't hiding anything.

"Is there someone living with you?"

"That's a very personal question, but no, I live alone," She looked up at him, "I'm in finance." Her eyes stopped moving. Now she was searching him for some reaction to that statement. Was she expecting to impress him somehow?

"Okay..." Sullivan thought she wanted to tell him something, and he wanted to give her the chance, "As I said, I investigate fraud. I'm not involved in building codes or building code violations in any way. I have no interest in any building codes." He was just trying to fill some time.

. . .

What does this guy want? He doesn't seem to care about her work. Who cares about building codes? She studied his face. He had a five o'clock shadow, and his hair was a bit messed. He seemed to be about thirty-five but his skin was smooth. The smile he started with disappeared as he seemed to be babbling on about building codes with no apparent end in sight. She decided this was some sort of mix-up. She remembered she had to get somewhere. Besides, her legs were getting cold.

"I'm sorry," she said, "I have someplace to be." She moved to get past him. He shifted slightly to remain in her way. He reached into his jacket and pulled out a small case.

"Please, take my card," he said, "If something comes to you, please let me know." She took the card and quickly stepped around him. When she was just passing him, he said, "Don't call me from your apartment." She barely heard him as she'd already begun to think about getting changed for her game. She moved quickly despite her heels and took the stairs two at a time.

58. March 19, 2001

Sarah rested her head against the bulkhead on the flight to Milwaukee. She was on her way for the sixth time in as many months. She didn't mind the travel. She liked talking with Maxwell and messing with Lloyd. Today was different. Rather than feeling excited about talking to the only people in the world who knew what she really did for a living, Sarah was scared.

She found a second nuclear weapon in California. That made three weapons she found including the one in Greenville.

She was worried after she found the first one in California. Sarah knew Maxwell wasn't quite telling her everything about the weapon she found in San Francisco. For only a fraction of a second, he was thinking something, but he wouldn't tell her. Yesterday, she stood in the middle of her office staring at the scan of another nuclear weapon buried in the foundation of a building in Fresno, California. She processed the data and confirmed she was right, but she couldn't get the image of Maxwell's face out of her brain. Was it a look of relief?

Sarah was trying to figure out how to play this with Maxwell.

She could barge in and demand to know what was going on. She thought about his office, and Lloyd, and the secretary at the front door. They were the only three people she'd ever seen in a building that should have held hundreds. She thought about how he got her unlimited access to the Hubble Space Telescope, and that he was able to build *KiteString*. She decided he was definitely up to something. She decided he wasn't just looking for whatever she found. He was looking for something in particular. She also decided she didn't know how Maxwell would react if she pushed him.

Was she scared of him?

She wanted to get a better idea of what he was doing before she pushed him too hard. It occurred to her she really didn't know anyone else in his organization. She had worked for Maxwell, for Department 55, for nine years, and she had not said the words Department 55 out loud to anyone, ever. Her paycheck still said Cornwall & Wallace.

Maxwell was able to get her anything she ever needed. She had long stopped questioning his ability to do whatever he said he was going to do. And she realized she had long stopped questioning what it was he was actually trying to accomplish. She never had any reason to.

Did she now?

She'd found her third nuclear weapon hidden inside the United States.

What did that mean? Did Maxwell lose three nuclear weapons and he had to find them?

They'd been buried in the foundations of buildings, so they weren't going anywhere.

The flight attendant handed her a paper cup with coffee. She sat up and looked around the aircraft. Luckily, the flight wasn't full and no one sat next to her. She rolled her head on her shoulders and felt the tension.

No, she wouldn't barge in. She had to play it cool. But to play it cool, she had to be cool.

59. March 22, 2001

Claire's relationship with Dr. Hans Walters came to an abrupt end when she reported what he'd told her to Linus. He thanked her and told her she was done, he would take it from there. Peter said he would break things off with Sarah, and Claire trusted he would. They spent their nights making up for all the time they lost over the past ten years, and she had never been so happy. They'd fallen into a comfortable routine as though they'd been together since that first night.

"Linus called me at work today," Claire announced as she walked into his condo. He'd given her a key.

"I know, he called me too," Peter responded. He kissed her as soon as she reached him in the kitchen. He was cooking stir-fry. "He had the plane tickets delivered via courier this afternoon."

"I was about to run a test on the new pulse generators we've been developing," Claire said. It was nice to share absolutely everything with someone. "Will I have time to do it in the morning?" She pulled plates out of the cabinet and piled silverware on them on the way to the table inside the large sliding glass doors.

In March, it wasn't quite warm enough to eat outside, even in South Carolina.

"No, we leave first thing in the morning. It takes all day to get to Southern California. We've got four flights to get to Fresno." Peter said, "I do have some plans for you tonight, though." Claire looked over her shoulder to see Peter looking at her legs. She remembered the way he looked at her that night in the hotel room. He still looked at her the same way. When he looked at her like that, she knew he was hers.

60. March 23, 2001

"This is Sarah Kiadopolis," Sullivan could hardly believe it. It had been two months since he met her outside her apartment in Virginia.

In that time he confirmed that Sarah was trained in Astrophysics but had worked for Cornwall & Wallace since leaving Virginia Tech. He found and attempted to read her journal articles at the University of Wisconsin library. When he called to inquire about what she did, Mr. Wallace himself said she was on special assignment in Washington DC. Everything he could find, which was not much, indicated that she was not who he was looking for. He was sad to have given up on Dr. Sarah Kiadopolis, but he figured he had the wrong address after all.

Linus had been traveling to California frequently, but there was nothing suspicious about it.

"Hello, Sarah," Sullivan had only spoken to her for a few moments, but he felt like he'd known her for years. She probably didn't share the familiarity, "Dr. Kiadopolis..."

"Who are you?" Dr. Kiadopolis asked directly.

"As I said, I work for the Department of Indian Affairs. I work on the internal audit staff..." Sullivan repeated to her, "I'm investigating fraudulent activities within both our agency and the building industry."

"Who bugged my phone?" Dr. Kiadopolis seemed impatient.

"I'm sorry?" Sullivan wanted her to reveal information, not the other way around.

"You told me not to call you on my home phone. That seemed silly at the time. Then I realized that my," she paused, "Someone I know works in the building industry ..." Sarah paused. "Where are you?"

"I'm in my office, I work outside Milwaukee, Wisconsin," Sullivan answered.

"*What?*" Sarah interrupted.

Why did she care he was from Wisconsin? He wrote his state on his pad and moved on, "You're not on your home phone, are you?"

"Of course not," Sarah said, "I checked my phone, and there's a listening device in it. I'm calling from a friend's place."

"When we talked before, you seemed nervous when I mentioned who I was," Sullivan said.

"What? No...well...I think I need to go..." Sarah said.

Sullivan shouldn't have pushed her. If she was involved, it was not his interest to prosecute her, his interest was Linus Brenner.

"Dr. Kiadopolis," Sullivan said, "I'm interested in fraud within our department. I'm not interested in your acquaintance. Have you, I mean, has he been approached by anyone? Has he been asked for anything?" Sullivan thought she wanted to tell him more. He was getting the feeling she was in some sort of trouble and was looking for help.

"No, no one has approached me," she said, "I told you, this is about my acquaintance. I'm calling you because you knew my phone was bugged," her speech accelerated, "I wasn't nervous when we met. I was just in a hurry." She continued, "I believe you have some information that I could use, and..."

Sullivan's FBI friend, Hector Feliz had told him that sometimes when a subject was talking very fast, they could be tripped up with some new information. Sarah was talking fast, and Sullivan said, "Linus Brenner."

"What, who's that? Is that who's working with Peter?" Sarah didn't seem to know the name. Sullivan wrote *Peter* on his pad. In fact, she seemed more phased by Sullivan working in Milwaukee than Linus Brenner.

"He's involved in a case I am investigating," Sullivan said, "and I wanted to see if you knew who he was."

"How would I know who he was? I told you, I don't work in the building industry. My acquaintance does." Sarah said, "Is this conversation going around in circles?"

"Who's Peter? " Sullivan asked. There was a pause. The longest pause of the conversation so far.

"Peter Howard!" Sarah said quickly. Sullivan wrote the last name. Sarah continued, "There's clearly something you're not telling me. I don't like that." Her speech was slower.

"I'm involved in an active investigation," Sullivan said, "I can't tell you everything, but I know who bugged your apartment. What I don't know is why," Sullivan intentionally slowed his speech to match her change in pace, "There's clearly something you're not telling me, and without more information, I can't help you."

"I don't know what else I could tell you," Sarah said, her voice low. Sullivan realized her soft voice was quite pleasant, and his natural inclination was to want to help her. He had to hold off from that inclination because he wasn't sure how she was involved. "I may call you again," Sarah announced. With that, the line went dead.

61.   April 5, 2001

"I told you," Peter said, "I'm with Claire now." Peter tried not to get mad at Linus. He'd been okay when Sarah broke it off a few years ago, why not now?

"So what?" Linus said, "I certainly wouldn't stop anything with a woman like Sarah ... Claire will understand." Maybe a punch in the face would make him understand.

"Yes, she might," Peter said, "But I'm not going to do it. I'm not going to do it to Claire, I'm not going to do it to myself, and I'm not going to do it to Sarah."

How could Linus be asking him to be unfaithful? They had

worked together now for years, and Linus knew Peter was a man of his word.

"Besides, in all the time I've known her," Peter continued, "I've never learned a thing about Sarah you would want to know!"

Over the years, he told Linus the three routes Sarah took to get to work. He didn't report that Sarah was faster at a mile run than he was. Sarah told him about her financial instruments, but Linus didn't care. Peter didn't report that Sarah liked it when he kissed her calves, but not her feet. He did report that she mentioned she did a lot of computer programming.

"I know that," Linus said, "Can you just call her and go out to dinner? I'm not even asking you to get it on with her."

"No, I can't," Peter said. He remembered when he told her they couldn't see each other anymore. She wasn't mad.

"Can you just give her a call? See how she's doing? See if she's seeing anyone new?"

Peter exhaled deeply. Linus needed something. He wasn't going to leave until Peter gave him something.

"Fine," Peter said. "I'll call her tonight." He'd do it with Claire listening.

62.   May 19, 2001

Cathy Henderson pulled up outside the Poinsett Hotel on a busy Saturday night. Her son, Bill, had failed out of the University of Pennsylvania and was living at home in her basement. Damn it. If he knew what it took to get him into that school. He failed to live up to his potential, but at least she got him a job at *The Artifact*, the hot wine bar in the basement of the hotel where she worked. She looked past him to the notice on the wall of the building.

The Artifact will be closed May 25th – 27th for renovations

"What's that?" Cathy asked her son.

"What?" Bill looked to the wall, "Oh, yeah, they're renovating the bar. It's good. I don't have to work next weekend. I'll get to be out for *DownTown Alive!*"

She was upset with her son. She had asked him to tell her if there was anything going on with the bar, and this was certainly something. But she had to remember, he had no idea why it meant so much to her.

He had no idea her family lived in Greenville so she could keep an eye on this very location.

He had no idea she was going to go home and notify Colonel Burkett.

He had no idea she was a sentinel for LV.

63. May 21, 2001

"This is Sarah Kiadopolis," Sullivan answered the phone first thing on Monday morning. He put down his coffee.

"Hello, Dr. Kiadopolis." Sullivan was hoping to hear from her. Linus was planning an overnight trip at the end of this week, and Sullivan planned to follow him, "I am glad to hear from you, is everything alright?"

"I'm fine," Sarah said, "Peter Howard and I were close." Sullivan had suspected that. He knew Sarah wasn't married, and she said she lived alone. "I know he knows my apartment's bugged."

"How do you know that?" Sullivan asked. Sarah paused and Sullivan was afraid she was about to hang up.

"We used to be … close," Sarah was carefully choosing her words, "He would never come to my apartment. Even if our plans changed, he'd never come up."

"Were you in a rush?" Sullivan asked, "Maybe he wanted to get where you were going?"

"No, he would want to come in," Sarah said, "Look, I know he knows. I'm not talking about this anymore. He called me a few weeks ago, and it got me thinking. He was very careful with what he said, and I put two and two together. Did he put the bugs in my apartment?"

"No," Sullivan said, "It was Linus Brenner."

"Okay, but somehow he knew about them. Maybe he knows this guy Linus Brenner? How did you know he bugged my apartment?" Sarah had a lot of questions but Sullivan had to remind himself that he was the investigator.

"I have access to his travel records. I followed him to your apartment before I met you." Sullivan opened a file containing Linus' recent travel itineraries, "I'm glad you called because he's taking a suspicious trip this Friday night to Greenville, South

Carolina."

"*Greenville!*" Sarah blurted.

Sullivan was taken aback, Greenville was meaningless to him, and he thought meaningless to her. With that, again, the line went dead.

I've talked to her three times, and every time she's ended the conversation abruptly. There's something she is not telling me, and I might find it in Greenville.

64. May 25, 2001

"This can't be the place," Sarah said under her breath to herself. She stood on the east side of Main Street in downtown Greenville looking across to the 12 story façade of the Poinsett Hotel on a bright Friday afternoon.

Greenville, South Carolina had been the heart of the textile industry until it all left for southeast Asia. The downtown fell into disrepair as the textile industry in the US collapsed under the pressure of cheap fabrics from Asia. Over the past ten years, Greenville experienced a renaissance as industries fled the unions of the northeast and relocated to more attractive places. Greenville's combination of low taxes, skilled non-union workforce, and location halfway between Atlanta and Charlotte made it a destination for business. The Poinsett Hotel was over one hundred years old and was now the cornerstone of a revitalized Main Street.

She'd purchased a map of Greenville's downtown and painstakingly laid out the geographic coordinates of the site she studied for so long. A picture of the building generated by her *Space Resonance* scans would've been helpful, but there wasn't a printer in her office. She had, however, studied the image so many times that she had it memorized. The *Space Resonance* image included the entire building and she looked at the unmistakable façade to determine that she was in the right place. The nuclear weapon was in the basement under the right front corner of the building. Despite the warmth of the afternoon, she felt a shiver when she realized she was so close to such a thing.

Sarah avoided the few cars and crossed the street to the building she'd always imagined was a research facility. The lobby was marble and reminiscent of its age but she could tell it was recently renovated. Like many old hotels, the check-in counter was out of view from the main foyer.

Sarah walked to the right and found the main stairway. She hesitated at the recognition of what was down there.

The wide marble stairs descended to a landing and Sarah walked around the corner. She felt unsettled to be there, but she was just like anyone else here today. She rounded the corner and could see below her a seating area with tables. When she reached the bottom of the stairs she was surprised to see she was in a bar.

The lone barkeep was lifting the chairs up onto the tables as though he was closing. Sarah looked at her watch. Two thirty in the afternoon seemed an odd time to be closing.

"Excuse me," Sarah called.

The barkeep looked to be in his early twenties. He was thin in a well-worn brown t-shirt with jeans and flip flops. At Sarah's call he stopped lifting a chair and flipped his hair out of his face to see her. He didn't hide his motion of looking her up and down.

Sarah looked herself up and down. She drove down from Fairfax this morning. Seven hours in the car. Her hair was windblown and she wore shorts, a pink Virginia Tech t-shirt and running shoes.

"I'm sorry, we're closing," the barkeep said, "But I'd be happy to fix you a drink!" he added.

"I'm just here looking around," Sarah felt oddly unprepared for this conversation, "I'm interested in the building."

"Oh, well you're early!"

"I'm early?"

"Yes, Agent Brenner told us to have the place cleaned up at four." He looked to another wall and a clock, "I've still got over an hour!" Agent Brenner? So Linus was coming to this bar tonight! She was right. There was no coincidence at all. The barkeep thought she was with Linus, and Sarah decided to go with it.

"He said he'd be here at four?" Sarah asked. She tried to ask casually.

"Yeah," the barkeep said, "I'm Bill, Bill Henderson." He walked over and extended his hand.

"Sarah Kiadopolis," Sarah shook his hand.

"Well, Sarah," Bill said, "You better get changed; you've got a long night!" Sarah didn't know what he was talking about, but she couldn't let him know that. She just nodded and took her hand away.

She looked around the bar. A large water fall dominated the

space but was recessed into an alcove in the wall. She walked over to it. There was a small stone box in the center. The sign over the bar said *The Artifact*, and this must have been it. The chill returned to Sarah's spine when she closed her eyes and imagined the picture she'd created of this place. She realized that small box, the centerpiece of this wine bar, was the atomic bomb! It was smaller than she'd imagined.

"That's the Indian artifact that gave us our name," Bill said, hanging around a little too much. Sarah knew there was nothing Indian about it.

. . .

Sullivan pulled out of the rental car parking lot a few cars behind Linus. Like before, he'd arrived at the airport on the flight ahead of Linus, got his car, and waited for him to come out with his rental.

This time Linus drove an Acura. Greenville was much smaller than Washington, and Sullivan found the reduced traffic a double edged sword. He had little difficulty following Linus but felt exposed.

Linus took Highway 385 straight into Greenville. The highway dissolved into a city street and Linus made a left onto Main, a street with one lane each way with two and three story buildings on each side. Sunlight dimpled the windshield through the trees lining the street.

A surprising number of people moved along the sidewalks for three-thirty on a Friday afternoon. Sullivan briefly lost himself in a daydream about Madison when he saw Linus hit his blinker.

Focus!

A young couple turned to their car. The man opened the door and dropped a shopping bag into the back seat. He waved to Linus and the couple returned to the sidewalk.

Linus turned off his blinker and continued down the street. Now Sullivan knew Linus was looking for a parking space. He decided he would take the next spot that opened to him.

A few moments later, a car signaled to back out in front of Sullivan, and he took the spot, jumped from his car, and saw Linus take a side street.

Sullivan walked down Main Street past restaurants setting up tables with white tablecloths. He wanted to find a place to sit where he could monitor the area but still not accidentally run into Linus.

Several bars along the walk had balconies on their second floors and Sullivan quickly made his way to the closest one. He hurried past the greeter and made his way to the stairs. He estimated about thirty seconds had passed by the time he stood at the railing. A glance at his watch told him it was four p.m.

Sullivan scanned the street, forcing patience. A large banner spanning the street announced *DownTown Alive* from seven to eleven. Ten restaurants were setting up tables along the street.

If he didn't re-acquire Linus this would be a short trip. Sullivan didn't want to repeat his failure in Fairfax.

There he is. Sullivan felt his body relax as he spotted his target just as Linus Brenner entered the Poinsett Hotel.

. . .

Linus had been here ten times in the past years. The town government worked closely with the business community to revitalize the downtown. It used to be a place he was happy he carried a gun. Now moms walked lazily with kids and mingled with young professionals coming off work while the bars got ready for the street fair. On very rare occasions he thought about what he'd do after this. He didn't like to think about it because he liked his job, but he thought Greenville might be a good place to end up.

Linus descended the stairs into *The Artifact*. He stood at the entrance and surveyed the scene. He remembered the first time he was here, ten years before. The building was torn apart. Peter and Claire had done a great job putting the place back together. Linus thought they were going to have to only use the space as a storage room. They'd surprised him by taking advantage of the device and accentuating it. The water running down the walls around it matched the feel of the street outside with the nearby Falls Park and the Reedy River. Since then, he'd come to know and respect both Peter and Claire. Now, he'd expect nothing less from them.

The device had served its purpose in this location, and the time had come to get it out of there. Ten years ago, he forced Claire to design a decorative box over it so no one would know they took it.

"You must be Agent Brenner?" a college kid said as he came from the store-room behind the bar.

Linus didn't like this kid already. The t-shirt and flip-flops made him look like a hobo. He was probably a dropout. He painted on a smile, "Yes, Agent Brenner."

"Well I think everything's ready for you. Mr. Pinkerton's pissed, but I don't care," Linus struggled to look at the kid. Why would Linus care about whether the owner was mad? Even more, why would he care about if the owner's idiot barkeep was mad? He just wanted him to leave. "Is that woman coming back with you tonight?"

Linus didn't answer but looked at him with a questioning look. "You must have a team coming in. One got here a little early. She said she'd be back later."

"Okay," Linus wasn't sure if he cared. Claire must have come early to check the place out.

"Yes, of course she'll be back. She's on my team," Linus said. He held his hand out indicating he was ready for the kid to leave the area.

He didn't seem to get the hint and just stood there with a stupid grin.

"Look," the kid said, "I'm obviously not working tonight. Can you give this to Sarah?" Linus accepted a folded note before he thought better.

Of course, Claire's pretty cute. He found himself feel some respect for this doofus. At least he was trying. You lose every game you don't play.

Did he say Claire?

"You mean Claire?" Linus asked.

"No, I mean Sarah."

"What was her last name?" Linus asked. He didn't have anyone named Sarah on his team.

"She told me, but I can't remember," he said, "How many pretty blonds will you have here tonight? Maybe I should come and help out! "

Linus laughed a little. "I can assure you, not many, but I do need to know who she was. Can you remember the name?"

"Look man, she was in here in shorts and a t-shirt. I almost fell over when she pulled the pencil from her hair. You can imagine I wasn't focused on her name. Something Greek, I don't know, a Greek city, polis," Kid said with a wave of his hand. "When she gets here, could you give it to her?" He indicated the note with his hand.

Sarah Kiadopolis. A Greek city.

He'd monitored her in her apartment with her pencil in her hair.

The only camera he had was in her kitchen. He once watched her cook. She was meticulous about following recipes, and she would check off the ingredients. She had a habit of twirling her hair and sticking her pencil through it to hold it in place. Then she would spend time searching for the pencil and sometimes get another one. He'd even seen her reach to place a pencil in her hair when there was already one there. For a woman he'd never seen in person or spoken too, he knew a lot about her. But she should not be here. Any chance of a coincidence was eliminated by Dr. Kiadopolis' pretending to be one of his agents. Linus collected himself and put a face on.

"Of course I'll give it to her, buddy."

. . .

By nine-thirty in the evening, the street was closed to traffic, and the bars were jammed with professionals. *DownTown Alive* was in full swing. Sullivan sat at the railing since four and hadn't seen Linus since he went into the hotel until just now.

Linus walked out of the front of the hotel dressed in work clothes and stood out compared to the partiers around him. Linus looked up and down the street.

Sullivan's attention was drawn to the building directly across from Linus. It was another bar with a balcony. A pair of legs caught his attention. Many of the people in the restaurant were nicely dressed, probably business people straight from work. Two men just left her table so the woman sat alone and was very focused down at the walk. She sat against the railing at a high table for three with her back to him. She was looking up and down the walk synchronized with Linus. When Linus looked to his right toward the street in front of Sullivan, Sullivan looked up to the woman and recognized Sarah Kiadopolis.

. . .

"Can we buy you a drink?" Sarah looked away from the street. Two young men in suits pulled back the chairs at her table. She couldn't say no, they were already sitting down. Sarah had checked into a hotel, changed into evening clothes and was nursing an hour old drink. She wanted to keep her wits about her, but she also knew the bar would ask her to leave if she didn't drink something.

"Sure, sit down," Sarah said. The guys would give her some cover from the waitress and help her keep the table. Instantly, the waitress arrived. They ordered beers and told her to get Sarah another of what she was having.

"We just started at Michaels and Michaels," the one sitting at the railing directly across from her said. Sarah looked directly at him. He was okay to look at. Dark hair, clean cut, nice clothes, lawyer.

"Really, where's that?" Sarah asked, looking him directly in the eyes. She could see his eyes tighten slightly, although his smile didn't move at all. He'd expected to impress her with his announcement.

He clearly didn't.

"Michaels and Michaels," the other one said. He sat in the chair at the head of the table facing directly over the railing, "The largest law firm in Greenville. We both just got back from training at the New York office." This one was less to look at. He had an odd shaped nose, but still had nice clothes. He was a bit thicker than the frozen face directly across from her.

"Well, that's very nice," Sarah said. She looked back to the street but didn't see anything new. She glanced back to Nose. He was looking down her low cut red blouse. His face reddened when she raised her eyebrows at him, but he managed a solid smile.

"Are you from around here?" Face asked, his smile still perfectly constructed, "You must work at one of the firms around, you must have heard of M&M?"

Sarah couldn't help but giggle at the name, even more as her suitors' faces briefly lost their smiles in disappointment.

"No, I'm here visiting on business," Sarah answered, wishing she had not...

"Really, what sort of business?" Nose asked. He didn't care, and she didn't want to answer. She could look at Face and still see the walk and the door to the hotel, but turning to Nose forced her to take her eyes entirely off the scene.

"Just visiting," She said, glancing at Nose and returning to the street.

Face's smile was wilting now. He turned to say something to his friend, but Sarah didn't hear what he said.

She saw a man step out of the hotel in jeans, work boots, and long-sleeved t-shirt. Face and Nose said something, Face looked at his watch, and they excused themselves with a big laugh, then a small grumble.

Sarah would not risk looking away from the man to address them. She saw him look up and down the block. She followed his gaze but couldn't see what he was looking at. He did this for about two minutes and then went back into the hotel.

. . .

After Linus re-entered the hotel, Sullivan quickly made his way from his bar over to Sarah's. He pushed his way through the crowd to the railing. He walked up to Sarah's table and looked over the railing to see what she was looking at. Sarah looked at him. "Was that Linus?"

"Yes," Sullivan answered, although Linus was no longer on the street below.

Apparently no introductions were necessary. Sullivan sat directly across from her, "What are you doing here?" He had to catch his breath. He looked at her leaning back in a high chair. Her red blouse was low enough that he could see the top of a black bra. Her left foot was visible on the side of the table. Her tan calf led to a black pump. Under normal circumstances, he'd barely have the guts to look at her from across the room.

"You told me you were coming to Greenville, and I wanted to see what Linus was doing," Sarah said. She looked across the table directly at him.

"Okay, but how did you know to be right here, right now?" Sullivan asked. He'd followed Linus very carefully and almost lost him. Sullivan tried to remember what he'd told Sarah about this trip. That he was going to Greenville. That was it. That was all there could be because he didn't know any more. She didn't have an answer ready.

"Will you be buying her a drink?" the waitress arrived quickly. Sarah and Sullivan both looked at the woman. She seemed hurried.

"Shit," Sarah said. She'd only briefly glanced at the waitress and looked back across the street.

Sullivan followed her eyes. She wasn't looking down at the street, but up at the building. The curtains were pulled on one of the third floor hotel rooms. Linus stood in the window and looked directly at them. He paused for a moment as he caught Sullivan's eyes. They stared at each other for a moment as Linus recognized him. Linus must have at first seen Sarah, but now saw him. There would be no explaining what they were doing together. The game was up. Sullivan would have to question him directly now. It would get messy.

Linus raised a walkie-talkie to his mouth. He spoke into it for about thirty seconds, never once taking his eyes off Sullivan. Linus was clearly giving direction to someone about Sullivan and Sarah. Sullivan believed Linus was involved in criminal activity, and probably worked with the mob, he still didn't know what Sarah had to do with it. He realized that he was no longer in danger of compromising his investigation. He was now in personal danger.

He looked back at Sarah who must have come to the same conclusion and was standing up, "We have to go."

. . .

Sarah didn't like what she saw. The color leaving Sullivan's face confirmed he didn't like it either, she decided she didn't want to be here anymore.

Sitting on that chair for an hour gave her a dead leg and tension in her back, and the crowd slowed progress to the stairs leading down to the first floor. She paused a moment to glance back to make sure Sullivan was behind her. He ran into her back and nearly pushed her down the stairs.

Thankfully the stairs were less crowded than the second floor and she could move quickly. She felt the need to run, and she felt fear, but she wasn't sure what she was running from. She had done nothing wrong. She didn't even know Linus Brenner. On the drive down, she figured if Linus saw her he would just let her pass to maintain his anonymity.

Then Sullivan found her. Sullivan said he knew Linus. Now Linus had seen Sarah with Sullivan while they were both following him. She wasn't sure why, but she was sure she didn't want to come face to face with Linus Brenner tonight.

Sarah reached the bottom of the stairs with Sullivan still on her heels. She turned the corner to head toward the door and stopped cold.

The first floor of the bar was nearly empty and she could see all the way to the front through the glass doors. She saw four men dressed in heavy jeans, work boots, and brown t-shirts quickly crossing the street from the hotel to the entrance to the bar. They didn't look like they were coming over to talk. The fear that a moment ago was abstract and potentially imaginary became very real.

She felt her elbow pulled. Sullivan had taken the lead, and she was being pulled back up the stairs.

"No!" Sarah said and tried to resist, but her fear was limiting her ability to resist.

"Follow me, there's another way," Sullivan said. Sarah's instincts told her that going up was a bad idea, but she had nothing better.

She followed him up the stairs back into the thick crowd, expecting him to push through to the front of the balcony.

Instead, he headed back toward the bar. Claustrophobia set in as she looked at the space with no openings and lots of people. Sarah was five-seven, and her heels made her five-eleven, but the crowd was full of tall businessmen. She could barely see around them. How could there be no emergency exit?

Sullivan pushed through the crowd as quickly as he could, but the going was slow. Sarah pushed tight to his back and put her hands on his waist, otherwise the crowd would close between them and she would have to push through on her own. Sullivan was taller than she was, maybe six-two and seemed to be going somewhere with purpose.

A glance told her the four men had reached the second floor. They stood at the top of the stairway scanning the crowd.

She wanted to go faster, but was happy to see that they didn't seem to know where they were.

Sullivan had come back upstairs to try to lose them in the crowd. Now they had to figure out how to get out of the crowd. She walked on her toes to try to see over Sullivan's shoulder to where they were going. The bar area was much darker than the balcony area.

Their pace slowed because the crowd grew impossibly dense as they approached the bar. Sarah looked back toward the stairs. She couldn't see any of the men. They were in the crowd with them like sharks in the ocean.

They reached the back corner of the bar. They were as far from the stairs as they could get. The corner of the room was occupied by a round booth table with a group of men and women smashed into it. Sullivan led Sarah past the booth against the back wall of the bar.

The decoration along the edge of the bar included a chair rail that in this corner was not a chair rail at all, but a push-mechanism like those on emergency exit doors! But this wasn't a door. Sarah looked up to near the ceiling. Behind a Samuel Adams neon sign was an exit sign. It was off. Her heart was pounding, but it still leapt when she began to make out the outline of the door in the wall. The door was well disguised, but it was a door! Somehow Sullivan had spotted it!

Sarah's mind briefly wandered and she considered that this doorway could not possibly meet fire code.

She looked down the bar to see that the style of the bar matched the decorations in this corner and that an emergency exit was probably a real problem for the interior designer that created this space.

Her mind was pulled back to the present when she spotted a man in a brown t-shirt staring directly at her from near the other end of the bar.

Sarah leaned into Sullivan's back to help push him through the door, but he didn't move. He was pushing the door but it was jammed against something.

Sarah pushed hard against his back, her panic returning. She knew they only had a few moments before the man reached them. She relaxed her posture and took her weight off of Sullivan's back. It didn't do any good. Sullivan looked back at her and for the first time, he didn't seem confident. His plan didn't work. She decided it was her turn to plan.

She decided she liked the anonymity of the crowd better than this little alcove.

Sarah grabbed Sullivan's hand and took the lead pushing into the crowd. Fortunately, the construction worker had only made it about halfway down the bar and his concentration was focused on pushing through the crowd. Sarah knew that the workers had split up. She pushed about ten feet into the crowd, maybe one quarter of the way to the stairs, and one tenth of the way across the room to the balcony. She stopped and turned to face Sullivan.

"Do you see them near the stairs?" Sarah asked him, but over the noise of the crowd she wasn't sure if he heard her. She looked past him to see if the construction worker making his way down the bar had changed his course.

He had not. He didn't see them leave the alcove. Then she spotted a second worker, who saw the first worker and was pushing in his direction. From the angle he was taking through the crowd, he was about to come within a few feet of them. Sarah dropped back down from her toes, but Sullivan was tall enough that she felt sure he would be spotted.

Sarah moved her head to her right, reached up to the back of Sullivan's head and pulled his head down toward her. She felt Sullivan tense, but she was quick enough, and strong enough to guide his head down to almost resting on her shoulder. From this position, she could look over his shoulder to watch the first construction worker, and her face was shielded by Sullivan from the second.

"Could you see any of them near the stairs?" She repeated.

"No," Sullivan said. He lifted his head to see, but Sarah still had a good grip on the back of his head, and pulled it back down.

"Stay down," the second construction worker came into view over Sullivan's shoulder. Sarah ducked her head in close to Sullivan hoping anyone around would think them amorous.

The first construction worker was just reaching the alcove and the second was about five feet from Sarah. There were only two people between them, "We're going to the stairs. Follow me, and keep your head down!"

Sarah broke from the relative comfort of their stance just as the two construction works reached each other and began to look around. She ducked behind some largish men talking next to them to get some bodies between her and the construction workers. She knew where two of them were, but not the other two. She hoped they were searching the balcony area. She pulled Sullivan by the hand and began to make an arc path toward the stairs. Now Sullivan had to pull up close behind her to not get separated in the crowd. He kept his head lowered, and Sarah could feel him bump into her back as she had to constantly be changing directions and speed to weave through the crowd.

"I see two of them on the balcony, but I don't see the other two," Sullivan said into her ear when they had to pause to weave around a small group. Sarah knew the other two were behind them, and with that information, she began to push harder toward the stairs. She made her path more direct and closed the ten feet quickly.

Sarah felt tremendous relief and fought the urge to laugh as they broke from the crowd and descended the stairs. Sullivan pulled back from her and she was glad to have no one within two feet of her for a moment.

At the bottom of the stairs, about to round the corner, she paused. Sullivan quickly stepped around her and looked out.

"I don't see anyone, and it won't take long for those guys to start coming down the stairs," Sullivan said, his eyes wide and a half smile on his lips.

He took the lead toward the front door. Sarah followed quickly. There were far fewer people downstairs and they covered the distance to the front door in only a few seconds. They were nearly running when they burst out onto the sidewalk.

Sullivan turned right out the door, and Sarah turned left.

"My car..." they both said in unison.

In the brief pause, Sarah glanced up to the third floor of the hotel. Linus was still in the window. He was banging on the glass with the walkie-talkie he had used to call his men to get them.

He pointed in the direction Sullivan was headed.

Three men were walking quickly toward them.

Sarah looked back up at Linus. Why would he have pointed out his men coming for them? He was now waving, beckoning them into the hotel.

"My car," Sarah turned and ran away from the men, away from Linus, and away from the bar. There was only one way to go. She was glad she could run as she covered about a block. Sullivan was right behind her, and she knew that the men were running now.

She couldn't believe it when a motorcycle appeared from a narrow side street and screeched to a halt in front of them. Sarah hit the back of the bike and pushed with her entire body against it and the rider.

They went down hard.

Sarah found herself lying on top of the bike and its rider. She looked into the helmet of a man who was grabbing at her. She struggled to get away but he had a hold on her.

Suddenly the hold released.

Sullivan had kicked the driver in the helmet. He pulled her up by the shoulders and they ran down the opening the bike had emerged from.

They ran about fifty yards at full speed, Sarah in heels. She knew she could keep this up for a while longer, but the collision with the bike had twisted her right leg a bit and now she began to feel her right quad burn. Just before she left the walk between the two buildings, she looked to her left, back toward where they had come, to see that the three men were still running toward them and the first of the construction workers was joining them from the bar.

There were now seven men chasing them, plus the motorcycle.

Sarah's leg was hurting, but she knew she could make it to her car about a block away. Sullivan was keeping up okay. At the end of the alley they reached another street and Sarah turned right. Her car was parked about fifty feet ahead. She pulled her keys from a small pocket in the hem of her skirt as she ran. She was never happier to have automatic locks and a remote starter.

She lost little time getting into the car and Sullivan did the same on the passenger side. She was in a parallel parking space and she quickly put the car in drive.

Sullivan pushed the automatic door locks just as the first of the men reached the side of the car.

The windows were down and a man reached through to grab Sullivan. The man on Sarah's side didn't reach in, but he had a gun.

The sight of the gun shocked her.

Sarah hit the gas and the car lurched forward. She turned the wheel, but didn't have enough room, and the corner of her car hit the rear corner of the car in front of her. She pushed harder on the gas. There were metal sounds as they pushed through the car in front. That car acted as a wiper to push the man off Sullivan, and she squealed her tires as she pulled onto the street. Sullivan pointed to the first left they came to, and Sarah took it.

. . .

"What's going on?" Claire asked as Linus hurried down the stairs. They'd been working steadily on extracting the burial cyst for a few hours. Claire didn't know what was inside, but she was sure it wasn't bones. Throughout the planning process for tonight, and for the two times they'd done this in California, she told Linus it would be much easier to do this if she knew what was inside.

He told her she knew enough.

One team was assembling rigging to lift the cyst onto a cart so they could move it to the stairs down to the back entrance. Another team was assembling a rigging system to get it down the stairs.

Claire didn't know what was inside but she knew it had electronics, it was heavy, and it was not to be tipped over or dropped.

A few moments ago, Linus had come down the stairs and demanded that the stair-rigging team go with him to *take care of something*. They were on a tight schedule and Claire didn't think she could spare the four men for long.

Now he returned without them!

"We have a bit of a situation upstairs," Linus said, "Mark, Chris and Jeff, I need your help!" The remaining three men stopped what they were doing and moved without question.

"Wait!" Claire complained, "What are we supposed to do?" She gestured between herself and Peter.

"You keep going as best you can," Linus said without looking at her.

"Can't we help you?" Peter asked.

"I've told you before," Linus said, "I've got these guys to help with this type of thing. I need you to stay here!"

Claire tensed. That meant there was something violent going on upstairs. She forgot that Linus and some of the others carried guns. It was just part of the process. They never once needed them. Peter moved to Claire's side and took her hand as the four men left them.

. . .

"You're bleeding," Sullivan looked at Sarah's leg. She was driving fast. She made a hard right to beat a light to follow the signs back onto highway 385. The road wasn't an interstate yet and Sarah squealed the tires as she came to a stop at a light.

Sarah's skirt was above the knee and it was torn on her right leg exposing most of her thigh. Her leg flexed rapidly pushing the accelerator and relaxing as her left leg worked the clutch. Her right hand moved quickly on the gear shifter as she accelerated onto the highway. The flurry of motion that was Sarah combined with the street lamps' intermittent light shining through the car made it difficult for Sullivan to assess her injury. But he knew there was a lot of blood.

Sullivan looked up at Sarah. Her face was intent on her driving. Her eyes were alternating between the road and her mirrors. She glanced at Sullivan and followed his eyes down to her leg. Her eyes returned to the road, but were wider now.

"The motorcycle," Sarah said, "I knew I pulled something, but I didn't think there was a cut, how bad is it?"

Sullivan moved closer to her leg, shifting his weight in his seat and lowered his head. He was tentative. His own shadow made it a bit darker, but also reduced variation in light level from the street lights. He could see there was blood over much of her thigh and that it had run down her leg while she was running. "It's hard to tell, can you stop?"

"I don't want to," Sarah accelerated to eighty as the highway began.

"I can't tell how old the blood is," Sullivan said, still trying to make out what he was seeing.

"There are wet napkins under my elbow," Sarah raised her elbow keeping her hand on the wheel, exposing a small console lid.

Sullivan looked from her leg to the console, and then up to her face, which was now about eighteen inches away. She glanced at him and wordlessly commanded him to proceed. He fumbled with the wet wipes lid but was able to get one out. He reached under her right arm with his left and moved her skirt to open the tear and expose more of the wound. He looked up at her but she stayed focused on her driving.

Sullivan hunched over so that he could get a closer look. He was having trouble distinguishing between the tan of her leg and the color of blood in the fluorescent lighting provided by the street lights. He was pretty sure he was seeing almost all blood. He couldn't see a large cut, or another origin of the blood, so he put the wipe directly in the center of her leg. Her leg flexed and her foot briefly pulled back from the accelerator. She inhaled sharply.

"Are you okay?" Sullivan looked up.

"It stings a little," Sarah bit her lip, "keep going." Sullivan pulled the wipe down her leg toward her knee. The wipe cleaned the blood away making clear lines between her skin and the blood at the edges of the wipe. There was no cut. In fact, her leg looked like there was no injury at all. Then, blood re-appeared, coming directly from her skin. He'd been looking for a cut, but he found an abrasion. Apparently, when she hit the motorcycle, it rubbed the top layers of skin off the top of her thigh. He wiped again, and again she inhaled sharply, her leg flexed, and this time her right hand reflexively pushed his hand away.

"I'm sorry," Sullivan said, "it looks like an abrasion." Sarah lifted her hand into the light and Sullivan saw the color in her face drop a tone as she saw the blood on her fingers.

"It's... It's fine ... I'm fine," Sarah collected herself. She held out her hand and Sullivan pulled another wipe from the container and wiped the blood from it.

"You need medical attention," Sullivan said. He pulled another wipe from the container. All he could do was clean her leg and apply pressure. That would at least make her feel better.

"No," Sarah pushed the wipe away, "The wipe hurts a lot."

Sullivan realized there was alcohol in the wipe, and over a large abrasion, the stinging would be much worse than *a little* as she had previously reported. "I have a towel in the bag in the back seat." Sullivan retrieved the towel and pressed it to her leg. Again, she inhaled, but not as sharply. Sullivan held the towel on her leg, applying some pressure. He studied her face. He was happy to see some of her color had returned. She was still studying the road and her mirrors intently.

Except for his hand on her thigh things were briefly calm. He turned his body back so that he was in his seat properly, always keeping the pressure on her leg, and thought about what had just happened.

"Sarah," Sullivan asked, "How did you know that Linus would be at that building?"

"What?" Sarah looked over at him. Her eyes were still focused, and her face looked hard, almost too thin, "You asked me that before..."

"Yes, I did," Sullivan said, "I don't know what you're doing here, but I do know I told you I was coming here, and maybe you decided to see for yourself what I was doing. But I can't figure out how you could know to come to the Poinsett..."

"Oh no," Sarah groaned, "I think were not alone." Sullivan nearly groaned himself. This was the second time he was asking her this, and the second time he couldn't get an answer. Sullivan followed her eyes to her rear view mirror. He looked behind them and saw a pair of headlights that was definitely moving aggressively through traffic. The car was behind a pair of cars driving next to each other. Sullivan was glad to feel Sarah accelerating her Civic, moving to the right lane. She was forced to slow down, but it was clear she was going to take an exit. Sullivan looked back and saw the follower moving to the right.

"Sarah, pass this car, move back to the left," Sullivan had an idea.

"I'm going to exit here, try to lose him in the neighborhoods," Sarah also had a plan.

"No, pass, *now*," Sullivan commanded. Sarah followed the instruction and mashed the accelerator, weaving back into the left lane and missing her opportunity to turn off. Sullivan watched as the car following them also quickly moved to the left lane.

"Get past this car, *fast*," Sullivan saw the end of the off ramp approaching. He looked back and saw the follower move into the shoulder past the left lane to get around a car. It was now next to the blocking cars and only about five car lengths behind them. "Get off!" Sullivan pointed to the end of the off ramp that was now impossibly close to them.

Sarah turned the wheel without slowing at all, and made a hard right turn from the center lane. Her tires squealed, and it felt as though the car would flip. Sullivan leaned to the right hoping to keep the car down.

The nose of the car missed the guard rail and they sped down the off-ramp. Sullivan looked back. The car they were passing slammed on the brakes and was rear-ended by the blocking car in the right lane. Their follower could do nothing but continue to pass the cars and get back into its own lane.

Sullivan put his head back on his head rest and exhaled. A smile crossed his face. They'd done it. They were going to get away. They'd drive somewhere safe and figure out who to call.

He felt a lot better until he looked over at Sarah.

Her eyes were wide, and her face pale. She gripped the steering wheels so tight her knuckles were white.

"Sarah," Sullivan said. She didn't respond as she turned left.

"Sarah," Sullivan said, a little louder, "Maybe we could stop now." Sarah blinked. She slowly looked over at him. She normally looked healthy, tan, strong … beautiful. Now she looked like she was in shock. Her cheeks were hollow; her lips tightly pressed together; her eyes still unable to focus on one thing.

"Sarah, Stop the car," Sullivan tried. Sarah looked away, returning to driving. She expertly took a right turn off the secondary road into a neighborhood. She pulled the car to a stop in front of a large home, next to a large tree. She efficiently took the car out of gear, pulled the emergency break, killed the engine, turned off the lights, and collapsed over the steering wheel.

Sullivan's hand was still on her thigh, and he could feel her body shake from light sobbing. He leaned back in his seat, unsure of how to proceed but happy to be stopped. He started to pull his hand away, but her hand quickly stopped him and held his pressure to her thigh through the towel.

. . .

"We lost them!" the walkie-talkie squawked.
Damn!

His team that was supposed to be quietly working in the basement was loudly roaring around town. This was not how tonight was supposed to go.

"They took the exit for, uh, Roper Mountain Road ... Should we come back?" The walkie-talkie asked.

"Find them!" He shouted into his walkie-talkie, "We've got to get them first!" He didn't know what Sarah Kiadopolis was doing here, and maybe he wouldn't have cared. It was entirely possible that she would know about the Greenville Poinsett Hotel, and maybe she had even visited it before. But why today, and why was she impersonating one of his agents? And what was she doing with that paper-pusher Sullivan Acer? Linus tried to remember what Sullivan did, exactly. They'd crossed paths a few times in the past ten years, and he didn't like him ... Ah yes, he was in *Special Audits*. The Special Audits Unit was responsible for looking into the behavior of employees within the agency. In the police, they called it Internal Affairs, and everyone hated them. Linus' eyes squinted involuntarily.

Sullivan must be investigating Linus! If he was with Sarah, Sullivan probably knew that Linus was monitoring her. That would bring him dangerously close to learning something. Linus decided that he was right to pursue them. He had to determine their connection and determine what they knew. It was unfortunate that he had to delay his primary purpose here, but that could wait.

He pulled off the highway onto Roper Mountain Road and consulted the tracking device he'd attached to Sarah's Civic seven years ago.

. . .

Sarah felt shaky all over.

She could feel the adrenaline fading and could tell that it was what had sustained her since she left the relative comfort of the bar table what seemed like days ago. Her head rested on the steering wheel while she tried to get a grip on her emotions. Yesterday, she was sitting in her apartment deciding to take a weekend trip to Greenville to do a little poking around. She hoped that maybe she would see this Linus Brenner. She hoped to get an idea of what he was doing. Now, she was sitting in her car, her leg was hurting, and she was being chased by men with guns who wanted who-knows-what. She'd caused a car accident, and her only comfort was holding the hand of this man, Sullivan. She knew she cried for a moment. It surprised her because she didn't normally do that. She thought Sullivan could tell, but she decided to let it go. Her head was spinning.

She lifted her head and looked at Sullivan. His head was resting back against the head rest, and his eyes were closed. Somehow he sensed her head lift because his eyes popped open, and he looked at her. He flashed a weak smile, but concern was visible on his face.

"I'm okay," Sarah said, "I just needed a moment. Thank you."

"No problem," Sullivan said, "Take all the time you need, I think we got away."

Sarah thought about what they'd done. Sullivan's maneuver worked on their chase car. They were on a random street, and their car was dark. She pulled the lever and let her seat recline back.

"I think we should go," Sarah said, "But I want to rest here for a moment." She wanted to look at her leg, but she realized she wasn't ready. She looked down at the towel. It was dark and she couldn't tell anything.

"I think it might actually be a burn, right under where I am pressing," Sullivan said anticipating her question "It looks deep. You must have hit the muffler on that bike."

"It feels like it, too," Sarah said, smiling a little.

"I think we need to find a hospital," Sullivan said.

"Okay," Sarah said, "But I think you're going to have to drive." Sullivan nodded relieved agreement and took his hand from under hers on her thigh. He sat up, looked around, and opened the car door.

The opening of the door was like opening the door of a vault that they were safely hiding in. Sarah felt the rush of the world return to her. Her senses sharpened. She tried to survey the area around the car. Were they still looking for them? Would they check hospitals? Did the driver of the bike know how badly she was hurt? Maybe they shouldn't go to the hospital?

She was startled when Sullivan appeared in her view out the driver's side window. He tried the door but it was locked. Sarah hit the button and all the car doors unlocked. Sullivan opened the door and paused. She felt like she was on display, stretched out in the reclined driver's seat with her skirt ripped. She reflexively tried to sit up, and the flexing of her quad sent bolts of pain that curled her toes and almost made her cry out.

"Hold on," Sullivan said. He moved to the back driver's side door. He opened it and knelt down. From this position, his head was nearly level with hers, "I'm going to push you up, ready?"

"Slowly." Sarah said. She hoped it was only the flexing of the muscle, and not any motion that set off the pain, otherwise she might not get out of this car.

Sarah felt the seat lever release, and she felt Sullivan slowly push her up into a sitting position. It was a struggle for her to let him do all the lifting. The pain was manageable as long as she didn't flex her quad.

Now she was sitting up, and she could look at her leg. She looked down at the towel. It was completely red with her blood. The sight made her queasy.

"Don't look under the towel," Sullivan said. He was at her side in the driver's side door now and he'd read her mind.

"I want to see it."

"No, you don't," Sullivan said. Sarah decided he was right. Maybe when she was in the passenger seat, and she had a little time to warm up to it. She thought the event of moving would be difficult enough without vomit to deal with.

Sullivan slid his right arm behind her shoulders while Sarah moved her left leg out of the car. Sarah let her shoe slide off and let Sullivan guide her bare foot to the curb. She let go of her skirt to use both hands to grab her leg at the knee and pull it out of the car. She was careful not to flex her quad. She was now facing directly at Sullivan.

"Ready?" Sullivan asked.

"Yes," Sarah said, "Thank you."

Sullivan heaved her to a standing position with surprisingly little effort. Sarah was briefly light headed and rested her head on his left shoulder. She opened her eyes and saw someone walking toward them down the sidewalk. He was about thirty yards away. The sight didn't immediately concern her because they were in a neighborhood. Normal people walked sometimes.

He passed under a street light. He was too far away to make out his face under his baseball hat, but he was wearing a long-sleeved t-shirt and work boots.

"Sullivan," Sarah said, "Linus Brenner!" They were so focused on moving her around in the car that they let their guard down and didn't see him approaching.

"Yes, we'll have to deal with him sometime," Sullivan said, "but right now it's just some people walking up the street." Sullivan had a view past the back of the car. Sarah lifted her head. Two people were approaching from the back of the car, about as far away as Linus Brenner was from the front.

Sarah felt herself lift off the ground.

Sullivan picked her up with an arm under her knees in a swift, fluid motion. He moved quickly around the back of the car.

Sarah saw the two men start running toward them.

She felt her heart rate accelerate. Seeing one of the men stop scared her more than seeing them both running.

The man on the left stopped running and pulled something from his jacket. He extended it in front of him. He was between street lights, so it was a little dark, but it looked like he was pulling out a gun!

Sullivan rounded the back of the Civic. Sarah forced her legs from his arm and they fell to the ground. The pain she expected was muted by her rising adrenaline levels.

"Duck!" For the first time, Sarah felt Sullivan rough with her as he pushed her down behind the car. She fell to her hands and knees. Her thigh pushed through the tear in her skirt, and she got her first view of her leg. In the dim light she saw the deep redness of her missing skin. She froze as her eyes focused on the sight. As Sullivan had described, she had a wide abrasion, but the bad part was near the top of her thigh. She had never seen under skin and was mesmerized. Was she looking directly at the muscle tissue of the leg? She felt her nausea returning in the brief moment of relative calm. She closed her eyes and became aware of the pressure on her back from Sullivan's hands holding her down. He was on one knee and had his head stretched up so he could see what was happening.

Sarah thought she would hear gunfire. She'd never heard it before but knew that it was very loud.

Instead, she heard an occasional popping sound.

Sullivan's right hand released its pressure.

She pushed up and looked over the door panel through the windows of her car.

To her left she saw the man who had stopped, holding a gun outstretched. He was behind one of the large trees for protection. He fired. A bright muzzle blast lit up the area around him for a brief instant. The shot was accompanied by a popping sound, and she realized they must have silencers.

She looked to the right and saw Linus had taken up a similar position behind another tree and was returning fire with a similar weapon with a similar popping sound.

"Where's the other guy?" Sarah asked.

Her question was interrupted by an electric sound behind Sullivan. His body tensed and his eyes rolled back in his head. He went limp and fell hard on the pavement.

Behind him, the third man held a Taser.

Sarah moved to dive into her car but her wounded leg failed her. She fell to the ground beside Sullivan.

The man ducked as a bullet hit her car so that he was crouched over her. Sarah was frozen with fear as the man extended his hand and applied the Taser to her stomach.

She briefly felt her body tense before she passed out.

June, 2001

65. June 1, 2001

Loud static.

Every muscle in Sarah's body fought the man above her. He didn't put his full weight on her, yet he seemed to be everywhere.

Her legs were pinned. Every time she flexed her right leg pain shot to her toes, and nausea returned. She fought through it. She was fast enough to keep her arms free from his grip, but he was fast enough to block every blow she tried to throw.

Sarah realized her eyes were closed. She couldn't remember when she closed them.

She thought of the shoot-out she witnessed. Sullivan must be lying right beside her, unconscious. She was lying on the pavement next to her car, fighting off this attacker who seemed to be everywhere. There were two of them. Maybe the second had arrived and was helping hold her down. That would explain the hands everywhere.

She focused on the tense muscles around her eyes to force them open.

They were open.

She could only see darkness, and she was having trouble

determining if her eyes were open or closed. Maybe the pain was interfering with her ability to concentrate, or maybe it was the men on top of her.

Her head flailed side to side as her arms and legs fought hard. There was nothing to grab, they were too fast. She couldn't see anything. She couldn't see her car, Sullivan, her attacker, the tree above, or the stars in the sky.

Then she saw a bright red light. It seemed impossibly bright. It was to her left at road level. She looked to her left pausing in her defense. She focused on the light, clearing her head. Her arms and legs moved on autopilot and seemed to hold off her attackers.

Transfixed on the light she then noticed that her head wasn't on pavement.

A pillow?

Next to the bright red light was a lamp?

She turned her head back to her attacker. Her eyes had adjusted to the faint light and she could see the outline of … a ceiling? Her fists unclenched and she could feel soft fabric. She grabbed it and realized it was a blanket.

There were no hands.

There was no attacker.

There was no second attacker.

She could hear her heart beating in her ears. She closed her eyes tight again. Sarah forced her arms to stop moving. Then she forced her legs to stop moving. Every muscle in her body was tense. She opened her eyes, still not moving, focusing all her efforts on determining where she was. She was in a bed. She was alone. Her eyes searched for anything familiar. There was nothing familiar about the ceiling.

She carefully released the blanket with her left hand and reached out to the lamp next to her bed. Her muscles remained tight and her head was filled with her heart pounding. She reached out slowly, like she was about to touch a hot stove. She reached to the red light. The light was part of a small device that she tentatively took into the palm of her hand. She found a slide-control and moved it a fraction of an inch.

The lamp came to life. Her eyes protested the bright light. She pushed the slider further. The room got brighter. She was holding a dimmer for the light next to her bed.

She was alone in a small bedroom. She lifted her head to survey the room. There was a small night stand next to the bed holding the lamp and the dimmer. Across the room was a chair. On the chair she saw a pile of neatly folded clothes.

Her clothes.

How did she get into this bed? Who put her there? What was she wearing? She slid her hands down her body and determined she was wearing a bra and panties. She lifted the covers enough to determine that it was her bra. Her muscles relaxed some. She tried to calm herself enough to think, forced her breathing to slow and hoped it would slow her heart rate.

She heard movement outside the door and she shot up to sitting in the bed. Her thigh protested. She had to remember to not flex it.

She was not alone.

Her heart rate accelerated. She quickly turned the light back off. Then she thought better of it and set the light to its minimum brightness.

She didn't want to be undressed when they came.

She threw back the covers in a quick motion and jumped from the bed. Pain shot through her thigh, almost too much to bear.

Almost.

At the chair, she set her blouse aside and grabbed her skirt. Hers was badly ripped the night before, but this one was not. It must've been a replacement. She quickly put it on. The movement seemed to be coming toward her.

She surveyed her room for options. There were no windows. There was nothing to use as a weapon. She didn't think she had time to put on her blouse. She ran across the room, less interested in noise now, grabbed the comforter from the bed, and pushed her body into the corner that would be behind the door when it opened. She wrapped herself in the comforter. She didn't know what she would do when the door opened, but her fight or flight reflex was active. There was no place to run, so she would fight. She looked back at the lamp.

She risked reaching out from her hiding place to grab the lamp. She put it on the floor, pinning it with her right foot. She turned it off with the dimmer, and yanked the cord free. She returned to her corner and wrapped the blanket tightly around herself. She held the exposed wires in her right hand and the dimmer control in her left.

. . .

Despite his eyes fighting to stay closed, Sullivan registered that it was dim in his room. He felt like he had slept for a long time and enjoyed the feeling of his pillow. His mind was groggy. He felt confident that he didn't have to be anywhere. He didn't get to sleep in often and was taking advantage of this opportunity.

Sullivan knew that this early morning dozing was delicate. He felt as though he was floating down a stream. He had to keep the stream clear of any difficult rocks. Once he hit the first rock, no matter how small, he knew the stream became turbulent and quickly he would be pulled into the present and wake up.

He thought of sitting on the deck of his parents' lake house watching the water and the boats slowly drift by. He thought of his Danny. He'd recently taught his son to spell his name leading to a series of high-fives that ended in Danny tackling Sullivan to the ground. There was little in the world better than a happy three-year-old. Wait, Danny wasn't three. He was twelve. That was years ago.

He could feel the rapids accelerating. Sullivan's eyes opened again. This time they stayed open long enough to focus on the wall. It was not his wall, and the night stand next to the bed was not his night stand. He was on travel. Often on travel his work didn't require him to get up early, so he'd sleep in. This had to be one of those mornings.

He remembered the airport yesterday. The rapids began to accelerate more. He clearly remembered Linus in the window of the Poinsett Hotel pointing down the sidewalk.

Of all the scenes to jump into his head, why that one?

The rapids slowed briefly as he remembered Sarah pulling his head down to hers.

He shot through all the rapids when he remembered shooting. Linus was shooting. Sullivan was carrying Sarah. Pain in his back. He must have been shot!

He looked more carefully at the room. No, he was not in a hospital. He willed his right arm to motion and felt around his back and found no bandages or other indication of injury.

No shirt, but that was normal for him.

Not his room. Not in a hospital.

The room had no windows, no television, and no phone. The clock blinked 12:00. Not a hotel either.

The door was a normal six-panel interior door like his parents had in their home. There wasn't any light coming around it.

He had no idea what time it was.

The last thing he remembered was crouching behind the car with Sarah at about eleven p.m.

Sullivan stood. He was wearing his boxer shorts as he normally did when he slept. He didn't remember getting into this bed, but he got in himself.

His clothes were draped on a chair. He searched his suit pockets for his wallet or watch.

Nothing.

His clothes appeared cleaned and pressed. He pulled on the slacks, his t-shirt, and his button down blue shirt. He picked up the tie but decided against it. He went to the door.

He half expected it to be locked, but it opened without complaint.

The room beyond was dark except for the light shining through the doorway. He found a light switch next to his door and two ceiling lights gave the impression the large, single space was divided in two. To his left, one light was over a living room with a couch and two over-stuffed chairs. The back of the couch further divided that space, and to his right, the second light was over a small kitchen complete with table and four chairs.

The entire space was carpeted in a beige carpet. The walls were bare white. Each had a door. Sullivan realized that there were no windows in this room either. He went to the kitchen. The clocks on the microwave and stove both flashed 12:00.

Crossing back to the living room, Sullivan turned the TV on.

Loud Static.

He quickly dropped the volume. The loud sound heightened his senses and called his attention to the fact that he had not heard any noise since waking up. He quickly went through a few channels and found no signal. Behind the TV there were two cable jacks, but there was no wire connected to either.

Two of the other doors were the same six panel interior doors he had on his room. The fourth door, next to the kitchen was not the same. It was a heavy exterior door. He began to cross the room but stopped short.

It didn't have a door handle.

This realization made him more uncomfortable than his inability to determine what time it was. No windows, a door he was not meant to open, and no clocks. He tried to remain calm. He had two more doors to try.

The door next to the TV opened to a simple bathroom with a

sink in a wide countertop, a toilet, and a shower. He went through the drawers in the vanity and found it stocked with toothpaste, toothbrushes, soaps, shampoo, and toilet paper. The sink worked. No windows.

He went to the third door. It opened as easily as the others. This room was a bedroom exactly like his. The bed was empty, but clearly slept in. Sullivan looked to the chair and saw the red blouse Sarah wore last night.

"Sarah," Sullivan said.

"Sullivan!" Sarah's voice called from behind the door as it pushed against him.

He let it close with them both in Sarah's room. It was dark. She pushed directly into him and he grabbed her. He found himself holding a lump of fabric. She must have been wrapped in the comforter from her bed. He felt her leaning into him, and he had to hold nearly all of her weight.

"Help me back to the bed," Sarah said. The three steps back to the bed were quick, but she limped heavily. Despite his efforts, she fell hard onto the bed. She moved away from him.

"Sarah, where's your light?" Sullivan asked.

"It's broken," Sarah said, "Do you know where we are?"

"No, it appears we're in an apartment with no windows, and no way out. Do you know how we got here?"

"No, can you hand me my blouse?"

Sullivan moved across the room carefully in the dark. He found the chair and easily found the silk of her blouse against the fabric of the chair. He stood awkwardly holding the blouse.

"Please, put it on the bed," Sarah directed, "Is anyone outside the door?"

"No," Sullivan answered as he tossed the blouse on the bed, "we're alone. Do you know-"

"Open the door and look into the next room," Sarah interrupted.

Sullivan followed the instruction. His eyes hurt briefly as his pupils re-adjusted to the light in the living room and he heard the blankets moving behind him. He assumed Sarah was dressing. She continued, "I don't know how we got here. The last thing I remember is a man Tasing you, and then me." Sullivan couldn't remember the Taser.

"How long have you been awake?" Sullivan asked.

"I heard rustling in the next room, I felt very groggy," Sarah said, "then I heard static, and I was awake. Maybe two minutes. I might need some help." Sullivan hesitated before he turned slowly, giving Sarah time to correct his interpretation. She did not.

Sarah sat on the edge of the bed with both bare feet on the floor. She was in her skirt and blouse.

Sullivan saw a clean bandage on her right leg. "Is your leg hurting?"

"Not bad, but I'll have to get used to it," Sarah said. She reached out her hand. Sullivan took it and helped her to her feet. He was relieved she was able to stand without much assistance. They took a step toward the door, and she leaned on him heavily. The next step required less assistance, and after they crossed the five steps to the door she was nearly walking without help. Then she paused.

"Are you okay?" Sullivan asked.

"Yes, I just don't know what's out there."

. . .

"What?" Peter opened his door to the heavy knocking. It was early, and he and Claire couldn't imagine who would be there first thing in the morning.

"I need your help," Linus Brenner walked past Peter and into the condo.

Claire pulled on a robe and stepped into the main room.

"No, we're not just going to drop everything every time you feel like it," Peter said. He tried to be tough, but he had a feeling he'd be doing whatever Linus asked.

"I need your help with Sarah Kiadopolis," Linus said.

Peter looked at the man. His eyes were open. He didn't seem to be his normal, manipulative self.

. . .

Any level of comfort Sarah felt after Sullivan showed her around their *apartment* immediately disappeared with the first sound of footsteps.

The footsteps were heavy. There were several people walking.

She looked to the door with no handle. She hoped it would open. Then she realized that she desperately hoped it would not.

Her flight instinct was kicking in, but she knew there was nowhere to go. The look on Sullivan's face betrayed the same feelings.

The footsteps stopped right outside their door. Sarah stood and turned to face the doorway. Sullivan joined her shoulder to shoulder. The door opened out of the apartment as she took Sullivan's hand.

Her heart beat into her throat. She saw a cement floor behind the door. She realized she wasn't breathing, and she could tell Sullivan wasn't either.

A woman's high-heeled shoe appeared in the space of the floor.

Sarah's eyes traveled up the woman. She had bare pale legs, a black pencil-skirt, and a red blouse. After a brief pause in the doorway, she stepped into the room, and the door closed behind her without her help.

Sarah felt Sullivan's body relax. Sarah was very wary, but she also couldn't help but relax a bit. She was prepared for a group of large, impossibly strong men with guns, or clubs, or knives to enter, but instead a disarming, almost familiar woman entered.

The three stood staring at each other. The woman had a soft smile on her mouth, but her eyes were tense. Her hair fell simply on her shoulders. She wore no jewelry and little makeup. She was a bit shorter than Sarah.

"Please sit on that sofa," the woman said after what seemed an eternity, but was probably thirty seconds. She gestured to the only sofa in the room. She spoke in a clear, strong voice with a slight accent.

Sullivan moved toward the sofa. His body pulled away from hers and Sarah felt exposed. Sarah tightened her grip on Sullivan's hand and allowed him to guide her to the sofa without turning her back to the new visitor.

When they both were standing in front of the couch, the woman began to walk into the room. After a hesitant first step, she broke into a comfortable stride.

She again extended her hand, "Please, sit." As she moved in a wide arc around the room, Sullivan and Sarah pivoted. When she stood next to the television, and they could see her from the sofa, they sat.

She reached behind herself and produced a cable in her right hand.

"Please remain seated," the woman looked at both of them to convince herself that they would not move. She then turned her back to them and worked with the cable and the television.

Sarah noted she no longer felt her heart in her chest.

"She's wearing your clothes!" Sullivan leaned to her and whispered. She looked down briefly at her own clothes and looked back up in amazement. Sarah's clothes were exactly the same as the woman's. The woman paused a moment at the sound, but then returned to her work without turning.

"Yes," Sarah said, squeezing Sullivan's hand. She wanted to focus and not talk to Sullivan.

The woman stood, turned to face them, ran her hands down her skirt to straighten it, and sat straight-backed on the edge of the closest over-stuffed chair.

She looked at Sarah with the same soft smile, but her eyes were still hard. She focused her attention on the television and the remote control.

The room filled with the static that woke Sarah up as the television came on. The woman placed the remote control on an arm of the chair and sat with her hands in her lap looking directly at Sarah.

The static on the television was replaced by the NBC nightly news. The anchor man stood on his set introducing the show. Sarah didn't watch the nightly news, but clearly she was supposed to watch tonight. She tried to focus on what the anchor was saying.

The channel changed to the CBS evening news, a similar looking man on a similar looking set, saying similar things.

Then the channels changed more rapidly. Sarah glanced at the woman who sat motionlessly watching her. Clearly, she wasn't changing the channels. Soon they were in the hundreds. The station stopped on channel 556.

Some sort of home-improvement channel. Bob Vila, or someone who looked just like him, was walking through a house talking about replacing some stairs.

The channel changed to 557. A new car commercial. That commercial was replaced with another, something about weight loss. Sarah glanced at the woman, who was only watching her.

A lot was happening, and Sarah couldn't figure out what she was supposed to be looking at. Certainly they didn't want her to watch some commercials. She was trying to take in everything not knowing what she was going to need later. She wanted to look at the woman, but the woman wasn't moving. There was something familiar about her. Sarah thought it was the clothes.

The TV changed back to 556, stairs. Then it changed back to 557, commercial.

Back to 556 and the stairs.

557, new commercial, telephone service.

The channel changing accelerated and was now moving back and forth between 556 and 557 fast enough that the image only briefly showed and there was little chance to see what they were watching.

The woman's hands were small. She was skinny, like a model. She didn't look like she worked out. She had a model's severe beauty, like Angie, not Sarah's athletic build. She tried to keep her face relaxed, but the tension in the tendons of her neck revealed her disquiet.

Did she know her from somewhere?

Suddenly an image appeared on the screen. It was not Bob Vila or the commercials. It was a large desk in a well decorated room.

Sarah felt Sullivan's hand tense. She'd forgotten she was holding it. Sarah looked at him. He was transfixed on the television screen. Looking back to the TV, she vaguely recognized the room.

Sullivan stood as a man settled into the chair behind the large desk. Sarah didn't know why, but she stood, too.

. . .

"Dr. Sarah Kiadopolis," the man now settled behind the desk called directly to her, "I am President George Bush. Six days ago, you were sitting in a bar across the street from the Poinsett Hotel in Greenville, South Carolina. You were taken from that location into custody by an organization called LV. During the chase you were injured on your right thigh, an injury I have been assured is being treated. For the past ten years, you've been working to prove your theory of *Space Resonance*, funded by the government. You are to provide your captors with any technical information they request related to your work on *Space Resonance*. Your complete cooperation is imperative in this matter. Good Luck."

. . .

"We're clear!" The camera crew chief called. President Bush relaxed back into his chair behind his desk in the Oval Office. Before him stood a camera man, a tech, and the crew chief. Thankfully the bright lights turned off, and his eyes began to adjust to the normal lighting in the room. The President watched as the camera man slowly moved out from behind the camera and all three support personnel stared at him in disbelief. He looked away.

"That will be all," Jim Williams said. He sat behind the production crew in front of the fireplace. The President heard immediate action from the three as they quickly collected their equipment and left the room. Finally the door closed and the President began, "Were they cleared to hear that?"

"Yes, Mr. President," Jim replied, "They're part of my team."

"What are we doing now?" The President asked.

Jim stood and walked quickly across the room, "Mr. President, we're doing everything we can do, but there isn't much to go on." Mr. Williams settled into the chair next to the President's desk, "Of course, we immediately collected all the surveillance tapes from the street where they were chased and from all the bars, hotels, banks, and businesses up and down Main Street and the side streets in Greenville. But we're getting amazingly little information. Teams interviewed every witness. Dr. Kiadopolis was the only remarkable person in the chase, in her skirt and heels. No one got a good look at anyone"

"You must be getting something," The President pleaded, "Don't hold out on me, Jim!"

Jim looked at his President with sincerity, "I never hold out on you. There were only three cameras looking at the street and only two on the path Dr. Kiadopolis took when she was trying to get away. All we see is her car. She was driving, and Mr. Acer sat in the passenger seat. He didn't appear to be taking her. By all accounts, he was running with her."

"Who's this guy? Mr. Acer?"

"He's a government bureaucrat. We're going through his records in his office in Wisconsin."

"Wisconsin? Near Maxwell Rassic?" The President leaned forward.

"Yes, actually, he also works at Fort Halishaw. But there doesn't seem to be any connection. Maxwell doesn't know him. Mr. Acer wasn't, isn't, a meticulous note taker, but we should be able to figure out what he was doing there. Clearly, he knew Sarah Kiadopolis somehow."

"Could he be with LV?" The President asked.

"I considered that," Jim said, "If he was, it wouldn't make any sense for them to take him too. They could have left him on the street in Greenville. That would've drawn much less attention to him. He could've claimed to be in the wrong place at the wrong time. And like I said, all the witness accounts are that he was helping her escape."

"What was she doing there?" the President asked.

"We don't know," Jim said, "No one asked her to go there. We've been through her apartment and her office and her car. There isn't anything to indicate why she was in Greenville that night."

The president considered this. "So now what?"

"Now, we wait," Jim said exactly what the President didn't want to hear. "I have the entire extended team working on finding clues. The division chiefs are coordinating the search calling in people with particular skills where necessary."

"What about the FBI and the CIA?"

"We're letting the FBI take the lead. This is a kidnapping for them. I've got people closely monitoring their work and trying to feed them information and get information from them as necessary, but I'm not bringing them in, yet."

"And LV?" The President asked.

"We got the letter that told us to do this," Jim waved his hand around the room indicating the video production they just sent out.

"The Doctor's work was paying huge dividends for us. It is, was, by far the best thing we've got going," Jim sighed and looked out the window, "This is the first time they've taken anyone like this. But Dr. Kiadopolis and her Fourth Option is the closest we've ever gotten to finding them."

An even worse question crossed the President's mind. What was to happen to these two people? He was about to ask but thought better.

. . .

The television station returned to 556 and Bob Vila talking about stairs.

Sullivan stared directly at the screen, wide eyed. The President of the United States knows they're here? Wait. The President of the United States knows Sarah's here?

Wordlessly, the woman stood, brushed her skirt down her legs, clicked the television off, and left the apartment.

"So," Sullivan turned slowly to Sarah, "This doesn't have anything to do with the Mob or with Peter Howard?"

"No," Sarah whispered, looking down at the floor. He turned

and faced Sarah directly. She looked down, her eyes moving side to side, processing information. She slowly sat down on the couch.

"You knew about all this all along? What is *Space Resonance*? Do you work for Cornwall & Wallace?" Sullivan had a lot of questions, and Sarah knew the answer to some of them.

"No, Yes, I mean no," Sarah said, "I figured a lot out last week." Sullivan knew this was not the time to feel insecure about being deceived by Sarah. He also knew it wasn't a good time to feel foolish about being the only one in the room that didn't know what the hell was going on. He realized that he didn't have the knot of fear in his stomach. He moved to the over-stuffed chair opposite the one the woman was in and sat.

"Can you tell me what's going on?" Sullivan asked.

"Sullivan," Sarah looked up at him. She was clearly unsettled by what was happening. "I'm not trying to keep things from you. Like I said, I just figured some stuff out last week."

"Can you answer my questions?" Sullivan asked.

"Oh, yes," Sarah said. She paused a moment and collected herself. "I do work for Cornwall & Wallace. I'm on special assignment in Washington DC."

"What's *Space Resonance*?" Sullivan asked.

"I'm a trained theoretical physicist," Sarah said. She looked away for a moment, "It's what I did my PhD on." Sullivan didn't like that she looked away from him. Was she lying to him? He decided to let it pass for now.

"Okay, what about Peter and the Mob?" Sullivan asked, "You told me you figured something out about Peter, and that's why you called me."

Sarah thought a moment, "I figured out that Peter wouldn't come into my apartment. I remembered that you said my apartment was bugged. So he had to know it was bugged. I don't know how Peter knew, but he did." Sarah paused and then said, "and *Space Resonance* is a powerful theory that would be worth a lot of money to whoever controlled it."

Sullivan knew she wasn't telling him something.

He felt a touch of frustration. Then he realized it had been a strenuous half hour. He shouldn't assume she was trying to hide things from him.

"Okay," Sullivan said, trying to sound stronger than he was. He flopped back into the chair with a thud.

He immediately felt uncomfortable in this lounging position

and Sarah looked at him hesitantly for a moment. Then she smiled and softly leaned back into a similar, although much less awkward, lounging position. Sullivan looked up at the ceiling for a moment.

Thirty minutes ago, he'd thought he'd be killed at any moment. The door would open, large men would enter, and that would be the end of him. Instead, a small, polite brunette entered, and they were addressed by the President of the United States. He was feeling an emotional high that came from the reptilian portion of his brain relaxing the fight or flight mechanism. He also knew that this moment could not last long and they would have to figure out what to do soon. What did Sarah know, and what would she tell them? When would they come back?

Sullivan sat up, startling himself. "Six days?" Sullivan looked to his right at Sarah. Her legs were stretched out straight to the floor as though she was lying down.

"What?" Sarah rolled her head on the back of the couch to look at him, "Six days!" She sat up as well.

"The President said we were taken six days ago!" Sullivan said, "I don't remember anything before today."

"I don't remember anything either," Sarah said, "I was surprised the wound on my leg appears to be more than a few days old. Have they been keeping us drugged?" She thought for a moment, "Are we drugged now?"

"I think it's safe to assume that we've been drugged," Sullivan said after thinking for a moment, "I had a lot of trouble waking up, and I feel a little too calm right now." He didn't mention that he was having trouble controlling his emotions and briefly thought she was lying to him. Did he still think that?

"Hmm," Sarah thought, "I don't think there's anything we can do about it. I think all we can do is be careful of our feelings."

"Agreed," Sullivan said. He turned back to the ceiling.

"Did the President say we were *taken into custody*?" Sarah asked.

Sullivan tried to remember, "I think so. Is that just language?" Sullivan thought of the other words the President could have used. *Kidnap. Hostage.* They made him wince, and he was glad the President didn't use them.

"I don't know," Sarah dismissed the question looking at the ceiling.

"I'll be right back," Sullivan wanted to move and there was only one place to go.

. . .

Sarah was alone in the room when she heard the footsteps outside the door. The sound forced her entire body to tense more than it was. She stood, turned to face the door, and stepped back. Her calves touched the coffee table. Her quads tensed enough that her right leg protested and pain curled her toes. Her heart began to pound. She looked to the bathroom door realizing that she wanted Sullivan here. *Now.*

The door again opened. She didn't want to face this door alone.

"Where's Mr. Acer?" The woman asked, her voice betraying concern. The door began to close behind her and she used her hand to hold it open.

"Restroom," Sarah was able to say. The recognition of concern on the face of the woman made Sarah feel better for some reason. The woman relaxed her grip on the door and allowed it to close.

"We will wait for Mr. Acer," the woman said, "I trust the accommodations are comfortable." Sarah was caught a bit off guard. Was this woman trying to make small talk? Sarah's heart was in her throat, and she was struggling to stop from passing out. She stood, frozen.

The bathroom door opened and both women looked to it. Sullivan strode out into the room as though he'd lived here for years. He stopped when he saw Sarah standing, then his face tightened when he saw the woman.

"Please, take your seats," the woman said, gesturing to the couch. She took a hesitant step along a wide arc away from both Sullivan and Sarah.

Sullivan also hesitated but walked back to the couch.

Sarah moved the two feet back to the couch and pivoted as the woman made her way around the room never turning her back. Soon they were back to the positions they were in thirty minutes previously.

"My name is Mary," the woman said. Sarah studied her "As your President said, Dr. Kiadopolis, you're to cooperate with us in every way," she turned to look at Sullivan, "You will be with us while Dr. Kiadopolis helps us, and your best cooperation will be to help her. This should only take a few days."

"A few days?" Sarah blurted. "What do you want to know, can we get this done faster?"

"In time," Mary smiled softly, "First, are your accommodations acceptable? Is there anything we can do to make your stay more comfortable?"

Sullivan was tense, but he laughed a little, "Is this a hotel? Could you call me a cab?"

"Certainly, there are parameters of your stay that will be out of your control," Mary said, "but you must recognize that we have no interest in your discomfort, and we believe that the more pleasant your stay, the faster and more productive it can be." Mary's eyes narrowed an almost imperceptible amount, and Sarah saw the rest of her face remained perfectly calm, "The more cooperative you are with us, the more cooperative we can be with you."

The relaxation Sarah could sense in Sullivan evaporated. He received the threat as well as Sarah and his body tensed.

"How did you get the television message?" Sullivan asked, "The government must be tracking the communications and will be breaking down that door any minute. We can't be here for days!" Sarah was glad Sullivan was thinking and not paralyzed with fear. Mary didn't seem fazed.

"We instructed the President to direct you to cooperate two days ago," Mary said, "The message you received was broadcast across the satellite TV system on a channel half way between two channels normally received by a TV. The message was broadcast across the entire globe. So, by your logic, yes, the US government can determine, conclusively, that you are on earth."

Sarah looked at Sullivan. He was thinking. As a few seconds passed, he moved onto another topic. "You said *two days ago*, and the President said you took us *six days ago*. We don't remember anything."

"You've been drugged," Mary said matter-of-factly.

"Are we drugged now?" Sullivan asked.

"The doctors assure me the affects you may be feeling will pass quickly."

"How did you *tell the President* what to do?" Sarah interrupted.

"We have an arrangement with the government that goes back decades."

"Are you part of the government?"

"No."

"Then who are you? What is *LV* ?"

"We do not believe that is something you need to know."

"Who's *we*? We only see you."

"Certainly I could not be doing all this myself," Mary's face remained completely composed, "Do you need anything in these rooms?"

"No, everything here is fine," Sarah didn't want to change the subject, "How many people are outside that door with you?"

"Are bagels and cream cheese a good breakfast for you?" Mary asked.

"Yes," Sarah said, "What country are we in?"

"Could we get lite cream cheese?" Sullivan interrupted.

"Certainly," Mary turned to Sullivan.

"Can we get a clock?"

"That clock is accurate." Mary looked briefly to the display on the DirecTV set. It read six fifteen p.m. Sarah was relieved to see the time. She guessed the TV system required an accurate clock to function properly.

"Have you bugged this, this," Sullivan held out his arms and looked around for the word, "this *apartment*?"

"No," Mary said, "but you will not believe me."

"You're right," Sullivan said, "Can I have my shoes?"

"No, you do not need them," Mary looked down at her watch, "That is enough for now. I will return at eight a.m. tomorrow. Good Night." She stood quickly and moved toward the door. Sarah began to stand, but decided not to. The door opened as Mary approached it, and closed after her without her touching it.

Sarah felt the sound of the door lock in the back of her neck.

. . .

"Sarah," Sullivan touched her shoulder.

Sarah found it more difficult to open her eyes than she'd expected. She looked up to see Sullivan standing behind the sofa looking down into her face. She sat up and looked around.

Sullivan had made a simple dinner out of bagels and some tomato sauce and cheese he found in the kitchen. Over dinner Sarah described the basics of the theory of *Space Resonance* and Sullivan explained how he got onto Linus Brenner. They both agreed LV was probably listening. Sarah had a few questions for Sullivan, but she just listened to him.

She was sure he had questions for her, but he did the same.

Sullivan offered to clean the dishes and Sarah moved to the couch and briefly closed her eyes.

Now the dishes were cleaned and put away. The clock under

the television read nine-thirty. She must have fallen asleep instantly.

"I guess I'll go to bed," Sarah said forcing her head up from the couch.

"That's a good idea," Sullivan said, "I don't feel tired, but we must be."

Sarah stood on wobbly legs. She balanced for a few moments and turned to face Sullivan, "Well, good night." She turned and walked to her room.

The thought of the room being bugged entered her mind as she unbuttoned her blouse. She and Sullivan had taken precautions throughout dinner in case they were listening to their conversations, but it didn't occur to her until now that there might also be cameras. She hesitated in removing her blouse, but realized that there was nothing she could do about it.

She quickly removed her blouse and skirt and climbed into her bed, pulling the sheet and comforter up to her neck. Once there, she removed her bra but kept it under the covers with her. She rarely slept in only panties but there were no other options provided.

She lay in bed and squeezed her eyes shut expecting to again fall asleep instantly. Sarah couldn't clear her mind. She put her hand on her chest and realized that her heart was pounding.

The back of her mind was processing thoughts, nearly in her subconscious, and those thoughts were keeping her up. She pulled them to the front of her mind. She thought of the second time Mary entered the apartment.

Sarah stood alone. Sullivan was in the bathroom as the door opened. At that moment, she was scared. She was very scared and her body was still feeling that fear.

She fought to slow her breathing and get her heart rate under control. She focused her thoughts back to a few minutes ago when she fell asleep so easily. Was it the couch? Was it the sound of the water? No. It was Sullivan. She was afraid when Mary came in, and that fear didn't subside when Sarah saw Mary. The fear persisted until Sullivan returned. They were in this together, and Sarah was depending on him more than she realized.

She lay in her bed trying to calm her breathing. She relaxed her eyelids, and allowed that relaxation to pass across her entire body, but she could still feel her chest rise and fall under the sheet as she was still breathing hard.

She tried this for what seemed like an hour before she got up.

Sarah wrapped her sheet and comforter around herself. She

pulled her pillows into her bundle. She crossed her room, and slowly, quietly, opened her door. The living room was dark but her eyes had adjusted and she could see enough. The door to Sullivan's room was open. She silently crossed the carpeted floor. She paused at the entrance to Sullivan's room and looked in.

Sullivan didn't have the same trouble falling asleep. Sarah entered his room and quietly closed the door.

66.   June 2, 2001

Sullivan sat up to test his need for sleep at six-forty am. He'd slept soundly, but awoke early as was his habit. He rubbed his face. He felt calm despite the situation. Mary said eight. He had some time to think.

Sullivan thought of his son, Danny. He was with Sullivan's parents. They would take care of him indefinitely. There was nothing he could do for him now, except not mention him. Clearly these people knew a lot about Sarah, but nothing about Sullivan.

Up until the President talked yesterday, Sullivan thought he was Linus' target. That Sarah was a bystander. He felt silly about that, but he knew he had to get over it.

He stretched out his arms and legs and remembered the day before when he was in the same situation. He lifted his head to see his clothes neatly folded over the chair. This time he'd put them there.

Sullivan lay there a few more minutes. He knew the day was going to be stressful, and he would need to be as well rested as possible.

His calm morning was interrupted by the unexpected site of a pile on the floor. In the dim light of the glowing alarm clock, he had trouble making it out. His body tensed as he leaned forward to get a closer look.

He relaxed when he recognized Sarah. She was lying on her stomach wrapped in her comforter on the floor. Her hair was spread across her pillow and the comforter was down so that Sullivan could see the top third of her back. The tan of her skin against the white of her comforter provided a contrast that his eyes could easily detect. Her left leg stretched out of the comforter. Her left arm was up under her pillow exposing the curve of her breast where it met her chest.

He wondered why she was here, but he didn't want to disturb her. He stood slowly and quietly. He adjusted himself in his boxer shorts, grabbed his pants from the back of his chair, and headed for the bathroom.

In the bathroom, he found two hanging bags on hooks next to the shower. He opened the first to find fresh clothes for himself. They were identical to what he wore yesterday. He confirmed the other bag was for Sarah.

Sullivan was showered and dressed by the time he paused shaving his face because he heard motion in the living room. He pulled the razor away from his right cheek and held his breath to concentrate on the sound.   He smiled and exhaled when he figured out it was rustling sheets. He could make out the quick pads of bare feet on the carpet and recognized the limp in her step.

Sarah closed the door to her room. He finished his shave happy that they had avoided the awkwardness of her waking up in his room. Sullivan put his old clothes in his bag and left them on the hook, brushed his hair and his teeth and walked out.

Sullivan felt the thick padding under the carpet below his bare feet and couldn't help the feeling of exhilaration that had persisted since he thought of Sarah running across the room wrapped in her bedding.

Immediately to his left was a tripod with a video camera on it. He must have almost walked into it on his way to the bathroom! He reached out and touched it to make sure it was real. It was. It was an unremarkable Sony model. The camera faced to the left across the front of the non-functioning television to the corner of the living area at a large dry erase board set on an easel. His exhilaration evaporated as he tried to figure out how he had not seen this stuff on his way into the bathroom.

Sarah's door opened and her head poked out. He could see her bare shoulder.

"Go in your room and close the door," Sarah commanded. Sullivan wordlessly complied. He heard the unmistakable sound of her favoring her right leg as she padded barefoot to the bathroom.

His stomach told him to look for breakfast. In the kitchen, he found bagels and cream cheese. He set them out on the table with two plates and a butter knife as he heard the shower water turn off. Sarah must have been in there less than three minutes. Sullivan also found an assortment of magazines next to the front door and selected an old Sports Illustrated to read. He tried to be interested by a story about the recent Super Bowl MVP Ray Lewis of the Baltimore Ravens, but he couldn't force himself to care.

As he scanned the article, he thought about the day they would have. He assumed today they would be talking about Sarah's work. Last night, Sarah described her theory of *Space Resonance*. It seemed a little farfetched, certainly not the kind of thing to get someone kidnapped. And what about Linus and Peter? There had to be more to what was going on. He wanted to ask Sarah more questions, but he could tell she was taking this situation with some difficulty. He wasn't sure why he felt so calm. He knew they weren't going to be harmed at least for a few days. So he had time to try to figure this all out. He shuddered at the thought that his life might depend on it.

. . .

Sullivan looked up when the bathroom door opened. Sarah stood halfway in the door way. She had her red blouse on. Her hair was still wet and clung to her head, brushed straight back. Where her skirt should have been, she wore a towel around her waist, "Sullivan, I need your help, if you don't mind."

"What do you need?" Sullivan flipped the magazine closed and stood.

Sarah stepped out into the room fully, "It's my leg," she said. Sullivan looked down. Her right hand held the part in the towel open so the towel would not touch her wound, "They left a dressing and some ointment, but I can't wrap it myself."

Sullivan could tell Sarah didn't want his help. She was standing very uncomfortably.

"Of course," he moved quickly around the table.

Sarah picked up a package of wrapping and stepped awkwardly into the living room to the coffee table.

Sullivan saw where she was going and sat on the edge of the overstuffed chair at the head of the seating area. Sarah handed him the bandage. It was a standard role of brown wrapping like people use to wrap a sprained ankle. It, in turn, was wrapped in plastic. When he had it opened, he looked to Sarah standing next to the coffee table.

They both didn't seem to know what to do. He waited for her next move.

Sarah took a deep breath, closed her eyes, and removed the

towel from her waist. A sharp intake of air betrayed the pain in her leg as she lifted it quickly and placed her toes on the corner of the table.

Sullivan couldn't help but stare at the long, muscular, tan leg presented before him. He felt he looked too long and forced himself to look up at her face.

Sarah looked directly back at him. She bent down to pick up the gauze and moved to place it over her wound.

Sullivan reached out and placed the end of the wrapping against her thigh just below the gauze, a few inches above her knee. He held the end there and reached around her leg to get the roll. Every time he passed the wrapping over the gauze she inhaled. He worked his way up her leg stopping with one full wrap above the gauze leaving less than an inch of exposed skin before her panties. Sullivan looked straight ahead and forced himself to focus on what he was doing. His neck tightened as he forced himself not to glance. He rolled the wrapping back down her leg and completed the circuit back to the start. The task was completed with the little metal clasps to hold the wrap in place.

With the job done, Sarah quickly dropped her foot back to the floor, wrapped the towel around her waist and turned to return to the bathroom.

"Thank you," Sarah said. Sullivan could tell the strength in her voice was forced.

"You're welcome," Sullivan said as the bathroom door closed, too quietly for her to hear. He sat back in the chair a moment.

. . .

"You know I hate you, right?" Angie Reynolds greeted Peter Howard at her door. Linus asked Peter to talk with Angie to see if she'd heard from Sarah.

"Hello, Angie," Peter said, "Can I come in?"

"Why would I let you in?"

"Look, I'm worried about Sarah," Peter said with genuine sincerity.

Angie's angry face broke and her eyes watered with sadness. She stepped out of the way and Peter entered her apartment. The layout was almost identical to Sarah's, but Peter had only ever seen Sarah's on Linus' surveillance pictures. Peter went to the kitchen peninsula and Angie stood next to the kitchen table.

"The FBI came by a few days ago and told me she was missing," Angie said, "How do you know she's missing? She told me she had not spoken with you in over a year."

"The FBI came to see me too," Peter said. That was a lie. "Do you have any idea where she is?"

"No!" Angie's shoulders were slumped. In the half dozen times Peter had seen her, he'd never seen her perfect poise crack until now. She was clearly devastated by Sarah's disappearance. "How could I know where she is?"

"Well, you're close," Peter said, "Do you two go anywhere, a favorite vacation spot? Anything like that?"

"We went to St. Thomas last spring," Angie began, "Wait. She was kidnapped. They wouldn't take her to a vacation spot. Would they?"

Peter knew she was right. It was a stupid question. Linus asked him to come here and talk to her to see if she'd received any communication from Sarah. Where ever she was, there was a chance she could get a message out, and if she could, Linus wanted to know about it. Like it or not, Peter was closest to Sarah Kiadopolis, and he was the only person who knew Angie. This was a desperation move, but Linus was desperate, and Peter was going to do whatever he could.

Even Claire understood.

"You're probably right, I'm just hoping she's going to contact someone. I hope we can find her." Peter looked around the apartment. It was clearly hard for Angie. She looked like she had not been out in days. It was a work day, and she wasn't dressed to go to work.

"I wish there was something I could do," Angie started to cry.

Peter looked around the kitchen. "Angie, why don't you sit, let me make you some breakfast."

"You know you wrecked her, right?" Angie said. She still didn't like Peter, but she liked the idea of breakfast, so she was going to be mean to him while he cooked.

That was fine with him.

"I'd set her up on dates," Angie said sitting on a stool facing into the kitchen, "but she never wanted to go. She said you were the perfect man. She said you did everything she asked, and left her alone. Her mom is pretty messed up, and she doesn't want to get dependent on any man, so she always said you were exactly what she needed. A man she didn't depend on. It was so sad."

Peter agreed. That was sad.

. . .

"I saw you had bagels!" It seemed like ten seconds had passed when Sarah opened the door again. This time she stepped confidently into the room. She walked around him and the back of the chair.

Sullivan could still hear she was favoring her leg. He looked at her from behind as she walked to the kitchen. Her skirt was short and as the fabric stretched against her leg he could see the bottom of the wrapping. When she stopped at the table and stood with her feet together, her wrapping was completely covered. Sullivan looked up to see her looking back at him.

"You can't see the wrapping below your skirt," was all Sullivan could say.

"I know," Sarah said, "I checked in the bathroom. You did a good job. Let's eat." She slid into a chair facing away from him and began to prepare a bagel. "What do you think is going to happen today?" Sarah asked as though she was asking about a book they were reading.

"Well, Mary said she would be back at eight, that's in," Sullivan looked around Sarah to the clock under the television, "five minutes." Sarah put her bagel down and sat with both her hands in her lap.

"I forgot she told us that," Sarah said, "They set up the easel and camera, clearly they want us to tell them something."

"*Us*?" Sullivan asked, "They don't want *us* to tell them anything, they want *you* to tell them everything!"

"Sullivan," Sarah said quietly, "I'm sorry I didn't tell you earlier. The work I do..." Sarah paused, "Look, when you came to me, you started talking about Peter, and I thought that was what this was all about, until I..." Sarah trailed off again.

"Until you what?" Sullivan asked.

"I haven't spoken to anyone about what I do. Not a single person in the last eight years!" Sarah said.

"What do you mean anyone?" Sullivan asked. He felt he was getting mad. Was she playing with him? "There must be someone, and you're going to have to start talking now!" Sullivan realized this conversation wasn't going the way he wanted. Right now, they had to stick together. Right now, there was no one else but them.

Before he could say anything further, he heard footsteps outside the door. If Sarah looked tense before, she looked absolutely terrified now. Sullivan could see the color draining from her face as she stood. He stood and moved quickly to be next to her, he thought she was going to faint. Sullivan found himself standing with the back of his legs pressed to the back of the couch in the living room. Sarah stood next to him.

"I'm sorry," she whispered.

Sullivan knew that they were going to be okay, at least today. Whoever Mary was, she still needed something from them, "It's going to be okay."

Mary stepped through the doorway and again the door closed without her touching it. She wore the red blouse and tight skirt matching Sarah with the same four-inch heels Sarah wore in Greenville. The only new feature was the attaché Mary carried.

Sullivan looked her up and down. He would have found her attractive except for the situation.

She stood very near the wall just inside the apartment. She was just as nervous as they were. The three looked at each other for a few moments. Sarah rested against the back of the couch.

"Please, sit on the sofa," Mary said in a pleasant voice. She made a sweeping gesture Sullivan thought was designed to convey confidence, but her shaking fingers betrayed her.

Sarah moved first and Sullivan followed around the couch. Sarah never turned her back on Mary and instead walked backwards or sideways when necessary.

Sullivan didn't. He was certain they weren't in any danger. They were held asleep for six days and had no idea where they were. Whoever had them went to a lot of trouble setting this place up. Mary was afraid of *him*. There was no need to be afraid at this point.

On the other hand, there might be plenty of reason to be afraid when LV got what they wanted. Sullivan knew he had to pay close attention to what was going on. He couldn't let himself be afraid.

Sarah looked down in shock at Sullivan when he sat down and leaned back into the couch. He barely stopped short of throwing his arm over the back of the couch and putting his feet up on the coffee table. He just smiled back at her.

She was very tense. She pivoted. Sullivan knew she was facing Mary coming to the living room. Mary moved into view and sat on the edge of the large chair near the dry erase board, opposite the one Sullivan had sat in to wrap Sarah's leg.

Mary looked around. She had to turn forty-five degrees in her chair to face the dry erase board. She stood, placed her attaché on the chair, and attempted to move the chair. Her body struggled and the stretch fabric of her skirt was pulled tight across her thighs and butt as she threw her weight into attempting to move the chair.

Sullivan attempted to move around Sarah to help.

Mary stood instantly and turned red-faced, "Please sit!"

"I was just going to help." Sullivan said.

"I can manage!" She said and moved quickly to the other side of the chair. She was afraid of him. What did she think he was going to do? He let out a burst of laughter.

"Please, Sullivan," Sarah shifted her weight so she blocked his path. She spoke softly, looking him directly in the eyes, "Please."

Sarah was still very uncomfortable with the situation. Both women seemed to share a sense of physical danger that Sullivan could not believe existed in this situation. He allowed the smile to drop from his face as he returned Sarah's look. He turned and carefully sat back down, this time on the edge of the couch.

The two women remained standing for a moment. They looked at each other. Sullivan thought he saw a connection between them. They seemed to take the same cue and turned to their seats at the same time.

"Dr. Kiadopolis," Mary began, "We will be very interested to hear everything about your work in the field of *Space Resonance*." As she said this, she pulled out a folder from her attaché as though she was going to take notes.

"The field of *Space Resonance* is a large topic," Sarah said, "Is there something specific you, your group, uh, LV, would like to know?" Sarah said the letters LV with an exaggerated gap between them to confirm she was saying it right. Mary didn't respond. "I could speak about it for weeks!"

"We would expect nothing less!"

Sarah let out a small noise. Sullivan knew she was only asking where she should begin so she could give them what they wanted, but instead she just learned that they, LV, had every intention of keeping them here for a long time. Sullivan found that this realization didn't surprise him. He thought it made sense with the amount of care they'd taken in setting up the place. He thought it odd of himself to be thinking of this in such a detached, academic way. He also knew that the longer they planned to keep him here, the longer he had to figure a way out.

"Sarah," Sullivan said, "Why don't you tell me about *Space Resonance*?" He knew he had to help Sarah through this. He also wanted to test Mary. He was getting the impression Mary didn't know anything about *Space Resonance*.

"What?"

"Imagine you're talking to me, a lay person, and tell me about it." He looked past Sarah to Mary.

"Mr. Acer, that is an excellent idea," Mary said, "Dr. Kiadopolis, why don't you explain your work to your friend? I will just listen." Sarah considered this. She looked at Mary and then at Sullivan. Then she smiled at Sullivan, and he knew she would be okay.

"All right," Sarah said, "Let me propose this: I gave a talk on the basics of *Space Resonance* to the Society of Women Engineers in Orlando last year. It was designed to work with technical people but not physicists. The talk took about fifteen minutes, and it gives a good overview of the concepts required to understand my work. We could start there and see where you want to go after that?"

Sullivan was struck with the odd expression on Mary's face. Just for an instant.

"That would be excellent," Mary said. It must have been nothing.

"So, the talk started like this," Sarah paused as she remembered it. It had been almost a year and a half, "This talk will focus on answering three questions, first"

"Please," Mary interrupted. She pointed to the dry erase board and reached her other hand into her attaché. She produced a TV remote. They forgot all about the video camera.

"Please give us the formal lecture," Mary directed with a smile.

They want a formal lecture?

Sarah stood slowly. Her leg didn't allow her to move quickly. She took a tentative step toward Mary as she had to pass close to her to get around the coffee table to the board and lecture position. Mary didn't object as she was focusing on the remote control. As Sarah stepped past her, Sullivan could see that Mary's fear of Sullivan did not extend to Sarah. Sullivan thought that if the rest of Sarah was as strong as her leg was, Mary had not judged her physical risk well.

"Please begin, Dr. Kiadopolis," Mary said after she returned the remote to her attaché. She crossed her left leg over her right so she could twist her body to face Sarah and folded her hands over the folder on her lap somewhat awkwardly.

After a few moments of looking at herself on the television, Sarah picked up one of the dry erase markers from the ledge of the board and wrote as she spoke, "This discussion will focus on answering three questions. One: which force is stronger, the force of gravity or the force of electromagnetism?" As she spoke, Sarah wrote *gravity* on the left side of the board and stepped across to write *electromagnetism* on the right. Sullivan had no idea the answer to this question and no idea how the answer to this question could lead to him being a captive in this place.

Sullivan started the talk paying attention to everything Sarah said. He tried to make sure he understood it so he could help figure out what was going on. Then something occurred to him. He didn't need to understand everything she was saying, because Sarah already did. Sarah understood it far better than he ever would. Even if he could follow the basics of this very basic and introductory talk, he wouldn't be able to follow along when they got into more detail. No, he decided it was important for him to understand why Mary was paying attention to this. He had to understand what Mary was interested in. So he focused his attention on her.

Sullivan wished he had paper so he could take notes on everything Mary said. She asked several questions extending what was supposed to be a fifteen-minute overview to over an hour and a half. Sarah was able to answer easily, filling the board with simple drawings.

Sullivan studied every detail of Mary. She was left handed. She wrote with her hand below the line she was writing on, the way modern lefties wrote, not the hooked over writing that got ink all over their hands years ago. The low cut on the blouse allowed him to occasionally see her bra. It was black like Sarah's although Mary's breasts were smaller. He tried to figure her accent. Her skin was fair like maybe a Norwegian and her accent was similar. Her English was good, but a little too formal to be her first language. When she asked questions she had no difficulty with the technical jargon, so she must have some technical training.

At the end of the hour and a half, Sarah said, "Mary, that's the end of the talk I gave to SWE." She had been moving around the board a good deal, but now she returned to standing with her feet together and her hands clasped in front of herself. Her right knee was bent, "Where would you like to go now?"

"Actually, I have a number of questions," Mary said. She pulled out a page from her folder. Sullivan could see that it was full of typed writing. Mary turned in the chair so she was facing straight ahead. She uncrossed her legs and studied the page in front of her.

"Sullivan," Sarah addressed Sullivan for the first time since she started talking, "Could I have a glass of water?"

"Yes, of course," Sullivan said. He stood, looking at Mary.

She looked up from her paper at him. He turned and walked around the couch away from her. As he rounded the couch he looked back to see Mary had returned to her notes.

"Could you also bring me a chair from the table?" Sarah called out.

"Yes," Sullivan called back. He realized she'd been standing for nearly two hours. He should have thought of her leg hurting and gotten her a chair before now.

Sarah grimaced as she sat down. She held her right leg out straight in an unnatural position. Sullivan wondered if he should move the coffee table over for her to rest it. Then she forced it down. She pressed her hand to where he could see the bandage under her skirt and let out a low sound as her heel hit the floor. Sullivan wanted to help, but he knew all he could do was retrieve the water.

"Perfect," Mary said when Sullivan returned to his seat. Sarah finished her glass of water in one continuous chug. "Now, could you please explain to me the concept of *Space Resonance* applied to *Right Packed Rings*?"

Sarah cocked her head and looked at Mary. "Yes, that is actually the title of one of my papers. Let me see, if we start with the natural frequency of a straight ring. Oh, I need to explain the rings, right?"

The description lasted for three hours. Mary asked several questions Sullivan could tell were directly from her list. She would check them off one by one. Sullivan noticed that the writing on the questions sheet was broken into groups, and Mary had asked the last question in the first group.

After Sarah answered the last question Mary said, "Thank you very much Dr. Kiadopolis. You've been most helpful. I believe that's enough for today. Let us begin again tomorrow morning at eight." With that, Mary fished out the remote and turned off the television. She closed her folder and stood.

Sullivan moved to stand as well.

"Please, Mr. Acer, you have been most helpful. Please stay seated until I leave. Good day." With that, she moved to the doorway. Sullivan noticed she moved directly, not hugging the wall and that she turned her back on him. The door opened as she approached without any signal he could see.

. . .

"Are you all right?" Sullivan asked as soon as the door closed.

"Yes," Sarah was rubbing her leg, "I'll be fine, just sore." Sarah was relieved to be able to sit and rest. She was actually kind of enjoying talking to someone about *Space Resonance*, even if it was only the stuff she did in college. She got lost in the discussion even though her participation wasn't voluntary.

"So, we should compare notes while this is all still fresh in our heads," Sullivan said.

It was easy for him to say, Sarah thought, he just sat there all morning. He was relaxed on the couch. She simultaneously liked that he was remaining so calm and was driven nuts by it.

"I agree, but we should do it over some food," Sarah stalled. She really wanted to take a nap, but she knew he was right. She looked at the clock. It was just after one p.m.

"Let me see what I can find."

Sullivan prepared a lunch of peanut butter and jelly sandwiches while she let her leg rest. It still ached, and the pain was wearing on her.

"LV?" Sullivan asked after they'd moved to the table.

"I've never heard of them," Sarah said, "Is it the name of a company?" Sarah studied his face looking for any sign of recognition. She was sure there was none.

"I've never heard of them either, why would you think they were a company?" Sullivan asked. He looked at Sarah closely. "Sarah, what do you need to tell me?"

Sarah had a bite of sandwich in her mouth, and she took her time chewing. She had never told anyone about her work and didn't know how to start. If she couldn't tell Sullivan, how was she going to tell Mary? She'd spent the entire day answering questions about what she did in grad school, basically stalling.

"I can't shake the feeling I've met Mary before." Sarah attempted to change the subject, to stall again.

Sullivan looked at her while he finished his sandwich. "No," Sullivan said, "I don't think she knew who you were before they took us."

"What?" Sarah asked. That didn't make any sense. Why would

they have taken them if they didn't know who they were? That was a pretty incredible statement.

"Sarah," Sullivan said after a drink of water, "I watched Mary ask you questions. She was reading off a script. She checked off each question as you answered it."

"So?" Sarah asked. She didn't have any idea where Sullivan was going, but she wanted to let him take her there. Besides, she was enjoying the peanut butter and jelly sandwich more than she should have been.

"You're having no trouble answering their questions," Sullivan said, "are you?"

"No..."

"So, these are basic questions about your theory?"

"Yes..."

"Probably things they could have gotten from reading your papers?"

"Yes, they are." Sarah had thought the same thing. "Yes, they are," she said again, "I was thinking the same thing while she was asking the questions. They, she, could have learned everything I taught her today by ready my papers that are available at the library at Virginia Tech."

"So why didn't they go to Virginia Tech and get them?" Sullivan asked.

"How should I know?"

"I think they didn't know who you were when they took us," Sullivan said. Sarah felt herself perk up as he continued, "I think they made that list of questions after they took us." Sarah sat up straight. She could feel the weight of her secret lift. Maybe he was right. He continued with her encouragement, "If they called you and asked you these questions over the phone, you'd have answered them, right?"

"Absolutely!"

"I think they took us and then had to figure out what they wanted to know about us. I think they researched us and your *Space Resonance* was the only interesting thing they came up with. But we both know no one would be chasing us over a theory."

Sarah was so excited that Sullivan could be right that for just a moment she forgot how much more there was to the story. She felt her face frown, and he saw it.

"What?" he asked. His smile broke.

She smiled a little smile but looked down at the last bite of her sandwich. "I think we should rest a little."

Sullivan nodded agreement and Sarah moved through her sore leg to the comfortable chairs. She put her feet on the coffee table. Sullivan sat in the opposite chair and also put his bare feet on the coffee table.

Sarah decided she'd let LV guide the conversation for a while.

Her eyes closed.

. . .

When Sullivan opened his eyes, Sarah was gone. He blinked a few times to clear the webs and looked to the clock under the television. Three hours had passed. He was glad for the break. He was receiving a tremendous amount of information and needed time to process it.

He looked around. Sarah couldn't have gone far.

It was a struggle to lift his head to look around. Nothing.

Now he was a little worried.

He could hear a faint rustling. Rhythmic, steady. It was accompanied by a weak creaking sound from the kitchen. He surveyed the room again and couldn't see anyone. Then he spotted knuckles on the edge of the kitchen table. He noticed the chairs were pushed away from the table. The table was moving slightly with the rhythm of the rustling.

Sarah's right leg was crossed over the left so no weight was on it. Her body was straight. She was pulling herself up to the bottom of the table pivoting on her left heel. Sullivan could see the strain of her tight left leg. Her blouse was un-tucked from her skirt and he could see a few inches of her stomach. She might have a six-pack. Her arms were likely as strong as his. Stronger. She had sweat stains in her pits and Sullivan realized that much of her body was moist with sweat. He could now hear her counting with the rhythm and see her hair touch the floor each time she extended her arms lowering her back almost to the floor.

He watched her with intense admiration. He didn't think he could do that move more than five times, let alone enough times to break a sweat. He also couldn't remember the last time he woke up and was motivated to exercise. This was certainly not one of those times.

Sarah paused at the top of a pull-up. Her head fell back and her eyes focused on Sullivan. Her speech was broken by her labored breathing. "Oh, I'm sorry, did I wake you?"

"No, you didn't wake me up," he sat up, barely able to move from his too-deep sleep. Sarah lowered herself so her arms were extended and relaxed her stomach so her butt hit the floor. She used her left leg and her arms to pull herself from under the table and up into one of the table chairs.

"I have to exercise or I'll go crazy," Sarah said as she sipped a glass of water. "This was all I could figure out with my leg. Sit-ups even hurt too much." Sarah was in a much more relaxed mood than she was this morning. Sullivan just smiled at her and then looked back around the room.

"I looked around in the kitchen," Sarah said as she walked past him into the bathroom. She left the door open, "I'm making spaghetti and meatballs tonight!"

"Spaghetti sounds really good," Sullivan said, "and I think I might be able to make it dinner and a movie."

He'd used the cable from the camera to connect the TV to the wall.

"Do you think that's a good idea?" Sarah asked leaning against the bathroom doorway.

"I think it's a great idea!" Sullivan said, "They left the wire here, what harm can it do? I'll put it back before I go to bed." He thought for a moment. "Besides, it'll give us a clue about their monitoring of us."

She wiped her face with a hand towel, "Okay, let's see if you can get it working. I'll freshen up and start dinner."

"Deal."

He knew they had some things to discuss over dinner, but he found himself looking forward to an evening where they pretended not to be prisoners. Sarah must have come to a similar conclusion. She didn't seem to be concerned about their predicament. They were both just bystanders who had to get through this misunderstanding and they would be released.

They made spaghetti to Sarah's recipe as best she could put together. Sullivan played with the lights to get it a bit dimmer in the kitchen. It wasn't romantic, but much more pleasant than the powerful overhead lights. They talked about anything except physics or chases or that they could not open the door and walk out.

Sullivan told Sarah about his ex-wife. He intentionally didn't mention Danny.

Sarah told Sullivan about her soccer team and explained the

origin of her need for exercise.

There was a tense moment when Sullivan commented on Sarah's much improved mood. That was a little too close to the current situation, but Sullivan was able to smoothly change the subject to his FBI friend who seemed to always need his mood improved.

After dinner it was a bit late, but neither of them wanted to go to bed, so they picked up *When Harry Met Sally* about ten minutes in. Neither of them had seen it, but they caught on quickly. They each sat on opposite sides of the couch.

. . .

Sullivan woke up in middle of the night. He heard the sounds in the living room. At first he thought it was Sarah, but listening closely he could tell the person didn't have a limp and was wearing shoes.

He held his breath and listened as the feet moved into the tile bathroom. He panicked when he thought of Sarah on the other side of them.

He sat up and looked over the edge of his bed. He breathed again when he found Sarah's pile of sheets like a big ball on the floor.

67. June 3, 2001

Sarah's shower woke Sullivan. He dressed in the clothes from yesterday and went to the kitchen to pull out breakfast. The clock read seven thirty.

As soon as he sat, he remembered the cable.

He jumped back up and returned it to the camera as Mary had left it. He returned to his seat.

He jumped back up to put the remote back in the drawer. This time he didn't immediately return to his seat but instead stood and examined the room.

He remembered Mary sitting uncomfortably and moved her chair to more directly face where Sarah would be. Sarah's chair was still there from yesterday. Sullivan told himself to remember to bring her water regularly. Satisfied everything was in place, Sullivan saw Sarah standing in the open bathroom door.

Again, Sarah wore her red blouse and a towel around her waist. She was holding the wrapping and gauze. Sullivan saw she was trying to look confidently at him. He responded with a nod and moved directly to the large chair next to the coffee table. Sarah followed the exact routine as yesterday, handing him the wrap and opening the gauze on the table top. When she saw he was ready, she quickly dropped her towel and lifted her leg to stand on her toes on the edge of the table. Sullivan worked quickly and efficiently. Her leg was wrapped without further ado.

"Thank you," Sarah said after her towel was returned to her waist. She returned to the bathroom.

Sullivan showered quickly and ate his bagel alone. Sarah found a pitcher and filled it with water. She set it and a glass on the coffee table just as they heard the sounds of footsteps outside. The routine helped. Sullivan could tell Sarah was less tense than yesterday, but certainly more tense than last night.

They met again to face the day at the back of the sofa.

Mary's questioning followed the same script as the day before. She started by asking questions from the same page as yesterday. Sullivan could see the check marks. Sarah answered the theoretical questions without difficulty. Sarah was filling the board with equations and figures, and Mary was taking notes. Sullivan noted Mary's predictable behavior.

By contrast, Sarah was erratic.

On a few occasions, Sarah would be starting to draw a figure that seemed would make a lot of sense to the discussion and then think better of it, erase it, and draw a figure with much less definition. Sullivan struggled to put his finger on what she was doing. She would be answering a question and get into a very specific example and then she would alter the course of the example to be more ... Abstract. That was the word he wanted. Sarah seemed to be intentionally abstract. Sullivan hoped Mary didn't notice, but he couldn't see how. She wasn't an idiot.

. . .

At three thirty, after seven and a half hours straight, Mary announced it was time to leave.

After she left, Sarah immediately went to the bathroom and Sullivan noticed the pitcher of water was empty. He went to the kitchen and found supplies to make cheese burgers and potatoes.

"What did you think?" Sarah asked. Sullivan turned around, she was leaning again on the door jamb resting her right leg and drying her hands on a hand towel. "You were mostly quiet all day." She seemed in a pretty good mood.

"I was thinking a lot about food," Sullivan said not wanting to get too deep.

"I've been working on these theories for ten years," Sarah said as she hung the towel back on the hanger. She looked to the dry erase board still crowded with her writing. "That's my life's work." Sullivan thought it was a profound statement to be made so casually. He tried to think what his life's work was. He decided he didn't need to go down that path.

"Burgers sound great. Get to work," Sarah commanded.

Sullivan watched her as she studied the door frame she was leaning on. She reached across her body and ran her hand along the frame. She leaned back as her eyes traced the inside edge to the header, across to the other jamb and back down.

She stood up straight and looked up again. She raised her hands over her head and grabbed the frame, testing her weight on her fingertips. She slowly bent her knees stretching out her body and lifting her feet from the floor. Her blouse pulled up exposing the smooth stomach muscles of an athlete. She slowly pulled herself up until her head disappeared behind the wall above the door. She held herself there momentarily and lowered back down.

She looked directly at Sullivan.

She winked at him and he decided it was time to stop gawking.

Sullivan pulled the food out of the refrigerator and turned on the oven while she did five more pull-ups with her fingertips.

He looked over when he heard her drop to her left foot. She smiled at him, "You were right, it was a long day. I had to get some exercise." She rubbed her hands together.

"No problem, you go right ahead," Sullivan said, "I might do twenty or thirty of those while the burgers are cooking." He smiled to himself. He had not done twenty or thirty pull-ups in his entire life. "On second thought, I'm not sure that frame would hold me."

"It's metal, a pretty heavy gauge," Sarah said as though that would help him. He looked at her sheepishly, as she looked at him expectantly.

"So, what are you not telling them?" Sullivan grasped at the first thing that came to his mind that wasn't about him not being able to do a pull-up.

Sarah's playful smile gave way as her face scrunched a little, "What?"

Sullivan wished he had said something else. The conversational lane change was abrupt, but he was into it now, "You were holding back in your explanations when it came to details. You're aware of someone testing something, maybe on a satellite?"

Sarah walked quickly from the bathroom doorway across the living room and right up to Sullivan. The look on her face told him to keep quiet. She whispered through clenched teeth, "Who said anything about satellites?"

Her apparent anger confused him, "No one did," he whispered back, not knowing why they were whispering, "All your examples were intentionally using terrestrial telescopes despite you starting to draw satellite pictures several times."

"Shit," Sarah showed frustration, then panic, then she let her forehead fall to Sullivan's shoulder.

"What's the problem?"

"Nothing," Sarah said. It wasn't nothing.

"Look, Sarah, all we need to do is be cooperative." Sullivan said. He enjoyed the feeling of her head on his shoulder.

"I'm not so sure," Sarah lifted her head and looked into Sullivan's eyes. He immediately missed the intimacy and warmth, "I don't know why they would release us. Once I tell them about my thesis work, they could just dispose of us."

"Sarah," Sullivan smiled, "They've taken great care to limit what we know about them. We only know what one of them looks like. We don't know where we are. We don't even know how they dress. That's why Mary always dresses like you. Why would they do all this if they were planning to *dispose of us*?"

"Sullivan," Sarah smiled softly, "You said this yesterday, but it's taken me most of the day to figure out what you meant. They don't know what I do. I don't think they know why they have us here."

"I still agree," Sullivan said, "but why do you say that?"

"They've been asking me about my thesis work and the papers I published. Their questions haven't strayed far from that, and I could go very far," Sarah said.

"I think Linus saw us together," Sarah said, "You said you met him before, so he knew you. He had my place bugged, so he knew me. So, when he saw us both in Greenville, together, he knew it couldn't be a coincidence. So he decided to pick us up."

"You're right," Sullivan confirmed and he continued because he couldn't help himself, "But Linus wasn't with these people."

"Yes, I agree," Sarah said. She leaned back into him this time leaning her head back so she could whisper into his ear, "He's been watching me, but LV didn't know me before we got here. That's why they're asking me about what I did in college."

Sullivan saw she was connecting the dots as he had. He continued, "I've been thinking the same thing, that Linus knew us both so he wanted to take us. He's clearly part of something very big, but he's some other part. He's not with these people. I think they don't know why they took us. No one kidnaps you to find out about your theoretical work from eight years ago. I think we've stumbled upon something big, but we're not part of it. I think you have to tell them everything, show them every example, or they won't believe we don't know anything."

Sarah looked him in the eye and smiled, "It's a damned good theory." Sullivan thought she was about to cry. She wouldn't quite look him in the eye. They were standing close enough together that it was an effort for her to look away. The normally smooth skin of her cheeks was flushing unevenly. "You're wrong. I've been trying to keep the examples simple and consistent. That's why I'm rethinking my examples."

Sullivan had to think. He saw her eyes. They were darting back and forth looking over his shoulder. He couldn't shake the feeling she wasn't telling him everything, but he couldn't imagine what. He stepped back from her and said, "I need to make the burgers, can you find us a movie for tonight?"

She stared for another moment. He felt the chill of the air in the space between them, although the room was plenty warm. "Yes, good idea."

Over dinner, Sullivan told stories about running track in high school. He always said he had the best view of the race, he could see everyone in front of him. Sarah seemed to enjoy the light conversation, although Sullivan knew they were both a bit distracted. When there was a break in the conversation that would be very awkward on a date, they both sat eating quietly for several minutes. Sullivan realized he had not been so comfortable eating with a woman since his ex-wife had left him.

"What is it?" Sarah asked. She had a soft look of concern.

"Nothing," Sullivan briefly missed Danny. He felt the frown on his face after she called attention to it and returned to a little smile, "I think I'm about done here," he said surveying his nearly clean plate, "What do you have for us tonight?"

Sarah didn't drop the look of concern in her eyes, but followed his lead that everything was alright, "I found one of my favorite movies, and one that maybe we should take notes on," he watched the concern fall from her face, "*Die Hard*."

"Excellent," Sullivan was happy. He liked the movie a lot. Last night he was careful to pick a movie he thought she would like. If she was doing the same, she did well.

Thirty minutes later Bruce Willis was on the TV screen standing barefoot on a floor covered in broken glass. Sarah had again sat on the right side of the couch, but on the inside of her cushion with her head against the back and her feet on the coffee table. Sullivan sat next to her and mirrored her position. They both looked over their toes at the screen. Sullivan had his right foot crossed over his left and Sarah's feet were side by side, only slightly smaller than his.

Sullivan turned to whisper in her ear. From their positions, nearly shoulder to shoulder, it was not difficult, "Is this *Space Resonance* really worth all this?"

"Yes," Sarah said matter-of-factly. Her head turned a few degrees toward him then returned to face the movie.

Sullivan wanted to ask what she wasn't telling them. He wanted to question her, but he wanted to trust her more. But he knew there was time.   After a few moments, Sarah slumped over to him so their shoulders touched. She said, "Sullivan, thank you, I couldn't do this without you."

. . .

The more time Jim Williams spent with the Vice President, the less he liked him.

He was pretty sure he just figured out why.

Throughout the history of Department 55, it was the role of the Vice President to spend nearly ninety percent of his time leading the organization toward its singular goal. That precedent was briefly interrupted with the resignation of Spiro Agnew as Nixon's Vice President. Nixon changed the protocol and assigned the job of leading Department 55 to his White House Chief of Staff, Bob Haldeman.

Dick Cheney was Gerald Ford's Chief of Staff when Jimmy Carter was elected President. The new President so disliked Cheney's maniacal approach to the search for LV that he returned to the previous precedent and assigned Department 55 to his Vice President, Walter Mondale.

The Special Secretary for Department 55 occasionally sought council with the former Presidents and VP's. Every one of them expressed regret for their failure, and every one of them expressed some discomfort about being asked to discuss it again.

Every one of them except Dick Cheney.

Fifteen years after running Department 55, Mr. Cheney was Secretary of Defense. In that position, he repeatedly asked the President to have Department 55 assigned to him. He was rebuffed. Now, defying all logic and probability, here he was, again running the Department as the Vice President of the United States.

Dick Cheney had no interest in becoming the President of the Unites States. Soon after the election, he told Jim that as long as LV was around, the President was actually the second most important person in government.

Since the Oklahoma City Bombing, Jim helped Bill Clinton work through his impeachment and Al Gore's defeat from the position of the President's closest aid. When George Bush came to office, President Clinton had joined Jim in the Oval Office for George's first meeting and told him who Jim was and what Department 55 was all about. George was shocked, but Dick was not. Since then, the Vice President had inserted himself between Jim and the President, as was his prerogative, but with a zeal that Jim found disturbing.

Jim sat in the Vice President's office helping Dick Cheney work through this crisis. They'd been there all night and the morning was breaking through the windows across the South Lawn. Jim respected that the Vice President had the stamina to continue through the night with no breaks and no interest except to solve the current problem. Dick's capacity for conspiracy and intrigue was unmatched. Jim didn't like that Dick relished the thought of commanding near absolute power in that goal. He carried himself as the master puppeteer with the President as his puppet and the media was beginning to catch on. This was a very dangerous game he played and the more dangerous it got the more the Vice President liked it.

"You've kept me here all night, Jim," the Vice President said, "I like you, and I enjoy our time together, but really?" The Vice President made a show of looking at his watch, "Ten hours ago I told you we were going to have to shut down *Hubble* and *KiteString* forever, and you haven't given me any other viable option to keep those programs alive."

Jim knew the Vice President was right.

Since LV demanded the destruction of the Desertron, every time they caught wind of a new scientific breakthrough, LV sent one of their damned letters telling the US to stop.

Now, LV had Dr. Kiadopolis. She was going to tell them all about her work on *Space Resonance*. So far, no one could figure out how LV found her, but once they knew about her work, they would certainly tell the USA to stop it.

"Sir," Jim was going to try again, "Dr. Kiadopolis' work is on the verge of the biggest breakthrough since Benjamin Franklin flew his kite! *KiteString* is actually living up to its name! And, it's our best chance of stopping LV!"

"I know all that," the Vice President said, "and LV is learning it right now. That's why we know they're going to demand we stop. I have a briefing with the President in twenty minutes. You and I both know that when we get the next letter, and it might be today, we're going to have to stop that work, and stop it fast."

Jim knew he was right. He looked down to the floor.

"I need you to figure out how to destroy those satellites, and fast," the Vice President seemed almost happy with this proclamation.

"Yes, sir." Jim accepted. He stood to leave. The Vice President began to jot notes on a scratch paper. That paper would need to be burned as soon as he had the President's approval.

Jim stood knowing he was about to figure out how to destroy the most promising work going on in the world. The human race was about to get a whole lot dumber.

Maybe the Department of Defense was closer to shooting down satellites than they let on.

Maxwell Rassic would be furious. Once the satellites were gone, he would have to destroy Sarah's office, all of her servers and data. LV would give them some deadline, probably a few days.

So in a few days, he would have to show them that he had complied.

Jim stopped with his hand on the door knob. He would have to show them what? How would he show LV that he had stopped Dr. Kiadopolis' work? Even if they destroyed the satellites and her work, and even if LV killed her, how did they know there weren't ten more like Dr. Kiadopolis and ten more satellites?

This was going to be a major problem.

"Mr. Williams," the Vice President said looking over the top of his glasses, "do you need something?" By the tone of his voice, Jim knew the VP really meant *Mr. Williams, Get Out*. But that wasn't what he was going to do.

He turned, "Mr. Vice President, destroying *KiteString* won't do any good."

"Oh, why the hell not?" The Vice President was growing tired now.

"Even if we could prove to LV that we destroyed the satellite, which is doubtful, we wouldn't be able to prove there isn't another *KiteString*. We wouldn't be able to prove that we had destroyed the capability. We could just build another one. It's not a seventy mile track in the desert!"

Jim knew it would be impossible to prove to LV that they had destroyed the satellites. They couldn't drive out to the desert and see a trench being filled in. They couldn't visit a research facility and see the equipment falling into disrepair. The unfortunate part about physics research was that it required huge, dedicated, tremendously expensive equipment. The CERN, currently under construction by the Europeans, was the largest machine on earth. It was easy to see whether it was being used or not. But a satellite? No one could see them except the Air Force Space Command. LV wouldn't believe them. They couldn't prove a satellite had been destroyed. And they couldn't prove a second, secret satellite had been destroyed. Just like they couldn't prove there weren't five more of them. No, destroying *Hubble* and *KiteString* wouldn't do any good. Jim knew it. He looked at the Vice President and could tell he knew it too.

The Vice President frowned. Jim fought back a smile.

68.   June 4, 2001

Sullivan woke up before Sarah and again stepped around her in her pile of bedding on his floor. He would say something to her tonight. He grabbed his clothes from yesterday and walked in his boxer shorts to the kitchen. He decided he would start the coffee first today. It was seven thirty-five and they didn't have as much time as they were used to. He showered and dressed quickly and didn't shave to give Sarah time.

Sarah was in her room when he got back to his. He closed his door so she could move to the bathroom in private. He didn't have to wait long for the sound of her characteristic limp as she padded to the bathroom. The bathroom door closed and the water came on quickly. Sullivan's hand slid from the handle when he tried to open the door. He was moving quickly so he grabbed it again.

Again the door did not open.

The doorknob turned. He looked at the crack between the door and the jamb and saw the latch retract.

Why didn't the door open?

He pulled hard enough to make the solid wood door flex and saw it move away from the bottom but stay fixed at the top.

Sullivan dragged his small chair to the door and stood on it. Looking again at the crack between the door and the jamb, this time across the top of the door, he could see a half inch metal rod protruding from an opening in the jamb into the door. He stood back up, still on the chair.

His heart rate was accelerating as he thought. This rod must have been from a locking mechanism in the top of the door. They must have been able to operate it remotely. Did all of the doors have this?

He quickly decided yes.

That's why the frame was metal and so thick that Sarah could do pull-ups on it. The metal frame and solid wood door would be too strong for him to break through. He was trapped in his room.

He thought his heart was pounding before, but then he heard movement in the living room. He knew it wasn't Sarah because he still heard shower sounds. He didn't know what to do. He decided to get off the chair before he fell off. He stepped down silently and listened through the door.

He thought he should call out, but he couldn't figure how that would help. He put both hands on the door and listened with his ear against the door. He heard the shower stop. Seven-fifty, the clock in his room only read seven-fifty. They still had ten minutes. The bathroom door opened.

"Dr. Kiadopolis," he heard Mary say.

"Oh, I'm not ready yet," Sarah said, "Where's Sullivan?"

"Dr. Kiadopolis, we need to talk," Mary said.

"Where is Sullivan?" Sarah asked with urgency.

"He's in his room being quiet. I assure you he is fine," Mary said. Sullivan tried calling out, but he choked on any words he tried to get out.

"Please, Dr. Kiadopolis," Mary said, "Please sit."

Sullivan heard Sarah padding, presumably to the large chair nearest his door.

"Wait, I'm going to dress," Sarah said. Sullivan thought she must be in her blouse and towel like the last few days.

"No, please, this will not take long," Mary said. Sullivan heard Sarah pause, then nothing. She must have sat quietly.

"Dr. Kiadopolis," Mary's voice was firm, but low. Sullivan had to hold his breath to hear. "I've enjoyed our talks these past few days. They've been very informative, but not really to the point of why we are all here."

"I thought," Sarah started softly. She stopped abruptly. There was a pause.

"Dr. Kiadopolis, why were you in Greenville?" Mary asked.

Sarah didn't answer at first, but then she spoke quietly. Sullivan could barely hear her, "I've done some work there, and I went to see it."

She did work in Greenville? Okay, Sullivan thought. That must be how she met Peter. He pushed that from his mind, it seemed irrelevant.

"What kind of work?" Mary asked.

"We've been talking about this, I'm a physicist," Sarah said.

Sullivan didn't think that was a good move. They had separated them for some reason. Either they thought Sarah wouldn't talk with Sullivan around, or they wanted to intimidate her, or they were going to do something they didn't want him to interfere with. Sullivan cringed. It wasn't yet clear which.

"We know you are a physicist. We read all your papers and we have studied you closely." Mary said, "You were in Greenville on a very interesting night. You were sitting in the perfect position to be watching a very interesting building."

"There must have been hundreds of people in that bar and there were many more in every bar up and down the street." Sarah explained.

"Yes but of all those people you and Mr. Acer were the only ones chased onto the street!" Mary said.

"That was you chasing us!" Sarah said in an uncomfortable voice.

"Dr. Kiadopolis, we want to know how you found the bombs." Mary said, her normal composure faltering.

"What bombs?" Sarah asked.

She tried to make it sound like a question but Sullivan could tell it wasn't, even through the door.

She knew about the bombs.

Bombs? Sullivan didn't know about any bombs. Mary was speaking quickly, urgently. She was worried, and that worried Sullivan. He hoped Sarah would come clean. *Bombs?*

"We believe you are using *Space Resonance* to locate nuclear weapons, and we must know how you do it." There was a long pause. Sullivan was holding his breath.

Nuclear weapons?

Nuclear weapons were way beyond anything he could have imagined was going on here. He thought he was investigating a mob bribery ring. Over the last few days, he thought they were here because of mistaken identity. Now he had to contend with *nuclear weapons?*

Mary spoke very slowly and softly, "Dr. Kiadopolis, you must know that the people I work for are going to find out what you have done. You must know that you are going to tell them." Another pause. "Dr. Kiadopolis, you must know that they don't want anything to happen to you."

Sullivan had trouble hearing what happened next.

There was the small sound of a woman.

It was gagging!

"Sarah?" Sullivan cried through the door.

Just as he did he heard rustling and a sudden explosion of motion.

Quick footsteps. Sarah's.

He heard both women moving quickly. There was some banging.

They were fighting!

"Open this door!" Sullivan called to no one. He grabbed the doorknob and pulled as hard as he could. It didn't do anything.

Gagging again.

He banged on the door. There was nothing he could do.

Sarah was on her own.

Sullivan fell quiet again trying to listen. As quickly as it started, the rustling stopped. Sullivan was glad to hear quiet talking between the women, but he couldn't hear what they were saying.

With his ear pressed against the door he heard the two women walking across the carpet. He heard Sarah's limp and Mary's heels.

"Sarah?" Sullivan called again, "Are you okay? The door won't open!"

He got quiet again. His entire body was tight. He thought his heart was going to explode out of his body. What was happening on the other side of this door?

. . .

Sarah's leg throbbed from her recent efforts. Mary didn't look good, but Sarah had done everything she could to help.

She waited while Mary composed herself in her chair. They were both back in their seats as though nothing happened. Sarah wanted to run, but there was nowhere to go, and Mary was in no condition to threaten her right now.

"Okay," Sarah wished they had just come out and asked her before. She struggled to remember why she was dancing around her work before.

She'd hoped she could keep it secret.

Stupid. Deadly Stupid.

"I'll tell you everything I've been doing. I'll tell you how I've been finding the bombs. But first, I need to get dressed, and you need to open *that* door." Mary knew she meant Sullivan's door.

"Very well," Mary looked at Sarah, her hair disheveled and her make up a mess. "I, too, need a moment. I will be back in seven minutes." Mary stood holding onto the back of the chair for stability. She clutched her attaché and a trashcan and made her way as gracefully as she could to the door.

Sarah felt a burst of emotion well up from her chest as tears poured from her eyes. She heard a small click and knew the lock mechanism was released.

By the time Sullivan came to her she was shaking uncontrollably. His hand on her shoulder was a lifeline and she wanted to hold on as tightly as she could. She struggled to stand and fell into his body.

They hugged for some time.

"I've never been so scared in my life!" Sarah wept into his shoulder.

"I know. It'll be okay." Sullivan said.

For the first time in two days, Sarah didn't think he was right. Sarah leaned back and looked into his face. His pure concern was comforting. He wasn't the kind of man who could hide his emotions, and she loved him for that.

No, she liked him for it.

She pulled her arm out from under his to wipe her face.

"What happened?"

"Mary threw up."

Clearly Sullivan didn't comprehend what she said because his look of concern changed to a look of bewilderment. He looked silly enough for her to laugh. Her emotions were certainly not her own. The pulse of laughter shook her body and she felt it in her thigh. The pain wiped the smile from her face and she bent over slightly.

"I need to get ready." Mary would return in a few minutes. She steeled herself and stepped three steps to the coffee table. She unceremoniously dropped her towel and put her foot on the coffee table.

"Sullivan, please." Sarah was regaining some control, but Sullivan didn't keep up.

He stood gawking.

She appreciated his awkwardness in this difficult situation. He looked down to her leg, and she saw his face snap back to the task at hand. He moved to his position on the chair and set about applying the wrapping.

The first day she watched him closely to see that he respected her. The second day she was a little less diligent. Now she found herself willing him to touch her leg.

"Mary tried to threaten me," Sarah said as Sullivan worked. "She opened her attaché and showed me a pair of handcuffs." Sullivan paused briefly.

The implication of the cuffs was that if she didn't talk the nature of their time here would change dramatically. LV also demonstrated their ability to control their two captives with the door lock. If LV got them separated and decided to use cuffs, this could get less pleasant very quickly.

"You're going to have to tell them everything. Whatever everything is," Sullivan looked up at her face, "You know that."

"Of course," Sarah looked away from his direct stare. Here she was, in her panties with the only person in the world she could rely on working on her upper leg, and she was afraid she was letting him down. He'd been honest with her so far, and she'd been keeping the most important detail from him. Now LV threatened to raise the stakes and Sarah learned she was playing with fire.

"She couldn't do it," Sarah said, looking back down at Sullivan.

He was almost done with the wrapping.

"What?"

"She couldn't go through with the threat." Sarah talked to the top of his head, "She took one look at the handcuffs and she got physically sick herself."

Sullivan finished her bandage and sat back in the chair. Sarah didn't move from her perch on the table. His work wasn't as neat as yesterday, but it would do.

"She threw up in the trashcan," Sarah said. For a moment, she forgot about her near nakedness. She looked at him looking at her, and for a moment, she felt secure in their connection.

. . .

"Sarah," Sullivan stood as she came from the bathroom.

Sarah kept the bathroom door open while she dressed and he tried as hard as he could to not watch her pull her skirt on.

He stepped directly in front of her. She stopped and he looked her in the eye. "No games. Whatever you know, whatever you've been keeping from them, whatever you've been keeping from me, tell them everything. I don't care that you've been keeping things from me, but they do."

She looked down. Her eyes started watering again, and her lip began to tremble. *We don't want anything to happen to you.* That was all Mary said. The sentence made ice run through Sullivan's veins and he wasn't even in the room. He didn't see her face. He didn't see the handcuffs. LV went out of their way to remind them that they had complete power over these two people.

Sullivan sat down on the couch. He sat heavily in his customary position. Sarah stood before him, her eyes still watering.

"Sullivan, I'm sorry." Sarah whispered. Despite himself, Sullivan felt betrayed. For three days, he was convinced this was a misunderstanding. He thought Linus was involved in something big. Whatever it was, Sullivan quickly decided that the less he and Sarah knew about it the better. They were just bystanders in the wrong place at the wrong time.

His entire strategy was predicated on neither of them knowing anything about anything. He looked up at Sarah who was still standing in the middle of the room. For the first time, he didn't see the beautiful woman she was.

Despite himself, he was mad at her for knowing things.

They heard Mary's heels clicking against the concrete floor. The tears that had been welling up began to roll freely down Sarah's cheeks.

"I'm sorry!" Sarah pleaded quietly.

The door opened. Sarah quickly wiped her eyes, but they were bloodshot from crying. Sullivan didn't turn to watch Mary approach. He watched Sarah's face follow her around the room. Mary settled into the chair as she had done the past few days, as though everything was the same. Sullivan looked at her and Mary looked away. It wasn't the same for her either.

Sarah took a deep breath, "So, this is all about finding nuclear weapons lost in the United States?"

Sullivan tried to pay close attention to Sarah but realized he wanted to see Mary's reaction to everything as well. He turned slightly to his right so he could see them both. Mary cocked her head at Sarah's question but didn't say anything.

Sarah took a cleansing breathe, "Five years ago, we altered the Hubble Space Telescope to allow me to detect gravitons using an experimental *Space Resonator* based on the theories we discussed over the past three days."

Sullivan wanted to look at Sarah and gawk but fought the urge and focused on Mary.

She gave little or no reaction.

"The resonator was able to see distant stars like normal satellites could see our sun. We did some really great work, but it was slow going. I spent most of my time on data management and software development. The amount of data available in a graviton stream is mind boggling. Then we turned the telescope to the Earth."

"You can do that?" Mary asked.

"Yes, Hubble is run from a command center at Lawrence Livermore. I was given authorization to task the satellite regularly," Sarah said. Mary looked like she didn't believe her. "There's an internet site where anyone could put in a tasking request, and they're sent to the satellite based on a priority number." Sullivan turned and looked at Sarah in disbelief. "Yes, even you could put in a request. But if you went to the site you could see that it's tasked for the next eighty years."

"How do you get priority?" Mary asked.

"Researchers can request priority numbers," Sarah said.

"No," Mary tried again, "I am sorry you did not understand me. How did *you* get *your* priority numbers?"

"Oh," Sarah understood now, "I never applied for a number. The administrator at Lawrence Livermore just sent one to me. I figured my project manager arranged it." Sarah stopped.

"Please go on."

"Forgive me, Mary, I haven't talked about this with anyone. It's difficult for me say these words."

"Okay, I understand," Mary said, "Just, *please*, keep going."

Sullivan looked back to Mary. She was begging Sarah to keep talking. What situation was she in? Sullivan had a sudden thought. What if Mary was also a prisoner?

"Okay," Sarah said. She took a few steps back toward her chair next to the dry erase board. "As I said, I received a high priority number code that allowed me to submit my tasks to the satellite and cut the line."

"And you looked for nuclear weapons?" These women seemed completely comfortable with those two words, but Sullivan was not. Every time one of them said *nuclear weapon,* it resonated through his spine.

"I never knew what we were looking for," Sarah said, "Actually, I wanted to keep looking at stars, but I was directed to focus on the Earth. I mentioned earlier that I did some work in Greenville, that's where I started to collect data."

Sullivan had a lot of trouble following the conversation because he was stuck between them. He decided to stand. He moved slowly so as not to alarm anyone. Neither woman seemed to notice him. He moved to the other side of the living room and sat on the chair Sarah had been using when she was lecturing. From there he could see both women.

"You started to collect your data?" Mary repeated in the form of a question.

"Yes, it took a long time to get the algorithms to work on the Earth as well as they did in space. We kept focusing on one spot until we got them to work, and then I quickly found," Sarah trailed off and looked at Sullivan.

"What did you find?" Sullivan asked, speaking for the first time. Sarah looked at him and he nodded at her. Don't stop talking now.

"I found a nuclear device in the basement of the Poinsett hotel!" Sarah said.

"When was this?" Sullivan asked. His mind was reeling. He was glad he was sitting down.

"Yes, when was this?" Mary asked. Sarah and Mary both looked at Sullivan then back to each other.

"The system first worked two years ago," Sarah said.

"And then you found the devices in California this spring?" Mary asked.

"Yes," Sarah said quickly, but then she looked at Mary with some concern.

Sullivan was trying to process everything that was going on. Mary didn't know when Sarah found the first device in Greenville, but she knew when Sarah found them in California? Why did Sarah look for a device in Greenville when she didn't know it was there?

"There was an atomic bomb in the basement of the Poinsett Hotel?" Sullivan asked.

Again, both women looked at him, but Sarah answered, "Yes. When I reported it, I was told it was an old device left over from past experiments. They told me it was in storage and it was a great place to refine the technology."

"But it was under a hotel," Sullivan pleaded.

"I didn't know that, not until the day I saw you there," Sarah said.

"So why were you there, after two years," Mary asked.

"After I found the two devices in California, I got suspicious that there were so many of these things lying around. I began to distrust my program manager." Sarah paused. She looked at Sullivan. Sullivan again felt panic that she was going to stop talking. "Then Sullivan told me he was going to Greenville to follow L-." Sarah stopped herself. "Sullivan was going to follow a lead, so I decided to see what was going on there myself."

Mary turned slowly and looked at Sullivan, "You were there following a lead?"

"I, I," up until now Sullivan had been regarded as just a bystander. Maybe he was Sarah's boyfriend, but certainly someone who was unimportant. This was the first time Mary had asked him a question in four days. "Yes, I was there working on a case."

"Never mind, it is not important," Mary said and turned back to Sarah, "So you can detect the devices from space."

"Yes."

"I'll need to review this with others," Mary said, "I will likely not be back until the morning, let us again resume at eight am?"

"Okay," Sarah looked at Sullivan and he looked back with his palms up. It wasn't up to them.

"Thank you for being so candid, please let us continue tomorrow," Mary said. With that, she stood up and left.

Sullivan looked at Sarah, and Sarah looked at Sullivan.

Sarah smiled, then she frowned, then her eyes started to water.

Sullivan didn't know what to do. He could feel himself starting to tear up.

Sarah started to cry.

Sullivan stood but she waved him off. Instead, he went to the kitchen.

He busied himself making coffee and leaned on the sink to think.

If Mary wanted to know how Sarah found the bombs, why didn't she just ask, why wait for Sarah to talk about her theories for the last three days?

Because Mary didn't know. That's why.

The only reason they got picked up was because Linus was chasing them. He was sure of it now.

Linus. Linus was chasing them and that's why LV decided to take them. So Linus isn't with LV. But Linus has been watching Sarah, and he has been traveling to California, and he was at the hotel.

Sarah's crying slowed. As Sullivan pulled out the bagels and cream cheese for breakfast, Sarah stood and joined him. She sat down and wiped her eyes. She looked terrible.

Sullivan put a cup of coffee in front of her.

She took a sip of the coffee and grimaced. Sullivan knew it was awful, but it was hot. She muscled it down and he was surprised she took another sip. She laughed at the look on his face.

"I'm desperate," Sarah said.

Sullivan smiled, "It's been a rough morning. I'm a little desperate, too." They spread cream cheese on their bagels and started to eat. Sullivan used much more than he normally did, but what the hell. There was no use trying to lose weight when you could be killed at any time. Strange thought. He had trouble gripping the knife.

"Sarah," Sullivan said after eating half a bagel in silence.

Sarah looked at him but didn't speak.

"Where did you find devices in California?"

"Why does it matter?" Sarah asked with her hand covering her mouthful of bagel.

"It was San Francisco first, then Fresno, right?"

"Yes, that's right," Sarah said with no hand covering the mouth still full of bagel, "How did you know that?"

"Because, I've been tracking Linus," Sullivan said. He put his bagel down, "He travels a lot, but he sometimes takes trips that don't make any sense. Most were pretty normal, but the two to California were overnight with no hotel."

Sarah looked around, "I'm tired, let's finish eating and watch some TV."

Sullivan was briefly disappointed, but then realized what she was saying.

They finished eating and were flipping through channels in five minutes.

At nine-thirty in the morning there wasn't much on. Sullivan settled on The Andy Griffith Show and turned the volume higher than necessary.

"The system only works when the power is out," Sarah whispered into Sullivan's ear. They had resumed their positions from last night. "The California energy crisis was a real boon for my work." Sullivan was vaguely familiar with the California energy grid troubles. They seemed self-induced.

Sarah moved up and used her hand to push his face away so she could whisper in his ear, "Wait, Linus was in California this summer?"

"Yes," Sullivan said. He couldn't help but be aware that her body was pressed against his. He could feel her breasts against his chest. The comfortable position overpowered his disappointment in her that she was keeping things from him. Wait, he didn't want it to be that easy for a woman to manipulate him. He'd made that mistake before.

"I found the devices this summer."

Sullivan shifted and Sarah pulled back. He looked at her, "Linus went to San Francisco on January 20, 2001. I remember it because I've been looking at the records for weeks."

"Shit," Sarah said, "That's three days *after* I found it!" Sarah looked at Sullivan as though she hadn't seen him in a month. She looked up and down at herself apparently just becoming aware of her position. She pulled herself back, "Did he go to Fresno on March 21?"

"No," Sullivan said, "He went the next day, on March 22."

"I don't think we know who Linus is," Sarah said, looking Sullivan in the eyes and close enough that he could feel her breath on his nose. "He's been watching me for years. And as soon as I find a nuclear weapon, he jumps on a plane and goes right to it. But what's he doing there, and how does he even know I found it?" Sarah asked.

"He's listening to you at your apartment and probably in your car, maybe he's listening at your work."

"No, that's impossible," Sarah said. "If he was listening at my work, he wouldn't hear anything. I never talk to anyone there. And I never took anything out of the office. No one ever came in and nothing ever left."

"What if he was watching you in your office? With a camera?" Sullivan asked.

"He has cameras?" Sarah asked. He immediately felt her body tense. He had never mentioned cameras to Sarah before. If Linus had cameras for her work, he must have had them in her apartment. He felt her lift herself away from him a bit more.

The both watched Andy Griffith in silence and thought for a moment.

"You found nuclear weapons and didn't tell *anyone*?" Sullivan asked.

"I told my program manager," Sarah said. "But he made me memorize the data and fly to him and tell him in person."

"So," Sullivan looked over at Sarah. Her forehead was creased with concentration, "How well do you know your program manager?"

Abruptly, Sarah got up. She moved quickly around the couch and into the kitchen.

"I'm going to exercise a little," Sarah explained as she pulled the chairs away from the table.

Sullivan must have voiced the concern she didn't want to admit she had.

He watched as she lay under the table and began to lift herself from the floor with intense focus. He certainly could fall for her, he had fallen for lesser women in the past. He might not even know any better women.

But he wasn't going to.

. . .

They spent the afternoon sitting on the couch and chair reading magazines. Sarah found a National Geographic that was far more interesting than Cosmo, so they took turns reading it. They completed the compatibility test in Cosmo and found that the experts at the magazine rated them *good for each other*. They exercised together, holding each other's feet while they did sit-ups and counted push-ups. Sarah could only use her left leg, but still out-performed him on every measure.

They took the time to look at her wound closely. It was healing well despite the continued discomfort.

Sarah practiced wrapping it a few times, and Sullivan was mildly disappointed that she could do a good job.

Sullivan enjoyed Sarah's straight forward approach to just about everything and Sarah laughed easily. At times they seemed to forget where they were and the afternoon passed quickly.

By five-thirty they were sitting side by side at the kitchen table working on a crossword puzzle when Sullivan had a thought.

Over the course of the past five hours, they'd surmised that Linus was stealing the nuclear weapons Sarah found and selling them to LV. There were some corollaries to that theory, but right now it held up to the information they had.

"What?" Sarah asked following Sullivan's quizzical look.

"LV is telling the President that they have these bombs, right?" Sullivan asked and Sarah nodded, "And that's how they got the President to tell you to help them, right?" Another nod from Sarah. "They could ask the President anything, right?"

Sarah's light smile continued, "Yes."

"They could ask for a billion dollars, release of their crazy leader from prison, that the army attack Canada, anything." Sullivan said.

Sarah put the pencil down and looked at him, "I suppose."

"Why in the hell would they ask for you to explain to them your theories?" Sullivan asked.

Sarah looked at him still smiling. Then her shoulders shrugged, "I don't know. Maybe they think I can teach them how to do it and they could find more?"

"How many could there be?" Sullivan asked.

"Maybe they're going to move the bombs and they don't want us to find them again?"

Maybe, Sullivan thought. Something still didn't fit.

They spoke openly because they didn't think it did any harm if the two of them figured out what LV was doing. Certainly, the government would have legions of people working on this too. But if it had to do with what Sarah knew, they were more careful.

Sullivan didn't have anything else, so he returned to the crossword. He was pretty good at them, probably the only thing they'd tried so far that he was better at than Sarah.

Sarah made stir fry while Sullivan picked a movie. They ate talking about the National Geographic article on Central Africa that they had read that day. Sullivan thought Sarah might be the smartest person he had ever known. Then he decided that made sense as she was also the only theoretical physicist he'd ever known.

After watching *The American President*, they each went to their rooms.

Sullivan thought of the day as he unbuttoned his shirt. Again, he couldn't shake the feeling of comfort he had with Sarah. Despite her intimidating looks, strength, and brains, she was easy to talk to and easy to be around.

He'd only been in his room for twenty seconds when he heard a strenuous knocking on the door.

"Sullivan, open up!" Sarah whispered that whisper that sounded like a shout. Sullivan stood in his t-shirt and pants for a fraction of a second as his heart rate skyrocketed and the edges of his vision turned red. He stumbled three steps to the door and threw it open expecting to see, to see what? He didn't have any idea what to expect.

He didn't see anything as she threw herself into his arms and squeezed him tightly.

"They could have locked us in our rooms!" Sarah said.

Oh, Sullivan's heart rate immediately began to slow as he processed her fear. As he calmed, he felt the bare skin of her back and the warmth of her body tightly against his. She was in her skirt and bra. Apparently she was at about the same point as he was when she realized they were separated in their rooms and panicked.

They stood like that for half a minute before Sarah collected herself. She pulled back, slightly loosening her grip, and looked up at him for a brief instant.

Sullivan saw in her eyes an acceptance he'd looked for in every woman he'd ever been close too.

Then, she turned and returned to her room.

Sullivan stood watching her walk away. He found himself still standing there a minute after she turned the corner into her room.

Sullivan took off his t-shirt and pants and folded them neatly on his small chair before turning the light down to its lowest setting and climbing into bed.

As soon as he settled his head into his pillow, he heard the characteristic shuffling of Sarah wrapped in her large quilt with the slight favoring of her right leg coming across the living room. Normally she waited until he was asleep, but he expected her earlier tonight. It was dark but he could see her enter his room, a blob of bedding with her head poking out the top.

Sullivan squinted to see her.

She looked at the floor and then at the wide space he'd left by lying on the far side. Sarah quickly lay down on her stomach in a smooth motion opening her quilt and pulling it down on top of herself. She settled in on her side of the bed facing away from Sullivan with his quilt below her and hers on top making an effective barrier between them.

Sullivan knew she needed good sleep, and he was happy she trusted him enough to lay there. He wanted to say good night, but he knew he shouldn't.

69. June 5, 2001

Sullivan woke up to the sound of Sarah talking in the living room. His eyes opened slowly and he sat up. His door was open. He heard what sounded like Mary laughing? Could that be right? No, he decided he wasn't hearing something right. He stood up in his boxers and peaked around his doorway.

Mary and Sarah were both sitting at the table. Both women were again wearing the exact same outfits with Sarah barefoot and Mary in heels. They were facing away from him. Sarah was eating a bagel and Mary was drinking coffee. Sullivan pulled back into his room quietly and looked at the clock.

Eight forty-five.

He'd overslept. He still couldn't process what was happening. He dressed quickly. He felt he entered a different world as he crossed into the living room.

"Good morning," Sarah said when she looked over to him. Mary looked over too. Sullivan could see both women was smiling broadly, honestly.

When Mary saw him, the smile melted from her face. She moved to stand up.

"No, please," Sullivan said, "Don't get up."   Sullivan had no idea what was going on, but he decided if Sarah was calm, he could be calm. "Good morning," he said.

"Good morning, Mr. Acer," Mary said, her smile returning.

"We overslept," Sarah said, "I tried to make it back to my room when I heard her at the door, but she caught me running across the living room." Sullivan found himself in an awkward situation. So he just smiled.

"As I was saying," Sarah turned back to Mary, "I started dressing professionally in high school. I found it gave me a confidence in myself. You said you normally don't dress like this?" She looked out of the corner of her eye at Sullivan. He was focused on keeping his face neutral.

"Yes," Mary said, "I was the type who wore sweats and a big wool scarf to class. Anything else and I couldn't get the boys to leave me alone!"

"But didn't you like the boys paying you all that attention?" Sarah asked.

Sullivan thought it was genuine.

"It could be nice, but where I attended university," Mary checked herself and spoke slowly, "Where I attended university, there were few women in the sciences and engineering colleges."

Sullivan knew she was taking great pains to not reveal anything about herself. He also knew that every university in the world had trouble attracting women in significant numbers to their sciences.

"It made me uncomfortable having those boys looking at me."

"Yes, I can see that," Sarah said, "I knew they were looking, but I knew that meant I could get them to do anything I wanted. Sometimes it came in handy. I always got the smartest groups for projects. I always got invited to every party and study group. Because I was invited to everything, I could pick and choose what I did, so I always got to be with the smartest most challenging people."

"Isn't that using your looks to get ahead?"

"I don't sleep my way to the top, if that's what you're asking," Sarah said.

Sullivan was afraid some tension would build, but it didn't.

"Think of it like this," Sarah went on, "Tall men get noticed more and get ahead. Not because being tall makes them better, but just because they get noticed. Some people have the right last name. Some people start out rich, and funny people get noticed. In the random world we live, you need every opportunity you can get.

Tall people don't stoop over to keep everything level. I like looking my best, and in some instances, it gives me an advantage. I'll be damned if I'm going to give up any advantage I can get!"

"I must admit, I had not thought of it like that," Mary said.

Sullivan noted that her precise conversation persisted outside of the scientific debates and into what seemed a casual conversation. Her tiny fingers seemed to barely hold the coffee mug as she held it in both hands to take a drink. She looked over the top of her mug at Sullivan. She seemed to be keeping close track of him. She was a pretty woman. Where Sarah was tall and muscular like an athlete, Mary was small and petite.

"Well, I'm afraid we are going to have to get started."

"Okay," Sarah said.

"We will have to resume our positions so I can record the conversation," Mary said in a very conversational way. She left her nearly empty coffee on the table and made her way to the living room.

Sarah stood and carried her mug and plate to the sink.

"My quilt got snagged as I ran in front of her and we stood staring at each other," Sarah explained quietly to Sullivan, "I was mortified until she busted out laughing." Sarah looked up at Sullivan who was still resting on the sink.

"I'm glad you had a good time," Sullivan said.

"She made the coffee while I showered, and we talked while I ate," Sarah said, "She's a nice lady."

Sullivan looked over Sarah's shoulder at Mary who had returned the camera to its correct orientation. They both looked at their captor. "If I wasn't held here under threat of death, I could easily be her friend."

"Yesterday," Mary began after they'd all taken their positions in the living room, "You gave me an excellent overview of your work in the field of experimental physics and the use of that work to locate nuclear weapons on Earth."

"Yes," Sarah said.

"Please start at the beginning and tell me how the physical system works."

Sarah thought for a few moments, likely trying to figure where to start. She stood and drew an arch signifying the surface of the earth, "First we installed a *Space Resonator* on the Hubble Space Telescope." She drew the Hubble Telescope with a big box, then a distant star. Sullivan recognized the picture Sarah almost drew a few days ago.

The conversation went on for eight hours. Sullivan reflected that it was a conversation, much less stressful than the previous lectures. He felt more comfortable because Mary didn't seem afraid of him. He was able to move around the apartment, bringing the women coffee and even peanut butter and jelly for lunch. The mood was light and Mary even laughed a few times.

"What happened?" Sullivan asked as soon as Mary left and the door closed.

"I don't know," Sarah looked happy and relaxed as she leaned against the sink, "When I first saw her this morning, I knew I was already late for the day, so I was almost running across the living room. She had just come into the room and was standing next to the door. I stumbled and my blanket got caught on the coffee table." Sullivan could see color flush to her cheeks at the memory. Sullivan pushed the image from his mind. "So, there I was," she made a gesture waving her hands down her body indicating her nakedness at that moment, "and we just stared at each other. I thought she was either going to throw up again or, or, I don't know what!" Sarah was clearly amused by the story she was telling. "So I said *'Can you make the coffee?'* and just stood there."

Sullivan focused on the image of Mary throwing up to get other images out of his head, "So what did she do?"

"She busted out laughing!" Sarah was almost laughing reliving the experience.

"What did you do?"

"I turned and went into the bathroom," Sarah said. "When I came out dressed, she had put my blanket in my room and had coffee waiting on the kitchen table. She was sitting and looking over her own notes. I sat with her, and we talked."

Sullivan idly washed the coffee mugs as Sarah described the small talk. They shared a lot of experiences being women in technical careers.

They discussed their understanding of LV to see if anything changed over a light dinner of assorted breads and cheeses. Nothing had.

Sarah dropped any pretense of going to her room to sleep and was already under her blanket and on top of his when Sullivan came from the bathroom.

He disrobed to his boxers noting that Sarah was on her side and facing the wall. As he moved around the bed to climb in, she rolled careful to not look at him and also to keep her blanket up around her neck.

. . .

Peter could see where Sarah got her good looks. He was sitting in Henrietta Kiadopolis' kitchen.

Henrietta agreed to meet him for dinner at her home, but only after she'd arranged for her boyfriend to be there.

She wore a skirt that was a bit too tight and makeup that was a bit too heavy, and she was a little thick around the middle, but he could see how she would be beautiful if she'd taken better care of herself.

"So," Dylan, her boyfriend, said, "You're here looking for little Sarah?" He asked Peter but didn't bother to look away from Henrietta's ass as she worked to get plates to serve the food Peter had brought. Claire was also helping, and Dylan didn't hide his glances at her behind either.

"Yes," Peter cringed, "I'm worried about her."

"Why? You ain't been with her in years, have ya?" Dylan slouched in the chair across from him and Peter could see a tuff of chest hair poking out of his collar. At the mention of Peter being with Sarah, he immediately looked at Claire. A few months ago, Claire was very sensitive to their history, but now Peter knew she was okay with being here. He checked anyway, and she didn't react at all.

"No, we haven't been together in some time," Peter looked back at Dylan, "But I still care about her. And when the FBI told me she was missing, I wanted to make sure there was nothing else I could do."

"Well," Dylan said, "If there was anything to be done, I'd be doing it!" Peter doubted it but smiled in agreement.

"Have you heard from her?" Peter asked Henrietta as both women returned to the table with the settings. Henrietta passed out the dishes with the practiced precision of someone who worked in the service industry.

"No, we haven't heard from her," Henrietta said. She looked up at Peter, "And it's been too long. When the FBI came here, I was already scared!" Her statement was the logical one for a mother whose daughter was currently kidnapped, but there was something about the way she was hanging on Dylan that made Peter think she wasn't that concerned.

"No letters? No calls?" Claire asked.

"No," Henrietta said. Peter studied her face and she was telling the truth about that.

"Any checks?" Peter asked.

He knew Sarah had been paying most of her mother's living expenses for years now. He looked around the kitchen and was disappointed by the state of dis-repair considering what Sarah had told him she'd invested in the place.

Dylan looked suddenly uncomfortable at the mention of the checks, enough that Claire glanced at Peter because she saw it too.

"Let's dig in!" Henrietta dodged and picked a fried chicken breast from the plastic tray Peter and Claire brought from take-out.

Claire followed her lead but neither man moved except for Dylan shrinking under Peter's stare.

Did they get a check from Sarah? Would she somehow get an opportunity to get a message out from captivity, and send a check to her mother? That didn't seem right. After a moment Peter selected chicken and a biscuit. Everyone ate in an unfortunate discomfort as the question hung in the air.

Not able to take it anymore, Henrietta laughed and said, "We haven't gotten anything from Sarah." She talked while laughing like she was saying something funny, but it was really embarrassment. "It's really hurting Dylan, actually, you see, he's got a big opportunity he's going to miss if we don't get a check soon!"

Dylan glared at Henrietta. Claire stopped chewing in awe. Henrietta was now the one shrinking under Dylan's stare. Clearly, she wasn't supposed to mention the *opportunity*. That's where Sarah's money was going.

Peter had a flash of realization. Henrietta was giving money to this guy, and despite that, she seemed to be desperate for his attention. He looked at her ridiculous dress and makeup, and how she did all the work while Dylan sat there, and how she was constantly checking on him to see if he was okay. She was totally dependent on him, despite the fact that she was providing for him, probably entirely.

Now Peter understood Sarah a little better. She said she wasn't going to be dependent on a man. She said it as an offhand comment, but her face hardened in a way it rarely did. That's why she broke it off with him when they were getting serious the first time. And that's why she wouldn't allow their relationship to move past *friends with benefits* this last time. He looked at Henrietta probably the same way Sarah had ten years before, as a caution for what Sarah might have become.

70. June 6, 2001

"Stay in here until about 9 AM," Sarah said.

Without really understanding in his groggy state, Sullivan was fine with that. He was content to open his eyes and see Sarah lying facing him wide awake. He smiled at her just as she rolled away and sat up. He enjoyed a view of her bare back with her hair falling to the middle of her shoulder blades. She looked back over her shoulder and smiled at him. She then stood and pulled her blanket around herself in a quick motion.

He listened through the open door as Mary entered and the women shared coffee. He listened for any detail that could be used to identify her if they ever got out of here. He didn't know if he wanted to hear anything or if he did not. If he did, it might help people find who took them. But the less he knew the better their chances of being released.

He didn't hear anything of any use.

Mary was remarkably adept at having a personal conversation with another woman and yet keeping everything generic enough that no personal information was conveyed.

Sarah would talk about her Ultimate Frisbee team at Virginia Tech and Mary would comment on her sports at university.

Sarah would describe the lecture hall in Robeson Hall and Mary would talk about the large classroom.

Sarah mentioned Tim, the backstabbing manager at her work at C&W and Mary would just say *men in her office*.

Sullivan decided that if he were not trying to hear detailed information, he wouldn't notice that none was being conveyed. The women continued to hit it off, and he thought that in any other situation, someone would think they were old friends catching up.

The routine continued for three days. In that time, Sullivan listened to Sarah describe her work, developing her algorithms, designing upgrades for the Hubble, the challenge to overcome the electrical grid, and finally finding the bombs in California.

Every morning, Sarah and Mary would have coffee, every afternoon, Sarah and Sullivan would discuss what they learned, and every night they would climb into bed together. Sullivan would ask Sarah each night how close she was to telling Mary everything. It was hard for her to estimate as this had been her full time work for many years.

71. June 8, 2001

The relationship is improving. Dr. Kiadopolis is following directions well. Any interruption of the power grid, anywhere in the United States, for any reason, for longer than ten minutes, will be viewed as a direct assault and will result in immediate action on multiple fronts.

- LV

Barbara delivered this letter to Jim ten minutes ago while he was in a meeting. He slipped it nonchalantly into his coat pocket.

He let the paper fall onto his desk and dropped down into his chair. He closed his eyes and rested his head back. He allowed himself to breathe deeply.

Damn.

72. June 9, 2001

"Sarah," Mary opened with Sarah in front of the camera and Sullivan sitting on the other overstuffed chair. Sarah and Sullivan were optimistic that they were about to enter the final phase of this ordeal and be released. They didn't discuss any alternative outcome. The conditions had been so consistent, and they had been so well cared for that they couldn't imagine anything else. "You have described in detail the challenges you faced with the power grid, and that it was lucky that you discovered that your algorithm worked only when the grid was off."

"Yes," Sarah said, taking a sip of water.

Mary looked up from her notes, "You have been compiling a database of the world so that when the opportunity arises, you can collect the *key* as you call it and decode the details of any region where the power has been off for a number of hours." She stopped and looked at Sarah with a pleasant smile.

"Yes, that's right," Sarah said. Sullivan recognized that Mary was summarizing, and he was getting excited. He could tell Sarah was happy too.

Over the past nine days, Sullivan had paid close attention to everything Mary said. He studied her every word. She never revealed anything. They had not seen or even met anyone except Mary. Sullivan knew they were being held in some sort of warehouse, that the cement floor was uniform. That was it. Mary and LV had been careful enough that Sarah and Sullivan didn't know anything about them. They couldn't possibly be a threat. They were about to be released.

Sullivan began to daydream about how that would happen. Then his daydream ended.

"I need you to tell me what it would take to get around the power grid problem," Mary said.

"Excuse me?" Sarah asked.

"I, I mean we, need to be able to detect objects with the power on," Mary said.

Sullivan sat up. This was the first time Mary had made a request for a capability rather than asking for clarification of what Sarah had done already.

"I know. That's what everyone would like, but I can't figure out how to make that happen. If I could, we would be doing it now." Sarah's comment was off hand. She was ready to get out of here. Sullivan was concerned that the question was not idle.

"Sarah, can we talk about what it would take? What is the limitation you are up against?" Mary asked.

"Mary, as I have described, I've been working for a government agency with significant resources. We've tried to accomplish this for the past two years," Sarah said.

Sullivan saw her look at Mary almost annoyed. The inability to see through the power grid was certainly a significant limitation to Sarah's system, a limitation that they were working with. Sullivan had to agree with Sarah that if the government could solve the problem, they would have.

"I assure you, LV is also an organization with significant resources," Mary said, "And when properly motivated, we can also get things done."

"I'm not sure what you're asking me to do," Sarah said, "I've talked you through everything we've done, and I told you everything I did to try to get the *Resonators* to work through the grid, but we can't do it."

"Sarah," Mary said with a soft voice, "I am sure you have been completely honest with me, and I assure you that your time with us is nearly complete." Mary paused and looked at both Sarah and Sullivan to let that sink in. "But I need you to help me with just this one last thing."

"Mary," Sarah was having difficulty concealing her disappointment now, "Are you asking me to show you how to beat the power grid? Are you asking me to solve a problem I can't solve?"

Sullivan interrupted, trying to help, "Mary, I think you're asking Sarah to explain everything she's done, and maybe everything she has been thinking of trying?" He looked at Mary who turned to look directly at him. "Right?"

"I am afraid I have very specific instructions," Mary said, "I have been asked to ask you, Sarah, to design for us a system that can see past the grid. I have been authorized to tell you that you will be released when this is complete." She looked at Sarah and Sullivan with a soft smile like she had just delivered good news.

Sullivan looked at Sarah. She looked at Mary in disbelief. Sullivan recognized that Mary had told them they would be released, something he knew would happen, but also something that had not been discussed previously. Now, at least, there was an end game. He believed Mary when she said the end game did not include their deaths.

Sarah was still quiet and didn't seem to be taking it as well as Sullivan was, or as well as Mary hoped she would.

Sullivan thought for a moment about how much he believed Mary. Could that be right? Should he believe her, maybe that was Sarah's trouble? No, Sarah had expressed to him just last night that Mary seemed to be completely trustworthy. Sullivan thought himself a reasonable judge of character under normal circumstances, and over the past three days, he'd come to recognize a level of openness with Mary that certainly didn't exist before.

Then again, she was holding them against their will.

But she also showed intense physical discomfort with the thought of hurting them, and she continued to be completely evasive even during the most casual of conversations about herself. Sullivan decided he had no reason to question her honesty. All they had to do was figure out how to see through the grid and they would be released. All he had to do was get Sarah to agree with that plan.

"Sarah," Sullivan said. Sarah had dropped her head into her hands. She lifted. "Sarah." Sarah held up her hand to stop him. She looked at Mary and Sullivan.

"Okay," Sarah said. Sullivan could tell she was not okay. He hoped Mary could tell what she was doing to her. "So, all we, all I have to do is figure out how to see through the grid and we can go?"

"Yes!" Mary was a bit bewildered by her reaction. She looked at Sullivan for support. Sullivan didn't have any to offer. "Yes, that's all you need to do!" Sarah looked at her blankly. "Dr. Kiadopolis, you're the smartest person I've ever met. I will help you, we can work together." Mary genuinely seemed excited.

"How long are you going to keep us here?" Sarah whispered through clenched teeth.

. . .

The rest of the morning was a bust.

Mary and Sullivan tried to help Sarah. They could not. At one point, Sarah went into her room and lay down on her bed.

Mary and Sullivan brainstormed on ways they could work out the problem. Without Sarah, Sullivan thought they were just making stuff up.

Sarah returned after about thirty minutes and apologized. She said she would give it a try. Mary was sitting on the stool in front of the camera so Sarah sat in her chair. Mary presented the brainstorming ideas. While Sarah was trying to be optimistic, Sullivan could tell she could easily see through each of their ideas.

At lunch time, Mary said she would return tomorrow.

. . .

Sullivan made sandwiches as had become his habit. He presented Sarah's to her while she sat in her chair. She didn't take it.

"Sarah," Sullivan said standing over her with his offering, "Maybe you'll feel better after you eat."

"I thought we were about to get out of here," Sarah looked up at him through wet eyes. She didn't move.

He knew there was no use trying to talk her into anything at this point, but he also knew he had to get her back functioning by tomorrow morning or all the good will they had earned over the past few days would be lost.

The last thing he wanted was another threat.

He decided the best thing he could do was get this off her mind for a while. He moved to the couch and turned on the television.

Sarah said she enjoyed the movie and seemed more herself by dinner time. They ate quietly, Sullivan trying to make small talk but not getting far.

"You know you're going to have to try to help," Sullivan said a few minutes after Sarah quietly slipped into bed that night. He wanted to bring it up all evening, but knew she was barely holding it together.

Sarah took a deep breath and turned on her side to face him, "I know, Sullivan. I'm sorry about today. I just want to get out of here."

"I know, and the best way to do that is to work as hard as you can to help them," Sullivan said. He almost continued and Sarah sensed it. He almost speculated on what might happen if she didn't give it her all. He decided she knew. He hoped she knew.

73. June 10, 2001

"Thank you for joining me," Linus said over breakfast at the Hampton Inn in Danville, Virginia.

Peter and Claire sat across from him, Peter with a plate of biscuits and gravy and Claire with a yogurt. They looked good despite the constant effort they'd put in for the past ten days.

"Have you made any progress?" Peter asked. If Henrietta or Angie had heard anything, Peter wouldn't have asked. It was a long shot that they would hear anything, but Linus was desperate. He had all his resources working on detecting any potential leak. If Sarah Kiadopolis was able to get a message out, it was imperative that he get that message.

"No, I've got people with everyone she knows in the world," Linus said, "Everyone on her soccer team is getting lucky this week, her colleagues in New York are meeting new people, and you're here with her mom." Linus didn't mention the less desirable actions he was taking.

He thought Peter and Claire were holding hands under the table. Of all the people he worked with, he liked these two the best.

He'd been rooting for them for years.

"Well, we're not learning anything from her mother," Claire said, "except that her boyfriend, Dylan, is a dirt bag!"

"Really, maybe I'll pay him a visit!" Linus said. "I speak dirt bag." Claire laughed a little. Linus knew she didn't really like him, but that she tolerated their professional relationship. He planned to visit Dylan, but he shouldn't have mentioned it here.

"Claire, I need you to go back to Greenville," Linus changed the subject.

"But she's helping me here," Peter complained.

Linus felt his eyebrows rise, but he didn't comment, "Ravi's made a lot of progress. He needs you to help him. In these times, we hope it won't come to it, but if it does, we're going to need as many as Ravi can make. So I need you to go help him."

Claire nodded and took the last bite of her yogurt. Linus was surprised by her standing up immediately.

She clearly knew this was a tense time, and he was happy she jumped right to it.

He was then more surprised when she leaned down and kissed Peter full on the mouth. She whispered something in his ear that made Peter smile before she left.

. . .

Sullivan woke up.

Sarah was already gone. It was eight fifteen and he could hear Sarah talking in the living room. He quickly dressed and peeked around the corner.

Sarah was standing at the dry erase board, and Mary was standing next to her. The board was already covered with multicolored writing. Sullivan walked into the room and joined them at the board. Mary looked at him standing next to her and didn't seem to mind.

"So, here's the fifth avenue I attempted," Sarah said, pointing to the number five on the board. "I was looking into the possibility that the *Space Resonator* could be specifically tuned to avoid the sixty hertz pattern. I worked through the mathematics and found a null set."

"Do you mean you couldn't solve it?" Mary asked.

"No, the math turned out to not be that hard. I mean there was no solution. There was no solution that oscillated space to excite gravitons and simultaneously not receive interference." Sarah explained.

"Okay, go on," Mary said.

For them to be on item number five out of twelve already, they must have started right at eight. Sarah must have been up early to create this list. Sarah took Mary through the entire list of everything she tried to solve the problem over the past two years by nine thirty in the morning.

"Thank you for your efforts, Sarah," Mary said. She was actually very happy. Sullivan realized she didn't want to have to make a threat just as much as they didn't want to receive it. Probably not quite as much, Sullivan decided. "I would like to take some notes here. You should make some breakfast."

"Good idea," Sullivan said. Sullivan and Sarah went to the kitchen. Mary sat in her chair focusing all her attention on Sarah's board and her attaché.

"I'm glad you did all this, you really saved us," Sullivan gushed.

"I know. I couldn't sleep and did all this in the middle of the night," Sarah said. "I know I need to help, but I just don't know if there's a solution. I'm not sure what they'll do if we don't find one."

"Let's not worry about that just yet," Sullivan said. They looked into each other's eyes for a few moments. Sullivan knew she was looking for a bit of wisdom from him, but he didn't have any. All he knew was that they had to go down this path. So he smiled at her. She looked for a moment, quickly squeezed his hand, and moved to the coffee maker.

. . .

Over the next three days, Sarah explained in deep detail how she had discounted each of the potential solutions to see through the grid. Sullivan was again very carefully studying Mary. He knew he couldn't contribute to the technical discussion, a fact he'd grown accustomed to a week ago.

He thought he noticed something odd about Mary's approach.

Mary would question every avenue vigorously. She would return the next day and return to a topic they had covered to dig deeper. She seemed to be working hard to find a solution, but Sullivan couldn't help but feel something was just a bit off with her. She seemed to be just as pleasant and friendly as she was since the incident with the blanket. During the few breaks they took, she was comfortable and the two women enjoyed a steady rapport.

After Sarah and Mary had exhausted the seventh avenue, Sullivan was struck with a look of relief on Mary's face. They just spent three hours debating the potential use of high energy lasers pulsing in the inverse of the grid blasting into the resonators to create a uniform field. Mary had just suggested they move on to the eighth avenue. When that happened, Sullivan could tell Sarah was elated. That made sense as this was territory she already covered and if she had it her way, Mary would have just taken her at her word days ago. What was odd was the similarity in their attitudes. Sullivan realized Mary seemed to be just as exhilarated as Sarah was. He decided he would pay close attention to this.

During the eighth avenue discussion, another three hours, there was a point where Mary was steadfast in her argument that Sarah made a logical error. There was a glimmer of hope that there could be a solution. Sarah was even beginning to get excited that it could work. They worked closely together at the dry erase board late into the day. Sullivan prepared dinner and ate by himself as the women were focused on the potential solution.

As he ate, Sullivan watched the two women. They were working together, but they seemed to be working against each other. Not in anything they said or did, but in the subtlety of their attitude. As Sarah seemed to get more and more excited that they might be onto something, Mary seemed to be getting more and more agitated. She seemed to fidget more and she seemed to be, what was it? Sullivan couldn't put his finger on it.

Then the discussion took a dramatic turn. Sarah began to write rapidly, deriving a lengthy equation. Mary watched intently. Mary suddenly stopped Sarah in the middle of a line. She physically stopped her by pulling her pen from the board. Sullivan put down his fork. Mary pointed to an earlier line in the derivation and Sarah agreed she had made a mistake.

Sarah quickly corrected the derivation and crossed off all the various terms from the board leaving a blue and red mess. Sarah turned to look at Mary and also faced Sullivan for the first time in two hours. She was devastated. It turned out she'd been right all along, the avenue didn't work. Sarah had, for a few hours, thought she found a way out of this, but no.

Mary had the exact opposite reaction. She was delighted. She was actually so happy that she moved to hug Sarah! But she caught herself, and pulled back. She looked back at Sullivan embarrassed but barely able to control her smile.

Sullivan couldn't believe his eyes. Mary had proved one of the avenues didn't work and she was happy? She collected her notes, pointed out it was after seven p.m. and left. Sullivan thought she almost skipped out the door. He decided not to talk about it with Sarah. He wanted her to form her own opinions.

The next day he continued to watch Mary closely. She continued to be happy with their failure to find a solution.

That was it.

She was happy that they couldn't find a solution.

74.   June 12, 2001

"Yes, Mr. President, we're covering everyone both Sullivan and Sarah know," Jim Williams sat on the plush sofa facing the door in the oval office. Across from him were three of his lieutenants, Maxwell, Thomas, and Eustis. The Vice President sat next to the fireplace and the President sat in front of his desk.

"It's been seventeen days, and we don't have shit!" George Bush didn't tend to use profanity, nothing like Bill Clinton, but when he did, it meant he was mad. "The entire US government can't find two damned people?"

"So far, we have absolutely no idea where they are," Maxwell piped in, "they could be anywhere on earth."

"So, unfortunately, all we can do is wait for LV to make a move," Jim said.

"And, in the meantime, we're going to take down our own satellites?" the President asked. Jim had spoken with both the President and Vice President every day. Now President Bush wanted a daily meeting with the entire team with the hopes that something would break loose. So far, nothing had.

"No, George," Dick said. He looked at Jim, "We could knock them down, but how would we convince LV that we did? Jim's right, there's no way we could prove we did it."

"Then how do we prove we're not using her technology?" the President asked, "and the more important question, how do we then get around it?"

"The technology has a weakness," Eustis, the gamer, spoke up, "the power must be off for the technology to work."

The group respected him, and everyone waited for Mr. Jefferson to speak slowly.

"LV must know this, that's why they demanded that we keep the power on. Dr. Kiadopolis must have explained that to them."

"So?" the Vice President asked.

"So, if we keep the power on, LV will know we can't use the technology," Eustis explained with his glasses in his hands. "We must keep the power on. That will be the proof we're not using our technology against them, even if we are."

"But, doesn't the power just go off sometimes?" Thomas asked.

"Yes, unfortunately, sometimes it does." Dick said.

"So, if the power accidentally goes off, we could end up dealing with LV detonating a nuclear weapon!" Thomas affirmed.

"We're going to have to make sure that doesn't happen," Maxwell said, "We're going to have to secure the power grid. That means massive investments in new power generation, smarter grids, everything. We can do that."

"It'll be expensive," Dick said.

"We can cover it," Eustis said, "besides, we've demonstrated we can manipulate the markets enough, we can drive the market through financial processes to create the incentives we need."

Jim knew not everyone in the room understood what Eustis meant, but he also knew they all believed he would take care of it.

"So, lots of new power plants?" the President asked.

"Yes," Dick said, "We're going to have to move the regulators to act quickly, we'll have to distance ourselves from any environmental regulations, including climate change, so we can push the new plants through."

"So we're going to have to be against the environment?"

"Not against it, just not for it," Eustis said.

"Fine, we'll deal with that later," the President said, "You've got all this moving?"

"We're setting it all up now," Jim said, "It'll take time to get the pieces in place, and we're not kicking off until we know what happens with Dr. Kiadopolis."

"Yes, are we going to get her back?"

"We're not hopeful," Jim was sad to report. He looked at Maxwell, the closest person to her. He was pained but kept neutral. "We'd expect them to be done with her by now."

75. June 13, 2001

As Sarah and Mary worked systematically through the twelve technical solutions, Mary was perfectly happy that they couldn't find a way to get one to work. Sarah wasn't happy, but she did stay focused and occasionally Mary did take her down a path that seemed promising. Nothing worked out and they completed the review on the end of the third day.

After Mary left, Sarah sat on her chair and put her head in her hands. Sullivan sat on the couch and smiled.

"What?" Sarah asked as she looked up. "Don't you understand? There's no way to see through the grid? They're going to keep us here for a very long time!" As she looked at Sullivan, her sadness was turning to anger.

"Sarah," Sullivan said calmly, "I'm as desperate as you are to find a way out of here. I haven't seen my -" He'd been thinking about Danny a lot lately, but he'd been careful not to mention him. He wasn't sure it helped, but he felt like it was his little bit of defiance.

"Then why are you sitting there with a smile on your face?" Sarah asked. She stood up. Sullivan could see she was getting angry with him. He was about to tell her he knew how to get them out, he opened his mouth to talk, but then reconsidered and closed it. That didn't make Sarah happy. She huffed and went to the bathroom sink and splashed water over her face.

"Sarah," Sullivan tried to pacify her, "Everything is going to be okay. We'll get through this."

"That's easy for you to say," Sarah was letting her anger show, "All you have to do is sit there and wait for me to come up with something!" Sullivan knew she wasn't actually mad at him. It had been a very trying three days for her. She knew there was no way out of this. She knew she had to review everything Mary wanted to review. She knew that their lives may depend on it. And she had worked harder than he had ever seen anyone work for three straight days. She deserved to let a little out, and he was prepared to take it.

She slumped heavily on the bathroom doorframe.

More importantly, Sullivan thought LV was listening to them and hearing how desperate Sarah was, how hopeless she thought their situation was. If he was right, and he was sure he was, then her outburst would help them in the long run. He just hoped she wouldn't hate him for it.

"Sarah, we're in this together," Sullivan said trying to emphasize that point. He became aware of his smile and forced a scowl onto his face, "We need to find a solution. Even Mary is on our side."

"She can be on our side all she wants! She gets to leave this apartment every night! This is like a job for her, and one she enjoys!" Sarah said. "Even you're enjoying this!" She looked angry at him from across the apartment.

He had to pause at her statement.

Was he enjoying this? He had to admit that the time they'd spent here had been pleasant. His position was to help Sarah. He didn't think they would be killed, and whoever these people were, they didn't seem to want to hurt them.

So was he enjoying this?

He wasn't dreading it as much as Sarah was. There were three key differences between their positions. First, Sarah was under the stress of answering all of Mary's questions. While Sullivan sat and watched, Mary and Sarah engaged in a technical debate that was way over his head. She seemed to be able to handle that stress well, and in fact, he would have said Sarah enjoyed those times. Second, while Sullivan was trapped here with Sarah, probably the most interesting person he'd ever met, she was stuck here with him! That had to be not as good for her. And third, and currently the most important, she thought she had to solve the transparent grid problem. He knew she did not. He also knew the more she felt it was impossible, and the more she showed it, the sooner they would be released. So, he couldn't tell her what he knew to be true. He had to choose his words carefully.

"Sarah," Sullivan said after far too long a pause, "Please make no mistake about it, I have spent every waking moment since we have been here struggling to find a way out. I agree that my role here is to help you, a role that I am happy to accept. Despite my efforts I can't find any way out that is not through your mind." He paused.

Despite her slouch, she looked great leaning on the doorframe.

"Please, I've made some dinner, please come eat some." She continued to look frustrated, but she couldn't think of anything better to do so she joined him at the table.

Sullivan retrieved her warm plate from the oven and poured her a glass of apple juice. Her first cut into her chicken was rough as she was still mad, but after a few bites she calmed. She ate quickly. She was hungry. Sullivan sat and watched her while pretending to flip through a magazine.

After half her chicken was inhaled, Sarah took two deep gulps from her juice and looked at Sullivan, "I'm sorry."

Sullivan let the cover close on his magazine and said, "Sarah, you have nothing to be sorry about. This is a difficult situation and you've handled it well." He paused and looked at her. "You need to know, I truly enjoy your company. Please don't mistake the ease with which I can fulfill my duty for a lack of determination to get out of here."

Sarah smiled. It was a half-smile, but Sullivan would take it. He felt he was walking a tight rope. He wanted her to know he was working for her, and that he liked her, but not that he was angling for anything more. He didn't want to put any pressure on her, or disappoint her in any way. She didn't need any of that. He returned her smile sheepishly.

Sarah reached over and took his hand, "Sullivan, I couldn't do this without you. Please don't change anything you're doing." They ate dinner and went to bed early. Sarah was exhausted from the long day and the mounting stress she was feeling. Sullivan was afraid their friendship was hurt by the fight, but his fears were dispelled when Sarah grasped his arm through his quilt after he carefully climbed into bed.

Sarah was exhausted and fell asleep quickly, but Sullivan found he was wide awake. As her breathing slowed, he would have pulled away and gone into the other room to think, but her grip on his arm remained tight. He decided he would not disturb her by moving but instead enjoy the intimacy.

He replayed the key events of the previous few days. Mary continued to show her pleasure in Sarah's failure to find a solution. They had discounted all twelve of the avenues Sarah had proposed. Sarah had been working on these twelve avenues for years, she said, so he wasn't so sure there was a thirteenth. He knew tomorrow they would start looking for one.

Mary's attitude was giving him hope. Mary was part of LV, an organization that they had surmised was buying nuclear weapons from old labs as Sarah found them. Linus was stealing the information from Sarah's program manager and taking the bombs. LV had significant resources, but Sarah's work required satellites.

Sullivan doubted any secret society had those resources, so what would they want with the ability to see through the grid? Besides, Sarah was working on seeing through it anyway, and if she eventually found a way to see through it, Linus would still be there to get the bombs as soon as they were found. So Sullivan knew they had no use for Sarah's ability to see through the grid.

They weren't trying to find a way to see through the grid.

LV wanted to make sure Sarah couldn't.

If LV buried the bombs in new locations, they would want to make sure the government couldn't find them.

They forced Sarah to explain how she found the bombs with the intention of finding a way to make her stop!

Sarah didn't have to find a way to see through the grid to get them out of this, she had to find a way to prove to them that she couldn't. That was why Mary was always so happy when each avenue didn't work. Sullivan had heard of scientists being happy when they could prove something was impossible. What did they call it? Proving the negative?

Sullivan drifted off to sleep at about midnight with Sarah still holding tightly to his arm.

76.   June 15, 2001

"Well, it's good to see you!" Claire greeted Peter at the door of his apartment. She'd been working fifteen hour days with Ravi, and Peter had been traveling between Henrietta and Angie. They had not seen each other since that morning at the Hampton Inn.

"Not as good as it is to see you!" Peter said.

His eyes were scanning up and down.

Claire wore the bra and panties she purchased ten years ago and wore that night at the Poinsett. She stood back so he could get a good look. The outfit was significant to her, but she didn't expect him to remember.

"I haven't seen you in that in, what has it been? Ten years!"

"These past few days have felt like ten years," Claire said.

"That's not what I meant."

"I know!" Claire laughed and felt more at ease than she had her entire life. Peter Howard was the one. They'd shared more in ten years of not being together than most married people did. And the last year together was the natural extension of everything that came before.

He walked up to her and she jumped into his arms wrapping her legs around him. Luckily, he knew the way to the bedroom because he couldn't see past her kissing him.

77. June 17, 2001

Over a fajita plate Sullivan didn't think he could pull off, Sarah said, "I think you're right."

"Thank you," Sullivan said, "about what?"

"You know what!" Sarah said, smiling, "About proving the negative!"

Sullivan had explained to her his theory.

"Oh, yes?"

"I think I can actually do it!" Sarah said, "I can't believe I didn't think of it a year ago. The derivation was straight forward."

"Are you sure?" Sullivan said.

"I would say ninety-five percent," Sarah said. Her hands worked quickly wrapping a fajita with only meat and cheese.

"What would it take to be one hundred percent?" Sullivan asked quietly leaning toward her, "You can't propose something like that and be wrong!"

Sarah thought about this. She knew he was right. They would only get one shot at a proof of the negative. If there was an error, it would be like crying wolf, and they would be trapped. Maybe forever.

After dinner, Sarah returned to her board, erasing it completely and starting over. Sullivan left her in quiet. He read the Nat Geo again.

In bed, Sarah moved close up next to Sullivan, pressing her body through the quilt, and wrapping her arm across his chest. "I'm one hundred percent sure," she whispered in his ear. He looked over at her. Her head and bare shoulder poked out of her quilt. Their nearly naked bodies were separated by only his quilt and he was beginning to feel the warmth of her body through it. Her eyes were bright and she was almost giddy.

"Okay," Sullivan said. He shifted himself so his hips were facing away from her, "So how do you bring it up to Mary?"

"I'll tell her first thing tomorrow."

"No, I don't think so," Sullivan said. Their close proximity allowed them to whisper. "I don't think you can spring this on her, and the math you had on the board looked like gibberish to me. Will she be able to follow it?"

Sarah's face stayed bright as she thought about what he said. "You might be right, but I want to get out of here. Let me think about it."

"Okay, but please don't spring it on her." Sarah pulled away from Sullivan. They both lay there facing the ceiling. Sullivan was about to tell her something when he realized she was asleep.

June 23 & 24

78.   June 23, 2001

Sullivan recognized the vividness of the dream. It had been nearly a month since he and Sarah were taken, and he could still remember the dreams he had that first night. The drugs they gave him during travel caused the most realistic dreams of his life. Maybe normally, with dreams this real, he would wake himself up. This morning he was back in that state, that state that normally lasted a few minutes when he was able to wake up without an alarm, but today it seemed to last hours.

Then he was struck with a realization. The realization was from his real brain, but he could tell the details were still foggy. If he was experiencing the extended wake-up that came from the drugs LV used to transport him, then they must be transporting him! Now he was asleep, but he wanted to wake up. He couldn't yet open his eyes. He tried to become aware of his body. He was not receiving any signals from his body that it was moving, but still he wasn't fully awake. He was about to panic.

He forced himself to be calm.

Sullivan felt his eyes open. It was dark. He allowed his eyes to adjust, and didn't force them to focus. He was in a comfortable bed. It was king-sized. He could see the simple furniture and large armoire of a hotel room. He was certainly not in the apartment. The new surroundings were at once concerning and a great relief. He looked to the night stand. He had no idea where he was, but he saw it was 3:45 AM.

Sullivan made an effort to reach for the phone. His muscles ached, just as they had when he arrived in the apartment. He held his breath briefly as he lifted the receiver and exhaled when he heard the very comforting sound of a dial tone. He mashed the zero with the same hand he held the receiver. It rang. It rang again. A third time. Sullivan began to become disheartened that he was still with them somehow.

"Hello Mr., uh, Mr. Acer?" a man's voice forced brightness in the middle of the night. Sullivan also recognized his inability to pronounce his last name. A wave of comfort rushed over him. Clearly LV knew how to pronounce his last name, so he wasn't one of them.

"Mr. Acer, are you there?" Sullivan must have been thinking for a bit for him to ask again.

"Yes, I'm here," Sullivan didn't know how to ask without sounding crazy, so he just did, "Where am I?"

"I'm sorry?"

"No, I'm sorry, what city is this?"

"Oh," he paused, "Don't be sorry, I get this question more than you would think, you guys travel a lot. You're in Houston, Texas. This is the Sheraton Westway."

"Thank you," Houston, Texas. Sullivan had never been to Houston. He didn't know anyone in Houston.

What was he going to do now? He had no idea.

"Mr. Acer, is there anything else I can do for you?"

"Oh, sorry, no, thank you, good night."

"Good Night, Mr. Acer."

Sullivan sat up. It wasn't easy, but he felt better after a moment. The cool air on his skin reminded him he didn't have a shirt on and he quickly discovered he was completely naked. He felt his body returning to his control as he reached over and turned on the light on the night stand. He had to cover his eyes to let them adjust. He must have been asleep for a long time. He let his eyes scan the room. There were no clothes on the two chairs in the room with him. He sat a moment.

Sullivan stood up. Again, not easy, but again he quickly felt better. He walked to the armoire and discovered that it, and then the closet, was empty. That added some complication. He decided to take a shower to feel better.

The hot water running down his back helped return full control of his muscles. He savored the feeling. He stood in the shower as the thoughts of his situation returned to him.

What was he supposed to do?

He was in Houston, Texas, with no clothes or belongings in someplace called *Westway*. He realized he didn't have a lot of time to waste. LV had at least one nuclear weapon, and they knew how to make the government stop looking for it. He had to tell someone. But who? Sarah probably knew.

Sarah.

He had to find Sarah. Maybe LV still had her. Maybe she was in a similar situation to him. Maybe she was in the same hotel.

Sullivan turned off the water, jumped from the shower still wet, and ran to the phone.

"Hello Mr. Acer, what can I do for you?"

"Can you connect me to Ms. Kiadopolis' room, K-I-A-D?"

"Hold on," a moment, "I am sorry, there's no Kiadopolis at the hotel."

Sullivan's heart sank. He felt like he was ready to start running, but there was nowhere to run.

"Is there anything else?"

"No …," Sullivan needed clothes, "Wait, yes, do you have a gift shop?"

"Yes."

"I don't have my luggage," Sullivan didn't know exactly what to ask for, "I need some toiletries."

"We have a *Lost Luggage* kit available for $49.95," he reported, "It has toothpaste, and tooth brush, a change of underwear and socks, a razor and shaving cream."

"Can I charge that to my room?"

"Certainly. Would you like me to send it up?"

"Umm," Sullivan needed more than just underwear, "I usually like to work out, but I don't have my exercise clothes."

"That is no problem, we're piloting a new program offered by Sheraton to allow guests to borrow them. They are, of course, freshly laundered. You can join the program for a month, and use it in any Sheraton Hotel for just $99."

"Shoes?" Sullivan couldn't believe the luck.

"Of course, we have several pairs for you to try. Just come down in the morning and we'll set you up."

"I have a very busy morning, and I'm awake now. Can you bring the lost luggage set and workout clothes to my room, men's extra-large, shoe size 11?" Sullivan was pushing now. There was a pause.

You only get what you ask for.

"Um," now the receptionist paused, "Um, yes, yes I think I can do that." he was figuring out that he could do it. "Give me about twenty minutes and I'll send it right up."

"Thank you very much." Sullivan said and set the receiver down. He dried off and tried to figure out what he would do when the clothes arrived.

. . .

Two hours later, it was almost six in the morning. Sullivan was showered, dressed, and ready to go. He just didn't have any place to go. He couldn't figure out where Sarah was, and he couldn't figure out what to do.

He considered calling the police. But what would he tell them? He was held hostage by a group with a nuclear weapon and he had to talk to the President?

He lifted the receiver and was amazed to find he remembered a number. It rang four times before it was answered. It was only five in the morning in Albuquerque.

"Hello?" a groggy man's voice answered. Sullivan recognized the slight draw on the ll's and knew he had the right man.

"Hector," Sullivan announced, "It's me, Sullivan." There was no response. He realized he'd often gone over a month without talking to his friend at the FBI and maybe Hector was completely unaware of anything being out of the ordinary.

"Sullivan?" Hector said after a long ten seconds.

"Hector," Sullivan knew he had to fill his friend in, "You're not going to believe what happened to me. Linus Brenner, I followed him. I met that physicist again!" Sullivan could barely remember thinking of her as *the physicist*, but that was what he called her before.

"Sullivan," Hector said, but Sullivan kept going.

"I followed Linus down to Greenville-"

"Sullivan!" Hector yelled. "Sullivan, you have to stop talking."

Sullivan was shocked by this command.

"Sullivan, I am going to tell you what I know, and I'm going to tell you what we're going to do," Hector said, "Okay?"

"Okay?" Sullivan didn't know what to think.

"Look, I don't think you know this," Hector said, "But you know the FBI Ten Most Wanted List?"

"Yes."

"Well, the FBI has a Secret FBI Ten Most Wanted List. We use it for all kinds of cases, high profile child abductions, people running from the mob, suspected spies, that sort of stuff."

Sullivan was beginning to be afraid he knew where this was going.

"About a month ago, you took over the number one spot on the list," Hector said, "You and a Dr. Sarah Kiadopolis. I assume she's *that physicist?*"

"Yes." Sullivan found it hard to listen.

"I thought so," Hector said, "Each name comes with specific instructions about what to do if they are found."

Sullivan really didn't like the sound of that.

"I know you've been missing," Hector said, "But I don't know why or where, and I'm not supposed to ask you about it. Please don't tell me."

"Okay."

"But, dude, are you okay?" Hector asked.

"Yes," Sullivan was glad to hear he still had a friend, "I'm fine. Do you know-"

Hector interrupted, "Don't tell me anything. But I will tell you this. When I saw you on that list, I set up surveillance on your parents and Danny. I've been checking on them every day, and they're fine."

"Thank you."

"I'm supposed to ask you where you are, and to send people to get you," Hector said.

Sullivan took a moment to answer, "I'm in Houston, Texas. I'm in a hotel."

"Great, I'll call it in, and some people will come get you."

Sullivan didn't like the idea of strangers. "No."

"No?" Hector paused, "Dude, I don't think you get to say *no*. You're wanted by the FBI. Whatever's going on, and *please* don't tell me, you are the most wanted person in America right now. Look, man, I trust you and know you're on the right side of this. We're coming to get you. Please don't run away. Let me help you."

"I want you to come get me," Sullivan said. "Not some strangers."

"All right," Hector paused, "That's a good idea. Let me make a call."

"Okay," Sullivan said, "and thank you for taking care of Danny and my parents."

"Hey, I've got your back!" The dial tone returned.

Sullivan dialed another number, and again it was answered with a groggy, "Hello?"

"Mom?"

It took just a moment, "Sull?"

"Hey, Mom," Sullivan said. No matter what, it always felt good to talk to his mother, "How are you?"

"Norm, get up, It's Sull," his mother said to his father, "I can't believe it! Where are you? Are you okay? I'm coming, where are you?"

"Mom," Sullivan called, "I'm fine. It's been a long month, but it's over now."

"What's over now?" his father asked.

Sullivan didn't know how to answer so he just ignored it, "How's Danny?"

"Marcia, go wake up Danny," his father directed, "Sullivan what's going on? We've been worried sick. They told us you were missing, that you fell into trouble with some bad people, drug dealers?"

Sullivan thought that was a stupid cover. They should have said the mob, his job was more directly related to that, but he had to go with it. "Dad, I'll tell you all about it soon, but right now I just wanted you to know I'm okay."

"Daddy?" Sullivan shuddered and instantly choked up at the sound of his son's voice. Danny was twelve but he still called him *Daddy*.

"Hey Danny," Sullivan forced out, "How's it going?" *How's it going*? He hadn't talked to his son in a month and all he had was *How's it Going*? Damn.

"Are you coming home?" Danny asked.

"Yes, buddy," Sullivan said. He realized he hoped that was true, "I'm on my way."

. . .

Sullivan arrived outside a private hanger at the George Bush International Airport and saw his friend Hector Feliz waiting alone outside. The sun rose on his ride to the airport and the temperature was already past ninety. Sullivan was happy to be in the shorts and t-shirt the hotel loaned him when he saw Hector in his customary suit.

His friend smiled when he stepped out of the cab. Hector paid the driver.

"Boy am I glad to see you!" Sullivan said as he hugged Hector. They had never done that before, but Hector responded with a strong greeting.

"Let's go inside," Hector stepped toward the single door in the wall of the hanger. Sullivan wasn't prepared for the inside where he was immediately greeted by a Lear Jet. The main hangar doors were open and Sullivan saw the tarmac and runways beyond. Sullivan focused closer to see a small table setup in the middle of the cement floor between him and the plane. A man in a lab coat was facing away from him preparing something at the table.

"I'd love to hear about where you've been," Hector said, "but I have strict instructions to not even ask. I'm glad to see you, too." Sullivan was struck by the formality of his friend. The hug showed him everything was fine, and he was sure Hector was being formal due to orders. "This is Dr. Humphries. He's with us." The doctor stood and turned around. He looked exactly like a doctor complete with greying temples, wire rimmed glasses, and a white lab coat. "He's going to take a sample of your blood."

Sullivan's comfort level dropped again. He wasn't afraid of needles; he just didn't like the idea of being told what was going to happen so quickly. He looked his friend in the eye. Hector held out his hand directing Sullivan to the table and nodded slightly.

"It's okay," Hector said.

Sullivan acquiesced and the doctor drew the blood with practiced precision. "Thank You," was all the doctor said.

"Now, you have a plane trip," Hector said. Sullivan looked to the plane.

"You're coming with me," Sullivan directed.

"No," Hector said, "This is all I do."

"But I said I wanted you to bring me in!"

"Look, brother," Hector stepped close to Sullivan as they

walked slowly toward the plane, "I asked a few questions. You're not suspected of anything. You're a good guy and everyone knows it. You know my number. If anything gets hairy, you call and I'll be there. You know I've got your back." The two men looked each other in the eye. Sullivan decided if it wasn't his friend standing in front of him he'd try to make a run for it.

"Here," Hector picked up a drawing pad and pencils off the table. Sullivan recognized them as the ones he left in Albuquerque the last time he visited. "I figured these might come in handy."

Sullivan took them without quite knowing why. "Thanks. Keep that phone on you." Sullivan hugged his friend again, turned and climbed the stairs into the jet.

Sullivan was greeted by an attractive young woman not dressed as a flight attendant or as an FBI agent, but in tight jeans, running shoes and a purple t-shirt with a large white flower stretched across her chest. Her hair was pulled back in a red ponytail and she had sunglasses on top of her head. Sullivan watched as she negotiated the airplane door. She seemed confident, and like she could handle anything, but she didn't know how to work the door. Sullivan almost offered to help just as she mastered the grip and heaved the bottom half of the door that served as the stairs up and into the closed position. Sullivan saw out the top half that the plane had begun to leave the hangar. The woman stuck her head out the opening to look back at the top half of the door to find a handle. Sullivan again felt the urge to help but waited a beat and she found the handle and pulled the door down.

"Claire Havers," she at once used her left hand to push a strand of hair out of her face, and extended her right to Sullivan.

"Sullivan Acer," Sullivan took her hand awkwardly.

"We have a lot to do and not much time to do it," Claire said. She moved past him into the aircraft. Sullivan turned around the bulkhead and for the first time saw the interior. He was expecting comfortable chairs like in the movies. What he saw was more of an office. There were desks on either side with swivel office chairs attached to the floor. On further inspection he saw it was less of an office and more of a laboratory. On one desk was a microscope; over another desk were bright lights. There were three other people in the space, all dressed in lab coats. Two men and a woman all were making preparations. The closest man was carefully laying out glass slides to inspect something under the scope, the woman was spreading blue sheets over the bright desk and one of the chairs, and the second man was working at a laptop.

The team moved easily despite the aircraft taxiing rapidly through the airport.

"Taking off," the pilot announced over the loud speaker, and with that, Sullivan saw out the windows that the plane was turning onto a runway. He and Claire had to grab onto the bulkheads to avoid falling. The lab woman was surefooted and was able to continue. The two men fastened their seatbelts.

The plane accelerated. Lab Woman completed her task, surveyed her work, and moved smoothly to the back of the plane taking one of the remaining seats. Claire was faster than Sullivan and began to move to the other seat in the back, leaving only the seat with the blue sheet over it for him. He looked around for another seat, and seeing none, began to panic. He felt sure he was supposed to sit, but he felt sure he was not supposed to sit in the only seat. Claire reached her seat and flopped into it.

After securing her seat belt, she looked up and was surprised to see Sullivan struggling to stay upright in the middle of the cabin.

"Sit!" Claire demanded. Just then the plane reared back and began to lift off. Sullivan struggled but was able remain standing with his arms extended to the bulkhead and the cabin ceiling. He wasn't going to make it to the seat but he could stay where he was. Then the plane banked hard, and Sullivan felt himself tossed. Briefly he didn't know if he would hit the wall or the floor, but gravity still worked, and he smacked against the floor. He was happy to be pressed to the floor for the remainder of the takeoff.

"Please stand up," Lab Woman instructed after the plane leveled off. Sullivan did as directed. He wasn't surefooted, "Where did you get these clothes?"

"At the hotel," Sullivan answered before it registered as a strange question. Sullivan saw Man Two respond by typing in the computer. He wasn't feeling comfortable with this situation.

"Okay," Lab Woman considered his answer, "It's good you didn't sit, then, thank you." She sized him up and asked, "Can I have your pants, shoes, and shirt?"

"What!" Sullivan answered. His brain registered that as an inappropriate request immediately. He took a step back, as though there was somewhere to go. He looked to Claire, but realized he just met her, too. The two Lab Men were unfazed. Man Two was looking at him, but didn't respond by writing anything. Finally, Claire spoke.

"Sullivan, without going into too much detail, this is a forensic science team. They're here to look for any physical evidence that may help us figure out where you were." She spoke softly and didn't make any move toward him. Sullivan thought for a moment. Claire must be involved in what was going on, but didn't want to share it with the lab team. He felt less secure right now than he did in the apartment. He decided he had no choice but to play along. His chance to run passed in the hangar. Besides, she had not asked for his underwear, yet.

He slipped off his shoes and pulled his shirt over his head. Lab Woman picked up his shoes and accepted the shirt and placed them on a table with no sheet. Claire didn't move. She sat in her chair, watching the scene with no expression. Man One was still working with his slides, and Man Two was watching and waiting. They were making no effort to make him comfortable.

He began to push his shorts down but then paused, "I took a shower, so you're not going to find anything on me." Man Two responded by typing.

"You'd be surprised," Lab Woman said. Now Sullivan stood in the center of the cabin of a Lear jet in nothing but the boxers he got from the hotel going who knows where with four strangers who weren't telling him anything.

He was directed to the chair with the blue cloth. Claire watched as Lab Woman took samples of Sullivan's hair, his ear wax, and swabbed his nostrils. She gave the samples to Man One who prepared slides. Then Lab Woman donned a pair of magnifying glasses and began a thorough search of Sullivan's body. She took clippings of his fingernails and toenails. She scraped under both to sample that material.

"I think I see spores," Lab Woman said to Man One.

"I agree," Man One was looking through the microscope at one of the slides, "We've got spores in the earwax. I'm sending the images to the analyzer, but they look subtropical."

She studied him while he sat, looking at his face, his arms, legs and chest. She dictated a few notes to Man Two. He didn't know how the details of his moles could possibly help them determine where he'd been. Occasionally, she would use a metal instrument to scrape a sample off his skin and pass it to Man One.

"I see sulfur and ammonia compounds," Man One looked over his shoulder at Sullivan. He paused briefly as he saw Lab Woman kneeling down between Sullivan's legs to inspect his crotch by pulling his underwear to the sides. "Uh, Mr. Acer, did you smell rotten eggs? Was there a gas stove or gas heating?"

Sullivan tried to act natural, "No, no smell, no gas stove." He stopped talking as Lab Woman rocked back on her heels. She was extremely efficient and completely unfazed by what she was doing. This process took about an hour. Sullivan answered a few questions and submitted to what in effect was a medical exam. Claire watched with no expression, and said nothing.

After the exam, Sullivan was allowed to put his clothes back on. He sat in the chair in the back next to Claire as the lab team continued to work with the specimens they gathered.

"Where are we going?" Sullivan asked Claire in a low voice.

After a moment of consideration, Claire looked at him and smiled, "Washington, D.C., don't worry, I don't think anyone will be taking your clothes again."

"Who are you?"

"I told you, Claire Havers."

"I mean, what are you? I know you're not a flight attendant, and I know you are not a lab tech, and I know you know more about what's going on than anyone else on this plane." Sullivan studied her face to see her reaction. She held her disarming smile, but he could tell he was right.

"I'm a courier. We had a global network ready for your release, and I got lucky."

"Who's *we*?"

Claire didn't answer, but instead pulled a pad of paper from beside her seat, "We need to know where you've been."

"Why didn't you ask me?"

"I was told you didn't know. Where were you?" Claire asked with her pen ready to write.

"I don't know."

"Thanks for that," Claire said. Sullivan felt like an idiot. Claire smiled and continued, "Why don't you tell me something you *do* know?"

"Okay," Sullivan stammered. He didn't know where to begin. After a moment, he started at the beginning. "I woke up in a room, a bedroom. I was in one bedroom and Sarah was in another." Claire was writing. Sullivan stopped. "Where's Sarah? Is she out?"

"Sarah, yes. Our physicist. I saw her give a talk once," Sullivan was taken by Claire's obviously emotional response to the mention of Sarah. Sullivan wanted to talk about it, but Claire didn't look up from her paper. "I don't have any information about her, please go on."

"Like I said," Sullivan sat back in his chair watching out the side of his head while Claire wrote, "I woke up in one room and Sarah was in another. There were no windows and only one door out of a small apartment."

Claire asked about everything that happened during their time in the apartment and took a lot of notes. Half way through, she stopped to scan her notes into an electronic system next to Man Two. Sullivan took the opportunity to collect his drawing pad that was still on the floor. He started drawing Mary while he listened to Claire talk to the lab techs.

"We've got sulfur and ammonia, so we think he was near an industrial center," Man One said.

"And the spores are from trees native to sub-tropical Amazon," Lab Woman reported. Sullivan looked up. Did she say Amazon?

"Is there a chance these trees would be somewhere else?" Claire asked.

"These are the canopy trees, not small plants. There could be one somewhere, but unless he was in the tree he wouldn't have this concentration on him unless he was in that region."

"No, he's been inside a single space for the whole time, no sightseeing," Claire reported.

"Then I'd say he was in Southern Brazil or Northern Argentina for the past month," Lab Woman reported.

Brazil, Sullivan thought about that. He'd never been outside the United States, except to Canada, but that barely counted. He catalogued the information but didn't know what to do with it. He returned to drawing.

"Who's that?" Claire asked looking at his drawing.

"It's Mary."

"I've seen her before!" Claire said. She studied the picture. "I know I've seen her before, but it's not coming to me."

. . .

"Doctor Sarah Kiadopolis!" A man crossed the most ornately decorated room Sarah had ever been in, "I'm Jim Williams." Jim stuck out his hand. Sarah, not knowing what else to do, stood and shook his hand.

The last five hours had been just as shocking as the previous month. Sarah found herself in Atlanta, naked, and confused. She broke protocol and called Maxwell from the unsecured hotel room phone. He arranged for her to be picked up. FBI agent Tyler Jacobs escorted her to a private airfield and a small jet. On the jet, a team subjected her to the most invasive personal body search she'd ever had. Agent Jacobs tried to be comfortable as he questioned her about everything that happened. Now she stood in a beautiful room in the West Wing of the White House shaking hands with a man named Jim Williams. He acted like she was supposed to recognize him. Everyone knew who she was.

"Hello," Sarah pushed out. Jim was older than she was. She studied his face to see if she'd seen him on television, or if she'd met him somewhere. His hair was a little longer than most, but still professional. He wore a stylish suit with a thin pinstripe that looked like he was from the west somewhere.

"Let's sit and talk for a bit," Mr. Williams said in a very casual, conversational way. He guided her to a couch with his left hand on her shoulder. The touch of her shoulder caused him to recognize what she was wearing. He seemed to make a mental note but didn't comment.

They sat on the couch with an empty cushion between them. Sarah was only in the room for about twenty seconds before Jim arrived, and she didn't get a good look at it.

A large, heavy wooden desk dominated the left side of the room. To the right was an ornately carved table with chairs. It didn't look like a conference room table. It actually looked like a dining room table. Sconces spaced evenly around the room illuminated heavy white wallpaper with leaf patterns. This was an office, but it was decorated to look like a living room. A chandelier hung from the ceiling over the dining room table. Pictures covered a large portion of one wall. Sarah had good eyes and she could see across the room that many of the pictures included Dick Cheney, the Vice President of the United States.

She came around to looking at Jim's shoes making deep imprints in thick blue carpet. Sarah moved to look at her own feet. She had spent the last fifteen years of her life dressing better than everyone around her, and now, she was in the White House, and she was wearing running shoes she got out of the lost and found at the hotel this morning. Her self-consciousness mounted as she looked up her bare legs to her hands resting on her knees. She wore exercise shorts, a pink Guns & Roses t-shirt, and a sports bra, all from the lost and found.

She looked back to Jim, and he must have seen her discomfort.

"Debra!" Jim called, not loudly. Quickly the office door opened and a smartly dressed woman appeared. "Can you get Doctor Kiadopolis some clothes?"

"Certainly," Debra disappeared before Sarah could offer her size or preferences. She guessed anything would be better than this.

"Doctor," Jim turned back to Sarah and spoke in a soft, pleasant voice, "I'm very happy you're back with us. It's been a very long month." He looked into her eyes, his eyes moving from one to the other. Sarah knew he thought she knew who he was, but she didn't. Then realization hit him.

"I'm Jim Williams," Jim Williams said again, "I run Department 55." Again Sarah didn't feel she had enough recognition to change her facial expression. "Maxwell Rassic works for me."

She did know Maxwell.

"Can I see him?" Sarah asked. The words came out before she quickly realized she hadn't seen a familiar face in over a month. She wanted to see someone she recognized.

"Yes, he's on his way," Mr. Williams said, "He'll be here shortly."

Sarah felt some relief at the idea of seeing someone she knew.

"I know it's been a tough time for you," Mr. Williams continued, "We're going to get you some time off shortly, but we need just a bit more of your help."

Sarah barely heard what Jim said. She was thinking about how she had not seen anyone in over a month. She felt some relief at the idea of seeing Maxwell, but not complete. Who did she want to see?

Her mother? No.

Angie? No.

Peter? No.

Sullivan.

Sarah wanted to see Sullivan Acer. That was strange. She'd just spent a month with a man she barely knew, and now she knew he was the one person she wanted to see most in the world.

"I'm sorry?" Mr. Williams said. She must have said something.

"Sullivan Acer," Sarah said with more force, "Can I see him?"

"I'll check on him in just a moment, okay?" Mr. Williams said. Sarah was happy he knew who Sullivan was, but decided his answer didn't give her any information about him. Was he released? Was he waiting in the outer office with Debra? No, he couldn't be, if he was nearby he'd be with her.

Mr. Williams produced a folded sheet of paper from his breast pocket. He began to extend his hand to her, but reconsidered.

"Dr. Kiadopolis," Jim said, "I'm going to show you this letter, and I need you to know only eight people in the world know of its existence. You will be the ninth." Sarah figured she'd earned some trust and extended her hand. She read the letter.

> *Doctor Sarah Kiadopolis has made great strides in improving our relationship. She has explained the nature of your betrayal of our trust. We regret the loss of life, but it is necessary to remind you of the importance of our trust and to test our new trust in the Doctor.*
>
> *- LV*

LV. Mary told her LV communicated with the government with letters. This must be one of those letters. *Betrayal of trust?* Was the government working with LV somehow? Wait. *Trust in the Doctor?* Was that her? She reread the letter. Yes, she had to be the doctor they were referring to. What trust did they have in her?

"What trust do they have in you?" Sarah was shocked to hear Jim Williams speak the question she'd just thought. She looked up from the letter. She could feel the crease in her forehead. Jim looked at her expectantly.

"I don't-" Sarah began, but she was interrupted by a soft knock on the door. The door opened and Debra stepped back in.

"Sir," Debra said, "The Vice President is between meetings and is looking for an update. And-" Debra let the door open. Sarah felt a wave of relief at the sight of Sullivan Acer standing in the doorway. She almost stood immediately, but her body didn't respond.

"Dr. Kiadopolis," Jim said. She didn't want to look away from Sullivan, but she did. Jim extended his hand. She handed him the letter and that motion gave her the control to stand. "I'll be right back. My boss is looking for me." Jim Williams said and walked to the doorway. He left with Debra and the door closed leaving Sullivan and Sarah alone again.

The last month had been very difficult and she immediately knew she wouldn't have made it without this man. She stepped forward and drove her arms between his arms and his body. She hugged him as tightly as she could as tears burst from her eyes. He wrapped his arms around her and they stood for a moment.

"Sarah, I'm so glad to see you," Sullivan was saying as Sarah moved her head up and kissed him on the mouth. It was a hard, impulsive kiss filled more with the emotion of relief than of love, and it might have been the best she'd ever had. She was aware of every inch of herself that touched every inch of him. She wanted it to be more as she squeezed as tight as she could.

At the moment the kiss was about to turn into a second kiss, she collected herself, relaxed her grip and pulled her head back.

He looked at her, straight into her eyes with a broad smile. He made no move, and she enjoyed another moment as she remembered what he looked like. He had the easy smile that seemed like they'd been doing this for years.

"I'm glad to see you too," Sarah said at last. Was she smiling as idiotically as he was? She quickly straightened her face and pulled back a step. The front of her body was struggling to retain the feeling of his closeness, but it was gone.

She looked him up and down and saw that he was dressed as inappropriately as she was.

"I woke up in a hotel in Houston, Texas," Sullivan said. His practical statement drew her back to the present. She returned to the couch and took her seat. Sullivan followed and took Jim William's spot. Sarah immediately scooted to the center cushion and turned her body to face him. She wanted to take his hand but decided against it.

"Atlanta," Sarah said, "I didn't think you got out."

"I knew they weren't going to hurt us, remember," Sullivan said, "What are we doing here?"

"I don't have any idea," Sarah said, "That man was Jim Williams. He told me he's my project manager's boss. He showed me a letter from LV. *About me*." She looked to see if the name registered. It didn't. "The letter said they were *sorry for the loss of life, but they had to confirm their trust in me*?"

"What trust in you?" Sullivan asked, "Oh."

"What?" She was glad he was here. He was good at this stuff. He thought a moment too long and the door again opened. Jim stepped back in accompanied by Maxwell Rassic. Sarah was again relieved to see a familiar face. She didn't feel the urge to hug or kiss him, confirming Sullivan was indeed unique to her. She smiled a little at that as she stood.

"Sorry, my boss can be quite demanding," Jim Williams said.

Maxwell crossed the room quickly, and Sarah realized he was going to hug her.

"Dr. Kiadopolis," Maxwell stopped himself a moment before he embraced her, "I'm glad to see you're all right." Sarah was surprised to see him almost tear up. "Lloyd will be thrilled to hear it too."

"Thank you, Maxwell," Sarah was glad to see him, "Maxwell, this is Sullivan Acer, he was with me."

"Mr. Acer," Maxwell stood up straight and turned back into the father figure Sarah was used to. He boomed, "Thank you for taking care of our most important... " Maxwell seemed to search for words, "asset."

"She got us out of that place," Sullivan said, "I was just along for the ride."

"Let's sit, shall we?" Jim Williams indicated the couch again. Sarah and Sullivan resumed their seats and Mr. Williams and Maxwell pulled chairs from the dining room table. "This is my boss's office, please make yourself comfortable." Maxwell and Jim both sat and crossed their legs. Sullivan and Sarah both were in workout clothes and neither were comfortable in the Vice President's Office, so they sat straight backed.

"Sarah," Maxwell began, "I'm sorry I never told you we were looking for nuclear weapons." Sarah wasn't expecting an apology. She thought about it at the apartment and decided it wouldn't have helped her with her work if she knew what she was looking for. "We didn't think it would help, and we've learned that through strict compartmentalization, we can closely control information."

"I understand," Sarah said. She wasn't sure she did.

"We're confused about the letter LV sent," Jim Williams took over, "Frankly, the last time we got a letter with wording like this was just after the Oklahoma City Bombing."

"The Oklahoma City Bombing?" Sullivan asked. Sarah had relied heavily on Sullivan's ability to remain calm and even comfortable under extreme situations, and she was glad to rely on it again. "That wasn't a nuclear explosion-"

"Yes, it was," Maxwell said. Sullivan stopped cold. "Fortunately, the bomb was defective. A problem with the pre-charge. Probably defective manufacturing."

"Maxwell's right," Mr. Williams took back over. Sarah thought about what Maxwell said. The Oklahoma City bombing was in what? 1995? Six years ago? LV had a nuclear weapon six years ago?

"LV detonated a nuclear weapon in the United States six years ago?" Sullivan asked.

"Yes," Jim Williams said, "and we think they're about to detonate another one, so can we focus on the present?" Jim pulled the letter from his coat pocket again.

Sarah was convinced Sullivan was right, and LV had control of one or maybe two nuclear weapons that she had found for them in the past few years. How could they have had a bomb in 1995?

"Sarah," Maxwell said in his very calm, but somehow very strong voice, "Last time we got a letter like that was just after they detonated the Oklahoma City bomb. We got this letter this morning. It was mailed from a post office box in Wallingford, Connecticut. That happens to be the hub for junk mail, and therefore it's one of the most efficient post offices in America. We doubt LV knew this. We think they tried to time their letter to when they plan to detonate another device, but the letter probably got here one or two days early."

"So you're expecting a nuclear device to be detonated in the United States in the next two days?" Sullivan asked.

"Now you're up to speed." Jim said, "So, we need any clue you have that can help us find them before they detonate that bomb." Jim handed the letter to Sullivan and they waited while he read it. Sarah found herself absentmindedly rubbing her thighs. Maxwell smiled at her. Jim Williams tapped his foot silently on the carpet.

"So," Sullivan handed the letter back, "They've got two or three nuclear weapons, and they're going to detonate one to prove that Sarah can't find them without the power going off?"

Sarah watched Maxwell and Jim Williams closely. They looked at each other, both in realization. It hit Sarah what they realized. They thought LV told the two of them what was going on while they were in the apartment. Jim had told her that only seven people knew about all this. He thought Sarah and Sullivan were two of them.

"No," Sarah said. She looked at Maxwell, "They don't have two nuclear weapons. They haven't been stealing the weapons we're finding." Maxwell looked at her. "They've had nuclear weapons all along. The bombs I've been finding have been in the foundations of the buildings they're in. The one in Greenville wasn't but that building was renovated..." Sarah trailed off and thought.

"This is good," Jim said, "but we really need your help now."

"If we're going to help you," Sullivan said, "we're going to have to know what we're helping you with!"

Sarah continued, "The bombs must have been there when the buildings were built." She looked at Maxwell. "You have me collecting data and storing it so we can use it later, when the power happens to go out." Maxwell watched her put things together. He smiled at her like an approving teacher. She watched his face closely. If she got something wrong, she knew he would flinch. "So, you've been looking for bombs that have been stationary for a long time."

"LV isn't stealing the bombs," Sullivan said. Sarah didn't look at him. She focused on Maxwell. "They planted the bombs!" Maxwell glanced down at their hands touching, but only for a brief instant.

"The bombs were planted in the foundations of buildings in South Carolina and California," Sarah said, "and Oklahoma City. They could be anywhere! You've got me searching the entire USA. You don't know where they are!"

"Correct, Sarah," Maxwell said.

"And," Sullivan added, "you don't know how many there are!"

"And LV is using the threat of the bombs to force you to do whatever they ask?" Sarah asked.

"Yes," Jim Williams answered, "Yes, you've got it. We thought you would already know this. Very few people know what you now know."

Jim looked back to the letter. Sarah relaxed her back and felt it touch the cushion. She almost crossed her legs but thought better of it.

"Who else?" Sarah asked.

"What?" Jim Williams asked.

"Who else has bombs? Is it just the USA?" Sarah remembered that her search was collecting information across most of the Northern Hemisphere, which included most of the land mass of the Earth and nearly all the developed world.

"The Soviet Union had one-hundred and twenty-five," Maxwell said.

"The *former* Soviet Union?" Sullivan asked. One-Hundred and Twenty-Five? Sarah thought that was a very big number. Sarah was about to ask how they knew how many, but she thought that might have to wait for another day.

"Yes, that's why they *became* the *former* Soviet Union," Jim said.

"I have a thousand more questions," Sarah said, "but we need to get going. What do you need from us?"

Sarah saw Jim's face soften, "Thank you Dr. Kiadopolis. We've reviewed the information collected on the plane." Jim uncrossed his legs and leaned forward. "We know you were held in South America. We've narrowed it down to Buenos Aires, Montevideo, and Porto Alegre from the combination of spores and pollution we found on both of your bodies." Sarah looked away as she thought of where on her body they found those spores. "We'll be able to narrow it down further between Argentina, Uruguay, and Brazil based on the food regulations, and the samples we took from your hair." Mr. Williams was looking directly at Sarah. "But you can imagine that's probably not going to help in the next day."

Jim produced a folder while Sarah was looking away. He opened it and pulled out an excellent hand sketch of Mary. "In the mean-time, we'll circulate this picture to all of the universities in those countries."

"Oh," Sullivan interrupted, "Claire Havers, the agent on the plane with me, she said she recognized Mary."

"Yes," Jim said, "She reported that, but she couldn't place her. It must be just a likeness."

"Yes, but she also told me she knew you," Sullivan turned to Sarah. Sarah didn't know anyone named Claire, Claire what? "She said she saw you at a conference a few years ago." He looked at Sarah expectantly. "You also said Mary looked familiar to you."

Sarah remembered the unshakable feeling that she knew Mary from somewhere, but she wasn't ever able to put her finger on it. The only conference she'd been to in the last few years was when she talked at the Society of Women Engineers in Florida. There were a lot of technical women there, maybe she was there. She looked around the room and found everyone was looking at her. She didn't have anything further to contribute to that line of questioning so she started somewhere else, "You must have leads here in the United States? What about the hotels we were in?"

Maxwell and Mr. Williams both frowned. She realized they did not. Maxwell took this question.

"Sarah, they carefully selected these two hotels. They have two of the most outdated security systems of any hotel in the country. We did get surveillance video from both lobbies though. You both checked in by yourselves."

Jim produced photographs of both Sarah and Sullivan at hotel lobby check in desks. They were both wearing their outfits from the night they were taken, and every day in the apartment. They both looked alert.

"From the chemical analysis of your hair, we found you were both given sodium pentothal and Rohypnol when you were taken a month ago. This combination would make you highly influenced by suggestion and also forget everything you did. So, they probably told you to go check in, you probably went to your rooms, they probably helped you out of your clothes, and you slept for a day or so while the drugs wore off." Maxwell looked away from Sarah at the mention of clothes.

Sarah remembered Rohypnol was also called the *date rape drug* because the women who it was slipped to didn't remember enough to bring charges against their attackers. She didn't like the idea.

She thought about it and was sure she was not accosted while in LV's custody. It surprised her to feel so certain about that fact. She decided LV wasn't a bunch of monsters. They treated her and Sullivan with the utmost respect.

Yet they had detonated a nuclear weapon in the United States and were threatening to detonate another.

So they were monsters.

The door again opened. Sarah didn't immediately register it because she was thinking about the duplicity of her feelings about LV. She looked to the door and the man standing in it. At first, she didn't recognize him. He wore a stylishly tailored suit and walked into the room with a confidence that told her he was supposed to be here. Her first realization was that he was carrying a hanging clothes bag. Sullivan shot to his feet.

"*Linus Brenner!*" Sullivan said. Maxwell and Jim Williams had both turned to look at the man entering the room and turned back at Sullivan's proclamation. Sarah felt her eyes widen as she realized Sullivan was right. It was Linus Brenner. Maxwell and Jim Williams both didn't seem alarmed by his presence.

Wait. If LV wasn't paying Linus Brenner for his stolen bombs, then what was he doing? And what was he doing here?

Before Sarah could process his presence, Sullivan stepped forward.

No, he *lunged* forward. Sarah saw him draw back his arm and throw a punch at the new visitor to the Vice President's Office.

Luckily for Linus, and unluckily for Sullivan, Linus easily dodged the punch.

He stepped to the side and re-directed Sullivan's arm past him.

He put out his foot and Sullivan fell hard to the floor.

The door opened and Debra stood in it with her hand over her mouth.

As quickly as it started, the fight was over. Sullivan quickly lifted himself from his face to a sitting position. Sarah found herself standing and so was everyone else. Linus was still smiling and had not so much as dropped the garment bag.

"Everyone calm down!" Jim Williams demanded with his hands out, "Mr. Acer, are you okay?"

Sullivan scrambled to his feet. Linus Brenner didn't step away from Sullivan, but also didn't move to face him.

Jim stepped between them. "Linus."

Jim looked at Linus.

Sullivan stepped toward Linus.

Sarah knew Sullivan was embarrassed and needed to redeem himself. She also knew he probably wouldn't succeed against this man who obviously could handle himself.

"Sullivan," Sarah said. She stepped forward, "Mr. Williams, Linus Brenner's been stealing the nuclear weapons I've been finding!" Everyone in the room looked at Sarah. She was standing closest to Maxwell and felt herself shift her weight to be slightly behind him. She succeeded in drawing everyone's attention.

"Of course he's stealing LV's bombs!" Jim Williams said, "What did you think we'd do with them when you found them?"

"Linus Brenner works for *you*?" Sarah asked. Sullivan stepped back.

"Yes," Jim said, "Can we all calm down?"

"But he's been spying on me!" Sarah said, "And he was in Greenville, he sent people to get me!"

"Sarah," Maxwell turned. They were very close together. He touched her arm. "Linus Brenner is in charge of our Operations Division. He's responsible for all field operations required by Department Fifty-Five. He wasn't spying on you, he was protecting you."

"*Protecting*?" Sarah burst.

"But what about Greenville?" Sullivan recovered himself and stepped back into the conversation.

"I saw the two of you together and decided I needed to have a chat," Linus Brenner said. "Then I saw people I didn't send coming to get you. I tried to call you into the hotel. Then I tried to stop them from taking you. Why did you think I was shooting?"

Sarah looked around the room. Sullivan didn't know what to do with himself. He still stood in an aggressive stance. Jim still had his hands out. Maxwell stood next to Sarah. Linus was looking past Maxwell at Sarah. He obviously didn't think of Sullivan as a threat because he turned his back on him completely.

She thought through everything he'd said. She spoke softly to Maxwell, "Why was he *protecting* me?"

"After LV demanded that we cancel the Desertron in Texas, we started taking extra precautions to make sure none of our technical assets were compromised."

Sarah crossed her arms over her chest. It was the only defensive posture she could take. She needed to think. She and Sullivan had not been much help here, but they had just learned a tremendous amount. She needed to process the new information and see if there was something she could offer.

Maxwell helped her out.

"Are those their clothes?" Maxwell asked, indicating the bag Linus carried.

"Yes," Linus said.

"Okay," Jim said, "Dr. Kiadopolis, why don't you take these into the other room there and get changed?" Jim took the bag from Linus and handed it to Sarah.

. . .

The other room turned out to be the Vice President's private wash room complete with shower. Sarah found that the clothes were actually hers. Linus must have gone to her apartment and picked them out for her. The thought of him in her apartment picking out clothes was creepy, but she was relieved to get out of her borrowed shorts and t-shirt. She didn't even have underwear.

She took a shower and felt better in her normal business outfit, white blouse, black skirt, and black heels. There was no hair dryer; Dick Cheney didn't need one, so she pulled her wet hair in a ponytail.

After Sarah, Sullivan changed into a suit that was also in the bag. His suit was slightly big and clearly brand new. He looked good.

They were led down the ornate halls of the West Wing of the White House. Sarah walked next to Sullivan behind Jim and Maxwell. Linus excused himself saying he had matters to attend to.

That was fine, Sarah knew he was on their side, but she still didn't like him.

They wove their way down several hallways, each a bit nicer than the last, passing people in the bustling complex of beautifully decorated rooms. She looked into each open door as they hurried by beautiful paintings, thick trim, and elegant wall sconces juxtaposed with metal filing cabinets and desks overflowing with papers.

After what seemed too long a walk, they entered a small room with three desks along one wall. The room was more of a wide hallway and Sarah stopped when she saw the open door at the other end. She'd never seen this view, but movies and TV shows had made the Oval Office familiar to her.

"Oh shit," Sullivan mumbled a tiny bit too loud. The woman at the third desk, fifty in a neat pant suit, stood and walked to the open door of the Oval. She looked in and nodded to the people Sarah couldn't see. Sarah and Sullivan were motioned forward.

Sarah didn't move at first. She took a moment to pull the ponytail holder out of her hair and wrap in on her wrist. She ran her fingers through her hair. Then she forced herself to step. She walked carefully forward and felt as though she were entering a cathedral. Her eyes were drawn to the desk set in front of the windows where she saw the President of the United States talking with, yes; it was the Vice President of the United States.

Maxwell and Jim Williams walked around the couch into the seating area without introduction. The quiet sound of the door closing behind them rang in Sarah's ears as President George Bush and Vice President Dick Cheney looked at her.

The President stood and rounded the end of his desk, "Dr. Kiadopolis, it's a real pleasure to meet you! I'm George Bush!" She wondered if he really had to introduce himself to anyone in the world. She shook his hand without saying anything. "Mr. Acer!" They shook. "Well, let's sit down!" He led them around the couch. Sarah and Sullivan sat next to each other on the couch facing the door. The President sat in a wing-backed chair in front of his desk and the Vice President took a similar chair in front of the fireplace.

Sarah couldn't believe the last five hours. Six hours ago, she woke up naked and confused in Atlanta, four hours ago she'd been subjected to an invasive physical exam on an airplane. Two hours ago, she was in the Vice President's Office in a t-shirt with no underwear, and now she was talking to the President of the United States in the Oval Office.

"We've been waiting for you to come back to us," the President started, "We understand LV's valuing your trust. Let me cut right to it. We need to know what trust they value."

"I ... I" Sarah couldn't find words. She also didn't know what words they were looking for.

"Let me," Sullivan said. He patted her on her hands crossed over her knees. "Mr. President. Sarah and I were in a tough spot. We saw a video of you telling her to tell them everything."

"Yes," the President smiled.

"So," Sullivan continued, "we figured out that LV didn't want us, I mean Sarah, to be able to find the bombs. We didn't know why, but we knew that. So, Sarah proved that if the power grid stays on, her system doesn't work."

"Well," Dick Cheney spoke for the first time. His gruff voice would have startled her, but Sarah had heard him on television many times, "We're working on seeing through the grid, but we can't do it right now."

"No," Sullivan interrupted. Sarah thought that was pretty bold. "Sarah proved you can't do it."

"Is this true?" the Vice President looked to Maxwell. Maxwell raised his shoulders and looked to Sarah.

"Mr. Vice President," Sarah said softly, "I've found a proof that shows you cannot see through the grid. I was able to convince Mary that it was true."

"Is it true?"

"Yes."

"Damn."

"It got us out!" Sullivan said.

"Yes," the Vice President said, "That's great, but we need that system to work."

"We're also no closer to finding LV," Jim Williams said, "We're following all the leads we've collected, but they're not going to help us in the next two days."

Suddenly Sarah had a flash of realization. Somewhere in the back of her mind, she'd been processing the new information that she'd seen Mary at the conference in Florida. "Mary was at the conference!" Sarah blurted. "That's where I recognized her. She was at the conference in Florida! She was in the front row. She took a lot of notes. She was the only one who asked a technical question after my talk!"

"What conference?" the President asked.

"Mr. President," Maxwell answered, "I know the details. I'll get this to Linus, and he can get some people on it. I still don't think it's going to help us today." Sarah was getting the feeling the President was hoping for a miracle. That somehow she was going to say she knew how to find LV, and how to stop them from setting off a bomb. She didn't.

"Mr. President," Sullivan said, "We were captives. We knew our only hope of getting out was to not learn anything about our captors. So we didn't learn anything. They also were very careful not to tell us anything."

The President sunk into his chair, "I understand." Sarah saw desperation on his face. Everyone was quiet while he processed this news.

The Vice President turned to Jim Williams, "Are the other plans in place?"

"Yes, sir," Jim Williams reported, "The cell tower detection net is up and operational. Three people are monitoring it full time waiting for a signal LV will send to start the bomb on its detonation sequence.

"Then what?" the President asked.

"From our study of the bombs we've already found, we know we'll have eighteen hours, that's how they're wired," Jim answered.

"So, when we find what cell it's in, we turn off the power," the President looked at Dr. Kiadopolis, "and she finds it for us?"

"No," Jim said, "we can't turn the power off, LV was clear." Sarah looked down. They couldn't turn the power off because of her.

Sarah shuddered. Was a nuclear weapon going to be detonated, and they couldn't find it because she told America's worst enemy how to stop her? Depending on where it was, a nuclear weapon could kill tens of thousands. Wait, the ones in Japan were tiny compared to modern weapons, and they killed seventy thousand each. Were they talking about not finding a bomb that could kill hundreds of thousands of people?

"So, what are we going to do then?" the President asked.

Maxwell stepped in, "We're going to find the bomb with brute force."

"We're going to dig up the foundations of every building in a cell phone cell?" Dick Cheney asked.

"Something like that," Maxwell said. There was no love lost between these two.

"No, no, no," the President interrupted. He had slumped forward so his elbows were on his knees. "Here's what we're going to do. We've got about a day, maybe two. Linus is going to get this *Mary* based on knowing she was at that conference, and he's going to find LV. Maxwell, you're going to work with Sarah on seeing through the damned grid. Call in anyone you need. Dick, you're going to figure out how to evacuate a cell phone cell once we get that signal. Jim, get your video equipment back in here, we're sending a message to LV."

"But, Mr. President," Jim said.

"No, we've only got a day," the President stood, "I'm not going to waste another minute. Dr. Kiadopolis, thank you for your service to our country. We need you to do what you think is impossible. We need you to see through the grid, tonight."

Sarah knew there was only one acceptable answer, "Yes, Mr. President."

79. June 24, 2001

"You really don't need to be here, that's what they're for," Peter kissed Claire on the top of her head. Three young engineers manned a bank of computers. Claire sat at a desk behind the three with a summary display. They were on the eighth floor of the Chamber of Commerce Building across the street from the Poinsett Hotel in downtown Greenville.

"I delivered Mr. Acer to the White House!" Claire said in a hushed voice. Her team was carefully monitoring the network of cell phone towers. They still had to constantly make minor adjustments based on weather and cell phone usage variations across the country.

Helping Linus remove two nuclear weapons from buildings in California brought into focus the severity of the work they did for him. He explained to them that he'd been searching for hidden nuclear weapons for the federal government after the first one. Since then, Claire had been working seven days a week with Ravi on a new project aimed at narrowing down the location of a device after the cell system detected that it had been activated.

"Okay, okay," Peter knew he couldn't talk her into leaving. She had not left since she returned from dropping Sullivan off, and he could see she was tired. He brought her dinner and they ate while she worked. She put her hand on his leg under the table, but she didn't look away from the screen. Peter didn't know what to do. He didn't think it was worth the time for her to train him in what she was doing, but he couldn't think of leaving her here.

Peter stood, collected their dinner remains, and carried them to the trash. He paused to look out the window across the street to the Poinsett Hotel. Behind it he could see to the river and even the balcony of his own apartment.

Their apartment. She sold her house and moved in with him.

He'd been looking at rings.

"Claire," Peter couldn't remember the name of the technician who called out, "You need to look at this!" With a flick of his mouse he moved his display up to the large monitor on the wall. Peter saw a detailed map of the cell phone system. One of the cells was highlighted red in the mid-western United States.

"Kassandra, can you confirm?" Claire spoke with the steady voice developed through dozens of drills.

Ten seconds later, a second screen on the wall showed a different set of information and Kassandra called, "Claire, confirmed! We have detected a signal!"

"Good," Claire said, "Run the triangulation and neighboring cell algorithms to confirm we have the right one."

"Yes, Ma'am," Kassandra said.

"Bill, pull the signal files and upload them to the control server," Claire was moving through her checklist. Now Peter saw why she wanted to be here. Her team had no idea this wasn't another drill. Her team would have done a good job, but maybe not a perfect job. Peter knew everything had to be perfect. He watched as Claire dialed a number. He knew it was Linus.

"Sir," Claire rarely called him Sir, "We've received the signal ... Yes sir, we're running the regressions now, but I'm certain ... Yes, we're ready. I'll have confirmation in about two minutes ... No, he's here, with me," Claire looked to Peter. He saw she was completely in control. One by one, her technicians raised their thumbs in the air indicating they'd completed their regressions and everything checked out. Claire had carefully choreographed this dance.

"Sir," Claire didn't take her eyes of Peter, "I have confirmation. The signal was received four minutes ago, at 12 Midnight, in Kokomo, Indiana."

. . .

"Mr. Vice President," the door to the Vice President's office opened for the first time in two hours. Sarah pivoted on her heel and froze when she saw a man in a suit with an ear piece, obviously secret service, with his gun drawn but pointed at the floor. "We're taking the White House into full lock-down. You need to come with us." It was only then that Sarah saw several US Marines in full battle gear behind him.

"Come on," the Vice President said as he stood from the conference table where he'd been pouring over plans with Sullivan and Jim Williams. Jim stood without hesitation. He pulled a purple index card from his inside coat pocket and clipped it to his shirt.

Sarah and Maxwell had been at three large dry-erase boards since dinner reviewing her technical work. She knew they weren't going to find anything, but Maxwell wanted to go through it. He thought there was still a chance to see through the grid. She knew there wasn't. He clipped a purple index card to his shirt.

"What's going on?" Sarah leaned close to Maxwell and asked. She was looking across the room to Sullivan who had stood with the others but didn't know what to do.

"We must have received the signal," Maxwell said. He looked at his watch. "Twelve-ten, we must have received it at midnight." Sarah felt a pit instantly form in her stomach. Somehow she still hoped this wouldn't happen. Maybe it still had not.

She made eye contact with Sullivan. Earlier in the evening, Linus told Sullivan he'd flown his son and parents in from Wisconsin and arranged a dinner with them. Sarah felt his absence immediately, but she kept busy eating with the Vice President, Jim Williams, and Maxwell while continuing work. Sullivan returned two hours later, and Sarah had to fight the urge to hug him.

"Sullivan," Sarah called. He was starting to follow the other two men out of the room, and she didn't want that to happen.

"Yes?" He asked expectantly.

"Good luck," she wanted to tell him more. He hesitated, but fell back in line.

"Sullivan," Maxwell interrupted and Sarah's heart leapt. "You're going to need this," he moved quickly across the room to hand his purple tag to Sullivan.

Just like that, she was alone with Maxwell in the Vice President's office. "Where are they going?"

"The Situation Room," Maxwell said as he walked to the Vice President's desk, "They'll complete the lock-down procedure and then someone will come and let us know the details. I've got some calls to make." He lifted the receiver and started dialing.

Sarah sat on the couch not knowing what to do. Maxwell was coordinating moving a team of technicians into the Situation Room.

She sat quietly trying to calm her breathing. It still felt abstract. They'd received a signal that said a nuclear explosion was going to happen somewhere in the USA in eighteen hours. There must have been something she should be doing, but, in the flurry of activity, no one gave her a job.

She looked over to Maxwell. He was talking quickly but precisely. He met her eyes, but didn't indicate he needed any help. The marine standing guard looked at her. She was just like him, a bystander. She let her eyes close. She let her mind wander through the work she'd done for the past ten years, hoping against hope that something new would come through that would help.

. . .

"Sarah," Sarah heard Sullivan say. It took her a second to realize it was a real sound and she opened her eyes. She felt she was too happy to see him. She stood.

"Yes?"

"We're going," Sullivan said, "I told Linus you should come with us."

"Going?" Sarah said. She didn't care. She just wanted something to do.

"We're going to Kokomo, Indiana," Sullivan said. Sarah started to follow him, but she paused. Kokomo? That must be where they received the signal. That must be where the bomb is going off? And they were going there? Sullivan stepped forward and clipped a purple tag to her shirt. His invasion of her personal space was welcome and Sarah forced her arms to her sides. "We need you," Sullivan said quietly, "I need you."

. . .

"Something isn't right," Sarah leaned close to Sullivan and whispered into his ear in the back of a black SUV with a rear-facing middle seat. Linus Brenner and Agent Tyler Jacobs sat directly across from them. Both were on cell phones working to coordinate the efforts when they reached Kokomo. Their jet was leaving from

National Airport as soon as they arrived.

"What's not right?" Sullivan asked. Jim Williams and the Vice President decided it would be impossible to evacuate the entire area in eighteen hours, and if they did, they would be telling LV they knew where the bomb was.

"The President told them he wouldn't turn off the power," Sarah spoke quietly. She didn't know if she was trying not to disturb Linus and the agent, or if she didn't fully trust them yet. "LV knows we can't find the bombs with the power on. I can't believe Mary would do this."

Sullivan took a moment to answer. The SUV had a police escort and they were going about eighty miles an hour in a thirty-five. Sarah noticed the side streets were blocked by police and that their path was clear, so she wasn't concerned. She could tell Sullivan didn't share her sentiment.

"Remember, LV isn't just Mary," Sullivan said, "This is a test. What better way to prove we can't find the bomb than to tell us they're setting one off?"

"I understand, but they're going to kill one-hundred thousand people just to prove we can't find their bombs?" Sarah felt exasperated, "Doesn't there have to be a better way?"

"I don't know," Sullivan said. The SUV took a hard left turn onto the bridge across the Potomac River, the tires squealed and Sarah was pushed into Sullivan. She saw Agent Jacobs and Linus Brenner use their free hands to brace and didn't stop talking into their phones.

"They made this plan before we left the apartment," Sullivan said.

"Why?"

"They must have made this plan a few weeks ago. That's why you had to prove you couldn't see through the grid," Sullivan said. Sarah was happy he was there and could figure all this out.

Sarah looked out the window and thought. "Even if we turned the power off, I couldn't find a bomb in Indiana, yet. The scans have only reached the middle of Nevada," Sarah said. She realized she hadn't lifted herself from leaning into him since the last turn, and she shifted her weight.

Sarah braced herself as the SUV navigated through the entrance to the airport. The police escort pulled away as they were now on controlled roads around the government hangars.

Sarah had difficulty holding on as the driver continued with his speed and swerved between the low buildings.

Even Linus ended his call and held on.

To Sarah's surprise, they emerged from the far end of the jumble of hangars.

Sullivan patted her hand and pointed out his window. Sarah followed his finger to see a Lear Jet moving toward the runway. She estimated that it was traveling about twenty miles an hour, the top half of the door was open with a man's head poked out.

The SUV pulled onto the taxiway and accelerated to eighty to catch up. To Sarah's relief, both vehicles came to a stop. The relief was short-lived because Agent Jacobs and Linus Brenner nearly jumped from the SUV with Sarah and Sullivan close behind. The engines were still ramping up with the plane held by its brakes. No one had any luggage, so boarding the four passengers took no more than twenty seconds.

Sullivan was the last aboard and the man closed the door quickly behind him.

Sarah took the first seat she came to as the aircraft immediately began to accelerate down the runway. She saw Sullivan pause in the aisle and she looked to find him a seat. That there was one at the back of the plane, but when she turned to point to it, Sullivan had already sat down on the floor at her feet. He pushed his back against the wall as the aircraft pitched back and rocketed into the air.

Sarah looked around the plane. She had to look over her shoulder and she twisted in her seat, making sure not to kick Sullivan.

She was in the right window seat in the first of three rows of four seats. Each seat had an occupant. Each occupant was studying papers. Behind the three rows the space opened. There was a large table against the left wall. Agent Jacobs had taken the seat at the table. Behind it, chairs had their backs to the walls, three on each side and at the back of the plane there were two chairs.

A video projector mounted on the ceiling illuminated a trapezoid on the wall above the table. A digital clock hung above the trapezoid. Sarah realized it wasn't a clock, but it was counting down. It read sixteen hours, three minutes, ten seconds. Nine. Eight. Seven. Sarah checked her watch. It was counting down to six p.m.

"Sarah," Linus Brenner was in the seat next to her, "do we need to know something?" Linus was reading quickly through a sheaf of papers. They seemed to be more important to Linus than her answer, and Sullivan was subtly shaking his head no, but she offered anyway.

"Yes, there is," Sarah began. Linus paused only briefly, but didn't stop with the papers. He cocked his head toward her. "Why would LV want to detonate a bomb *now*? They know we can't find it." Sarah stopped abruptly as Linus raised his hand.

"Sarah, we have to act quickly. Finding the bomb is my top priority, not understanding why," Linus stopped with the papers and looked at her. He'd been going full speed for the past two hours, and this seemed to be the first time he paused. "You and the investigator here," he motioned to Sullivan who was still sitting on the floor, "If you two work something out that affects the path I'm on, let me know, otherwise, you'll get instructions on approach like everyone else." He looked directly at her again for the briefest of pauses, "Do you have something I can act on?"

Sarah was still intimidated by him, but she made sure her answer was strong, "Nothing yet, we'll let you know."

"Please do." With that, Linus unbuckled his belt, stood and walked to the back of the plane. Sullivan took the opportunity to move to the chair and almost fell back to the floor. He flopped into the seat and quickly buckled his belt. He put both hands on the arm rests with his eyes closed. Sarah put her hand over his and they sat for a moment. She watched as the tension melted from his face. Then she returned her hand to her lap.

"We've got to let the bomb go off. I don't see any way around it," Sullivan said with his eyes still closed. He spoke softly, but Sarah still looked around to see that no one was listening. Everyone was working their papers as fast as they could. She could've taken her top off and no one would have noticed.

"If Linus finds it, he's going to stop it. No way he lets a city disappear," Sarah said.

Sullivan opened his eyes and looked at her, "If we stop this one, then what stops LV from detonating another, and if we find that one, another? I heard Agent Jacobs say that in Kokomo we only have about a one in ten chance of finding it. They could easily pick a larger city and make our chances one in a thousand, or one in a million."

Sarah was discouraged, but something Sullivan said stuck. They could easily have picked a place where it would be harder to find it. Why did they pick Kokomo? It couldn't be the largest city with one of their hidden devices. Greenville was larger, and it was still small.

Was it the smallest? Sarah thought of the places she'd cleared in California. They were large, densely populated areas. If they'd picked one of them, the death toll would have been ten times Kokomo.

Sarah decided Kokomo was the smallest city with a device, "Sullivan, they don't want to kill a lot of people, that's why they picked Kokomo." She was excited by the revelation, but didn't know what it meant.

"Fifty-thousand is still a huge number," Sullivan said. He looked at her again, waiting for something more.

"So, did you hear Linus say in the SUV that they were going to focus their efforts on the buildings downtown?"

"Yes, that makes sense, you start where the most people will be affected," Sullivan said. His eyes squinted a little, trying to understand what she was getting at.

"Not if they're trying to kill as *few* people as possible!" Sarah looked around. Agent Jacobs was hunched over a large map making notes as he flipped through other pages. Sarah unbuckled her belt, stood, got her footing, and walked over. Sullivan didn't follow, but watched intently. No one else seemed to notice.

Not until Sarah was at the agent's side did she notice the projected image. It looked like the inside of an identical airplane. Directly in front of her was another table with a woman sitting at it. Sarah felt like she could reach through and touch the woman. She had a large map of a city, presumably Kokomo. She'd drawn a large hexagon over the city's east side. It covered downtown and reached east past the highway into the cornfields beyond an industrial area.

The woman and Agent Jacobs each had a stack of faxed pages that looked like county records. The records were the building information. She was making notes on the large map, identifying the age of the buildings. She then traced the outline of any building built in the sixties.

Agent Jacobs was feeding her information. They focused all their efforts on the downtown. There were about one hundred buildings, and they were through maybe fifteen. The work was slow as the records were not complete or standard in any way. They had to read through several pages of documents to find anything useful.

That's what everyone on this plane was doing. They were helping read building records.

Sarah looked into the other plane and saw it was configured the same, full of people similarly studying.

The man sitting in the chair next to the woman handed her a page, "Claire, what about this one? It has the right date, and large foundations."

Even with his back to her and only the side of his face on the screen, Sarah saw the man was Peter Howard. She was dumbfounded. What was Peter doing here? Sarah looked back at Sullivan who didn't react in any way.

"I think you're right, I'll mark it," Claire took the page, found the building, and carefully outlined its foundation.

"Peter?" Sarah whispered. Peter's head turned around and poked onto the screen. It took him a moment to see her, to refocus his eyes.

"Yes?" Peter said. Sarah was even more shocked that Peter wasn't shocked to see her. "Hello, Sarah. I'm glad you're back with us." With all their history, she thought she deserved more. She also knew this wasn't the place.

Peter was in on this? She was looking at Peter and he was looking at her. He seemed genuine in both his happiness to see her and also in his indifference to their past. She had been looking at Peter so it took a moment for Sarah to see the almost violent look on Claire's face.

"Hello?" Sarah looked directly at the woman she didn't know, "I'm Sarah Kiadopolis."

"Yes," Claire said, "I know who you are." Everyone had been nice to her until this moment. Sarah had no idea what was wrong with this Claire. She saw Peter put his hand on Claire's hand. It was more than the calming touch Sarah had just offered Sullivan. It was personal.

Oh, they were together, Sarah thought. She didn't have nearly enough evidence to make that determination, but she knew it was right. If they were, then Sarah's connection with Peter certainly could have been difficult for her. While they were intensely physical, Sarah and Peter knew they were only close friends. Sarah knew no one else would understand, so she never told anyone about their relationship except Angie. She certainly had not told any dates. Clearly, Peter had been more forthcoming with Claire.

Linus noticed what was going on, and now he put his papers down. Peter looked at Sarah, waiting for her to speak. Sarah looked at Linus. Sarah decided that whatever got Peter onto this plane wasn't important right now. It was another puzzle piece in her past that she would be trying to decipher for years to come, she hoped. What was important was finding the bomb, figuring out how to stop it, and figuring out how to convince LV they didn't use *Space Resonance* to do it.

Sarah turned back to the map on Claire's table. On the eastern edge was an industrial complex. Further east of it were corn fields. The complex was centered on a factory of some kind. To the north was more industrial buildings and to the south a small apartment complex. The plant sat on the east side of highway 31, so it was several miles from downtown with much lower population density around it.

"Claire, when was that plant built?" Sarah asked.

Claire still had the same angry look. Peter's hand didn't help a bit. "Sarah, that plant is outside our focus area," Claire seethed, "Not many people live out there, and the bomb is timed to go off at six in the afternoon on a Sunday. The plant will be nearly empty. Everyone will be home, on the West end."

"Sarah," Linus had had enough, "Claire's very busy. Do you have something?"

Sarah considered what she had. She had a hunch that LV wouldn't want to hurt people with the nuclear weapon they had just commanded to detonate. No, she didn't have anything. She looked at Linus. She looked at the count down. It read 15:30:05. He waited expectantly, but she turned and returned to her seat next to Sullivan.

"That was Peter Howard," Sarah said to Sullivan.

"Oh," Sullivan craned his neck to see his face. Sarah didn't look back. "He's still looking at you. The woman is Claire Havers. She was the agent on the plane with me. Linus sure didn't like it when you were talking to Peter!" Sullivan turned back with a concerned look.

Sarah wasn't sure what to make of that. Claire saw Sarah at her talk in Orlando, the same talk Peter showed up at. That was the talk where she started seeing him again. Peter must have told Claire about their relationship. Now Peter and Claire were together. And Linus knew all this? Linus was watching Sarah in her apartment. But Sarah knew Peter never came into her apartment, despite her promising enticements. That's how Sarah knew Peter knew Linus was watching. Did Linus know Peter and Sarah were together? Did Peter work for Linus?

Sarah closed her eyes and realized she was tired. She was

surprised to find she didn't have any feelings for Peter, but couldn't shake a bit of jealousy toward Claire. Just a bit.

80. 14:15:00

Sullivan patted Sarah's hand. She was surprised to find that she was almost asleep. He unbuckled his belt and stood up. Sarah did the same, not knowing what was going on. They turned and faced the back of the plane toward the make-shift conference area.

Linus sat in the same chair, and was collecting a few notes from those around him. Everyone was stopping what they were doing and assembling as best they could. Agent Jacobs stood and crossed to Linus, handing him a final note. Linus nodded. The man on Linus' left gave him a dirty look and Agent Jacobs returned it. Sarah realized she was a stranger among a close group. The countdown passed 14:15:00.

"Okay," Linus began, "So we're all straight, Claire, give us the background."

Sarah saw the people on Claire's plane similarly arranged. "We've received a credible threat that a nuclear device will detonate at 6PM today in this target area." Claire held up her map with the large hexagon. "That's in fourteen hours, fourteen minutes, and ten seconds. We've all been researching the buildings in the target area of Kokomo, Indiana. Tyler, Peter, and I assembled your work into groupings and you've been timing the groupings out so we can optimize the search patterns. Thank you. We're almost done with the final assignments so we'll be ready when we land." Claire stopped and looked back through the screen to Linus.

"Thanks, Claire," Linus picked up, "We'll be landing in Kokomo in thirty minutes. We'll be broken up into pairs. We have twelve sets of search equipment. That's the good news. The bad news is that Claire calculates that with all twelve scanners going full speed, we're only going to be able to search about 15% of the foundations." Linus nodded to Claire. Several people looked and she nodded back. "So, we'll start with the most likely candidates and work our way down. Our chances aren't good, but we're going to try."

Sullivan leaned to Sarah, "Have they done this before?"

"Seems like it," Sarah said, "I wonder if they've ever found one this way." Sullivan shrugged his shoulders. She noted that Claire didn't explain how they knew the bomb would detonate at 6PM.

Maybe not everyone here knew all the details she did.

"Claire will distribute the lists to each team when we land," Linus continued, "Mario, is the cover ready?" Linus turned to the man Agent Jacobs didn't like.

"We've nearly all the papers ready. The ground water flows from the north so we found a small machine shop named Innovated Solutions. It's about seven miles north of the cell, so the dispersion pattern is believable. We're going to need some hydrofluoric acid. We're going to say they were illegally developing a new leaching process and spilled a bunch into the ground water."

"Excellent," Linus said, "Is everyone clear on that? If we're lucky, this will only be a bad day for one machine shop owner."

"We can't reveal what we're really looking for," Sullivan read Sarah's mind and spoke quietly to her, "I hope we'll somehow take care of that poor slob!"

"What else do we need to take care of?" Linus asked.

"Two questions," a young man in one of the rows of seats announced, "What's the disarmament plan? And what is the fail-safe time?" Sarah half expected him to turn and point to her and ask *what is she going to do?* She had no idea how to answer that question. Everyone seemed to know what was going on better than the two of them. Now she tried to remember if everyone was busy, and she wished she had made a note of anyone who wasn't doing anything.

"Excellent questions," Linus answered, "The disable method is still in process. I'm assured we won't need more than thirty minutes. So the fail-safe time is five thirty, or thirty minutes remaining."

Everyone was silent, waiting for more.

"Good luck," was all Linus said. The people around Sarah greeted each other like they'd known each other for years. Some asked about kids. No one talked to her or Sullivan.

"Sarah and Sullivan, get with Claire and Peter for your assignments, now." Linus called across the cabin.

Sarah followed Sullivan to Agent Jacobs' desk and they waited in silence as Claire and Peter reviewed assignments on their plane while Jacobs did the same next to them. They'd ordered the assignments not so each team had the same number of properties, but so they each had the same number of square feet of foundation. Also, each pair's area was roughly arranged to minimize travel time. That must have been what everyone was doing, Sarah thought, everyone was calculating areas and travel times to make good routes. Amazing.

"Sarah," Peter said, he paused. He offered a brief smile to acknowledge their past. If they were together, Sarah knew he would have taken her hand. Maybe even hugged her. But across this video connection, this was all they got. He exhaled and continued, "We have a busy day planned for you and," even through the video feed, Sarah felt his eyes break away as he turned to Sullivan, "Sullivan, is it?"

"Yes," Sullivan said. Sarah thought Peter was the first person they'd encountered since the apartment who didn't know who they both were. She almost mentioned it.

"You two will come with us to the first site," Peter directed. Clearly Claire didn't like the idea. She scowled at Sarah. "We'll have scanning equipment that takes at least two people to operate. We'll be spacing emitters and detectors in patterns that should be able to detect the device if we get within ten feet."

Sarah thought about the size of some of the basements, "Ten feet, what are the chances of that?"

"Our goal is to maximize our chances of finding the device. We can't search everywhere so we're not going to search every square foot of every foundation," Peter explained. He spoke as though he developed the system. "Sullivan, your clothes will be okay. Sarah, go in the bathroom. There are sets of work clothes there."

. . .

As Sarah was pulling on the tennis shoes she selected, she felt the plane pitch down. It wasn't the gentle throttling back normally experienced on a commercial flight. The pilot pointed the nose at the ground and kept the throttle on. He wasn't wasting any time. She quickly made her way to her seat. Everyone was studying their pages, reviewing their routes. It seemed they were going to jump from the plane and start running as soon as it hit the ground.

"Nice outfit, Claire," Sullivan said as he handed her some pages. Sarah was confused until she looked over her shoulder and into the screen at Claire. It turned out she was wearing the exact same jeans and red long sleeve t-shirt. She briefly remembered that there were other options. Either they had similar taste or she had selected the outfit based on her subliminal memory. That didn't matter. She turned back, closed her eyes, and rested her head in the chair.

"Peter told me they have only practiced this before," Sullivan said. Sarah looked over at him but his eyes were closed, "They've never done this for real. No one really knows what's going to happen."

The plane hit hard and wobbled momentarily as the pilot got it under control. Before the plane stopped rolling, Sarah heard the clicking of all the seatbelts and people were standing and moving around. Sarah didn't have any place to go so she stayed in her seat. A large man opened the top half of the door and Sarah felt air blowing in.

The plane barely stopped before the man pushed the bottom half of the door down. Everyone moved to the front and off the plane. Sarah and Sullivan were last and just as she stepped off saw the clock tick 13:44:59.

81.   13:40:00

The other plane landed a few minutes before theirs. Claire and Peter were directing teams unloading their plane into twelve identical brown pickup trucks.

Sarah jumped behind the wheel of her truck and Sullivan was in the passenger seat.

It took all of Sarah's concentration to keep up with Peter as he raced off the airport property.

"Sullivan, look at the bottom folder in the stack," Sarah directed as she completed a pass of a slow car on a two lane road. Sullivan shuffled the papers on his lap and found the bottom of her stack.

"What is this?" Sullivan asked. He opened the file. It was the original data file for the Delco Electronics Plant on the east end of the cell phone hexagon. Claire and Peter had not even gotten to it in their review process. It was two miles from the next closest potential site.

Delco must have built the plant out in the middle of nowhere, and now the town was growing out to it. "Sarah, why am I looking at this?"

"We're not going to follow their plan," Sarah accelerated to close the gap with Peter, "Claire said we got lucky, that almost half of the cell was not developed. The eastern half never developed because a block of farmers refused to sell. She said that the town's natural urban sprawl was lopsided. In the 1960's, LV would have thought the new Delco Plant would have invited tremendous growth around it, and it would have made a great place to hide a weapon. They couldn't have known it would end up with very little development around it."

"They're only trying to see how we'll react to their threat," Sarah followed Peter into an underground parking garage. They wound their way down two floors to the lowest level. "They have no need to kill a lot of people. We're going to the Delco Plant. LV could test us by detonating a device in the desert, but they don't have one there. They must've picked a bomb that was placed somewhere that didn't develop as expected."

"But what about the plan we have?" Sullivan asked.

"First thing we have to do is learn to use the equipment," Sarah ignored him, "Let's go." With that, she pulled the key from the ignition with the truck parked across two spots five down from where Peter and Claire were already pulling a large case from the back of their truck.

"Are we going to tell anyone we're down here?" Sullivan asked as they approached.

"Put on a baseball cap from our truck," Claire answered. Sarah now saw that Claire and Peter each had matching brown baseball caps with EPA in large white letters across the front. They must be as close as they could get to uniforms in this rush. Sullivan followed orders and handed Sarah a hat as she looked at the sensor equipment. She pulled her ponytail through the hole in the back of the hat and fit it into place.

Peter pulled out a heavy plate mounted on casters and set it on the ground. He then opened another case with a box full of electrical equipment. He pulled out three small electrical boxes and one larger cylinder. He mounted the cylinder to the center of the plate over a hole. The cylinder protruded though the hole to come within an inch of the cement floor below. He then mounted the boxes in their pre-designed places. He connected the three with cables already supplied.

"This is the *pulse generator*." he pointed at the cylinder, "These are power packs. There are more in the truck. As the resolution fades, change these regularly."

Sarah had spent many hours with Peter Howard. As their relationship developed, they spent almost all of them in his various hotel rooms. She knew he was a building contractor, but that was an almost abstract reality that was hitting her now. He moved with the practiced precision of someone who knew how to use his hands.

Claire pulled out and explained the *receiver*. It was another plate with a rubber mount and a video display mounted to it. There were two other *ears* in the case. They looked like the receiver, but without the video display, and instead had twenty foot long cables. Claire and Peter looked around the bottom floor of the parking garage they were on. Forty of fifty spaces had cars, Sarah estimated. At four in the morning, this must be an apartment building.

Claire must have also had similar training to Peter. She moved quickly with no wasted effort.

"We need to measure out a pattern," Peter said as he handed Sullivan a tape measure, "Come on." They moved to the nearest corner of the garage and began the painstaking process of measuring out fifteen foot centers and marking the floor with chalk. Claire and Sarah were left to carry the equipment to the first square.

"I've hated you ever since I saw you in Florida. Peter had just told me he was assigned to you,"

Sarah stopped at Claire's comment.

Assigned? What did that mean? She looked past Claire to Peter working with Sullivan. He glanced at her and smiled. Claire looked over her shoulder, struggling with the load.

Claire was in good shape, but Sarah was bigger and stronger and had little difficulty with the equipment. She was a nice looking lady, obviously with Peter. The comment was clearly intended to hurt. Sarah decided she had more important things to worry about now, and forced it from her mind.

She saw the first square had about one and a half cars in it. The generator was to go in the center, with the receiver and two ears spread out to form a triangle around it. This was going to be difficult around the cars.

"Why don't we use the parking spaces as the pattern, and measure around each car?" Sarah asked.

Claire looked at her. It took a moment for her to adjust to a normal conversation and Sarah could see some conflict still in her. Thankfully, she was able to have the technical discussion.

"These parking spaces are only nine feet wide, it would mean taking more samples than we want to," Claire answered as she traced the wire from one of the *ears* to the *receiver* around a car. Sarah estimated another corner, and had to adjust the pattern around the parked cars. Claire watched Sarah and placed the *receiver* as close as she could get to a third corner of an equilateral triangle.

Sullivan and Peter stopped measuring and came to help by connecting the cables from the *ears* to the *receiver*.

Claire and Sarah studied the shape they made.

"Let's do it," Claire said when she was satisfied that this was the best shape they would get, "Peter, are you boys ready?"

"In a minute," Peter called out. Sullivan and Peter were both studying the *receiver* and Peter was doing a lot of talking.

Sarah knew Peter was explaining how it worked as he made gestures to show the shape of the triangle the women made. She watched as he gestured to the *Generator*. Sarah could tell from the gestures that a signal would go from the generator into the ground, bounce off something, and go back to the *receiver* and *ears*.

Wait. How was this going to work? The bombs were hidden from any form of detection. If they were detectable, she wouldn't be looking for them from space.

"What sort of signal are we generating?" Sarah asked. Claire looked at her. Sarah felt it unfair of Claire to hate her. Sarah didn't want to think about what it meant that Linus had *assigned* her to Peter. Claire seemed to be deciding whether to tell Sarah how this system worked.

. . .

Peter looked up from the receiver to see Sarah and Claire waiting. They were dressed in identical outfits. Claire was cute and petite with a lean body that he was growing to love. Sarah was at least four inches taller, with her t-shirt stretched across her chest and muscular legs in her jeans. These were two very similar women, and he knew he needed them to become friends if they were going to get through this day.

So far, he could tell they weren't. He wanted to stop and stare. He wanted to tell them he loved them both, Sarah in the past, and Claire now. But they didn't have time for that.

. . .

Sarah looked away from brief eye contact with Peter and back to Claire as she started to explain her system, "These devices, the bombs, had state-of-the-art electronics when they were installed, in the 1960's, but electronics have evolved a lot. A key improvement in electronics over the years has been their ability to tolerate electrical interference. Any operating electrical device puts out a magnetic field that could affect the magnetic field of any other electrical device nearby. Affecting the second electrical field would affect the electronics on the second device. The FCC has developed standards for how much interference a device can send out, and how tolerant a device must be to others. We realized we could *interfere* with the electronics of the bomb. That's been my day job for the past three years."

"So, you can interfere with the bomb?" Sarah asked, "Could we accidentally set it off?"

"No," Claire said, "Our interference doesn't affect the bomb's electronics. That's why our generator can only measure a small area. A stronger pulse could set it off. Our pulse of electromagnetic energy is altered by the interference from the bomb, and we can detect that alteration with the *ears*."

"Okay," Peter called, "The *receiver* is warmed up and calibrated. We're ready."

Claire moved quickly to the *generator* and found a button near the top of the cylinder. She pressed the button for about a second. She looked to Peter who was studying the results on the screen.

"Nothing," Peter said unceremoniously and began to disconnect the wires.

"What?" Sullivan said, "That was it?"

"That's it." Claire announced.

Sarah shared Sullivan's disappointment. They'd been racing for the last four hours to get to this one second *nothing*. Sarah checked her watch. It took twenty minutes! As they moved the equipment to the next space, they had to negotiate the new shape created by the next pair of cars because their pattern didn't match the previous pattern. The four of them got the system set up, and Sarah timed that Claire pushed the button this time ten minutes after the first one. *Nothing* again.

After that, Peter and Sullivan returned to measuring and Sarah and Claire set up the next pulse. They did it in ten minutes by themselves. Sarah realized they had just checked five spaces in forty minutes with four people. At this pace it would take five hours to complete this one garage! The setup time was taking too long.

"Why not do every two cars?" Sarah said as they worked frantically.

"We won't cover everything. The spacing would be too large."

Claire responded.

"We're not trying to check every square foot. You said it yourself. We're only trying to maximize our chances by maximizing the amount we cover." Sarah said, "It could be we're being too careful, we need this generator to fire much more often."

"I see your point. Let's try two spaces at a time," Claire said. Sarah briefly noted that Claire was getting over her hatred. The two women created a pattern where the *generator* was placed between the side mirrors of two cars, the *ears* were place at the outside front bumpers of the cars and the *receiver* was placed between the two rear bumpers. They fired the generator. *Nothing*.

They moved on. Without having to think about a new pattern every time, the two women got down to firing the *generator* every minute. And they didn't need the men to measure anything. The men joined in and the four of them each carried one piece to the next spot. Sarah ran the *receiver* and acted as the drum major setting the pace. The four of them got a shot every thirty seconds.

The pace was frantic, and Sarah's heart was pounding, but she enjoyed the focus. She realized she held her breath for each second the generator fired. She guessed the others did the same. She was appreciating the exhilaration, but she wasn't sure they could all keep up the pace. They finished the garage in one hour.

The four of them stood around smiling at each other, allowing their breathing to settle down. Sarah felt triumphant until she realized they didn't do anything. They didn't find the bomb, and they had to quickly move to the next assignments. She began to worry that Peter and Claire would want to continue as a foursome rather than break into pairs because of their efficiency. At this pace they could clear much more than Claire planned. If only they had started sooner, they could find this stupid thing! Sarah stopped smiling as she thought.

"What?" Claire asked.

"Why didn't we start this a long time ago?" Sarah asked.

"Sarah, they just found out there was a bomb in Kokomo six hours ago," Sullivan answered over his shoulder. The men were already replacing the equipment into cases in the back of the truck.

"With the money these guys have been spending, they could have been checking every building in the country!" Sarah said, "You wouldn't believe how much my work cost!" They were all around the back of the truck fitting pieces into their cases and strapping them shut.

"We tried," Claire said while fitting an ear into its case. "Before the bomb gets the activation signal, it's dormant, it consumes no power. That's how it doesn't run out of batteries. So, if no power is passing through its circuits, there's no magnetic field, and we can't detect it by this method. When the bomb receives the detonation signal, it starts its irreversible 18 hour countdown, and the circuit is active enough for us to detect it."   Claire could have smiled at Sarah, but did not. She wasn't quite over it.

"I guess we better go to our next assignments," Sarah said.

"That's a good idea," Peter said. Sarah glanced at Peter. If anyone was going to suggest they all work together, it would be him, but he didn't. She wasn't about to wait around for him to get the idea.

Sarah abruptly turned and moved quickly to her truck. She got in the driver's seat and started it up. She looked back and saw Sullivan hustling around to get in.

As Sullivan buckled his seat belt Sarah put the truck in reverse, pulled out of the space, threw it into drive and pulled away. Sarah looked in the rear-view mirror to see Claire and Peter moving to their truck.

She could feel Sullivan staring at her.

82. 12:15:00

"We did a good job back there," Sarah said, "We checked the space about twice as fast as they were expecting, and probably three times faster than they would have done." She glanced over at him as she navigated to the top of the parking garage, "I was afraid they would want to continue to work together."

"What would be wrong with that?" Sullivan and Sarah were both thrown airborne for a moment as the truck flew over the ramp at the exit of the garage and landed on the street. Sarah drove at about thirty.

Too fast.

She threw the wheel to the left and the tires squealed as they struggled to grip the road through the hard turn. When the truck left the ground, she knew she took the turn too fast, and as the truck nearly tipped over, she was concerned she'd made a serious mistake with the speed. Just as she thought they were going to tip, she straightened the wheel and the truck settled into a casual drive down the road. Outwardly, they looked like any two people driving down the road. Inwardly, Sarah's heart was racing, and she thought for a moment she was going to throw up. A quick glance at Sullivan and she could tell he felt the same way.

"Shit!" Sullivan said, "No matter where you think you're going, we won't get there if this truck ends up on its side!"

"Sorry, you're right," Sarah said, "I got a little excited."

"Okay," Sullivan said, "Just take it easy. We'll get there. What was the deal with you and Claire? I thought you didn't know each other?"

"We don't," Sarah didn't tell anyone about the details of her relationship with Peter, certainly not Sullivan. She glanced at him as she realized he was still special to her. "We don't," is all she wanted to say just then.

Sullivan faced front and Sarah knew he was considering this. She desperately hoped he'd drop it. "Where are we going?"

Sarah's tension dropped a bit, "I saw a sign for the highway on the way here, and I know the plant is right off the highway to the south, I'll get us there. You need to review the information to figure out where we have to look." Sarah wasn't sure why Sullivan wasn't arguing about not following their instructions, but she was glad to not have to worry about it. She expected they would be at the plant in about ten minutes. They would have to figure out how to get in.

"What day is it?" Sullivan asked. Sarah was about to answer when she realized she didn't know for sure.

"I think it's Sunday?"

"Yes, I thought it was Sunday too."

"Why?" Sarah asked.

"We're going to have to figure out how to get in, who to talk to, and how to search an operational factory," Sullivan said as he sorted through the thick stack of pages in the Delco file. He handed her one. She was driving down a deserted four lane east-west road at six o'clock on a Sunday morning so she took the risk to hold the paper on top of the steering wheel and look at it. It was the schematic of the overall plant on eleven by seventeen pages.

Thick black lines showed the boundaries of the various buildings and small detailed labels indicated what kinds of products were made in each of the buildings. Delco Electronics was the electronics arm of General Motors and the plant made many of the over twenty electronic modules in the automobile.

Sarah couldn't read the paper and drive at the same time, so she handed it back to Sullivan.

"They'll require badge access. We can't just walk in and start searching like we did in that parking garage," Sarah said as she turned south onto route 31. She still had to fight her own adrenaline and stay close to the speed limit. They would be there in a few minutes.

"So, as we approach from the north, we'll want to get off at Lincoln Street. This will bring us along the south of the complex and to the headquarters building. That's where we'll need to gain access," Sullivan said.

"Okay, but we're going to have to start searching in the part of the factory that was built in the sixties," Sarah said.

"I don't see any historical documents in here," Sullivan said, "We're going to have to get them to tell us what part of the factory was built then."

"How are we going to do that?" Sarah was beginning to wonder how this could possibly work. The factory was enormous. They couldn't possibly search the whole thing. Plus, there would be people working there. The idea that they were looking for some sort of underground chemical spill was not going to let them focus on a specific place. "If I were them, I'd let us search for a chemical spill in the parking lot. Anything that passes under the plant would have to pass under the parking, and then we wouldn't disturb their processes. This isn't like a bank or law office downtown. We'll be dealing with technical people."

Sullivan stopped looking through the papers and closed the file, "You're right, we need better cover. Much better cover." Sarah pulled off at Lincoln Avenue. She wished they had more time. She was happy when the light was red and they had to wait to turn under the highway.

She looked at Sullivan. His face was relaxed, and he slouched comfortably in the seat next to her. She had been with dates, most of her dates, more nervous than he was. If she had learned anything about him in the past two months, it was that he was cool under pressure. His coolness had gotten them through the apartment, and it would help her get through this.

83. 12:00:00

"Yes, we're done with our first site," Claire spoke into the briefcase sized phone on the seat between her and Peter. It wasn't a phone, by the traditional definition, but two specialized communications systems built into a single package. Claire had designed it, and knew the encrypted, high-power radio signal was bouncing off satellites on its way to the White House Situation Room. "Yes, I expected we'd be the first ones done. Sarah was very helpful." Claire looked out the side of her head at Peter. "We'll check in after our second site." She ended the call.

Peter pulled into another basement parking garage. This one was an office building. Claire had about thirty seconds to let her mind wander. She thought about Sarah. She had some good ideas and she was very efficient in her work. Just as she was starting to get comfortable being around her, she caught Peter checking out her chest, and she knew she might never like Sarah Kiadopolis. Well, that didn't really matter now. Peter was with her. As he parked the car, Claire leaned over the phone and kissed her man. Then she jumped from the truck to start another site.

. . .

"No," Sullivan said, "Pull right up front." Sarah wasn't sure he had a plan, but she followed his instructions.

She parked next to the flag poles in front of the large glass clad administration building and they both stepped from the truck. As Sarah rounded the front of the truck, Sullivan sized her up, "I wish you still had your other clothes on," he said. Sullivan wore khakis and a button down shirt. He pulled on a jacket that covered the scuffs on his shirt. Sarah was suddenly self-conscious in jeans, sneakers, and a t-shirt

Sullivan turned and started walking toward the building.

She remembered last night. Sullivan's son and parents were flown in to meet him for a late dinner. The only time she'd been separated from him since yesterday afternoon. He changed into the outfit he had on now for that dinner. She'd stayed in her skirt and blouse and ate in the Vice President's office.

That was just last night?

Sarah decided there was nothing she could do about her attire and jogged five steps to catch up with him. They walked in silence to the building. The sun was coming up and light reflected off the huge glass panels they passed. Sarah could see her reflection in the glass and was concerned that Sullivan carried the folder with him.

He was surely not going to show them the contents. It must be a prop. Sarah saw Sullivan look at them in the windows.

"Give me your hat," Sullivan held out his hand as they walked. Sarah pulled the hat from her head and pulled her hair from the hole in the back. She handed it to him. He removed his matching hat, surveyed the area, and threw them behind a bush just as they reached the door.

Sarah looked at herself in the reflection of the door for a split second and realized that without the hat, she looked even worse.

They entered a large atrium. There was a frame of a car with electronic modules called out; a display that would have been interesting to look over on any other day. They walked quickly past the car. Sarah struggled to follow Sullivan's lead like they were dancing, but she still couldn't hear the music. She held her breath as they walked up and stopped at the reception desk.

An older security guard sat at his station. He looked at Sullivan first and then spent more time looking at Sarah. Sarah stared back at him, not knowing how she was supposed to act. She tried to breathe through a nervous smile.

"Welcome to Delco Electronics," the guard said, pulling his quizzical expression from Sarah back to Sullivan, "This is Delco Electronics." Clearly he thought they were in the wrong place. He must have expected Sullivan to say, *Oh, sorry, we are on a long trip, and we were looking for the public restroom.*

Sarah was shocked when she heard Sullivan say, "Where's the restroom?" She felt her eyes go wide, the guard looked at her, and she quickly returned her face to its original expression.

"Sir," the guard said, "This is not a public facility, and we do not have-"

Sullivan interrupted him, "I assure you, I know this is Delco Electronics, and that I mean to be here." He gestured to Sarah, "My assistant needs to freshen up while you and I figure out who I need to talk to!"

The man glanced to his right, past the car. It was only an instant, but Sarah took the cue and immediately turned and walked that way. She was happy to be away from there, she felt like a stupid little kid, and if Sullivan didn't succeed, she'd let him know it. She found the women's room. She was a mess. She needed to calm down, to remember that Sullivan must have a plan. He seemed to trust her completely and was helping her deviate from Linus' plan without question. She took a deep breath and splashed water on her face. As she pulled her hands away, she realized her face had smudges of grease on it. She used the soap and paper towels in the bathroom to wash, careful not to get her clothes wet. She also ran water through her hair and pulled it back into a tight ponytail.

She realized that they were trying to talk their way into the factory. They had no back-up because they were outside of Linus' plan. If they couldn't get in, they would have to leave, and there would be little or nothing they could do about it.

She calmed herself and left the bathroom.

By the time she walked back into the atrium, Sullivan had stepped away from the security guard and was talking to a middle-aged heavy-set man in a suit. She tried to gauge the tone of their conversation, but it was surprisingly quiet. Sullivan held out his hand signaling for her to stop. She stood literally twiddling her thumbs as the man in the suit looked her up and down and a small smile crossed his lips. What was Sullivan doing? Again, she was standing there, feeling small, but sure there was nothing she could do. Sullivan finally looked to her and gestured for her to join the conversation.

She walked up and made a point of not standing directly next to Sullivan, but instead forming a third side of a triangle with Sullivan and the man.

"I'm Frank Saunders," he extended his hand. "I'm the plant facilities manager. I take any threat to this facility very seriously, just as I take any potential impact of this facility on the community very seriously."

Sarah shook Frank's hand firmly. Certainly, Sullivan and Frank were conspiring when she arrived. He continued, "But, you must know that we take industrial espionage very seriously as well."

Sarah's heart sank. She was frantically trying to find something to say, some way to interrupt. Once someone said no, it was nearly impossible to get them to say yes. She was about to start talking, some sort of stream of consciousness, when Frank made a hand gesture to the security guard. He held his thumb and pinky extended from a fist and waved it pantomiming signing in.

He turned back to Sullivan, "I'll call your Mr. Feliz as you suggest, and if your story checks out, we'll show you around. If not, we'll have a different kind of discussion."

Just as he said that, two security guards entered the atrium. "Please, have a seat." With that, he walked past the security desk and disappeared into the building.

Sarah watched as the two guards took up positions next to the front door. She tried not to look scared. She looked at Sullivan who looked back at her and winked with a small smile. She was amazed that he was so calm. If they were detained, they could be arrested. If they were arrested, they would have no one to call. She didn't have any money or even a phone with her. They had a phone in the car to call back if they found something. They each carried fake EPA badges, but no one at the EPA knew who they were. They could end up in jail, in Kokomo. She began to wonder where the police station was. It could be downtown! How ironic would it be to be arrested in Kokomo? She knew the rest of the team wouldn't find the bomb, because she knew it was here, so they could die here, locked in a jail cell at 6PM.

What had they gotten themselves into?

84. 10:45:00

Sullivan and Sarah sat on the comfortable but modern looking sofa in the middle of the Delco Electronics atrium. The sun poured through the large windows over the door as it crested the horizon. Sullivan sat quietly with the relaxed manner he had developed at the apartment. Sarah wanted to know his plan. She wanted to know who Frank was calling. She thought the guards were too far away to hear them, but she wasn't sure. She thought about leaning into Sullivan and asking. She wanted to sit closer to him than she did, but she didn't have any idea what their cover was. She was nearly certain it would not involve them sitting close together and whispering.

They sat in silence for what seemed to Sarah about ten minutes. She checked her watch and saw they had been sitting there for over half an hour. She tapped her fingers on her knee nervously. They started with only eighteen hours to find the bomb. They left the garage with twelve hours left. Now it was 7:15 in the morning and they were down to less than eleven hours until…

Sarah began to doubt herself. Maybe Claire had another criterion for selecting places to search. Maybe she also selected places that they had a chance of getting into. If they could only search a fraction of the available sites then why spend time trying to get into those that would be very difficult to gain access? They got to the parking garage and were firing the *pulse generator* in twenty minutes. They had been sitting here in this stupid atrium now for half an hour, and their hyper valuable *pulse generator* was sitting unused in the back of their truck in front of the building!

She looked at Sullivan who seemed very happy with himself. The more she showed frustration, the more he seemed pleased. He had developed a confident air in the time they spent together, and she thought she was really beginning to appreciate it, maybe even like it, maybe even more. But now, all she wanted to do was punch him in the face! He looked back at her lazily with a nod and a wink.

. . .

"What do you mean they haven't checked in?" Claire asked.

"I mean every team has cleared at least two sites, except Dr. Kiadopolis and Mr. Acer," the technician reported over the phone. Claire looked at Peter who was driving to the next site.

"But Dr. Kiadopolis was with us for the first site," Claire tried to think, "Was their next site big?"

After a moment, "No, Ma'am, the next site was a small apartment building. It was scheduled for thirty minutes." Claire knew Sarah would be able to complete it much faster. They should have completed maybe four sites by now. "Bill and Kassandra are near that site, should I ask them to check over?"

"Yes," Claire said quickly, but then reconsidered, "Wait, no. We can't divert a functioning group to look for a team that's not getting its work done. That would mean two teams down. Keep everyone going." She hung up. Damn that woman.

. . .

Finally Frank returned. Sarah jumped to her feet. Sullivan saw her stand and made a show of slowly looking to the security desk to see Frank returning, closing the magazine he had been reading, and standing. Sarah stood shifting her weight between her feet not knowing whether to move to Frank, stay where she was, or bolt for the door hoping to get through the two security guards stationed there. No decision is a decision, and she stood still. Sullivan waited for Frank to cross the large atrium to them.

"Agent Acer," Frank said, "I'm sorry to have kept you and Agent Kiadopolis waiting for so long." He smiled at Sullivan and only looked out of the corner of his eye at Sarah. What was going on? Did these two know each other? Was this all some big joke? Did Sullivan tell this guy that she was a stripper? Well, that might get them into the office, but then what?

"I first called a buddy of mine and confirmed that your Agent Feliz is actually with the FBI," Frank was certainly proud of himself for having the resources to check that himself. "He's in the Governmental Affairs and Oversight Office. I then called Agent Feliz and confirmed that you worked together. I told him where we were and we both agreed that you could conduct the inspection you planned."

"Good," Sullivan said. Sarah was certainly happy that he agreed, but she was still completely baffled as to how Sullivan pulled it off, and what secret they shared. "Now, as I said, we don't want anyone here to know what we're really doing, so we need complete discretion. I trust you can hold my plans in confidence?"

"Certainly," Frank was again proud of himself, "I served in the Navy."

"Excellent," Sullivan said, "We're lucky to have met you here. Now, we have two objectives, first, to conduct a cursory search of some of your factory floors in order to verify the claims made by our informant. Second, to root out the person who's been impeding our investigation." At this, both Frank and Sullivan glanced at Sarah.

"Yes, whatever you need."

"Okay, so, we need someone we can trust on your staff to show us around. And we need to get to your facility records."

"That will be fine," Frank said, "Let's get you signed in, I'll take you to the office. Then I'll send in one of my team to help you." He led them to the security desk and they signed in. Frank then led them around the corner to a stairway and down into the basement. After a hundred feet of corridor, he opened the door labeled *Plant Facilities.*

Sarah thought this was Frank's kingdom. He strode through the open room with purpose. There were six desks in the front half of the room and the back half of the room had four large rows of stuffed book shelves. The overhead florescent lights made the room seem smaller than it was, but the space had to be about a thousand square feet. There was a large table at the head of the rows of book shelves and Frank stopped at it.

"It's still early, my team will be arriving in the next few minutes," Frank announced, louder than necessary for the three of them. "You can work here. These are the records. My office is over there. Make yourselves at home," again he looked suspiciously at Sarah, making her almost blush. She looked away and instantly regretted it, "I'll be in my office."

"Fine, thanks," Sullivan said. With that Frank went to his office. Leaving the door open, he sat at his desk.

"Let's see if we can find the records we need," Sullivan said clearly for Frank's benefit. Sarah looked in Frank's direction. He studied his computer screen. Sullivan moved into the closest row of book shelves, Sarah followed, and finally, they were nearly alone.

"What's going on?" Sarah nearly screamed, but held her voice down. Sullivan looked around, again confirming that there was no way Frank could see them, and he put his hands on Sarah's shoulders.

"Sarah, we're in!" Sullivan beamed for two seconds. Then his face returned to a stern look, "Calm down."

Sarah forced herself to take a breath and enjoy Sullivan's hands on her shoulders. She realized she did trust him, and that they were almost out of the woods, but she still wanted to know what woods they were almost out of.

"What did you tell him? Who is Feliz?"

"Remember that I'm an investigator for the Bureau of Indian Affairs? That's my real job? I realized we needed a cover fast, and the only one I could pull together was no cover at all," Sullivan said, "I have a friend that I've worked with at the FBI, Agent Feliz. He knows I was missing, and he knows I'm with you. I told Frank we were investigating a cover up of buried artifacts and that I was here to run a sting operation. I told him that we received a tip that artifacts were recently discovered under a section of the plant during routine upgrades to the facility. That actually happens more than you would think. It told him that someone had covered up the first discovery, and that I was going to find the artifacts and the conspirator."

Sarah considered what he said as he looked at her, "Okay, that seems pretty complex, and Feliz followed all this?"

"Feliz and I have run similar operations before. I gambled he'd play along. He did."

"What if he didn't?"

"How fast could you run?" Sullivan smiled.

Sarah returned the smile and realized she wanted to kiss him again.

This plan was genius, and it seemed to be working.

"And the conspirator, how are we going to find that person? Are we going to ruin another person's life?"

"It's you!" Sullivan said looking like he swallowed a canary. Sarah processed this for a moment. That's why Frank kept leering at her. That was their shared inside joke. Sarah really understood now.

"Why didn't you let me know?"

"How could I? This is the first chance we had alone, and even now, we have to be careful," Sullivan glanced over her shoulder, the first time he took his eyes off her, to make sure no one was there, then the smile returned, "Besides, the more uncomfortable you looked, the more guilty. I know you're not a good actor, and I needed you to feel out of place. I told Frank that I woke you up early this morning and didn't give you time to dress. I told him this was an emergency investigation and we had to move fast. That way you would be off balance, and not able to notify anyone, or cover anything."

Sarah would have been mad if the idea hadn't worked. He'd gotten them in, explained her casual clothes, and built a story that should allow them access to the facility and these records. Under his simple smile he was a sharp man.

She took his hands from her shoulders into hers, squeezed them, and said, "Okay, so we need to find the right place in the facility to search. We need to find the construction records." They quickly surveyed the four rows of shelves to get a feel for what was where. For a building records office, Frank ran a pretty tight ship, and Sarah was happy to quickly find the section with the building construction history. She pulled a large file set and hefted it to the table. Sullivan joined her quickly, and they began to search through it.

. . .

"What part of EPA don't you understand?" Peter was trying to be forceful with the guard outside the bank. Claire sat in the truck and Peter was talking through the PA system.

"Sir, it's the weekend," the guard said, "you're lucky I'm even here. I'm just on my rounds. I need to get over to First National in twenty minutes."

"I understand you have a routine, but this is an emergency!"

Peter complained. "That's why you're here, in case of an emergency!"

"Uh," the guard paused. He'd clearly never thought about the nature of his job. "I guess you're right. Let me make a call."

"No, wait," Peter tried, but the speaker went quiet. Peter looked back to the truck to see Claire talking on the phone. He knew she was coordinating with Washington. They'd made a lot of progress, if you could call it that. They had not found anything, and because they didn't have time to search everywhere, they could still end up running out of time. But he knew they had to try.

"Okay," the speaker came back on, "I've got my boss on. Can you explain to him what you want me to do?" Peter forced himself to calm down.

. . .

As Sullivan and Sarah sat and searched, the desks began to fill up in the office. Every person who came in looked at them, but didn't spend much time and went to their desks.

"Kyle," Frank called. Sarah looked up to see the last person getting to his desk stop as he was about to sit and quickly answer Frank's call.

Sarah was close to identifying the full search area when Kyle and Frank arrived at the table. Sarah looked up to see Kyle staring at her. Clearly, Frank had told Kyle the total plan. This was fine with Sarah, but would not be perfect for Sullivan if he were actually investigating her. Sarah decided that if she were worried she would be exposed, she would want to keep her head down and let Sullivan take the lead. So she returned to reviewing the documents and making calculations while Sullivan filled Kyle in on what they were looking for.

The total Delco Plant covered fifty acres and included over a million square feet of foundations. If they had to search it all, and actually clear it all, they would have to do it in ten foot triangles, or fifty square feet at a time. Sarah figure that they could probably do one shot a minute for about eight hours before they would become exhausted, so she figured they could only clear about twenty five thousand square feet.

She found that Delco Electronics built three of the buildings at this site during the nineteen-sixties. Buildings eight, nine, and ten. This discovery confirmed her belief that the bomb was here. This was an area undergoing tremendous growth. LV would have expected that this plant would be a perfect place for a bomb. It also meant that she only narrowed their search area down to about four-hundred thousand square feet, an area twenty times what they could search at maximum speed. They needed to narrow down further.

"Can we get the building drawings for buildings eight, nine, and ten?" Sarah interrupted Sullivan, Frank, and Kyle. She looked up from her seated position. They were all standing. Kyle and Frank looked at her with contempt until Sullivan repeated exactly her request. Frank nodded and Kyle left for the third aisle.

"So," Frank asked, looking out of the side of his head at Sarah while talking to Sullivan, "You're going to search the plant?"

"Yes, we have ultrasonic equipment that we can use to detect artifacts in the floor. The procedure doesn't harm your facility at all."

"We're in the middle of an outage, the plant is shut down. All the line workers are home while we change over for the new model year. You can do whatever you want, but I cannot fall off schedule." Frank gestured to his office, now full, "That's why we're all here so early on a Sunday morning."

The plant was empty! Sarah knew this was the place! Not only was it Sunday so the industrial complexes would be empty, but the factory floor would be more empty than usual. LV wanted to minimize how many people it hurt, and this was the place to do it.

"We understand completely," Sullivan said, "We'll stay out of the way, but it will help if Kyle can show us where we want to go and help with our equipment."

"He's a coop student," Frank said, "He's all yours," Frank leaned in to Sullivan, "We all have personnel issues."

Kyle returned with three large books of drawings. Each book was three feet wide by two feet high, and held about a hundred pages. Kyle struggled to carry them and he dropped them on the table.

With that, Frank took his leave.

Sarah immediately pulled over the top set of drawings, building ten.

"Kyle," Sullivan said, "We're going to need to bring our truck into the plant to get to where we need to conduct our inspections, can you see to it that we have whatever passes we need?" Kyle looked at him with a completely blank look, but then turned and went to his coworkers to ask for help.

"What are you looking for?" Sullivan asked Sarah quietly.

"Anything that will narrow down the search. I can only narrow it down to about ten days' worth of searches!" Sarah looked through the drawings, "I really wish Claire was here, I don't know what I am looking at."

"Really?" Sullivan mocked her but sat down and started studying the book for building nine.

Sarah was looking through the books but not seeing anything. She was looking for anything that would give a clue to where the bomb might be, like she would see a big red circle with an arrow. She looked at the foundation drawings, the steel structure drawings, the electrical drawings, the heating, ventilation and air conditioning drawings, nothing stood out to her. This was a factory and to her it looked like every factory she had ever seen. She glanced at Sullivan and saw that he wasn't getting anywhere either.

Sarah was getting nervous, and her nervousness caused her to jump physically when she looked at the clock and saw that it was eight o'clock. They'd been in this basement for an entire hour!

85.   10:00:00

"Eve Burkett?" Linus looked up from the piece of paper Agent Jacobs handed him. He was in the chair at the back of the plane. Now the plane served as his command center. The projector wasn't showing the other plane anymore. Instead it showed a copy of the projected image from the White House Situation Room where the teams were reporting in on their progress.

"Yes, sir," Agent Jacobs responded, "We found the conference director and woke her up this morning. Two agents were with her all morning and they found the picture." Linus looked down at the comparison. Sullivan Acer was a pretty good artist and his sketch matched the picture of the young woman sitting in the auditorium.

"Find her," Linus said.

"Should we continue the search for Dr. Kiadopolis?"

"No," Linus said. He looked at the wall. Eleven of twelve teams were making progress. The Doctor and the Investigator were failing. "Finding Eve Burkett is our top priority now. Tell the pilot we're taking off. We'll circle until we get an idea where to go."

. . .

"We need to get moving!   We could have searched another parking garage by now!"

"Two parking garages by now," Sullivan said grimly. He was not as excited as Sarah was. It was eight in the morning and they were down to ten hours left. Maybe he was not as sure the bomb was here as she was.

Sarah closed her eyes and rested her face in her hands, her elbows on the table. The drawings replayed in her mind. As she replayed the images, some of the images in her mind didn't fit.

She realized that she had been looking at other images that looked like these plans. She began to replay the images she had generated with *Space Resonance* and stared at in her office in Virginia. A lifetime ago. The images she generated when she was focused on California. She was looking into the foundations of buildings and locating bombs without knowing it. She thought about the images of the foundations. How did she know they were foundations?   Looking at these drawings, everything looked so random and when she looked at the images from California, it looked like the plutonium was tucked neatly in the corner of a lab. At the time, she wasn't looking for bombs. She wasn't looking for anything. She was testing her system, so she paid little attention to the actual results and the structures surrounding the nuclear weapons she stumbled upon.

She decided that the answer to where this bomb was, the clue they needed, was in the images from the California bombs that were in her head. She strained her memory to make very clear mental images. She had cleared twelve power outages, but only found two bombs. Nothing was special about the location of the bombs. As she remembered some of the details, she could now see that they were underground, and that in the same plane as the bomb there were re-enforcing steel bars.

Concrete was strong in compression, but could be pulled apart relatively easily. Consequently, all large concrete structures had steel re-enforcing bars, called rebar, running through them. At the time, she thought it was some sort of fencing or security system, some shielding. The rebar stood out brightly on her images.

Something stuck.

Sarah opened her eyes and starting flipping through the book in front of her. Sullivan stopped what he was doing to watch her. She was moving the pages, but her eyes had to quickly adjust to being open, so she had to pause. She found the foundation specification sheets.

"There," Sarah said, "What is this? It's the rebar, right?"

Sullivan looked at the detail she was pointing to, "Yes, I'm not an expert, but I think rebar is pretty standard in these sorts of foundations."

"How would you hide a bomb under a thick layer of rebar? How long does it take to lay rebar like this?"

Sullivan thought a moment, "I worked a job, an investigation, where we found artifacts after the rebar was set. The contractor was furious, he said it would take five days to redo all of it. I told him he was crazy, rebar didn't take that long." Sullivan was getting excited. He talked quickly, "The guy said this was an industrial, heavy duty foundation. It was for something heavy, some kind of test lab or something. He said on a normal job, he could put down the rebar and pour cement the next day, but on a job like that, the rebar took a week!"

"So, if you wanted to hide a bomb under the rebar," Sarah was excited as well, "you'd want a place where the rebar could be put down in a day! Where you could cut through the stuff at night, and pour some concrete to cover what you'd done! You couldn't put it somewhere that would take days to get through the stuff!" Sarah started thrashing through the drawings. She was looking for anywhere where the rebar wasn't called out as dense as the rest.

"Kyle!" Sullivan called. Kyle was not excited. He'd been dispatched to figure out the truck situation, and returned to his desk rather than returning with an answer. He was a fat kid, and when he finally made his way back to the table, he sat down heavily in the chair directly across from Sarah. Sarah looked up from the drawings and glared at him.

He seemed to have seen her for the first time as something other than the potential criminal she was supposed to be, and his eyes moved down to her chest. He made no attempt to hide his distraction.

Sarah noted that she might need that later, so she didn't make an issue, but instead returned to her drawings arching her back a little.

"Kyle!" Sullivan didn't share Sarah's tolerance, "Look at me! I need you to help me find something!" Sarah felt Kyle look to Sullivan, "I need to find anywhere in these three buildings where the foundations have less rebar than average. And I need it *now!*"

Kyle didn't move. He didn't look at the drawings, "That's easy. I don't have to help you find anything!"

"What?" Sullivan started to rise from his chair. Sarah looked up to see the scene. She thought she was going to have to break up a fight. She wasn't sure a few punches to the face wasn't what Kyle needed right then.

"Everyone here knows that building eight has the area converted to offices," Kyle said, "It was originally designed to hold lighter equipment and the contractor did a sloppy job, so the floor can't hold any heavy weight. We can only put offices in it now."

Sarah looked up at Kyle. She smiled broadly and Kyle smiled back just as broadly. He looked at her face for about two seconds before glancing to her chest, and back. Sarah asked, "How do you know that?" She hoped he was right.

"Last summer, I was in this office then too," Kyle said, clearly happy to be talking to her and not Sullivan, "that summer, there were cracks in the floor, even with only the offices, so I worked with the maintenance crews to patch them. Great summer job." His sarcasm crunched his already ugly face into an even more unattractive grimace. Sarah didn't care. She kept smiling because this was it! "Roger, over there, told me that the floor cracked because it wasn't made as well as the rest."

"Show me!" Sullivan said and pushed the building eight drawings in front of him. Kyle frowned, almost pouted, really, but started to flip through the drawings.

Sarah realized if they were going to get anywhere with this kid, she would have to take the lead with him.

He moved slowly, maddeningly slowly. Sarah stood, moved around the table and looked with him. She let her hand rest on his shoulder. He glanced out of the corner of his eye at her and moved faster.

"There," he said. He sat back and Sarah moved forward. The northwest corner of the building, also the northwest corner of the entire facility, was an office area and the foundation specification was less dense than the rest. Sarah tried to remember what she had seen.

"Roger said the contractor set the rebar even less dense than this called for. Said he was running late and needed to pour quickly. Did a crappy job," Kyle said.

Sarah looked at the dimensions of this neat rectangle and

calculated in her head, about thirty-thousand square feet, "This is it!" She put both hands on Kyle's shoulders.

This odd kid might have just saved fifty-thousand lives.

86.   9:10:20

Nothing.

Sarah checked her watch, nine hours left. Kyle was huffing and puffing due to the exertion of moving as quickly as they could around the plant, but they just fired the *pulse generator* in the office area on the North West corner of building eight.

The office area was broken into two large rooms, east and west, each with walled offices along the edges and a large area of cubicles in the middle.

They'd run to their truck, driven around the complex, and Kyle helped them carry the equipment in. They quickly devised a pattern for the cubicles and fired the first pulse. Sullivan read the *receiver*.

Nothing.

Sarah was again disappointed, but it made no sense that they would find it on the first try. Sullivan moved the receiver and Sarah took one of the *ears*. Kyle needed little direction, he quickly figured out what was going on, but he was not in any hurry. Sarah moved the other *ear* while Sullivan helped Kyle with the *receiver*. It took five minutes to prepare the next pulse.

Nothing.

Sarah was disappointed that it took so long, but she knew they would get into a rhythm. After the third shot, Sullivan announced that it took another five minutes to get ready, and that it would take three days at this pace. The next pulse only took four minutes, and Sullivan responded with high-fives for Sarah and Kyle. After the next one, at three minutes, high fives were exchanged all around, and the spirit almost seemed fun.

Sarah was happy that Sullivan was managing their spirits with jokes. Kyle seemed to respond well to the team atmosphere. Sarah noticed him stealing glances at her, and she did everything she could to help out.

"One minute!" Sullivan shouted at the last cube in the first row. There were eleven more rows in this room. Sarah was feeling the energy and hugged Sullivan. She enjoyed the sudden closeness, but only let it last a moment. She made no eye contact with Sullivan, and as she looked away, she looked directly at Kyle who stared wide eyed. He was breathing hard from the exertion and took the opportunity to flop down in a desk chair.

After a one minute break, they completed the next row of ten cubicles in fifteen minutes. Sarah was in good physical shape and she knew she could keep up the pace, but her leg was starting to hurt.

Sullivan seemed to be keeping up, but Kyle was really struggling. He again flopped in a chair, his body jelly in the seat in complete contrast to his eyes alertly watching Sullivan and Sarah.

"What, no hug?" Kyle joked. Sullivan smiled sheepishly and they all exchanged forced high fives. This break took two minutes and the next row took twenty-five. Sullivan was beginning to look tired, Sarah's leg was hurting more now. She was afraid Kyle was about to pass out.

87.   5:00:00

They continued to work through the first room, completing all twelve rows by one p.m.

Five hours left.

By then, Kyle was talking about food, Sarah's leg ached and Sullivan was more determined and less funny. Sarah knew they needed a break, but she also knew they couldn't take one. She hoped that they would stumble onto the bomb, it could be anywhere, but they hadn't had luck yet.

"Kyle," Sullivan said after they gave each other fives for completing the first room, and all fell into chairs, "Is there somewhere you could get us some food?"

His face lit up, "Yes! Let's see."

"Whatever's closest," Sullivan said and pulled out his wallet and gave him forty dollars. Sarah didn't know where he got money, but didn't care right then either. He also gave him the keys to the truck.

Sarah wasn't as trusting as Sullivan was, Kyle was proving to be a pretty good worker, but he was still just a guy they met a few hours ago.

Sarah stopped rubbing her leg, something she knew Kyle was watching, and stood as he did. She took his hand with the forty dollars in it and looked him right in the eye, "Kyle, we need your help. We need you to hurry, and to keep what we're doing to yourself."

Kyle looked at her quizzically, "Look, I don't have any idea what we're doing here. But I do know that thing is not an ultrasound generator, it's some sort of electromagnetic pulse generator. I also know that Sullivan has been watching you, and not because he thinks you're guilty of anything, but because he's into you." He looked at Sullivan as Sarah tried to drop his hand, "Sorry man." Kyle looked back at Sarah, now he was holding her hand, "And I know this is not some sort of Indian artifact search, or we wouldn't be going so damned fast!" Sarah didn't know what to do.

"Okay," Sullivan said, Sarah looked at Sullivan hoping to see his confidence, but he also didn't know what to do, "So, you know more than we thought you did, although you're wrong about this." Sullivan pointed to Sarah then back to himself.

Sarah saw his confidence return to his face. She couldn't tell what it was about his look, but she could just tell.

"What I told Frank was the truth, that Sarah here is in on something, something big. What I didn't tell him was that I'm in on it with her. This is big, and we need your help, and if you help us, we'll help you."

Sarah and Sullivan both looked at him waiting for his answer. He only thought for a moment, "Okay." With that, he let go of Sarah's hand and headed for the door.

Sarah wasn't sure if they would ever see him again, but she realized there was nothing they could do but keep searching. She looked at Sullivan, he nodded to her, and they continued with the search. Without Kyle, they progressed more slowly, but they did move all the equipment and clear the first row in the west room. At the end of the row, they stopped as was now habit, but without Kyle they hugged.

Sarah took a chance and gave Sullivan a quick kiss.

. . .

Just north of the Delco Plant was a collection of small industrial buildings. On the western corner was a small burger store aptly named *Hamburger Store*. Colonel Burkett would have preferred a coffee shop, but the *Hamburger Store* actually had reasonable coffee and no one bothered him. He looked out the window across the street to the Delco Plant and thought about losing control.

He didn't want to be here, but his lieutenants demanded it. It wasn't that long ago that he had a firm command of his organization. Emboldened by their ability to push him into the Oklahoma City bombing, and his failing health, a faction of his organization was engaged in a power play. They believed things were going too slowly, and that they needed to push things along at a faster pace.

Their latest attempt to wrest control from him was to threaten his granddaughter, Eve.

She'd graduated top of her class from Princeton and was still as devoted to their cause as she was when her father first told her their secret fifteen years ago.

He stirred his third cup of coffee of the day. The chocolate square was melting in the bottom.

Ironically, it was Eve who'd deciphered what the government was up to, and it was Eve who got Dr. Kiadopolis to tell them everything. The lieutenants had cowered outside while Eve spent day after exhausting day learning what the physicist had been doing.

The Colonel considered the case closed, but his lieutenants demanded that they couldn't trust the Americans with the responsibility of not using their technology. They had to be tested. His lieutenants had convinced him that a test was required, but not a test like this.

At least they let him pick the site.

Colonel Burkett watched as a roundish man emerged from the gate of the plant. He went straight to the only truck in the parking lot. The Colonel noted that the truck was there, but was disturbed with himself that he didn't see it arrive.

There was tremendous debate, but the Colonel couldn't come up with a better test than this. If the Americans had the ability to find one of his, one of LV's, nuclear weapons, surely they would do it and not risk the lives of thousands of its civilians. His lieutenants said these people would be casualties in a war that needed some casualties.

The Colonel didn't agree. Then they told him his granddaughter's life was at stake. A chill ran up his spine at the threat.

The truck made its way across the parking lot and the Colonel was surprised to see it pull up to the *Hamburger Store*. The roundish man turned out to be little more than a child. He hurried into the store and up to the counter.

The lieutenants were convinced that this demonstration would both test the Americans' ability to find a weapon and force them to move faster toward their ultimate goal. The Colonel had acquiesced in order to save Eve. He told himself it was a fair trade. Eve was quickly emerging as his most competent advisor, and soon she would take over his position as leader of LV. He could trust her to guide them toward their goal. But there was a power struggle going on, and she wasn't strong enough, yet. The problem was he wasn't strong enough to protect her any more. Thousands of lives to save Eve. And Eve would save the world.

He looked to the young man waiting for his food. He was clearly in a rush.

"What's the hurry, young man?" Colonel Burkett asked in his best american accent.

"Huh?" the boy asked. Americans, always so sloppy.

"The plant's shut down, isn't it? What's the big hurry?"

The boy thought about this. He looked sideways at the Colonel, almost as if he knew what the Colonel was doing there. Then he answered, "We need to get the change-over done. We're just a little behind schedule, that's all."

"Good luck," the Colonel raised his coffee cup to the boy as he ran out the door. In four hours, the Colonel would leave, and in five, the boy would be dead.

. . .

"Nothing going on?" Kyle called with bags of fast food in his hands. Sarah was surprised to see him, both for the timing and also because she thought he might just go home.

She pulled away from a brief embrace. She hadn't planned to eat, if she didn't the fatigue would get worse, and they would lose more time.

Kyle met them halfway down the row and they each grabbed greasy burgers from a local shop. They shoved the food in their mouths as fast as they could.

"What are we looking for?" Kyle asked between bites. Sarah had no intention of telling him.

"Buried treasure," Sullivan said.

Kyle considered this, "Why do we need to go so fast? How much money?"

"Lots," Sullivan ended the conversation by turning his back and moved down the aisle.

Kyle looked at Sarah without chewing. Sarah swallowed the bite in her mouth, wrapped up the last third of the burger, and moved down the aisle following Sullivan, placing the bit of burger on a desk on the way.

"I want in!" Kyle called from the end of the row.

"We'll see." Sullivan didn't look up as they cleared the first cube in the second row. Sarah was worried Kyle wouldn't help, but she was going to let Sullivan work it out.

"I want money," Kyle picked up one of the *ears* to move it to the next cube. Sullivan nodded slightly. Kyle pushed a little more, "and a date."

Sullivan and Sarah both stood and looked at him. Sarah wasn't sure what he had in mind, but she was sure she wouldn't be going on any dates with Kyle. She couldn't believe what he was implying. But then, they needed his help, and they could be dead before she had to go on any dates.

Sullivan looked like he was going to get rough. Sarah waved him off.

"Kyle, dates can be arranged," she deflected.

The roundish twenty-year old thought a moment while looking her up and down, then smiled at her as he walked past her.

He looked back, "Oh, and we're going to modify the pattern here a little." He placed the *ear* not following the pattern they'd been using in the previous room, but in the center of the aisle between the two rows of cubes. Sullivan and Sarah watched as Kyle placed the *generator* and *receiver*. Sarah picked up on his pattern. He was going diagonally across the aisle. She realized that it would mean moving the *receiver* and each *ear* only every other shot, greatly increasing their speed. Sarah picked up the last *ear* and moved it into Kyle's pattern.

Sullivan didn't quite follow, but he knew how to fire the *generator*. He moved to it, but Kyle was in the way, "Well?"

"Well what?" Sullivan asked, "Oh, yeah, money and girls. With how much money we're going to give you, you'll have girls much prettier than her after you!" Kyle smiled and got out of Sullivan's way.

Sarah didn't know how to react to the objectification, so she just looked at the *receiver* display. She was happy Kyle was on board, and happy that Sullivan had deflected his interest to other women.

He even had some brains to add to the effort. But he seemed to have a dark side and it was coming out.

## 88.	4:00:00

"Jim," Linus looked down and spoke into his cell phone.

"Yes, Linus," Jim Williams answered, "We're all here, what do you have?"

"Mary is certainly Eve Burkett," Linus said. He held up both the sketch Sullivan had drawn and the picture from the conference for comparison. He'd flown to Chicago as soon as they had her address. He was in her apartment, staring at her.

"That's great news!" Jim said, "You need to get her to help us." Linus knew what Jim was implying. It didn't bother Linus to rough someone up, but he wouldn't have relished abusing a young woman. He knew they needed information, and he knew they didn't have a lot of time to get it.

"She's not going to talk," Linus reported.

"But she has to," Jim said, obvious disappointment in his voice, "We're not getting anywhere. The teams are searching, but there's not much hope they'll find it. You're our best hope now. You need to make her talk."

"She's not going to talk," Linus allowed his eyes to focus on the woman sitting in the chair before him. Her hands were bound to the arms of the chair and her feet to the legs. He might have put her in this position, if she wasn't this way when he got here. He looked at her head leaning back with her mouth open. "She's dead."

## 89.	2:10:00

With Kyle's pattern, they were able to clear the entire west room in two hours, and they were done before four p.m. That was a success, but they didn't find anything. They only had ninety minutes left before they were supposed to drive out of there and report in. Could they search the twenty offices they had left in ninety minutes? It didn't seem likely.

"We only have an hour and a half," Sullivan said, in sync with Sarah, "Which offices should we search, we won't get them all." Sarah's leg hurt, but she still climbed up on top of one of the desks so she could see over the cubicles.

"Let's start here and work to the outside of the building," she said. She had no idea where to start, but without a plan they would waste time trying to create one. They moved quickly to the first office. Kyle threw the door open and they stormed in with the equipment. They completed the office in eight minutes and moved to the next. Eighty-two minutes.

Sarah was certain the bomb was here, she was sure they were in the right place. At eight minutes per office, they could clear only ten, only half. She thought about the history of the place, the contractor who did a rush job in this area. She thought about Mary and how she had no intention of hurting her. She had an idea LV was a religious organization, not a bunch of killers. She replayed in her mind all the information she had about LV and this place and was even more confident that the bomb was here.

As they cleared the third office, Sarah decided to herself that she was not leaving. She decided she would have to clear ten offices herself, that she could probably get through half herself, so she had a fifty-fifty chance of saving maybe ten thousand lives. It was a bet she was going to take.

They worked frantically, increasing their pace to one office every three minutes. At five thirty they had cleared eleven offices.

"Is it time to go?" Kyle asked. He didn't know why they had a deadline, but he knew they did.

Sullivan and Sarah looked at each other, "I think we can push it a little," Sullivan said. Sarah could have cried. She was ready to continue alone.

"Kyle, you should go," Sullivan said.

"I don't think you realize how important the girls are to me!" Kyle said jokingly and moved into the next office.

Sarah knew he was blissfully unaware that he might have just committed himself to his own death. There was no time to argue with him, and they could use his help, so Sullivan and Sarah continued.

90. 0:20:00

At twenty minutes to six, in the thirteenth office, Sullivan looked up from the *receiver*, shock on his face.

"This is it." He looked at Sarah, "We found it, this is it!"

Sarah ran to the *receiver* and confirmed the four green lights where they had seen five red lights all day.

She fired the *generator* again.

Again they got four green lights. Sarah allowed herself to feel the strain that her body felt, and allowed herself to feel the pain in her thigh. With the relief of pressure, she sat back against the desk in the office. They'd done it. They found a secretly placed atomic bomb under a factory in Kokomo, Indiana. Sullivan came to Sarah.

"Now what?" Kyle interrupted, "There will be plenty of time for you two later, what do we need to do before six o'clock?"

Sarah tried to remember what Linus told them to do through the fog of the relief she felt. The fog got thicker as she realized she didn't pay much attention to that part as she never thought they would get this far.

Luckily Sullivan remembered, "There's a portable phone in the pile of boxes, we need to call Jim Williams." Sullivan ran from the room. Sarah remembered it looked ridiculously large compared to the cell phones they had, but didn't care at the time.

"Jim Williams?" Kyle asked, "Should we put this stuff away?"

Sarah sat down in the desk chair and rubbed her very sore leg. She ignored Kyle's questions. She'd lost feeling in her foot. "Don't bother with this stuff. I think we need it here." Kyle tried to make small talk, but Sarah wasn't interested. She continued to rub her leg although her arms were so tired even that took effort. She looked at the ground and thought that a nuclear warhead was a few feet below her feet, and was set to detonate in about ten minutes. She was oddly at peace because she knew there was nothing she could do at this point.

Sullivan returned after about a minute.

"We have less than fifteen minutes," Sullivan said as he put the briefcase sized phone on the desk. Sarah stood and moved next to him. Kyle moved to the other side. Sullivan opened the lid of the metal briefcase. Inside, on the left was a phone receiver, very similar to the one on the desk in the office. Next to it was a keypad, and luckily, above the keypad was a printed label with a phone number. On the right was an LED display with the count-down, a miniature version of the one on the wall in the airplane. It read 00:11:35 and as she watched, 11:34, 11:33, the seconds were ticking away.

"Wow," Kyle said.

Sarah realized that although she had never seen this thing before, it was entirely consistent with the bizarre nature of what was happening. She also now understood that this was not only a cell phone. Sullivan must have felt the same way. He stared down, but was taking it in, not surprised.

The device in front of them, though, didn't make any sense to Kyle.

Sullivan lifted the receiver to his ear. Sarah held her breath. They would be in trouble if the phone didn't work. Sullivan nodded, Sarah exhaled, and Sullivan dialed the number from the label. He took Sarah's hand and waited for someone to answer.

91.   0:11:00

Jim looked at the clock counting down in the Situation Room under the White House.

00:11:00.

President Bush sat at the end of the table with his head in his hands.

The small team in this room, the President, Jim, Maxwell Rassic, and a team they'd preselected for this purpose, had done everything they could, but there was nothing left to do. They'd worked constantly for the past eighteen hours, since the signal was received.

In the last fifteen minutes, they received calls from eleven of the twelve search teams. They were clear of Kokomo. The last team, their newest, Sullivan Acer and Sarah Kiadopolis, had not called in.

They were a long shot anyway. They were new to Department 55, had no training, and were both desk people. Jim thought he saw something in the pair and decided they should be on the ground in Kokomo in case they saw something no one else would.

His gamble didn't pay off.

Each of the other eleven teams was referring people who questioned them to a special number. That number was answered in the next room by Thomas Kirk and his team posing as the EPA. No one called to check on Dr. Kiadopolis and Mr. Acer.

They probably just took off. Jim was disappointed. He expected more from Doctor Sarah Kiadopolis. He knew Maxwell was more disappointed.

The President had just given the order to recall the bomber from its station over Kokomo, the final act of giving up. In fifteen minutes, a thermonuclear device was going to destroy the town of Kokomo Indiana, killing fifty thousand Americans, and there was now nothing anyone could do about it. There was absolutely nothing left to do.

Jim looked at the President. This would be the largest terrorist attack the world had ever known. President Bush would have to retaliate with aggression, he would have to select a country, even though they didn't know what country to attack, and destroy it.

Jim knew they had a few days to work that out. The President also knew that. Jim would assist the President by again reviewing the very limited data on where LV could be hiding, but after that, it would be up to the Commander in Chief to retaliate. Jim would return to his efforts to find LV.

At least they had a new clue. Unfortunately, the clue was a dead body. But it was a clue.

He realized that everyone in the room had nothing to do. He and his team were assembled around the large table, a table with twenty seats. Fourteen of them were empty. These were the only seven people in Washington who knew exactly what was going on. These were the only seven people who knew fifty-thousand were about to die, and they all sat there looking at their hands. The room seemed enormous with so little activity.

The phone rang at 00:10:20.

Jim looked to the large screen on the near wall that displayed the origin of the incoming call.

Team : 7
Sullivan Acer & Sarah Kiadopolis
Signal Register: No

So, Jim thought, they're finally calling in, too late.

"Sarah!" Lloyd Jansen lifted the receiver to his ear and answered the phone.

Everyone around the table looked at him. He looked around the room and reached out to the phone base. He pressed the speaker phone button and the room was filled with a click and then a brief moment of silence.

"Hello," a male voice filled the room over the speakers, "Oh, hello, yeah. This is Sullivan, I'm here with, uh, who is this?"

Jim was annoyed that he had to deal with this now, but he nodded to Lloyd.

"This is the Situation Room at the White House. You have reached our dedicated line."

Jim was impatient with this. The President immediately grew tired and his pleading eyes looked away. Jim interrupted, "Sullivan, this is Jim Williams, are you clear?   We only have," he glanced at the clock, "Ten minutes."

"No, we are not clear," Sullivan said, "We found it!"

"What?" Jim looked again to the readout that read *Signal Register: No.* He knew that meant they had found nothing, "What do you mean *you found it?*" Jim looked across the table. The President looked up. His eyes filled with a false sense of hope.

"I mean WE FOUND IT!" Sullivan repeated louder, "We decided that it would be at the Delco Plant."   A woman's voice spoke in the background, probably Sarah Kiadopolis. Sullivan returned quickly, "Right, no time for a story, how do we disable the bomb? As you said, we don't have a lot of time!"

"I don't know what you think you did," Jim's annoyance was raising, "But you did not find any bomb, or we would see it in the electronic register here."

"Look," Sullivan barked, his annoyance beginning to show, "I don't know about your register there, but we're looking at the receiver, and it is showing us four green lights! We searched all day, and we found the damned bomb! Now, tell us what to do! How do we disable it?"

"You can't disable it," Jim responded, "There's no way from there."

There was silence. Then they could hear Sullivan talking rapidly to Sarah.

"This is Sarah Kiadopolis," the woman's voice came over the speaker, "Look, we found the bomb! Now you're telling us there is nothing we can do about it? What the hell are you-"

"Dr. Kiadopolis, this is President Bush." The line fell silent. The president looked at Maxwell, "Could the system be malfunctioning? Could we just not be receiving the signal?" Maxwell didn't answer.

"Oh, shit!" Ravi, the system architect answered, "The bomber has left his station, remember, the signal is sent so the bomber can target, and then the bomber forwards that signal here to us, so-"

"What bomber!" Sarah shouted.

"So they could have found it!" The president stood up, "Get that bomber turned around!"

The third team member, Colonel Minetti, lifted a phone in front of his desk, "Reconnect me to flight fifty-five." A few seconds later, "Yes, Captain, this is Minetti, return to station."

"*What bomber!*" Sarah yelled again.

Jim lifted the receiver, taking her off speaker, "Hold on, Sarah, we're calling the bomber back." He couldn't remember if the teams knew that the bomb would be destroyed when, or if, it was found. He was happy that Sarah fell silent. Jim watched as Colonel Minetti completed his conversation with the Captain. He looked at the clock, 00:07:55, now time was going too fast. The Colonel returned the receiver with the steady hand of a man who had been in this type of situation before.

"The bomber is returning to station," Colonel Minetti said with slow precision. He looked to the clock, "But he's eight minutes out." The President's mouth fell open. He wanted to shout something, but nothing came. The Colonel continued, "He's going to full after burner to cut the time down, but he'll be running on fumes, so either he'll make it, or he'll run out of gas."

The President's eyes cleared, "Is there anything more we can do?"

Jim couldn't decide if he was hoping the answer was *yes* or *no*. If there was more to do, then they would have to do it, if not, they had to wait, and hope. Jim wished there was more, but he was certain the answer would be *no*.

"No," the Colonel responded. Jim looked around the room just as the President did. No one said anything further and the frenzy of activity suddenly died back to nothing. Jim ran through the situation in his head and agreed there was nothing further to do. He found he was standing and sat back down. On his way down, he remembered the phone handset in his hand.

"Sarah, are you still there?"

"*Still there?*" Sarah burst, "Where do you think I'd go?" She was panicked. It was understandable.

"Okay, so, we have a bomber inbound to your location. The *Receiver* is equipped with a transmitter that will guide the bomb in," Jim said to Sarah not knowing if he was repeating what she already knew.

"Okay," Sarah said. She seemed to be taking it well, "If there is a bomber coming, what do you need us to do?"

"I'm going to put you back on speaker," Jim waved his hand and Lloyd pushed the button on the base station, "Sarah, Ravi's here, and he is going to tell you exactly what you need to do."

"Okay." Jim was amazed how much she seemed to have calmed down. 0:5:59. He expected she didn't hear the comments about the gas, so she was more confident than he was.

"Doctor, this is Ravi Kumar. The *receiver* and the bomber require authentication to confirm the target is located. The system requires base coded physical assertion."

"What?" If Sarah didn't understand, Jim could not blame her, he didn't either.

"Speak plainly," Jim said, "What does she need to do?"

"Sorry," Ravi thought a moment, "on the *receiver*, are there four green lights?"

"Yes."

"Okay, below those lights is another LED, it would be red, but it's off at this time, correct?"

"Correct."

"Next to it is a red button without a label."

"Correct."

"Good, when the Bomber gets in range, the red light will begin to flash. At that point, push the red button, and the light should turn solid. When that happens, the bomber is locked on."

"Then what do we do?"

Ravi looked up, he didn't know. Jim looked around the room. Lloyd was struggling to control himself. Jim realized he personally knew Sarah Kiadopolis.

The Colonel spoke.

"You should get about one hundred meters away, two hundred would be better." Colonel Minetti said.

92.　0:05:30

Sullivan stood next to Sarah while she talked to Jim. She seemed to be going through a whole range of emotions, and with each one, he felt like an amplifier. She seemed to be calm now while she received instructions about a bomber on its way. He looked at Kyle. His face had gone white. Sullivan wasn't sure his face had any color either. Sarah looked at him and covered the receiver with her hand.

"You two need to get two hundred meters away from here," Sarah said. Sullivan thought she was repeating. He didn't move. She studied the receiver for a few more moments and looked at the briefcase phone.

"What's going on?" Kyle asked. Sullivan looked at him. His face was white and his eyes were wide. But, Sullivan thought to his credit, he didn't move either. He was part of this now.

"Look," Sullivan pulled Kyle away with a hand on the shoulder, "Obviously, there is more to this than you know. Actually, there is more to this than I know." Sullivan looked Kyle in the eyes, he was telling him the truth, "I think the less we try to figure out right now the better. If you look at that timer, you know something real bad is going to happen right here in five minutes. So, if I were you, I would do as the lady says and get about two hundred meters away from here. If I were you, I would go home."

"Okay," Kyle said. He looked around the room. He looked at Sarah, who was listening to the phone, but not saying anything. Sullivan looked at Sarah as well. With both of them looking at her, she recognized the staring and waved them toward the door.

"Get out of here," Sarah said, "Both of you. I'll be out in a minute."

Sullivan returned to Kyle, "Kyle, go home, we'll be in touch." He didn't think that was true, "Until then, don't talk to anyone about any of this."

"Okay." Kyle said, and he left.

That was one thing done. Now, what was Sarah hearing? Sullivan knew he wasn't going to leave this room without her. He thought that two hundred meters would be out the door of the complex to the north, across the large parking lot, and the far road, into the parking lot on the other side. He thought it would take about two minutes to get there at the most. He wasn't concerned with the time. 00:05:00. Then he thought what if the bomber didn't come? He guessed they were going to blow this place up. What if that didn't happen? How far would they need to be then? Ten miles, probably, and they couldn't make that in five minutes.

That bomber needed to come.

"Lloyd, calm down. I'm not going to leave Sullivan here. No," Sarah said, "Jim, where's that bomber? The light's not flashing." Sullivan looked at the phone box. There was a red LED next to a button.

"Four minutes!" Sarah said. She dropped down into the desk chair. Sullivan moved around the desk. He wanted to do something, but there was nothing to be done.

93.   0:01:30

Sullivan didn't think they had time to make it.

But they were waiting for a stupid red light to start flashing. Who would design a system like that?

Sarah's arm relaxed and the phone dropped to her hip. After all they'd been through, this was going to be it. Sullivan enjoyed the feeling of holding her hand. They looked into each other's eyes.

He desperately wanted to kiss her, but he didn't want to take his eyes off of her. They moved closer, to where they were almost touching. Her eyes didn't move. She smiled a little.

He wanted to say something, but there was nothing to say.

No, this was perfect. If this was it, he'd be okay with it.

"It's flashing," Sarah lifted the phone to her ear. Sullivan looked down to see the red LED flashing rapidly. He was glad she saw it.

Sarah said it with the calm of someone giving traffic directions, "Pushing the confirmation button now." With that, she took her hand from Sullivan and pushed the red button. A half heartbeat later, the red flashing light became a red solid light.

"We have a solid light," Sarah reported.

Jim said something to her, "Yes, good luck to you two."

Sarah placed the receiver on the desk, not hanging it up. She looked at Sullivan and kissed him quickly.

When she pulled away from the kiss, Sullivan saw her eyes were full of fire.

The next thing he felt was her hand pulling him toward the door. He fell into a run after her. She raced out the door and turned immediately right. Sullivan followed, not sure that right was the way to go, but racing after her all the same. As they reached the end of the row he saw the path she was taking. She turned left into the center aisle between the cubes toward the door to the east room. She was moving with the practiced ease of someone who had this all planned out. That must have been what she was thinking about while they stood there! Sullivan recognized this was the second time he was running after her with their lives on the line in two months. The last time did not end well. He also remembered that he was not as fast as she was.

Sullivan could see Sarah limping. Her leg was obviously in more pain than she was letting on. He was able to close the distance to her as they passed into the western room of cubicles. He looked to the right and saw the double doors leading to the parking lot. Sarah stumbled and almost fell. Sullivan grabbed her waist and pulled her up before she hit the ground.

"My leg," Sarah said in a low voice. She wasn't breathing hard. She continued to push toward the door and threw his hands off her. She returned to a run, Sullivan next to her. He could see pain in her face when she glanced at him. He tried to help her, but she again shrugged him off and broke into a full sprint. This time she pulled away from him easily and was a full stride ahead of him when she turned quickly to the right toward the exit doors.

They burst out the doors into the sunlight of late afternoon in the summer. The heat hit Sullivan in the face, and he was pulled into remembering that there was still a world all around them. He held his left hand up to block the sun as he looked forward and remembered the security gate ahead of them. On their way in, Kyle had to badge them through.

They were stuck.

The tremendous sound of tearing metal forced Sullivan to cover his head and drop to his knee. The screeching lasted about two seconds followed by a few sounds of collateral pieces falling. Then quiet.

Sullivan had never heard an explosion before, but that didn't sound like the ones in movies. Did the bomber drop a dud? He looked up to see nothing different, no cloud of smoke rising over the factory, no broken windows. Did the bomb go off, and everything was over?

"Sullivan, come on!" Sullivan turned around back to the gate. Sarah was outside the gate calling for him. He was confused. Then he saw their truck with the driver's side door open. Then he saw Kyle! He was standing at the turnstile waving for Sullivan to move. Sarah turned to the truck. Sullivan ran to the turnstile and pushed through as Kyle swiped his badge.

Sullivan piled into the truck and slid across, followed by Kyle and Sarah drove. She floored the accelerator and slammed the door shut by turning the wheel hard, straight away from the building.

The parking lot had concrete stops in the parking spots and the truck bumped over them.

"They dropped the bomb," Sarah said, "It's a bunker buster. It's timed to go off one second before the time runs out!" Sarah explained as she held onto the steering wheel. Sullivan wasn't sure how much control she had.

They were not clear yet. Sullivan looked ahead to the street and thankfully didn't see any other cars on the road.

Kyle looked at his watch and counted down, "Three, two, one." Sullivan looked back. He thought he saw the building shutter, then he saw the walls of the building flex inward for a fraction of a second.

94. 0:00:02

The GBU-28 Bunker Buster bomb was designed during Desert Storm to penetrate deep into enemy strongholds. They had been known to penetrate hundreds of feet into the ground. The bomb dropped on Delco was designed with a five hundred pound charge of chemical explosives that was detonated with a timer, rather than on impact or open space. In theory, the bomb could be dropped, lodge in the ground, and detonated the next day or the next year. In this case, it was timed to detonate at 00:00:02. The five hundred pounds of high explosives were designed to not only destroy a bunker, but to do it at such high temperatures that everything in the immediate vicinity was vaporized. This would ensure that the bomb would destroy any building above its detonation point by eliminating the support structure below it.

At exactly 00:00:02, a military grade, impact hardened microchip inside the head of the GBU-28 changed pin 12 from ground to plus 24 volts. That signal traveled three quarters of an inch to the digital multiplexer that converted the signal into twelve individual 24 volt signals. The twelve signals were routed to transistors that signaled capacitors to release static charges of five thousand volts to the firing caps spaced around the solid chemical explosive charges. This electrical process occurred in less than four ten-thousandths of a second.

The explosive was a mixture of high speed fuel and solid oxidant. It was remarkably stable at room temperature. It had to be to survive the violence of the impact without detonating. When hit with five thousand volts, an area the size of a pin head reached a temperature of ten thousand degrees Fahrenheit. At that temperature, the mixture was very unstable, and the oxidant and fuel reacted to release tremendous energy. The energy release heated the mixture around it, causing it to ignite and release more energy. The process propagated through the explosive charge at greater than the speed of sound, resulting in a detonation.

The GBU-28 was lodged twenty feet below the surface of the factory floor. The detonation blasted unburned fuel and oxidant upwards. As the fuel rose, it consumed all oxidants it could find, including the organic matter in the clay of the earth. A wave of heat at five thousand degrees propagated upwards at one thousand feet per second.

The nuclear device and its protective housing designed and installed by LV in 1962 sat six feet below the floor of the office. The detonation wave took less than a hundredth of a second to reach it and begin heating. The circuitry that was designed to fire the detonators failed to keep time as it passed two hundred degrees. At twelve-hundred degrees the wires connected to the detonators melted, breaking the connection to the explosive dome surrounding the plutonium with one second remaining. As the nuclear device passed three thousand degrees, the small dome of explosives surrounding the plutonium also detonated. In order to create a nuclear explosion, the plutonium needed to reach one million degrees, a feat that could only be accomplished by precise detonation of the ten pounds of explosives that formed the dome. The heat wave from the bunker buster forced the dome to ignite in an uneven way, forcing the plutonium to one side of the detonation chamber. The plutonium was pressurized and heated, but reached a temperature of only twenty thousand degrees, nowhere near that required for critical mass. At the time when the nuclear blast was scheduled, two seconds after the bunker buster detonated, the plutonium was a cloud of superheated vapor exploding outward, its temperature dropping safely to five thousand degrees.

. . .

The first sign of an explosion on the surface came when the super-heated fuel broke the surface of the office. The detonation wave sucked the air from the room, consuming the fresh supply of oxygen. The low pressure briefly created ahead of the wave was strong enough to suck the exterior walls, shrinking the building an inch. The electronic circuitry of the timer on the phone vaporized with zero point eight seconds left as the pressure wave changed directions and the explosion of fuel and super-heated debris erupted from the expanding crater.

Once the blast reached the relatively easy passage of open air, it expanded in every direction, heating the walls, carpets, cubicles, books, and everything else in the office area to five thousand degrees in half a second. The first breach of the exterior face of the factory occurred just before the last second would have ticked off the timers and within two tenths of a second, the entire north face of the two office areas was vaporized, replaced with a ball of fire expanding outward and upward. Outside the confines of the building, the explosion slowed below the speed of sound and erupted as a fireball that rose to five hundred feet above the original factory floor.

The pressure wave of the explosion hit the truck just as it bounced into the air over the curb into the street north of the factory lot. The back window of the truck burst forward through the passenger compartment showering the three passengers with glass. The weight of the truck slowed its acceleration briefly giving the passengers a brief sensation of weightlessness followed by the tail of the truck being pressed into the ground, and the engine compartment lifting into the air. The three saw the ground disappear and the sky take up their view as the truck flew wheels first across the road.

After an eternity in the air, the tail reconnected with the ground, sending the truck into a spin. The driver's door flew open, and the rotation ejected passengers from the truck. The tail of the truck hit a barrier, catapulting the truck and smashing it roof down on the pavement.

Epilogue

95. July 4, 2001

"Thanks for having us out here," Jim Williams looked out over the Chesapeake Bay from the deck of Bethany's Dream. It was the Fourth of July and boats of all sizes were positioning themselves for the fireworks.

"We all needed it," Thomas Kirk stated the truth. They had barely avoided catastrophe in Kokomo and the President wasn't letting up on them to get a new plan together. So far, they had not come up with anything good.

"You're all going to need it a lot more, I suspect," Eustis said.

"*You?*" Maxwell challenged him from his standing position against the railing. "You're not going to retire."

"We all have to go some time, and this might just be the bang to go out on!" Eustis said. "I don't want to get that close again."

"You were a big part of stopping us from going over the edge," Jim said. "Don't forget that." Eustis devised the response to LV's demands. The capital markets would artificially build demand for increased power generating capacity to stabilize the grid.

The President made an address over the satellite TV system. He detailed the American plan to guarantee the electricity stayed on.

He described the billions of dollars the government would spend. With the power on, Dr. Kiadopolis would be unable to find any more of LV's hidden nuclear weapons. LV's next letter reasoned that one hundred billion dollars seemed a small price to pay to keep its cities intact.

The threat rose was back down to four.

"Hey," Linus came up from below deck, "Can I drive?"

"I don't think we'd be able to handle you at the helm!" Thomas said. Everyone laughed, but everyone knew Thomas was right.

Jim knew this team had gotten them closer to stopping LV than anyone had in the past forty years. He also knew they almost went too far. Eustis' comment reminded Jim that this team wouldn't be at the helm forever. The past few years had taken a toll on all of them. He looked out to the horizon and thought of the young men and women who had helped them. They were smarter, faster, and more capable, and they already knew more about what was going on than he knew after years on this job. Even if he didn't know how today, for the first time in a long time, he felt confident they'd win.

. . .

"Thank you, Bill," Claire thanked the barkeep at *The Artifact* as he delivered their second round of drinks. The basement bar was clearing out as the time for fireworks approached.

"I don't know about you, but I'm not sure I need to see another explosion for a while," Sullivan Acer declared. After the explosion, Claire and Peter went in to retrieve any of the team that had survived. They loaded three people into the bed of their pickup and sped back to the rendezvous point.

Sullivan called Peter this morning to ask if he could stay the night on his way to Florida with his son. Claire felt certain he hadn't told Danny any details of what happened. She could also tell it had not been long enough for Danny to let Sullivan out of his site. He sat close to his father sipping on a cranberry juice.

"Let's just keep it to fireworks," Peter said. With that, the first explosion of the night erupted outside and several tables of patrons stood and began to move to the door.

"I'll drink to that!" Sullivan said patting his son on the back. They all sipped their drinks. Claire looked at Danny, a handsome thirteen year old. Normally kids were awkward looking, but he was solid and sure of himself. Claire decided he wouldn't have much trouble with the ladies. She felt herself a bit envious of Sullivan. She smiled as she felt the new engagement ring on her finger. She and Peter had not discussed kids.

"So, that's it? That's where this all started?" Sullivan pointed with his glass to the empty box in front of the waterfall.

The box that used to hold a nuclear weapon. Claire and Peter had completed the removal on the night Sullivan was taken. Claire knew there was something like one hundred more of them scattered around the United States.

"That's it," Peter said, "We did all this," he motioned to the bar, "for that box."

Claire knew Sullivan wore a brace across his broken collar bone and saw him wince when he moved his shoulder to point. Of the three, though, he was doing the best. Linus still had agents in Kokomo waiting for Kyle to wake up from a coma. If he woke up.

The President was able to convince the public that the explosion was the result of a massive natural gas leak.

Claire was now part of the team tasked with devising upgrades to the power grid to make sure the lights stayed on. It was a tremendous task.

Sullivan stood up and watched Doctor Sarah Kiadopolis come down the stairs.

Claire bristled at first. She would have objected to Sarah joining them, but Peter didn't tell her until ten minutes ago. She knew Sarah and Sullivan were close friends, but there must have been something more for her to go with Sullivan and Danny to Florida.

But then, she realized she didn't feel jealousy seeing this woman effortlessly making every man in the room look her way. Instead, she was grateful for the woman who had, at the last possible moment, used her brain and her instincts to save them all.

Claire knew she had a big job to secure the power grid, but she knew it was a job that required planning, investment, and diligence.

Sarah had a different job, to defeat LV by finding their bombs. Her job required invention, cunning, and creativity. Claire was proud of what she could accomplish, but at the same time she couldn't shake her admiration for Sarah Kiadopolis.

Proof

Made in the USA
Charleston, SC
13 August 2015